CAT

Frances Anne Bond was born, brought up and still lives in the town of Scarborough, North Yorkshire. She has worked in shops, as secretary to a headmaster in a private preparatory school and in the social services. She is married and has two grown-up daughters. She has been writing since she was a child, and has previously had articles, short stories and three novels, *Darling Lady*, *Dance Without Music* and *Return of the Swallow* published.

Also by Frances Anne Bond

Darling Lady
Return of the Swallow
Dance Without Music

Catching Larks

Frances Anne Bond

HEADLINE

First published in 1993
by HEADLINE BOOK PUBLISHING PLC

First published in paperback in 1993
by HEADLINE BOOK PUBLISHING PLC

10 9 8 7 6 5 4 3 2 1

ISBN 0 7472 4117 1

Phototypeset by Intype, London

Printed and bound in Great Britain by
HarperCollins Manufacturing, Glasgow

HEADLINE BOOK PUBLISHING PLC
Headline House
79 Great Titchfield Street
London W1P 7FN

This book is dedicated to my three-year-old grandson

JOE

Because I love him and he makes me laugh
and because he is the youngest
'link in the chain'

A beginning . . .

Kate Gallantree pressed the back of her hand to her throbbing forehead and focused her gaze on the ceiling. The thin pencil of strip lighting suspended above the hospital bed seemed incredibly remote and ice-cold, a million miles away from her own sweating body. As she stared upwards, the fluorescent tube flickered and made a buzzing sound. She blinked.

'It needs a new starter.' She heard her own voice, husky, like that of a stranger, but then she was hardly herself at the moment. Her own tiny giggle shocked her. 'Maybe you could plug me in,' she said, 'I've enough gas and air inside me to ignite a hundred lights.'

'Now then, Mrs Gallantree.' The voice held mild disapproval. 'Let's keep our minds on the job, shall we?'

The midwife's round face swam into Kate's line of vision and hung above her like a child's pink balloon. She was sweating, too. The realisation alarmed Kate. Had something gone wrong? She frowned, opened her mouth to speak and then saved her breath and surrendered to the rhythmic demands of her body.

'Good girl. A couple more pushes and we're there.'

Who's we? thought Kate. The flare of rebellion she

experienced swept away thoughts of faulty lighting. There's just one person in labour, one woman on this bed, she thought, and that's me. And it's a damned hard bed, too. Why does it have to be so hard?

She shifted position slightly and tried to breathe in the way the hearty woman who ran the relaxation class had advised. Oh, to hell with it! She stopped trying to relax, reached up and grabbed the iron bedhead with both hands and hung on. That was better.

'Good girl.'

Another wave of rebellion counterbalanced the ebb of the labour pain. Kate gritted her teeth and decided being angry was good for her; it made her more positive, more in control of the situation. 'I'm not a girl,' she said nastily.

The midwife's eyebrows rose above the top of her spectacles but all she said was, 'Rest a moment. I want to take another look.'

Kate rested and nursed her anger carefully. She remembered how nervous she had been on her first visit to the surgery, when she thought she might be pregnant. Oh, she had wanted the baby but it was so soon. A baby would force more changes in her life, and during the last year she had experienced nothing but change.

Marrying Jack and moving to Yorkshire had meant giving up her job and friends and acquiring a twelve-year-old stepdaughter, as well as the obligatory new dentist and doctor – she hadn't had time to make new friends yet. Remembering her previous doctor, Kate sighed. She could have talked to him about her fears, but not this new one, not Doctor Freeman. On her first visit he had made her feel guilty.

She had murmured that she thought she was

pregnant and he had examined her and confirmed that she was and then he had asked her questions. Hearing she was almost thirty-five years old, he had looked pensive and muttered something about special tests. He had said something about career women, and Kate, flushing, had found herself explaining that she wasn't a career woman, far from it. It was just that she had only been married for nine months. She had listened to her own apologetic voice and felt appalled. What was she apologising for?

Her baby decided to have another try at being born, and its struggle to enter the world brought her wandering thoughts back to the business in hand. She tensed.

The midwife gave her a light, encouraging tap on her leg. 'A few more minutes, love, and you'll have your baby.'

Kate gave a weak smile and wished she hadn't snapped at the woman, then she stopped thinking logical thoughts and surrendered to pure sensation. Ten minutes later, a thin wail announced a new presence in the room. Kate blinked the sweat from her eyelashes and raised herself on one elbow. 'Is it all right? What is it, boy or girl?'

'A beautiful boy.' Beaming, the midwife dumped the infant on his mother's upper body. 'A good size, too, considering he's a little early. You two take a minute to get acquainted, and then I'll clean you both up.'

Kate checked out her own personal miracle. He had the right number of toes and fingers and his tiny nails were so perfect she felt tears threatening. She looked at his tight-shut eyes and his pouting mouth and marvelled, and then she slumped back to lie flat on the hard bed. She was delighted, but also desperately tired.

'I'll get you a cup of tea, shall I?' The midwife whisked the baby away then returned and laid her hand flat upon Kate's stomach. 'Just a couple of minutes and you're all through. Nurse Simpson will sponge you down while I see to the little one.'

'Thanks.' A cup of tea. Kate ran her tongue round her dry lips. Tea would be heaven. Five minutes later, as the young nurse helped her back into her own night-gown, Kate heard clicking noises. She turned her head and saw that Daniel Gallantree was being weighed.

Daniel, the name Jack had chosen. They had agreed Kate would have first choice if the child was a girl, Jack if it was a boy. He had insisted it didn't matter what sex the child was, but she knew how delighted he would be to learn he had a son. If only he had been here . . . Her forehead creased.

'Six pounds, five ounces, that's a reasonable weight.' As if sharing Kate's thoughts, the midwife clicked her tongue. 'Such a pity his daddy couldn't have been with you.'

'It's the weather.' The midwife had been with her through most of the night, Kate felt obliged to explain. 'My husband works on an oil-rig, but he'd made arrangements to be at home for the birth. Only I went into labour two weeks early and even though the company was agreeable to him flying over, the weather was too bad. The helicopter couldn't take off.' She choked, suddenly tearful.

'There, don't upset yourself. He'll be here soon enough, I don't doubt. And look on the bright side. This young man here will look even more handsome tomorrow.' She handed Kate her son.

She sat up and held the child in her arms. He too had been smartened up. His hair had been brushed up into a tiny quiff and she saw one hand had worked itself loose from the hospital blanket. She stared down at him. 'He's red, isn't he?

'He's beautiful.' The midwife leaned over and beamed at the child. 'It was a long labour for him too, you know.' She laughed. 'You're right about the colour though. Haven't you noticed yet?'

'Noticed what?'

Puzzled, Kate turned back the cover from her baby's head. 'Oh!'

'You see, a definite tinge of red. I haven't had a red-headed baby for ages. Most of them nowadays seem to come out bald!'

Kate wasn't listening. She stared at the auburn fuzz decorating the small head.

A smiling young woman, Nurse Simpson, came into the room, carrying a cup of tea. She placed it carefully on the trolley within Kate's reach and then took a peek at the little boy. 'Isn't he lovely? Red hair runs in your family, does it?'

'I've no idea.' Kate stared down at Daniel's button nose and his busily working mouth. She touched his cheek with a gentle finger as her earlier euphoria drained away. Yes, it was sad Jack had missed the birth, but it didn't really matter, because she had done it! She had given birth to a perfect child. She was a mother. But now, because of one kindly meant, interested comment, her happiness was flawed. As she hugged her son, she suddenly realised this was the first time she had touched someone who was actually related to her. She was thirty-five years old, and Daniel was her first experience of true 'family'. She swallowed hard to get rid of the lump in her throat and forced herself to smile at the young nurse still waiting for her reply.

'My husband's blond. I don't think there's red hair in his side of the family. As for me, I don't know anything about my natural family. You see, I was adopted.'

'You should have seen my second one, over twelve pounds he was. God, he nearly killed me.'

The strident voice and the laugh that accompanied it jerked Kate from her sleep. She yawned and stretched. Apart from slight stiffness in her limbs, she felt wonderful. She opened her eyes.

The ward held six beds and all were occupied. The girl wearing a blue dressing-gown, seated on the bed to her right, was Asian and very young. Her hair was plaited into a long braid and her huge brown eyes were beautiful. She smiled and Kate returned the smile before looking round.

The room had a cosy feel. There were vases of flowers and cards of congratulation on the bedside lockers. The temperature was pleasantly warm and the curtains at the windows were a cheerful rose pink colour. But when Kate looked towards the windows, she saw the rain was still pouring down outside and heard the scream of the wind as it buffeted against the glass. She shivered. When would Jack be able to come? When would he be able to meet his son?

Her heart bounded. Her son! She sat up. Yes, at the foot of her bed stood a small cot. She bent forward until she could see Daniel's head. Yes, it was true.

'You've a little cracker there.' It was the strident voice again. Kate looked to her left.

Her other neighbour, a large lady with sausage-like blonde hair and a florid complexion, gave her a friendly nod. 'Your first, is it?'

Kate nodded.

'Oh, he's special then. There's never anything to compare with your first one.' The woman's mouth opened when she laughed, showing large white teeth. 'Oh, I say – that sounded cheeky, didn't it?'

Kate didn't know whether to blush or to laugh. Since moving to Leeds, she realised Northern women had a robust, friendly outlook on life. Look at the way everyone called you 'love' when you went shopping. It was an attitude a million miles away from the way in which Kate had been raised. She thought of her adoptive mother and her genteel circle of friends and smiled to herself. Mother would have been appalled by this woman, she thought. And then she laughed, because she wasn't her mother, she had a child of her own now, and she liked a touch of earthiness.

'It's a little lad, isn't it?'

'Yes.'

'I knew it. I can always tell. Mind, I've just had my fifth, so I should be able to, shouldn't I?' Again, that booming laugh.

Kate looked back at the cot. Daniel was moving and making a snuffling noise. What should I do? she wondered.

'You can pick him up, love. Don't be scared. He looks a little 'un, but that doesn't matter. If he'd needed special attention they'd have put him in the nursery for observation.' Her neighbour watched with interest as Kate swung her legs over the side of her bed, stood up and hesitantly approached the cot.

'That's right, give him a cuddle. Lovely, ain't it?'

Kate's adviser settled herself back on her pillows with a satisfied sigh. 'You wait until you see the nurses with 'em. Makes your blood freeze, it does. They toss 'em about like parcels sometimes. And speaking of nurses, I expect one of 'em will be along in a minute to give you a few tips on feeding. I suppose you're going to breast-feed? Not going to stick him on a bottle, are you?' Again, that laugh. 'Could never see the sense of bottle-feeding meself, not when you've got the stuff on tap!'

At that moment, an outraged howl rose from the cot at the foot of the big woman's bed. Kate held Danny and watched as her neighbour heaved herself up and padded on trunk-like legs towards her child. She plucked from the cot a screaming, scarlet-faced miniature of herself, and Kate stared. Why, the child even had a mop of tight sausage-like fair curls.

Feeling a bubble of laughter rising inside her she turned away and found the young girl on her right watching her. She, too, was smiling. Seeing she had Kate's attention, the girl, with a graceful gesture of her hand, wordlessly asked for permission to join her. When Kate nodded, she tossed back her plait of hair and came to sit next to her, on the side of the bed. She stared down at Daniel.

'He's a beautiful child, and a boy, you say?'

Kate nodded.

'Then you are lucky.' She sighed. 'I have a beautiful baby girl which makes me happy, but my husband Sadaf is disappointed. He wants only boys.'

'Oh, surely not?'

The girl shrugged slim shoulders. 'He pretends, but I know.' She pulled her plait of hair over her shoulders again and played with the thin blue ribbon securing the end.

'He is the only son of his family, you see. It is important the line continues. Still,' her face brightened, 'there is plenty of time.' She looked shyly at Kate. 'My name is Zita and my husband is called Sadaf. He is very handsome. When he visits tonight, you will see.'

'Yes.' Kate shifted Daniel to her other arm and went back to studying his face. His eyes were half-open now and she could see they were blue. But hadn't she read somewhere that all babies had blue eyes at birth? Realisation of the depth of her own ignorance on the subject of babies swept through her. She had read books and attended classes and she had thought she was well prepared, but now Danny was here, she felt scared. Oh, Lord – there was so much she didn't know.

During her childhood and early teens there had been no babies, no cousins to play with, and no infants living nearby she could take for walks. What if she made a bad mother? She looked across at the blonde woman who had climbed back in bed and was reading a magazine with every evidence of enjoyment as her fat, pink baby nuzzled at her huge breast. Five children!

'Your husband, he must be so happy?' Zita was speaking again. 'He will be coming tonight, to see his son?'

'I hope so.' Kate glanced towards the window. It was still pouring, she could see the raindrops running down the glass, but the noise of the wind was abating. She explained, 'Jack, my husband, works away and the baby came early. He hasn't seen Danny yet.'

'Oh, that's sad, to miss the birth of his child! Families should be together at times of importance – births, marriages, death.'

'Yes.' Kate was quiet, remembering her earlier feeling of sadness. She wondered, for the first time in many years, about her natural mother. How old had she been when she, Kate, had been born? Was she still alive? She probably was. Was she married with children? She would be going about her usual tasks today, totally unaware that she had a new grandson.

Brow wrinkled, Kate forced her thoughts into a different direction. What on earth was the matter with her? Why was she suddenly asking questions about what happened years ago? The past was over and the present was marvellous. She had everything she needed – a happy marriage, a stepdaughter she got along with and her new baby.

She started. Helen, her stepdaughter – had anyone thought to contact her? She looked round as the swing doors to the ward banged open and a nurse hurried in and headed towards her bed.

'Ah, Mrs Gallantree, you're awake.' The nurse smiled at her, stood back for a moment to allow Zita to scuttle back to her own bed, and then drew the curtains to allow them some privacy.

'Let's take a look at you, shall we?'

Kate asked, as the nurse took Daniel from her arms, 'I was wondering . . . my stepdaughter, Helen, has anyone been in touch with her?'

With an economy of movement she could only admire, the nurse flipped Daniel back into his cot, covered him up, pulled back the bedclothes and gestured to Kate to get back into bed.

'Yes, everything's under control, Mrs Gallantree. I gather Helen is staying with some friends, a family called Abbey?'

'Yes. Their daughter Eileen is Helen's best friend.'

'Well, they rang earlier, when you were asleep.

Sister told them the baby had arrived safely and Mrs Abbey's bringing the girls over when they leave school so that Helen can see you and the new baby.

'Oh, and apparently your husband has also received the good news. He's delighted and hoping to be with you in a few hours. Now, if you could just lie flat . . .'

Kate had thought the rest of the day would drag, but the reverse was true. She had a lesson in breast-feeding, which wasn't as easy as she had anticipated. Then, in company with the other mothers, she was put through a series of exercises by the hospital's physiotherapist and then it was time for tea. Although she still felt tired she found it hard to relax. Every time Daniel snuffled or squeaked or moved she leapt in her bed like a startled rabbit.

When Helen finally appeared on the ward, walking towards the bed with a look of embarrassment on her face and clutching a bunch of flowers, Kate was lying down and fighting an overwhelming desire to sleep.

Helen laid the flowers on the bedside locker and looked under her lashes at Kate. 'How are you feeling?'

'Tired, but happy,' she answered honestly. 'Oh, the flowers are lovely. Thank you.' She pulled herself up in bed and gestured to the cot.

'There he is. You can lift him out, if you like.'

Helen jumped as if stung by a wasp. 'Oh, no. I'll just . . .' She approached the cot warily and eased away the covers so she could look at the baby. 'Goodness, he's tiny.'

'Not really. He's quite a good weight, considering.' The slight feeling of hostility Helen's words had evoked in Kate faded as she studied her stepdaughter's closed-in face.

Poor Helen. The past year had been full of changes

for her, too. Kate smiled at her and patted the side of her bed. 'Come and sit down.'

Helen sat down, but on the chair, not the bed.

Kate persevered. 'You're all right? With the Abbeys, I mean?'

'Yes.' Helen's fingers pleated her school skirt. 'Mrs Abbey's taking Eileen and me to the cinema this evening.'

'Good. I hope you enjoy the film. And tomorrow, I'm sure your dad will arrive, then you'll be able to go back home.'

'Yes.'

Kate bit back a sigh. Normally she got on well with Helen but occasionally a blank wall seemed to spring up between them, and today seemed to be one of those times. She knew Helen must be feeling a mixture of things, it's not every day you are presented with a half-brother, but she was much too tired to try to be extra-nice with the girl. She put her head back on the pillow and closed her eyes.

After a short pause, Helen re-opened the conversation. In a small voice she asked, 'Does it hurt?'

Kate opened her eyes and put out her hand to touch her. 'Yes, it does rather, but mostly it's just hard work. Mind you, he's worth it, don't you think?' She squeezed the girl's hand. Helen did not return the pressure, but neither did she remove her hand.

Kate hesitated and then said, 'I hope we both enjoy this baby, Helen, and I'm counting on your help, you know. I haven't a clue about babies, and I'm a bit scared.'

Helen blushed and stood up. 'I guess we'll manage.' She paused. 'Do you mind if I dash off now? If we're going to the cinema, I'd better not be late for my tea.'

'Yes, off you go.' Kate watched her rapid retreat and decided she just couldn't start worrying today.

The ward was peaceful for once. No one was visiting and the new mothers were all resting or reading. Kate yawned and snuggled down on her pillows. She felt she could sleep for a week.

She managed three hours. Mother and baby wards are busy places. There was babies' feeding time, and then dinner, and then visiting. No visitors for Kate. She sighed, put her head on her pillow, closed her eyes and fell asleep again. When she did wake, with a sudden start, she realised it was late evening. Her fellow patients were all asleep and only a dim light was showing in the ward. She rubbed her eyes and looking down the room, noticed that the swing doors at the bottom of the ward were silently closing and a tall, dark-clad figure was tip-toeing towards her bed. She looked more closely then sat up and stretched out her arms in silent welcome. Her husband knelt beside her bed, put his arms around her and kissed her.

'Jack. Oh, Jack.'

'I woke you.' He spoke in a whisper. 'I'm sorry.'

She choked and gave his shoulder a little shake. 'I would have killed you if you hadn't.'

He relinquished her in order to sit on the bed, but then caught hold of her hand and held it tightly. 'Kate, I'm so sorry I wasn't with you. I've been going frantic. First the terrible weather and then, when the storm died down, the bloody air pressure was all wrong. It was too dangerous for the helicopter to take off.'

'It doesn't matter, you're here now. Oh!' She started up and looked towards the foot of the bed. 'The cot . . .'

He bent forward and kissed her again. 'It's all right,

the babies are in the nursery for the night. The ward sister let me take a peek at him before I came in to see you. He's wonderful. But what about you?'

'I'm fine, really I am.'

They gazed at each other, smiling. Then Jack sighed.

'I can only stay for a few minutes, and I've got strict instructions to be quiet. The sister wasn't going to let me in at all, but when I explained the circumstances, she relented. Anyway, darling, I just want to thank you for our gorgeous child.' He squeezed her hand. 'I'm so proud, of him, and of you.'

She relaxed against her pillows. 'He's feeding well,' she boasted quietly.

He grinned. 'I'm sure he is. Has Helen seen him yet?'

'Yes.' She thought for a moment and then said carefully, 'She seemed interested.'

Immediately he picked up on what was unsaid. His ability to do that was one of the things she loved about him.

'It will take her a little while to adjust, I suppose. We knew that, love.'

'I know. I'm not worried.'

'Anyway.' He moved closer to her, so she could hear him whisper. 'I'm home now and I don't have to go back for a month. We'll sort everything out. Do you know how long it will be before you can come home?'

'A week, I think.'

'That's not too long, although it will seem it. Anyway, I'll keep busy. I'll lay in some groceries tomorrow and Helen can come back home and we'll sort out the nursery. I'm sure if we involve her in everything, she'll get used to the idea of having a baby in the house.'

She sat up again and snuggled close to him. 'Daniel Gallantree . . . it sounds strange, doesn't it? He was just a bump but now he's a real person.'

Jack nodded. 'I know. When I saw him, I was amazed. There's real character in his little face already and you can tell he's a boy, I think.' He laughed. 'The hair was a surprise.'

'Yes.' She frowned. 'I've never particularly liked red hair. Do you think it will stay that colour?'

'Who knows?' He grinned. 'I think it's cute.'

The irritating niggle started inside her again. She asked, 'Jack, does red hair run in your family?'

'Not that I recall.'

Kate was silent.

'Hey, what is it? It doesn't bother you, does it? I mean, what does it matter what colour his hair is? He's a strong healthy baby.'

'I know, and it doesn't matter. He's beautiful and I know how lucky we are. But . . .' She moved restlessly in the circle of her husband's arms.

In the half-dark, he gazed at her, trying to read her face.

'Something's bothering you. Tell me what it is.'

'Nothing, really.'

When he caught hold of her chin with his fingers and made her face him, she capitulated. 'Ever since the midwife handed him to me I've felt really strange,' she confessed. 'It's not that I'm unhappy – how could I be?' She shook her head. 'I can't explain.'

Seeing the worry in his eyes, she realised she must try. 'I keep wondering about my mother, my *real* mother. Somewhere there's a woman who is Daniel's grandmother, and yet she doesn't even know he exists. She knows nothing about him, she knows nothing about me . . .' She choked.

Jack's forehead creased and for a few moments he was silent. Then he rocked her in his arms and asked, 'Why now, Kate? You've known for years that you were an adopted child.'

'Yes, and when Dad told me, I remember I was shocked. But it's only now I realise how *much* I was shocked.' To her own surprise, Kate found slow tears were spilling from her eyes. She sniffed. 'I suppose I deliberately pushed the knowledge out of my mind, but now it's important.'

She broke free from his embrace and with an irritated gesture, mopped her eyes on the sleeve of her nightdress. 'And I've decided I want to find out what happened, Jack. I want to know where I came from.' She stopped speaking, surprised at her own words. Then she looked at him and said slowly, 'You can find out things about your adoption. The laws regarding adopted children have altered. I remember, I read an article in a magazine once. You can find out,' she repeated.

Jack's brow creased. 'Well, it's certainly a thought. But now is hardly an ideal time, is it? We've a brand new baby to look after, remember? Perhaps you'll feel differently in a few weeks. Let's face it, having a child is a pretty traumatic experience, emotions run rife. I should think, when you get home, you'll forget all about these feelings. And looking after Daniel will keep you too busy to spend time raking over the past.'

'But having Daniel's *part* of it all.' Kate gripped her hands together, willing him to understand. Then, seeing his total incomprehension, she sighed and bit her lip. 'You're probably right. It's all the fault of my stupid hormones.'

Jack's face lightened. He kissed her soundly and then tucked her up in bed. 'I'd better go before Sister comes gunning for me.' He smoothed back her hair. 'Thank you for my son, darling. I'll see you tomorrow.'

She smiled as she watched him tiptoe from the room, but she lay awake until the dawn lightened the room and when she finally slept, her mouth was set in a stubborn line.

PART ONE

Chapter One

Behind the chattering of her friend, Pauline Verrill could hear the sound of the slow wash of the waves against the shore. She turned her head and looked outwards, towards the sea.

The night was dark. No moon, just the glimmer of far-away stars in the velvet blackness of the sky, and yet the scene spread out before her sparkled like fairy-land. The Whitby fishing fleet was putting out to sea and the bay was ablaze with lights. She watched them as they twinkled, disappeared and then flashed out again. There's a swell on, she thought, and the boats will be beyond the shelter of the harbour now, cresting the larger breakers as they moved out to sea.

Pauline acknowledged the sailing of the fleet was a fine sight. She knew the holiday-makers who came to Whitby enjoyed the spectacle. She had lived all her life in the town and had always enjoyed seeing the boats go out, but recently her pleasure at the sailing of the fishing fleet was due to more complicated reasons. She sighed. It wasn't the beauty of the scene that enthralled her, but the fact that her dad was out there, on board *The Enterprise* and wouldn't be back until morning.

Thinking of her father, Pauline experienced the

now familiar sharp tug of anguished affection. Why were things so strained between them? Why was it that with every day that passed he grew more distant from her? She shook her head, perplexed. Look at the way he had criticised her new dress.

She looked down at herself. It was a perfectly respectable dress, made of pale blue linen and with a box pleat at the front of the skirt. The sweetheart neckline was positively modest. She had saved up her coupons for ages to buy it and had been so excited when she brought it home from the shop and tried it on. Yet her father's eyes had started out of his head when he had seen her in it.

'A young girl like you shouldn't wear low necklines,' he had stormed. 'You're sixteen and a bonny young lass. Why try and look like a woman of thirty?'

He should have seen what Mary was wearing. Pauline suppressed a grin as she glanced sideways at her friend. Mary was dressed in an eye-catching red, silky off-the-shoulder blouse and one of the new tulip skirts, which consisted of a plain skirt with over-lapping curved panels. She could get away with it though, thought Pauline. She had the confidence and the figure.

Her dad didn't like her being friends with Mary. Pauline leaned against the wall of the Spa building and chewed her thumb nail. But then, what did he like? She looked again at the sea. The lights were still there – glowing, lovely – and yet she knew all about the reality of fishing. It was hard, dirty and sometimes dangerous work. She wouldn't want anything to happen to her dad, even though they were always falling out.

All right, sometimes, after a row, she told herself

she hated him, but she didn't really, because occasionally he could still be lovely. She recalled his lean, tanned face and oddly slanting smile, the way he would ruffle her hair and laugh at what he called 'her pretensions'. She crossed her fingers behind her back and wished him a good trip.

And she also wished herself a good night out. It had been three long weeks since she had been able to go to the Spa, for she could go dancing only when her dad was away fishing, and for the past two weekends he had stayed in port, carrying out repairs on *The Enterprise*.

Oh, why was he so old-fashioned? She frowned as the grievances surfaced again. She'd be seventeen in two weeks' time, but he treated her like a child. Ignoring the fact she had no savings and nowhere else to go, she thought, If things don't get better, when I'm eighteen, I'll move out. In fact, if it wasn't for Gran, I'd go now, I surely would!

Mary nudged her. 'Will you stop day-dreaming? Didn't you hear me?' She shook her head in exasperation. 'Those chaps, just a bit ahead of us in the queue. Not locals, are they?'

Pauline narrowed her eyes in a vain attempt to see them. She was short-sighted but would have suffered torture rather than admit it. Last year, her gran had persuaded her to go and get some spectacles, and she used them in the house but would rather die than wear them in public!

'The one wearing the trilby, do you mean? His pal's wearing a blue suit?'

'Yes.'

She shrugged. 'They look OK.' She wasn't going to tell Mary the two figures were just a blur to her.

Her friend blew out her cheeks in a comical sigh. 'They're the pick of this bunch, Pauline. The rest are just lads we were at school with. Where are all the visitors, that's what I want to know?'

'In the boarding houses putting the kids to bed and drinking mugs of cocoa,' Pauline laughed. 'You know it's mostly families that come to Whitby. Anyway, I don't care what they look like, just so long as they can dance.'

She glanced impatiently at the queue in front of them. Surely the doors should be open now? 'I want to let my hair down and dance and dance,' she said. 'It's ages since I've had a bit of fun.'

Mary gave her a sympathetic glance. 'I know.' She touched Pauline's hand. 'What's up with your dad? Have the chapel people got their clutches into him? He didn't use to be so mean.'

Pauline shook her head. 'No, he doesn't go to church or chapel. He stopped going when Mum died.' She shrugged her shoulders. 'I suppose that's when he started to change.

'You know, they weren't like most married couples.' She hesitated, trying to make herself understand as well as Mary. 'They'd been married for seventeen years and they were still in love with each other.' Pauline glanced shyly at her friend. 'Dad's never been one for friends, mixing with people, but he was crazy about Mum. He wanted to be with her all the time.'

'I know *that*. You could tell. It was an awful shame when she died. She never looked as though she had a bad heart, did she? But it's four years ago now, he should be getting over her. And anyway, what's your mum got to do with the way he treats you?'

'He's . . .' Pauline bit her lip. 'He's still very lonely.

When Mum died, he tried to make it up to me. He was away a lot, because of the war, but when he was home he used to spend a lot of time with me. I liked that, of course I did, but as time went by it got harder and harder.' She sighed. 'Sometimes, he'd come home when I was doing something with other kids and go really quiet when I went out. I always felt guilty, but Gran told me to go anyway. She said I needed my friends.

'But it's even worse now. He doesn't seem to realise I'm grown up. Do you know, if he sees me wearing lipstick, he goes mad? Honestly, Mary, I'm about fed up with it all. The only time I have a bit of freedom is when he's away fishing. My gran does her best to keep the peace but . . .'

'Can't you get him off with someone?' Mary interrupted her. 'He's still a decent-looking chap. He could get married again, and then you'd be off the hook.'

'Oh, I don't think . . .'

But there was movement in the queue and Mary had stopped listening.

'Hurray, they've opened the doors.'

Patiently, the queue of young people shuffled forward. The dances at Whitby Spa were popular. Indeed, they were the highlight of the week. The resident band numbered fifteen and both orchestra and dancers took their pleasures seriously. The dance floor was always crowded and the regulars enjoyed showing off their dancing prowess.

'Look,' hissed Mary as they inched closer to the paybox. 'That chap's taken his trilby off. My goodness, I could fancy him.' She nudged Pauline in the ribs. 'He looks like Errol Flynn. He even has the moustache.'

Pauline nodded. Although closer to the two men, she still couldn't distinguish their faces.

'The other one's not bad either.' Mary knew of Pauline's short sight. She grinned understandingly. 'He's not as good-looking as mine, but he's lovely and tall. I'm sure you'll like him.'

The objects of her interest had disappeared through the plush curtains which guarded the way to the ballroom and now the girls were at the paybox. Mary's words had made Pauline cross. Colour heightened in her cheeks as she searched in her handbag for her purse.

'Don't push me into things,' she snapped. 'I'll make up my own mind, thank you!'

'My, we are quick-tempered tonight.' Mary handed her money to the woman seated behind the glass partition and received her ticket in return. She stepped back to allow Pauline to pay. 'It's only a bit of fun.'

She linked arms with her friend as they walked up red-carpeted steps and through the draped curtains. 'I know what's up with you.' She squeezed Pauline's arm. 'You couldn't see them properly, could you?' She paused. 'Well, the tall chap looks nice. He's clean-shaven with a straight nose and good teeth.' She paused. 'And he's got lovely curly dark red hair.'

'You don't *mind* dancing with me, do you?'

His voice sounded cool, amused rather than concerned. Pauline ducked her head so he wouldn't see her blush and concentrated on a tricky foxtrot turn before answering him.

'No, of course I don't.' Her voice was noncommittal. Mary had been so blatant in her approach to the two young men, Pauline had been rigid with embarrassment. Even now, an hour later, she still felt self-conscious.

'I'm glad of that. It was just, well . . .' he laughed. 'You didn't seem too keen when I asked you.'

'No, really – I'm pleased you asked me.'

He nodded, exerted a touch more pressure to the small of her back and twirled her off in a different direction. He was an excellent dancer. Cautiously, she began to relax and enjoy herself.

He seemed disinclined to talk so Pauline closed her eyes, content to take pleasure in the music and to follow his confident lead. The band went into a waltz and she was glad when he continued to hold her easily but not too closely. Truth to tell, she felt a little in awe of him. She could see his suit was of good quality and his accent was quite posh. She wondered why he had come to Whitby and was spending his Saturday evening dancing at the Spa?

All she knew about him was that his name was Grahame and he was tall and slim. She was dying to have another look at his face but she was only five foot three in her high-heeled dancing shoes and in order to do so, she would have to step away from him and crane her neck, so she looked around her instead.

Many couples on the floor had used the change of tempo as a chance to smooch.

The lights had dimmed romantically, and Pauline saw some of the girls had linked arms around their partner's neck and were holding up their face for a kiss. In one case, a couple dancing nearby, the initial swift kiss had turned into a passionate embrace and the man's hands were now roaming possessively over the girl.

Because she was dancing with a man she didn't

know, Pauline felt a little embarrassed but gave the couple a sympathetic grin before looking away. She knew Penny Jackson and Brian Jennings. They had been courting ever since schooldays and were desperate to marry, but their parents had told them they must wait until Brian was twenty-one.

She saw her partner looking at the couple and felt obliged to explain. 'They're childhood sweethearts,' she whispered, and then felt silly when she saw the lift of his eyebrow.

'How quaint. I suppose,' he paused and did a complicated spin which she followed effortlessly, 'in a place like this, the locals all know each other. Do you all congregate here every Saturday?'

'No, we don't.' Even to her own ears, her voice sounded sharp, but he needn't be so patronising. 'And not everyone knows everyone else. Whitby's only a small town but we're close to other resorts – Scarborough and Filey. And there's the summer visitors.'

'Sorry, I didn't mean to upset you.'

Again, she caught a note of amusement in his voice. Thereafter they danced in silence.

Tonight, the band was in erratic mood. Without warning, the dreamy tempo of waltz-time changed to the rousing strains of a military two-step. Her partner sighed. 'Let's sit this one out.'

She nodded and followed him back to their table.

Mary and the look-alike Errol Flynn had their heads together but sat back in their chairs when Grahame and Pauline approached.

'I'm off for more drinks.' Grahame looked at his friend. 'Coming?'

Errol – Pauline now knew that his name was Jim, but she still thought of him as Errol – nodded. 'Sure.

It's my shout, isn't it?' He stood up and the two men went towards the bar.

'Well, what's he like?' Mary leaned forward in her chair to hear what Pauline had to say.

Before answering, she glanced back at the dancers galloping round the floor. There were shouts and laughter as three young lads skidded across the highly polished dance floor and bumped into a group of young girls. The military two-step was getting boisterous.

She looked back at Mary. 'He seems all right.' Her voice was cautious.

'He's a super dancer. You two looked fantastic together. Give you a swanky gown and him a top hat and tails and it would be Fred and Ginger all over again,' Mary laughed.

'It's not me that's ginger.' Pauline sat down and surreptitiously eased her left shoe off her foot. The soles of her sandals were practically worn through and her feet were killing her, but she had no coupons left to buy new ones. The blooming war's been over a year, she thought, and there's more shortages now than when it was on.

'What have you got to know about him?'

'He's called Grahame Lossing. He didn't talk much. He was concentrating on his dancing. Don't think he's on holiday though.'

'Jim's a commercial traveller. I bet twinkletoes is, too.'

Pauline looked towards the bar where Jim and Grahame were waiting to be served. A commercial traveller? Yes, he could be one, she thought. He had enough confidence.

The young men joined them again and conversation

became general. As the evening progressed, Pauline's annoyance with Mary for pushing her into a foursome began to fade. There was a small but ugly incident when the manager and the doorman had to be called to the youngsters who had disrupted the dancing; they started annoying two girls and so were thrown out. It made Pauline glad they had escorts.

At least we didn't get landed with roughs like those, she reflected. And it was nice to meet someone new. She found out Grahame was indeed a commercial traveller, for as the evening wore on he became more talkative.

'I'm visiting the farms in this area,' he told her. 'I travel in farm equipment. The firm's office is based in Middlesbrough, but I travel all over the Midlands and the North-East.'

'That must be interesting.' Pauline clasped her hands together. 'I'm just stuck in a shop all day.'

'Not as interesting as *my* line.' With a flourish, Jim produced a slim packet from inside his jacket and dangled it before Mary.

'Nylons, my dear. Take them with my compliments.'

'My God!' With a whoop of joy, she pounced on them. 'Fifteen denier, too. You wonderful man.' She flung her arms about Jim and kissed him on his lips. He grasped at her hungrily.

Pauline looked away, discomfited. She saw Grahame looking at her. His eyes twinkled and he shrugged his shoulders and gave her a swift grin. She smiled back. She had been more or less forced into his company, and certainly he wasn't as handsome as his friend, but she liked him better. And she was glad he travelled in farm equipment rather than ladies' underwear. Studying him from beneath lowered eyelashes, she decided he was quite attractive and his hair wasn't so much ginger as auburn.

'We've struck lucky tonight, old bean!'

'Maybe.' Moving away from the urinal, Grahame buttoned up his trousers and went over to the basin to wash his hands. 'Old bean'. Trust Jimmy Redder to use an expression like that. God, how he disliked the man, and to think, the first time they had met, Redder had impressed him! Of course, Grahame hadn't been in a fit state to judge anyone that day.

It had been eleven months ago and he had only been out of the army two months. They had met at a sales convention in a hall at Leeds and he had been both elated and terrified: elated because he had landed a job and terrified because he had lied to get it. He had told his prospective employers that he knew all about selling. In truth, he knew nothing.

But he had wanted the job so badly. The war in Europe was over. Soon there would be thousands of demobbed soldiers, sailors and airmen wanting jobs. He had been lucky, being in the very first wave of men to be demobbed. Lucky? He smiled sardonically. If you could call suffering from bad asthma attacks being lucky. North Africa had got him, not with a bomb or a bullet but with its climate. Well, it wasn't so bad. His limbs and his mind were intact and the frequency of the asthma attacks was decreasing.

So he had moved from being a soldier to a salesman and hadn't known which career had terrified him more. At the convention Redder had spotted him as being a new boy and had offered to give him a few tips. He had laughed at Grahame's murmured doubts.

'Sure, women's underwear and farm equipment are different products,' Grahame remembered him saying. 'But selling is selling, old boy. The principle is always the same!'

That, thought Grahame, was the only time he had heard Redder speak the truth. For example, his last remark, 'old bean', meant that he was still peddling his pretence of being a former RAF officer. Grahame knew that was a lie. He had met enough of the genuine article to recognise a sham. The bugger had probably spent the war years selling army surplus on the black market. Probably still did, he thought. He straightened up and smiled grimly at his reflection in the glass.

Because, whatever Jimmy was, he could *sell*, by God, and everyone in the trade *knew* it! Jimmy always knew where the action was. He had contacts everywhere. That's why Grahame kept company with him, even though he hated his guts.

If he'd been his own boss, Grahame would have made some excuse when he had bumped into him in the bar of the Royal Hotel. But he wasn't, so when Jimmy had suggested they go to the 'local hop' together, he had agreed. It might be to his advantage to stick with Jimmy a while.

Grahame never forgot he had landed the job as commercial traveller for Manner's Farm Equipment after tight competition and he'd only keep it as long as he produced results. If that meant drinking with bastards like Jimmy Redder, then he'd do it. And, after all, tonight he had already gained his reward.

After a few drinks, Redder had spoken of a buyer at a departmental store near Redcar. She was an attractive woman and Jimmy had treated her to a meal. During the sweet course she had mentioned her husband who was a farmer.

'From what she said,' Jimmy grinned, 'he sounded a lousy husband, more interested in his pigs than in her. But he's a workaholic, Grahame. And currently he's thinking of investing in more labour-saving machinery. Might be worth a visit, old bean.'

He had laughed. 'If he's as co-operative as his wife, you'll do all right!'

Women, reflected Grahame, liked Jimmy, but men did not. Did Jimmy know what the other salesmen on the North-East circuit really thought of him? He shrugged. Jimmy was shrewd, so he probably did. He was such a sleaze, he probably got a kick out of knowing; watching them buy the drinks, return his smiles, knowing that although they couldn't stand him, they were in awe of his sales technique, and all, at some time or another, were beholden to him.

Drying his hands, Grahame noticed they were trembling. He took a deep breath as he moved away from the roller towel. Silly to let Jimmy upset him. Jimmy was nothing. If Grahame could cope with four years of war, plus a ghastly childhood with a bastard of a father, he could put up with an oily grub like Jimmy. One day he would leave people like Jimmy far behind him. One day, when he had money.

'Time we were getting back to the ladies,' he said. 'Come on, my turn to buy a round.' It wasn't, of course, but Jimmy wouldn't argue.

Waiting with Grahame at the bar, Jimmy nodded to where the two girls waited. 'Nice bits of skirt, don't you think? Little beauties, both of them.'

Grahame glanced over his shoulder. 'Yours is.' He gave his order to the barman. He had felt sour when the girls, after giving them the eye, had sidled up and immediately the tall brunette had come on so strong to Jimmy. He'd been stuck with the little quiet one who had simply stood next to him and looked embarrassed. He sighed. He didn't feel comfortable with wholesome girls.

But when he carried the drinks back to the table and looked again at the girl he had been landed with, he felt a touch of shame because she seemed a nice kid. And then he looked more closely at her and felt something else, because really she wasn't too bad. He watched as she talked to her friend and cast shy glances at him across the table, and he smiled at her and began to revise his earlier opinion.

Mary was the showy one, that was for sure. She had a fantastic figure and had made great efforts, make-up wise, to look vampish, but the other . . . Grahame had to wrinkle his brow in order to remember her name . . . Pauline, that was it, was also good-looking. She had regular features, good skin, and her fair hair was fluffed prettily around her oval-shaped face. She looked very young and vulnerable.

Thank God Jimmy hadn't taken a fancy to her, he suddenly thought. She wouldn't have stood a chance. Feeling he had been cast in the role of virtuous hero for the evening, which was an enjoyable thought, he stood up.

'Feel like dancing again?'

She nodded and blushed, very prettily.

My, but she could dance. They circled the floor in an old-fashioned waltz and then the bandleader assumed a foreign accent, shouted 'Carreba!' picked up a pair of maracas and they were swirling to the beat of a Latin American set.

Grahame, hesitating, missed a step. He had half-expected Pauline to excuse herself and leave the floor. In his experience girls were usually a bit embarrassed about dancing to Latin American music. But she wasn't, not one little bit.

They danced the samba and the cha-cha-cha and finished with a tango. She followed his steps perfectly. When they finally went back to their table, they were both flushed and laughing.

'Where did you learn to dance like that?' He pulled out her chair for her.

Mary answered for her. 'It's a natural gift, isn't it, Pauline?' She fluttered her eyelashes at Jimmy. 'You didn't ask me to dance, Jim?'

'No, can't stand "wop" music. Too bloody fancy for my liking.' Redder's voice was curt.

Grahame glanced at him. Could it be that Jimmy the ladies' man was no good at dancing?

But he didn't smile, for Redder's words had awoken a memory in him. He was twelve years old and his father was towering over him, screaming: 'No bloody son of mine is taking dancing lessons! What do you think you are, a bloody wop – or maybe you're turning into a pouf, is that it?'

He re-buried the memory. It had been a long time ago. His dad was dead now, and Grahame was glad.

'I've always loved dancing,' Pauline's soft voice distracted him. 'I used to go to ballet and tap lessons when I was tiny.'

'You won a couple of gold medals, didn't you, Pauline?' Mary was generously singing her friend's praises. 'Say, hold on a minute – I've just remembered.' She jumped up and ran across to where the members of the dance band were taking a well-deserved break. A few moments later she returned to their table, a leaflet clutched in her hand.

'I wondered if they had one left. Remember last

week, Pauline? No,' she clicked her tongue, 'of course you don't. You didn't come, did you?' She waved the piece of paper in the air. 'A competition was announced, a dancing competition – next week. Here you are.' She thrust the leaflet into Pauline's hand. 'See, three sections, Latin American, modern and old-time. And they're offering twenty pounds for first prize. Just think what you could do with twenty pounds! You two *must* enter, you'd win easily.'

Grahame, watching Pauline's face, saw the colour rise beneath her fair skin and then recede, leaving her pale.

'Oh, I couldn't!'

'Why not?' Mary was insistent. 'You're easily the best dancer I know. And the two of you,' she glanced at Grahame, 'would wipe the floor with the rest of them.'

'I just couldn't. Anyway, Grahame,' Pauline looked at him shyly as she said his name, 'probably wouldn't be able to come, and I certainly couldn't. My dad . . .'

'Oh, bugger your dad! He never lets you have any fun. Whoops!' Mary put her hand to her mouth, her eyes sparkling mischievously. 'Pardon my French!'

So Pauline's dad was a miserable old devil? Grahame felt a comradely pang of sympathy for her.

'I think I *could* manage next Saturday,' he said. He mentally flicked through his programme. He had plenty of calls within the area and might as well spend next Saturday night in Whitby as in Redcar, Saltburn or Runswick Bay.

He turned to Jimmy Redder. 'Why don't you come along, too?' His smile held a touch of malice. 'If you don't want to enter, you could sit and watch.'

Redder didn't answer, but Pauline did.

'Could we possibly win, do you think?'

'I think we would stand a very good chance,' Grahame answered her gravely.

She twisted her hands together. 'Twenty pounds – ten pounds each. Oh, what couldn't I do with ten pounds!'

He opened his mouth to tell her that, if they did win, she could keep all the money, but decided to remain silent. She might pull out if he did, and anyway, he too could find a use for ten pounds.

'All right.' She had made up her mind. 'I'll . . . *we'll* do it!' She looked both scared and happy. 'What about you, Mary?'

Mary giggled. 'You must be joking. However,' she tossed back her head, 'there's another competition, before the dancing, and I've already put my name down for that.'

'Oh?' They looked at her.

'Yes. I've entered the "Rita Hayworth look-alike" competition. Colouring's a bit off,' she grinned. 'But it's the face and figure that counts, isn't it? What do you think? Do I stand a chance?'

Chapter Two

After her late night out, Pauline enjoyed the luxury of a lie-in. It was after nine when her gran tapped on the door, entered her tiny bedroom and placed a mug on the small table beside her bed.

Pauline yawned, opened her eyes and then protested, 'Oh, Gran, you shouldn't have.'

'Why shouldn't I?' Eliza Verrill sat on the side of the bed. 'You're up early every other day of the week. And anyhow, I want you to stay put for a few minutes and tell me about last night. Were there lots of people there? Did you have a good time?'

She really did want to know. Pauline, looking up at her gran's rosy, wrinkled face, chuckled. 'Why so interested, Gran? Remind you of when you were a girl, does it? I bet you did a bit of gadding about before you were married?'

Eliza's face took on a dreamy look. 'I had my moments, Pauline, although they were few and far between. My generation didn't have the free time you youngsters have now. When I was sixteen, if I wasn't at work, I was looking after the younger nippers for me mam, or skeining flithers and baiting the fishing lines for me dad. Still, I did enjoy life.'

Pauline sat up and, reaching out, gently took hold

of her grandmother's hard hand. 'Yes, I know.'

Her grandma was very dear to her. Eliza Verrill had lived in her own little cottage in Skinner Street, Whitby, until the death of Pauline's mother in 1942. When that happened, she sold up and moved into the family home to look after her grand-daughter.

Pauline's dad, devastated though he was, had continued to do his duty. During the war he had served in the Royal Naval Reserve and was away from home for long periods, patrolling coastal waters in a minesweeper.

Eliza, being a practical woman, had wasted little time in bemoaning what couldn't be changed. Instead, she kept the house clean, cooked good, plain meals and saw to it that Pauline went to school looking decent. And when her son was home, she darned his socks, tried to fatten him up – he had become awfully thin – and watched him as he struggled silently with his grief.

Pauline often wondered if Gran and her father had talked about her mother's untimely death, because Gran had never actually mentioned her mother's last illness to her; but in her own way, she had administered comfort.

There were times, during those first dreadful weeks of bereavement, when Pauline had woken in the night crying, and when that had happened, Eliza had always come to her. She had slipped into the bedroom, wrapped up in a feather quilt, and sat on the self-same bed she was on now to tell Pauline a story.

She spoke of smugglers and dark deeds in caves close by the sea. There had been a bit of smuggling still going on when she was a lass, she had said, brandy and such-like. 'Everyone was so poor, you see.' Her father had been a fisherman and, in time, so had her two younger brothers.

They had lived in a cottage by the sea at Robin Hood's Bay. The folks with money had big houses and lived at the top of the village, up a steep bank. Eliza's family had been poor.

Pauline, tears drying and snug in bed, would watch the dark shape that was her grandmother talking about when *she* was twelve. How she would rise at five in the morning to help her mother with the washing. How the women would then go out to gather 'flithers', limpets, which were used to bait the fishing lines.

'We'd get mussels, too.' The soft voice of her grandmother conjured up word pictures for Pauline. 'We'd walk four miles sometimes, to find the best ones, and when there was snow and ice about, we'd shuffle down the banks on our rumps, because it was so slippy.' She had laughed and then sighed. 'Then we'd hump 'em back home and open the mussels with sharp knives and soak them in a big tin bath to make them bigger, before putting them on to the hooks. Eh, Pauline, it took ages. Two hundred or more hooks we'd bait for every line.' She had sighed again. 'And me dad used up to twelve lines every fishing trip in the winter.'

Nose peeping above the covers, Pauline had asked why the men didn't bait the hooks themselves.

Eliza shook her head. 'Nay, lass, the men had enough to do. They came home from the fishing grounds frozen and dog-tired. So it was only fair the women and bairns worked hard, too.'

And then Pauline had snuggled even further down in bed, thinking of her father, out there in the North Sea. And sometimes, with a chill of fear, she thought about her great-grandad, Eliza's father, who had drowned in that self-same sea many years ago, together with one of her brothers.

And Eliza, perhaps following the track of her thoughts, would pull the quilt tighter about her shoulders and talk of happier things. How she would dress up in her best clothes on a Sunday and go to Bridlington to see the Pierrots on the sands, and about the never-to-be-forgotten day she took a trip on a steamer running down the coast from Scarborough.

And occasionally her voice would soften and she would talk of the best day of all, the day on which she had met an upright young man with saucy eyes and beautiful corn-coloured hair who was playing in a band concert at Whitby. That was a red-letter day, all right, the day she met the man she would marry. Thomas Verrill had been his name. He had courted Eliza, married her, fathered a son and then died a few short years later, fighting in the trenches somewhere in France in a war and for causes he did not understand.

How strange, thought Pauline now, clasping her grandmother's hand, how strange that Eliza, despite her hard life and the loss of her father, brother and husband, was still the most joyous person she knew. Oh, she was no saint. She was sharp-tongued and liked a bit of gossip as much as anyone else. But beneath all that, she retained a certain sure joy, a love of life.

It surfaced all the time. You had only to bring her back a handful of early primroses from the cliff tops in the spring, or take her to tea in that posh cafe in Royal Crescent, and you could see the pleasure rise in her, and her eyes would sparkle like a child's.

And right now it was she who was waiting for a

story. Pauline released her grandmother's hand and did her best to oblige.

'We had to queue to get in. Mary was wearing a new blouse – I can't think where she gets all the coupons. It was bright red and a bit daring, but ever so pretty. Anyway,' she paused and took a sip of tea, 'by ten o'clock the place was packed. We knew most of the dancers, of course.' She chuckled as she told Eliza about Penny Jackson and Brian. 'He couldn't keep his hands off her, Gran. It was embarrassing.'

Eliza shook her head. 'They should let those youngsters marry. They're crazy about each other. Crying shame, it is.'

Pauline hid her smile behind her mug of tea. Gran had not let her down. She remembered what it was like to be young and in love, just as she accepted that Pauline was no longer a child. Unlike some people!

'Yes. And, oh, the band looked lovely. They were all wearing black trousers and short red jackets.'

Pauline knew her grandma had an especially soft spot for bandsmen. She chattered on as she finished her tea. Then she said, 'I had a lovely time, Gran. And I danced practically every dance. I did enjoy myself.'

'I knew you would, you were always one for dancing.' Eliza smiled. 'Remember when you went to Miss Havers' dancing school? Me and and your mam used to sit up half the night making your costumes for the shows.'

'Yes, I remember.' Pauline replaced the empty mug on the bedside table and reflected that now might be a good time to mention the dancing competition.

'Mary and I met two young men at the dance. They told us they were commercial travellers. They had lovely manners. The one who danced with me was called Grahame Lossing. He was a fantastic dancer and nice and polite, we got on ever so well. I danced with him all night. Then Mary told us about a dancing competition they're holding at the Spa next weekend. She said we should enter. Grahame was interested, and I wondered . . . it would be a bit of fun, Gran, and we'd get twenty pounds if we won.'

Eliza frowned. 'I don't know, Pauline.' She stood up. 'You'd have to ask your father.'

'Oh, Gran!'

'I know, I know. But it's only right. You wheedled me into letting you go dancing last night and I'm glad you enjoyed yourself. But,' she paused, 'I've felt guilty ever since.'

'But Dad had gone fishing when you said I could go, so it wasn't as if you lied to him.'

'That's splitting hairs, and you know it.' Eliza shook her head. 'I know your dad's hard on you, Pauline, but some men are like that with daughters. But I tell you this – I'm getting sick of being "piggy in the middle" between the two of you. I think it's time you sorted things out with him.'

She walked to the door. 'Pick the right time, that's all. Wait until he's in a good mood and then sit down with him and quietly explain your point of view. You might find him more understanding than you think. I know he's a stubborn man, but the way you flounce about sulking when he won't let you have your own way only makes things worse.'

She gave Pauline a sideways glance. ' "Actions speak louder than words", you know. Act grown-up and maybe he'll come to see you are. At least give it a try. Then, when he's thought about things, I'll put in my half-penny's worth, back you up.'

Pauline sighed and pulled moodily at her bottom lip. 'I'll tell him about last night, if you think I should.'

'I do.' Eliza opened the door. 'And another thing, while I'm laying down the law.' She pulled a humorous face. 'If you *do* get his permission to enter this contest, and if you *are* going to see this Grahame chap again, ask him round to tea next Sunday.'

'Oh, Gran!'

At Pauline's exclamation, Eliza laughed. 'Oh, I know you think you can handle everything, but a commercial traveller's a different kettle of fish from a local lad. I want to meet this wonderful dancer.' She went out, closing the door softly behind her.

Were all families so difficult? Pauline drew up her knees beneath the bedclothes and brooded. Even Gran thought she still needed looking after. What nonsense it was. She was a big girl now. She knew all about the birds and the bees, what lads wanted and what girls were prepared to give.

Anyway, Grahame wasn't like that. Very cool, he had been when he walked her home last night. Pauline's brows drew together in a straight line. Too cool. He hadn't even tried to kiss her. It was a bit insulting really.

She bet Mary and Jimmy Redder had kissed, and more. In fact, she thought she might go round to Mary's house later and find out. She threw back the bedclothes and got out of bed, then went to the window and drew back the curtains.

She had a splendid view from her bedroom and today, because the weather was serene and the sea gentle, it was particularly fine. Even without her glasses, she could appreciate the way the cloudless blue of the sky met the deeper blue of the sea, and how the mass of red-roofed buildings, which clung to the sides of the cliffs leading down to the bay, shone cheerfully in the sunshine.

Pauline looked and felt a sense of happiness growing inside her. What an idiot she was, staying in bed on a day like this. She went along to the tiny bathroom her father had installed a year ago to wash and brush her teeth, and then she returned to her bedroom to dress. As she did so, she hummed a little tune to herself. With Gran's help, she would manage to persuade her dad to agree to her entering the competition. She and Grahame would win, and he would want to see her again, and then, maybe, he would want to kiss her.

She decided to wear her new outfit, it was perfect for today. It was a pity the mirror in her room was so small. She tied herself in knots trying to see how she looked then gave up, ran down the stairs and into the heart of the house.

The kitchen was a poky little room dominated by a large old-fashioned fireplace which today, because it was warm, held only a pleated paper fan. The high mantelpiece was cluttered with two clocks, a luridly painted vase, brass candlesticks and a pot pekinese dog, the only survivor of a pair.

Faded photographs in black frames jostled for room with two ornate mugs, one commemorating the coronation of George V and Queen Mary, the other the birth of Princess Elizabeth. Pinned around the mantelpiece was a dark green velour runner, and below that, hanging from a string, a row of thick, grey fishermen's stockings hung up to air.

There were two sagging but comfortable armchairs beautified by the exquisitely worked patchwork cushions upon them, two hard-backed wooden chairs and a footstool. A solid, square table occupied most of the remaining space. There was linoleum on the floor and two rag rugs in soft muted colours. Eliza had made those years ago, using up scraps of discarded clothing. The cream-painted walls were decorated with pictures showing seascapes mounted in heavy, gold-painted frames.

It was a room in which with two people it was necessary to side-step to pass each other, but it was Pauline's favourite place in the house. Her room upstairs was so small it held nothing but the bed and table, with a stool to put her clothes on, and she knew she was lucky to have that. Most of the fishermen's cottages only had two rooms upstairs. The scullery, which held the sink and gas cooker, was cold and draughty with a stone floor, and the front parlour was so uncomfortable she found it impossible to relax when she was in there.

And yet, the front parlour was Gran's pride and joy. Pauline grimaced. If Grahame did come to tea, she knew they would eat in the parlour, a room in which the sun rarely penetrated and which always felt cold. The best china would come out and everyone would be terribly stiff and polite.

She shrugged away the thought. She wasn't sure she would even see Grahame again. He might have just been being polite when he said he would turn up for the dancing competition.

She glanced at her grandmother who was seated by the kitchen table industriously cleaning a set of forks with a soft cloth which she kept dipping into a saucer of vinegar.

'Oh, Gran, don't bother with them now. It's such

lovely weather, why don't you have an easy day? Dad won't be back until late and I don't want a cooked meal, it's too hot. In fact, I think I'll pop round to Mary's and ask her if she wants to go to the beach and sunbathe. Why not let me lift your chair outside, and then you could sit and enjoy the sunshine for a bit and watch the world go by?'

'Aye, I'll do that later, but I'll finish these first.' Eliza looked up. 'You're not going out like that, are you, Pauline?'

'Why not?' She twisted round to examine her rear view. 'Doesn't it suit me? I wondered if the stripes would make my bottom look big?'

Eliza laughed. 'No, you look right bonny. But – shorts, and that top! Fine for larking about on the sands, but maybe you should slip a skirt and blouse on, until you get there?'

Pauline sighed. 'All right, if you think so.'

She had finished sewing her sunsuit two nights ago and it was the first time she had worn it. She was proud of her efforts. The halter-necked top and matching shorts suited her, but she supposed Gran was right. The neighbours would be twitching their net curtains at the sight of skimpy clothing, particularly on a Sunday. Miserable old biddies, didn't they know the war was over? She dashed back upstairs again and pulled on a short-sleeved button-through blouse but then decided against wearing a skirt. She was young, the sun was shining, and she had nice legs. Why should she cover them up? She bounded back down the stairs and dropped a kiss on Gran's forehead. 'See you later.'

Her grandma gave her an old-fashioned look but made no further comment.

Ten minutes later, she turned into Grey Street and spied Mary, who had just opened the front door of her house and was bending down, collecting the bottle of milk from the step.

Pauline waved to her and hid a smile. The morning Mary looked quite different from the girl of the night before. A flowered apron hid her curvy figure, her long dark hair was screwed into tight pin-curls and her pale face devoid of make-up.

Mary gave her a limp wave back and waited for her to come up to the house. She nodded. 'You're out early.'

'It's nearly ten o'clock.' Pauline was unable to contain her curiosity. She asked, 'How did it go, then? How did you get on with "lover-boy" last night?'

'Don't ask.' Mary clutched the bottle of milk to her chest and shuddered. 'He brought me home the long way round, and when we got to the dark bit, you know . . .'

Pauline nodded, she knew the popular courting area.

'I had one hell of a tussle with him. Talk about hands! He was like an octopus.'

Pauline showed little sympathy. 'What did you expect? You led him on, Mary, you know you did. *And* you took those nylons.'

She tossed her head. 'Don't be a little prude. Of course I took them, anyone in their right mind would have, but that didn't give him the right to maul me about. I don't mind a bit of fun, as you know, but he turned nasty when I wouldn't . . .' She stopped and pressed her lips together. Then she said, 'I had to fight him off.'

'I'm sorry.' Pauline's brow creased.

'So was I. Who would have thought it? He was lovely at the dance.' She stared at Pauline. 'I suppose *Grahame* remained a perfect gentleman?'

'As a matter of fact, he did.' Pauline's chin lifted. She wasn't going to apologise for his good behaviour. And hearing about Mary's experience made her feel glad her partner had behaved himself. Anyway, it was the dancing they were interested in. It sounded as though Mary had had a bad time last night, but some of it was her own fault. She shouldn't have been so obvious. Everyone knew there were rules to be followed.

The image of her father rose before Pauline. How horrified he would have been if he had heard their conversation. Dad thought she knew nothing about men, but she hadn't mixed with other lads and lasses without picking up a certain amount of street knowledge, even though the most she'd ever done was a bit of kissing and cuddling in the back row of the pictures.

Dropping the subject of last night, she asked, 'Can I come in?'

'If you want.' Mary opened the door a little wider.

Pauline entered and stood in the passageway. 'It's such a grand day, I thought we could go to the beach.'

'I have to look after Angela and Malcolm. Jill and her husband are going on that brewery trip.' Mary pulled a face. 'If we go to the beach, the kids will have to come with us.'

Pauline thought for a moment. 'All right.'

Mary's face brightened. 'Great. And you'll play with them, too, won't you, Pauline? You're good with kids, I'll give you that. You have more patience with them than I have.'

Mary's family was a large one and so, last year, she

had moved in with her married sister and her husband in order to make more space at home.

Angela and Malcolm, her niece and nephew, were nice kids. Pauline thought it would be fun to take them on the beach. We'll paddle, she thought. Sea-water was supposed to make you tan more quickly. She wanted a tan. She was a bit pale-skinned and when you were brown, you looked more glamorous. She didn't want too much sun, though. Too much of a tan and you looked tarty.

The sunshine was wonderful. It soaked down into your bones and melted them, like jelly. Pauline felt marvellous. She put her hands behind her head and closed her eyes. She wriggled her bare feet in the warm sand and listened. Children were shouting and laughing and, further away. she could hear a dog barking.

She smiled. That would be the little brown and white mongrel that had been racing in and out of the sea earlier, trailing a great length of seaweed behind him. He had been playing near to their little group but Mary had chased him away. They had all been covered with sand for he shook the seaweed so ferociously, you would have thought he had a rat. We could do with him in our street, she thought. She was sure there were rats in the concrete air-raid shelters which stood at the top of the road. During the war, she had only been in the shelter in her street once. Whitby had been lucky, really. There had been nothing important enough there for the Jerries to bomb.

Someone, she didn't open her eyes to find out who, ran past and splattered her with sand. She wasn't bothered, she didn't mind anything today.

All through the war, the beach had been a sad place, festooned with barbed wire with boards up warning about mines. This year the visitors were back, not too many, but enough, and there were kids sticking paper flags in sand castles again, and fat ladies with their dresses tucked in their knickers, paddling.

'Are you asleep, Pauline?'

'No.' She opened her eyes.

'Oh, I thought you might be, you've been so quiet.'

Mary sat upright on the sand. Pauline thought she wouldn't lie down because she didn't want her hair mussed up. It wasn't a catty thought, she just knew Mary. She sat up.

'When does the brewery trip get back?'

'About six, I think.' Mary brushed sand off her legs and then critically examined her finger nails. 'They'd better not be late. I'm off to the pictures tonight.'

'Oh, who with?' Pauline was constantly amazed at how many chaps Mary seemed to meet. Pauline herself rarely did. Maybe it was because Mary worked behind the counter at a local dairy where lots of milk roundsmen came in to pay their money, whereas she herself worked at a dry-cleaner's. Or maybe, a little voice whispered, Mary's just that bit more attractive, and exciting, and *knowing*!

'He's called Mark Deakin, I don't think you know him.' Mary shrugged. 'He's all right, nothing special. Still, after last night . . .'

Pauline said nothing. She called four-year-old Angela to her and pulled up her drooping knickers, the only garment the little girl was wearing. Angela wriggled impatiently from her grasp and went back to building sand pies.

'Don't you get fed up of this place, Pauline?' Mary

was staring at her, a discontented expression on her face. 'Don't you get sick to death of doing the same old things and meeting the same old people all the time?'

'I've never really thought about it. Surely it's the same wherever you live? Whitby's not bad. It's better than being stuck out on a farm, up on the moors.'

'We might as well be.' Mary's full lips drooped disconsolately. 'We're so cut off from everywhere else. Just think of the other girls we know – they're either married or courting strong, all with local lads. Nobody ever seems to get away from here.'

'But that's what people do, grow up, get married, start raising their own families. What else is there?'

'Oh, Pauline.' Mary looked suddenly angry. 'That's what I mean. Everyone's stuck in the same old rut. Well, I've made up my mind, I'm not going to do that. I'm going to start looking for a job somewhere else. I want to move somewhere bigger, somewhere like Manchester. That'll do for a start. Then, later, I might go to London.'

Pauline didn't know how to reply. She had never realised Mary entertained such thoughts. London? She remembered Gran's remaining brother had come to see them once. He had lived in London for a year. Mucky place, he had said, rows and rows of houses and no green anywhere.

She looked around her at the sparkling blue sea, the birds soaring high in the sky and the high cliffs behind them, and knew she didn't fancy London at all.

'Well, if that's what you want,' she said lamely, 'I wish you luck.'

Mary didn't answer, just stared out to sea, and Pauline felt as though she had let her down in some way.

But there was nothing else she could say. She didn't want to go gadding off anywhere. She looked over to where Malcolm and Angela were intent on building a huge sand-castle. They looked so sweet, their strong little bodies and the sweet curve of their necks as they put their heads together to plan their next move.

She was happy living in Whitby. She liked going shopping and passing the time of day with the local people. She liked climbing up the steps to the Abbey and sharing a picnic with friends. She liked hearing the sea as she fell asleep each night and awoke each morning. She liked doing ordinary things, like going bilberrying up on the moors in the summer. You couldn't do things like that in London. You'd be surrounded by strangers there.

She sighed and guessed she was a boring sort of person. All she wanted was for things to stay the same for a couple of years. And then . . . she lay down and closed her eyes . . . then she wanted to fall in love, settle down and have two lovely children, like Angela and Malcolm.

An enormous wail shattered the tranquillity. Her eyelids jerked open. Malcolm was on his knees howling, his hands holding his forehead. A thin trickle of blood was sliding down his left cheek. Angela, her pert features frozen in a scowl, watched him. She was holding her iron spade like a club.

Pauline sprang to her feet. 'Angela, what have you done?'

'He stamped on my side of the castle.' The child's voice was cool and showed no sign of repentance. 'He only did it because my side was better than his.'

'Oh God, I'd better get them home before their parents come back.' Mary stood up and went over to Malcolm. 'Stop being a baby, let me see.'

Unceremoniously she pulled his hand away. 'It's all right.' She looked at Pauline. 'There's a cut, but it's not deep.' She turned back to her nephew. 'Haven't you got a hankie, or something?'

'Here.' Pauline produced a handkerchief and gave it to Malcolm. He nodded, his howls diminishing. He mopped his forehead, looked at the blood and then felt strong enough to let fly a kick at his sister's ankle.

'Stop that.' Mary clipped his ear. Pauline looked away. An only child, she decided she had a lot to learn about children.

They gathered up their belongings and made their way home.

'I'll see you before the weekend, won't I?' Pauline lingered outside Mary's home.

'Yes.' Her face wore a harassed expression. 'Get inside, you two, but empty your sandals first.' She dumped the buckets and spades outside the door and turned back to Pauline.

'About the dancing competition . . .'

'Yes?' Pauline froze. Mary wasn't going to go! And if Grahame didn't turn up, she'd be stuck there on her own. But what if Jimmy Redder came with him? And if Mary did come, what would she say to Jimmy?

'I'll see you about seven, all right?'

Pauline relaxed. 'Yes, if you're sure?'

Mary shrugged. 'I'm sure. I talked you into it, didn't I?' She hesitated. 'And if you want to come round one night and see if any of my frocks fit you, you're welcome to try them.'

A rush of affection filled Pauline. She squeezed Mary's arm. 'Thanks, that's nice of you, but I don't think they'd be any good. You're so much taller than I am.'

'Well, if you change your mind.' Mary looked back

at the house. 'I'll have to go and clean up Malcolm. His mum'll have a fit if she sees the blood.'

'All right. See you.' Pauline started down the street, then turned to wave. 'Mary . . .'

'Yeah.'

'Have a good time with,' Pauline searched for the name, 'Mark.'

Mary laughed. 'I'll do my best.'

The sand in Pauline's sandals rubbed against her heels as she toiled up the steep bank that led to her home and she hoped fervently that none of Malcolm's blood had splattered on her new sunsuit. She stopped for a moment to check and breathed a sign of relief when she couldn't find any. Then she took off her sandals, shook them and replaced them on her feet. That felt better.

She walked on. Fancy Mary wanting to leave Whitby. She'd miss her if she left, but more likely it was all talk. Surely she wouldn't really want to leave her mum and dad and all her brothers and sisters? I couldn't, thought Pauline. It would be awful not seeing Gran every day. And even Dad. She still fancied the thought of renting a room for herself, having a place of her own, but when she was a bit older. And she'd want to stay in Whitby. Because she did love her dad, even when he was being pig-headed!

Dad . . . he might be back in the house by now. She'd have to come clean with him, tell him she'd been dancing and ask him about next week's competition. Pauline's steps slowed. She knew she ought to think about her dad and how to approach him, but she didn't really want to.

It was funny, but lately, when she thought, *really* thought about him, it felt as though there was some kind of band wrapped around her head and it was getting tighter and tighter. Gran hadn't noticed it yet, but Pauline knew that something was happening, something wrong between herself and her father. It was bad enough that he flew into tempers with her when she hadn't done anything, or if she had, it had been something really small, not worth bothering about. But this new thing was worse.

There were days now when he would sit in his chair and watch her, whatever she was doing. When she was drying her hair in the kitchen or playing on the rug with the kitten they had recently acquired. He only did that when Gran was out, visiting her friends.

He never said anything strange and he never touched her, but she would feel his gaze burning into her and then if she looked back at him, he would look away. And his face would be set and hard and she didn't know whether he hated her or . . . She shrugged. Maybe it was her, maybe she was imagining things.

Anyway, whatever mood he was in, she was going to make herself really talk to him. She would tell him about the competition. And, her lips tightened, whatever he said, she was going in for that competition, with Grahame.

He was there, waiting for her. She thought he must have just got in, for he was still wearing his fishermen's boots and his old gansey. He was standing by the window and when she entered the kitchen he turned and looked at her. His face was tired and looked pale behind his stubble. Pauline remembered Helen had called her father a decent-looking chap. He was, she supposed. His features were regular and his hair fair and curly, very much like her own, but his face was too thin, and scored by deep, bitter lines.

He nodded. 'Now then, Pauline.'

'Hello, Dad. Did you have a good trip?'

He didn't answer her. He was staring at her legs.

She flushed.

'You never walked up from the sands dressed like that?'

Her head came up. 'Why not? Shorts are perfectly respectable. Everyone wears them nowadays.'

'Your mother never did. She'd have died of shame at the thought of it.'

She didn't reply, but she shrugged, and the movement said a lot of things. She wasn't her mother. Her mother was dead. And she was alive and young and it was now 1946.

His eyes narrowed. 'It's not a sight I care to see. You'd best get upstairs and cover your nakedness.'

'Oh, Dad. Don't be so old-fashioned.' The words burst from her. She stopped, surprised at her own show of defiance, but at the same time felt a flicker of satisfaction. She *wasn't* afraid of her father and she *was* going to ask him about the dancing competition.

She modified her tone. 'I'm sorry, Dad. I don't like upsetting you, but you have to understand – I'm not like my mother was. I enjoy dressing up. I enjoy going out with my friends. And I want to ask you something.'

She knew her words had surprised him because he looked at her warily, as though she was some strange creature that had wandered in from nowhere. Then he looked down at his boots and rubbed his chin with his hand. She could hear the scrape of his whiskers.

'What bee have you got in your bonnet now?'

His voice sounded surprisingly mild. She put her hands behind her back and crossed her fingers. 'There's going to be a dancing competition, Dad, at the Spa next Saturday night. Can I enter for it? There's a cash prize for the winner, and we think we have a good chance.'

He studied her face. 'Who's "we"?'

'Pardon?'

'We?' His eyes had gone cold and narrow. He trapped her in his gaze like a cat playing with a mouse. 'You've got a partner lined up, have you?'

She shuffled her feet. 'Er, yes.'

'Who is it, a local lad?'

'No.' She took a deep breath. 'I went to the Spa last night, with Mary, and I danced with this young man called Grahame Lossing. He's very polite, very respectable. And he's a wonderful dancer. And when we heard about the competition . . .' Her voice withered into silence. Her father's face had become a stone mask.

'You went dancing, without my permission?'

'You weren't here to ask. You'd gone fishing. I asked Gran.'

'Did you? And she agreed, I suppose?'

He went to the door leading to the scullery and flung it open. 'Tell her to come in here.'

'I persuaded her, Dad. She said no at first but then . . .'

'You don't have to make excuses for me, Pauline.' Eliza came through from the scullery, wiping her hands on her apron. She looked at the two of them and sighed.

'Pauline asked me if she could go dancing and I said yes.'

'Then you're a wicked old woman! You know my feelings about the Spa. It's a pick-up place. A place for loose women. I don't want my daughter anywhere near there.'

Eliza faced up to her son's anger. 'That's nonsense, Walter. It's just a dance hall. The youngsters go there on a weekend to dance and enjoy themselves. They come to no harm.'

'You don't know. I do. I've had some of these "youngsters" working on *The Enterprise*. You should hear them, the filthy things they say, the boasting about the girls they've picked up.'

'Pauline knows better than to go with anyone like that. Anyway, you don't want to believe everything you hear. Young men have always boasted, and usually they make up half of what they boast about.'

'If half of it's true, it's still filthy whoremongering.'

Eliza fixed him with a steely look. 'And you think Pauline would act that way? Don't you trust your daughter, Walter?'

'I . . .' He glared at her.

She shook her head and sighed. 'Why don't you go upstairs and wash and shave, son? We'll eat and then discuss this matter in a reasonable way. There's no need for raised voices.'

'I'll raise my voice if I want to.' But the sting had gone out of it.

'Aye, that you will. But I still reckon you'll feel better when you're washed and changed. And while you're at it, you remember a few things. Your Pauline's a good lass. And she's a good dancer, too. She could win this competition. You should be proud of her, not accusing her of things she'd never do.'

Eliza turned back towards the scullery. 'Now it's

time I finished peeling those spuds, or we'll never eat this day.' She reached the door and then paused. 'And another thing, Walter. Just remember who took your Pauline to dancing lessons in the first place. It was your Margaret. And I recall, even if you don't, how proud she was when Pauline won those dancing medals.'

She went through into the scullery, shutting the door behind her.

'The Spa's all right, Dad. It's perfectly respectable. They don't allow anyone in who's had too much to drink. And my dancing partner, Grahame,' Pauline swallowed, 'he's a gentleman. Gran says I should invite him to tea next Sunday so you can meet him, but he might not be here then. It's just the competition he's interested in, see. And we do dance so well together. I'm sure we'll win.'

Her father sighed and passed his hand over his hair. 'Do what you like. I'm sick of the whole subject. I'm going up for a wash.' He stared at her for a moment and then turned to leave the room, but at the door he paused and said heavily, 'Don't you ever let me down, Pauline, because if you do,' he shook his head . . . 'we'll both regret it.'

Chapter Three

Mary tapped on the door, expecting Pauline to open it, but it was Eliza Verrill who answered her knock.

'Come on in, love. Pauline's just getting her coat.' She ushered Mary into the kitchen.

Mary was not a perceptive girl, but even she sensed the atmosphere in the room was tense. She looked across at Pauline's dad, who was in his chair reading the local newspaper, and squeaked a timid 'Hello'.

He did not respond immediately but looked her up and down before giving her a tight smile and telling her to sit down.

Mary sat on the nearest chair. There was silence. Eliza, who had resumed her seat in the other armchair, picked up her knitting. The wool was thick and navy blue in colour, so Mary knew she must be knitting a new gansey for her son.

'You're well on with that, Mrs Verrill,' she ventured.

'Aye, lass. It's summer now, but by autumn Walter will be needing a new one. I'm on the tricky bit now.' Eliza held out the garment for Mary's inspection. 'See, I'm up to the shoulders.'

Mary admired the work. Coming from a fishing family herself, she knew the high value put on fishermen's ganseys. The best ones were always hand-knitted by those nearest and dearest to the wearer, and it was considered a terrible thing for a man to have to buy his gansey. She also knew the significance of the distinctive pattern developed for each community. If there was an accident at sea, and there often was, a corpse trawled up days later could be identified by its clothing.

She watched Eliza's busy fingers, the large ball of wool slowly unravelling upon her aproned lap. There was no printed pattern to follow, the skill was handed down from mother to daughter, but Mary knew the garment would be knitted in the 'Bay' style. Her own mother knitted the 'Whitby' style, in rope and cable pattern.

Mary shifted her feet and glanced back at Mr Verrill. He was reading his paper and his face was set in stern lines. He looked remote from them and his surroundings. He was nice-looking for his age, she thought. As if mind-reading, he suddenly looked across at her and her face reddened. She looked down and nervously smoothed her skirt over her knees.

Where was Pauline? It was time they were off, and why on earth was she taking a coat? It was lovely and warm, no wind, thank goodness. Mary's hand went up to pat her hair. She had spent hours coaxing it into the Rita Hayworth style.

There was the clatter of feet on the stairs and Pauline rushed into the room.

'Sorry I kept you waiting. I'm ready now.' She swung round to face her father and grandmother. 'We'll be off then.'

Eliza smiled and nodded. 'Have a good time, and the best of luck, Pauline.'

'Thanks, Gran.' But Pauline was looking at her father.

There was a pause and Mary noticed the knuckles of Mr Verrill's hands whiten as he grasped his newspaper. Then he folded it and looked at his daughter. 'Yes, have a good time, love.'

He glanced towards his mother and from the corner of her eye, Mary thought she saw Eliza give a small nod of approval. Then he looked back at Pauline. 'But you're to be back before midnight, mind. I'll wait up for you.'

'There's no need.' Pauline's face flushed, but then Eliza's steel knitting needles stopped clacking and in the small silence that followed, she bit her lip and crossed to where her father sat.

'OK, Dad.' She dropped a kiss on the top of his head. 'Thanks for letting me go.'

He nodded.

Away from the house, Mary snorted. 'I wouldn't have sucked up to him like that. Why should he lay down the law about when you're to come in? You're working now, bringing money into the house – I'd like to see *my* dad behaving like that to *me*.'

'Your dad's not my dad.' Pauline's reply was brief. 'And anyway, you're lucky. You're not living at home.'

Mary considered. Pauline was right there. She thought about her father. Her mum had the devil's own job getting money out of him, but he was easy-going with his children, particularly when he was half drunk. But how much did he care about them, really? She remembered how often he mixed up the names of his numerous offspring, and sighed and thrust her arm through Pauline's.

'Sorry. Tell me to mind my own business.'

'Mind your own business!'

But Pauline smiled.

They walked along the road and Mary asked, 'Why the coat, Pauline, you must be boiling?'

She looked mysterious. 'Show you later.'

They came in sight of the Spa.

As they bought their tickets, Pauline read the notice board in the foyer and saw the function was to be held in the Spa Theatre. She froze on the spot.

'Oh, no!' She turned to Mary. 'Why didn't you tell me.'

'I didn't know. Anyway, what difference does it make?'

'All the difference in the world. There'll be a great gawking crowd watching.'

Mary shrugged. 'They'd do that anyway.'

Pauline twisted her hands together. 'If I'd known it was going to be held in the theatre, I wouldn't have entered the competition.'

Mary wondered what she was fussing about. Everyone knew the theatre at the Spa was sometimes used for dancing when two separate functions were being held. At such times, the theatre seats were removed to make room for a large dancing area and the balcony area was open to spectators, giving them a fine view of the scene below.

Pauline had thought of something else to worry about. 'Grahame – he won't know where to go.'

Mary snorted. 'Don't be daft, Pauline. If he can find his way around the North-East of England, he can find the Spa Theatre.'

Pauline said no more. She followed Mary into the cloakroom and with clumsy fingers fumbled in her handbag for lipstick and powder compact.

She's got stage fright, thought Mary. Oh, well, she'll have to get over it. She was feeling a bit funny herself. The thought of parading with ten other Rita Hayworth look-alikes was doing things to her stomach. She muttered something and disappeared into the toilet.

When she came out again, she saw Pauline had removed her coat and was leaning over one of the washbasins trying to get a close look at her face in the nearest mirror.

'My God!' Mary's eyes widened in surprise. 'Where did you get the dress, Pauline? You look fantastic.'

She gave her nose a last dab with her powder puff before replying. 'It looks all right, does it?' She turned and faced Mary.

'It's . . .' Words failed her. 'It's . . . gorgeous!'

The praise obviously lifted Pauline's morale for she grinned. 'It is, isn't it?' She took another quick look in the mirror and then ran her hands down over the shimmering fabric of the dress. 'There's certain advantages to working at a dry-cleaner's,' she whispered.

Mary stared for a moment then began to laugh. 'You *didn't*!' she said. 'Who does it belong to then?'

'Me – for tonight.'

'No, really. Whose is it?' Mary stopped talking and blinked. '*That's* why you wore your coat?'

'Yes.'

Her attack of nerves forgotten, Pauline's grin turned into a Cheshire cat smile. 'First I put on my best dress,' she grimaced, 'you know, that old pink thing, and then I paraded before my dad and gran and got their approval. Then, just before you arrived, I dashed upstairs and changed. I'll have to change back again, of course, before going home – that's why I've brought my big handbag.'

Mary shook her head. 'You little devil.'

'Good idea though, don't you think?'

Pauline turned and squinted at her reflection in the full-length mirror at the end of the room. 'At first I was a bit worried in case it made me look too old.'

'No, it's perfect.' There was a touch of envy in Mary's voice.

Pauline was her friend and she was pretty in a sort of 'girl next-door' kind of way, but Mary knew, when they were out together, it was *she* who drew the most wolf-whistles. But in that dress . . .

It was a proper evening dress made from palest blue and silver lamé brocade. The widely gathered skirt swung to just below knee length and the fitted waistline made Pauline's slim waist look even slimmer. The shirred bodice, panelled with self-piping, clung sweetly to her upper body, emphasising her shapely figure.

Mary saw how Pauline's fingers were drifting about the bodice, plucking at the thin straps, hitching up the front. She's self-conscious, she thought. Casting aside her envy, she captured her friend's hands in her own.

'Stop messing with it,' she ordered. 'It's perfect as it is. You look an absolute knockout. If the judges for the competition are men, you've won already.' She grinned. 'Unless you fall on your backside or something.'

Pauline laughed as Mary stood back and took another look at the dress. 'Wait a minute – I saw a dress like that one in the window of Rowntree's about two months ago. I remembered it because it was so smashing. I remember the price, too.' She screwed up her face. 'It was all of fifteen guineas.' Her eyes narrowed. 'Go on, tell me whose dress it is?'

Pauline lowered her voice. 'Mrs Saunders.'

Mary stared. 'The Town Clerk's wife? Good grief!'

'It's all right. She'd never come to a dance like this one. She came into the shop two days ago. She'd been to a town hall function with Mr Saunders and some idiot had spilled a drink over her.' With a dramatic gesture Pauline placed her hand on her heart. 'Bless him, whoever he was. I stuck it into the machine straight away, and bingo! She's not coming to collect it until Tuesday, so I've time to clean it again and bag it up.'

'Pauline, that's brilliant.' Mary was full of admiration. 'I bet it doesn't look as good on her as it does on you.'

'Thanks. I'm inclined to agree with you.' She giggled. 'Mrs Saunders always wears clothes too young for her, I'm pleased to say.'

Mary looked at her watch. 'We'd better get a move on or your Grahame will think you're not coming. And, remember, I'm in a competition too, and I want to see what I'm up against.' As she pushed open the door, she began to giggle.

'What is it?'

'Just think, wouldn't it be a hoot if Mr Saunders was one of the judges!'

Pauline closed her eyes. 'Don't even think it.'

'We won, we won!'

Swinging her bag – a large clumsy thing, Grahame wondered why she had brought it – Pauline danced her way along the star-lit promenade oblivious of the stares she was attracting. Fortunately, there were few onlookers about.

She had kept Grahame waiting so long at the end of

the evening that by the time they left the Spa, the majority of the evening revellers had already departed. Not that she would have bothered about people watching her. Grahame's eyes crinkled with amusement as he watched her twirling about. Success had dispelled her shyness.

She saw him watching and, unabashed, danced back to him.

'We won!'

He smiled at her. 'Yes, we did.'

'And we deserved to win, didn't we? We were the best dancers in the competition.' Face sobering, she stopped dancing and walked along next to him, looking up into his face.

'You know we were. Why ask?'

Pauline tucked her free hand beneath his arm. 'Something Mary said. Nothing important.'

His smile deepened. 'I shouldn't let anything Mary said to you tonight upset you. She was awfully miffed when she came second in her competition.'

'Yes, poor Mary.' Pauline's attempt to look sad misfired. Her grin reappeared. 'She was livid, actually. She said the judges must have been blind and that the winner looked more like Bette Davis than Rita Hayworth!'

Grahame laughed out loud. 'Oh dear, is that why she left early?'

'Perhaps. She stayed to see us do our stuff though, didn't she? And when she did leave, I think she was feeling better. She'd found someone to take her home.'

Grahame reflected that it was unlikely Mary was ever short of an escort.

'Jim Redder didn't come, after all.' Pauline glanced at him.

'No.'

'Do you know why?'

'No.' Grahame winced. Pauline had now transferred her big square handbag on to her right arm, and as they walked along it rhythmically thumped against his left hip bone.

'I don't see Jimmy that often,' he said. 'We cover roughly the same area but his contacts have nothing to do with mine. It was mere chance we met up with each other last weekend.'

'Oh, so you're not really good friends?'

'No. Why?'

Pauline evaded his question but tightened her grasp on his arm. 'I'm glad.'

Grahame smiled to himself. Here was one young woman who hadn't been swept off her feet by Redder's charms. He looked down at Pauline's halo of fair hair as she walked with short steps beside him, and slowed his pace. She was so petite, it was a wonder she had managed to keep up with his long steps when they had danced.

'You were marvellous tonight,' he said.

At varying intervals, as they walked along, they passed through pools of light shining from the widely spaced street lamps. They were passing through one of the lighted areas as he spoke. He saw the pleasure which dawned on her face.

'Was I?'

'Yes. You're a smashing partner, Pauline. I feel as though we've been dancing together for years.'

Her look of pleasure disappeared, but perhaps he was wrong. It was probably because they had turned off the promenade now and were walking through a less well-lit area. He opened his mouth to say something else but instead, as they stepped off a pavement, he let out a cry.

'Ouch!'

She stopped. 'What's the matter?'

He rubbed his hip. 'Can you either swop sides or swop that damn handbag over?'

She looked at him uncomprehending.

He explained, then said, 'Why on earth are you toting that around with you?'

She bobbed her head, embarrassed. 'It's my dress.'

'Oh, yes.' Belatedly, he realised he should have complimented her on her appearance. When he had seen her all dressed up, he had thought she looked terrific and had meant to tell her so, but then they had rushed to collect their numbers and chattered to the other waiting couples, and in the excitement, he had forgotten.

She was explaining. 'I borrowed it.'

He bent his head and listened. 'My dad hasn't seen it, *mustn't* see it – so before we left, I had to change. That's why I kept you waiting outside for so long.' Her voice was quiet, tinged with embarrassment. 'I have to get the dress back into the house without him seeing it, so I brought this bag.'

'But it was a lovely dress.' At least he managed a compliment. 'And you looked beautiful in it. So why should he object?'

'It's . . . he's not used to seeing me in anything so . . . modern. He's a bit old-fashioned, my dad.' She shrugged. 'And I'm his only daughter.'

'Won't he be in bed? When you get home, I mean?'

'Oh, no.' She shook her head. 'He always waits up for me.'

Well, I can't blame him for that, thought Grahame.

He remembered again how much the dress had suited Pauline and how it had revealed her creamy skin and entrancing curves. She wasn't just pretty, he decided, she was desirable. There had been moments, during the slow waltz, for example, when he had held her and thought of things other than dancing.

But there was something else about her, a kind of vulnerability, which kept him at a distance. A chap should only get involved with Pauline, he thought, if his intentions were strictly honourable. She was sweet and innocent. She deserved a proper courtship, an engagement ring and a date set for the marriage. He frowned. And he wanted none of those things.

Of course, plenty of blokes would laugh at his thoughts. Jimmy Redder, for example. Grahame shivered,and was glad for the second time that Pauline hadn't taken to him.

But there again, life was simpler for blokes with Jimmy's attitude towards women. And maybe, if his mother hadn't drummed it into him when he was young that ladies were to be cherished and respected, he's have thought more like Jimmy. And certainly he would have had more fun. Not that he was inexperienced, but the few girls he had laid . . . well, they certainly hadn't been ladies!

If I was more like Jimmy, he thought, I'd have coaxed Pauline into one of the seaside shelters by now. And because she does like me, his thoughts continued, at this very minute I could be sliding my hand up beneath her skirt . . .

'Penny for them?'

The blood drummed in his ears. He coughed.

'I was wondering why your dad should object to the dress? There's nothing tasteless about it.'

'I know, but Dad's like that. I had an awful time trying to persuade him to let me come tonight. In his eyes, Whitby Spa is like the Temple of Babylon.'

'What? You mean full of wealth, luxury and dissipation?' He laughed.

'Yes.' Her laughter was timid, lacking conviction. 'I really thought I wouldn't be able to come, but Gran stood up for me and eventually he agreed.'

'I see.' Grahame thought he did. Another bullying, self-centred father. He remembered his own father laying down the law about what his wife and child should do. He remembered how his face would redden with temper until it matched his hair when they did anything without first obtaining his permission. God, how often he had wished he could have inherited his mother's colouring. Every time he looked in the mirror his hair was a constant reminder of his father, and every day he swore he would never grow to resemble him.

And yet how difficult it had been to respect and cherish his mother when he daily observed the ignorant oaf she had chosen to marry, chosen to father her child.

'We're nearly there.' Pauline cleared her throat. 'Are you leaving Whitby tomorrow, Grahame?'

'Yes. I was hoping to get away about nine, but my car's in dock and the man at the garage said it might take until afternoon to fix. Damn' nuisance, really.'

'So, you don't have anything planned for tomorrow?'

'No. Not really.' Was she waiting for him to ask her out? He considered. It might not be a bad idea, he enjoyed her company. But she mustn't get the idea he would come and see her regularly.

'My gran . . .'

Her voice had gone squeaky, she was nervous. He felt a small rush of protectiveness towards her, just the kind of feeling his mother had tried to foster in him.

He took her hand. 'What about your gran?'

'She wondered if you would like to come for tea tomorrow?' The words came out in a rush.

'Oh!' He bit back a sigh. He could hardly refuse. He had already said he was doing nothing all day.

'What about your father?'

'Yes, he seemed to think it was a good idea.'

Wants to check me out, thought Grahame. A spark of malicious amusement flared inside him. And I'd like to check *him* out.

'I'd be delighted,' he said.

'You would?' Pauline sounded incredulous.

'Sure. What time should I arrive?'

'About five?'

'Five it is. And here we are.'

They had reached Pauline's home. The neighbouring houses were in darkness but light still shone from the parlour window.

Grahame stopped by the door and put his hands lightly on her shoulders.

'Thanks for a smashing evening and for being a wonderful partner, Pauline.' He laughed. 'And thanks for the ten pounds.That'll pay my garage bill tomorrow.' He stooped and kissed her.

He felt her tense and then she stood on tiptoe and enthusiastically kissed him back. Her lips were full and moist and Grahame, who had kissed her partly because he wanted to, and partly for the benefit of the man he presumed was peering through the net curtains, forgot all about her father.

Dropping his hands from her shoulders to her waist, he drew her towards him in a closer embrace. As he did so he smelt the flowery perfume she wore and felt the softness of her body against his, and when he released her, they were both breathing hard.

He stared down at her and touched her cheek. 'Until tomorrow, then?'

She nodded. There was a smile on her mouth and her eyes were shining. He hesitated, then left her, his shadow elongating beneath the street lights, as his long legs ate up the pavement with quick, impatient steps.

Pauline stood and watched him until he was out of sight and then quietly she entered the house.

Grahame might have felt a moment's shame if he had seen what Pauline saw when she went into the kitchen. Walter Verrill was not in the front room spying through the window, he was in his usual chair, reading. When he saw his daughter, he let the book fall face down on his knee.

'I left the front light on for you.'

'Yes, thanks, Dad. I've turned it off.'

'And did this Grahame chap see you safely home?'

'Yes, he did.'

Walter looked at the clock. 'You're ten minutes late, Pauline. I said to be in before midnight.'

'I'm sorry.' She smiled in his direction but with blind eyes.

His brow furrowed. 'What happened then?'

'Sorry?'

'The competition, girl – did you win?'

'Oh, yes, we won. It was wonderful, Dad. Everyone clapped us like mad when we danced, and then they cheered when the result was announced. And,' she glanced at his impassive face, 'it was well organised and very respectable. Mr Keyes,' she mentioned an official from the Whitby Food Committee, 'was one of the judges. And look.' From her coat pocket she took a handful of notes. 'Ten pounds. Isn't it great?

'I've been thinking, I'd like to treat you and Gran. I thought maybe I'd get tickets for you to go to the orchestra concert at the floral Pavilion next week?'

Walter made an impatient gesture. 'Keep your money, Pauline. Best put it in the bank.' Then, obviously noticing the look of disappointment which flitted across her face, his voice softened. 'Buy your gran a present if you like. She still enjoys a bit of frippery. But I don't want your money.' He paused. 'Why not buy yourself that portable radio you've been wanting?'

She smiled and went and put her arms around his shoulders. 'Shall I?'

He allowed himself to smile. 'Why not? You won the money fair and square. I'm proud of you, lass.'

She beamed at him and kissed him on his cheek. He sat very still and his body tensed, then his arms went around her and he clutched her to him so tightly she gasped for breath. Immediately, he released her and there was an odd embarrassed silence.

She moved away from him. 'I'd best get to bed.'

He stared down at his book without replying.

'Dad?'

'What is it?'

'Grahame . . . I asked him, like you and Gran said.' She stared at a point above his head, reluctant to meet his eyes. 'He's coming to tea tomorrow.'

'Is he?'

'Yes.' She took a deep breath. 'You'll be here, won't you? I mean, you're not going fishing until Monday? I'd like you to meet him, Dad.'

Her father took up his book. 'Yes, I'll be here.'

'Oh, good.'

She blew him a goodnight kiss and a moment later he heard her footsteps as she ran lightly up the stairs. There came sounds of water running in the bathroom, then a few snatches of her humming a popular song as she prepared for bed. The creak of the floorboards and then silence.

Walter stayed in his chair. For thirty minutes he stared down at the book in his hand and in all that time he never turned a page.

Chapter Four

It took a lot to frighten Eliza Verrill but now she was frightened, because she didn't know what was happening to her. She wiped the cold sweat from her forehead and tried again to move her feet but, as before, they remained stubbornly rooted to the ground beneath her. Not only that, there was a strange buzzing in her ears and black spots floated in front of her eyes.

'Steady on, Eliza,' she whispered.

She took a deep breath, closed her eyes and fought down panic. After a few seconds the buzzing noise faded and her heartbeat, although still erratic, had slowed down. She opened her eyes.

It was nothing serious. She had overdone things, that was all. She was a stupid woman and deserved a fright. She should have known better than to try and shift furniture around at her time of life. Walter and Pauline would have helped, but she had been too impatient to wait until they came home. She had wanted to get on, wanted so much for the place to be spick and span when her grand-daughter's young man came visiting.

A commercial traveller, Pauline had said. He'd be used to staying in hotels, used to a nice standard of living. Forgetting her scare, Eliza smiled and then frowned. Fancy their Pauline walking out with a professional gentleman. She had thought Walter would be pleased his daughter had met someone with prospects. But no, all he had done was to frown at Pauline and then grumble to her, his own mother, telling her she allowed her grand-daughter too much freedom.

She sighed and said aloud, 'Poor Walter.'

The framed studio photograph on the wall facing her caught her eye and she studied it. How shocked her mam had been when she found out how much it had cost.

'Spending all that money on a baby's picture.'

But Eliza had never begrudged the money spent. The early death of Tom had denied her the joy of other children, and Walter, like all babies, had grown too fast. But she still had the photograph, reminding her what a bonny, smiling infant her son had been.

Her eyes narrowed. Today, the picture looked different. The frame looked lop-sided, and Walter's baby features were hard to make out, sort of fuzzy. She blinked and tried to move, to investigate, but her treacherous body refused to obey her commands. Biting her lip, she reached out to a nearby chair, pulled it closer to her and sat down. A little rest, that was what was needed.

She closed her eyes briefly, opened them and looked at the photograph again. That was better – she could see him clearly now. She could see his dimpled arms and legs and that wide, toothless smile that always made her want to smile back. How rarely he smiled now. The happy baby had turned into a morose, drained, middle-aged man.

Trying to turn her mind from her momentary

weakness, it wasn't as if she was in pain, Eliza pondered over her son. It was hard to admit it, but she was disappointed in him. When he was growing up, she had constantly found excuses for his morose behaviour, but she had stopped doing that many years ago.

She acknowledged that his upbringing had something to do with his nature. He had been a lonely boy and, because she had worked so hard, she had not always been there when he needed her. But she had done the best she could for him. And some of their neighbours had been kind to him during his growing years, although not many.

Eliza sighed. Like many tight-knit communities, the fishing folk of Whitby had never taken kindly to strangers coming to live in their midst, particularly back in 1919.

She had alighted from the bus on that first day full of foreboding. She knew what to expect, but there was nowhere else to go and she couldn't stay in Baytown. She had trudged along the streets at the back of Whitby harbour dragging her three-year-old son behind her, both of them laden with bundles containing their possessions. If only she could get a job and somewhere to stay, they would manage. She began knocking on doors.

The response were always the same.

'Thoo's not a local lass?'

'No, my pa fished out of Baytown.'

'That so? Well, thoo's in t'wrang part o' town. Thoo'd do better up at West Cliff.' And the doors would close.

Useless to explain she couldn't afford lodgings on the West Cliff. Useless to say the only skills she possessed were connected with the fishing industry.

But then one of the kinder women had listened to her, and offered her a room for two weeks, and later on, that woman's cousin found Eliza her first job.

Yes, there were *some* kind people and Mr Fitter had been one of them. He was their next-door neighbour when Walter was sixteen and struggling to raise the money to buy his first coble. He had called round one night. He had heard Walter was a good worker and a good fisherman and offered to advance a goodly sum of money to buy the boat on condition Walter gave him a percentage of the catch.

It had been a fair offer but Walter had refused it. Eliza had always remembered his words.

'I want nothing from you or any other family in this town. I'll not be beholden to any of you. What I do, I'll do on my own.'

He hadn't even thanked Mr Fitter for his offer but had slammed out of the room in a temper.

It was only after he had met Margaret and married her that he softened his attitude. Fittingly, his future wife had also been an 'outsider'. She had been on a visit to her aunt when they first met. Walter had adored her from the first moment he clapped eyes on her, and Eliza too had loved her. She was such a quiet, gentle little creature and easy to love.

When she died so suddenly, Eliza had cried, but not in the company of her son. He would allow no one to share his grief. He had shut himself away for twenty-four hours after Margaret's death, leaving Eliza to comfort Pauline. Then he had roused himself only to deal with his wife's funeral arrangements. When the time came for him to go back to sea, he had gone eagerly. Mine-sweeping was a dangerous business and

Eliza often wondered if he actively sought death.

But, unlike thousand upon thousand of others, death had rejected him and he had been forced to take up his life again, albeit reluctantly.

His reluctance had caused Eliza despair. She admitted she would never understand him. He had cause for grief, but he still had his health and strength, and he had Pauline. There were lots of people worse off than him, people who had lost everything in the war, and they picked up the pieces and went on with their lives.

She rested her hands on her knees and looked grim. Walter should have learned by now grief did not go away, but it should occupy a smaller space in your life. Even after thirty-odd years, there were still times when she grieved for Tom, her dad and young brother Wilfred. But no one knew it because going about with a long face was no answer. Her hands clenched. At least Walter was able to take flowers to his wife's grave, which was more than she could do for her lost family.

She shivered, then straightened her back. What a misery she was, thinking sad thoughts when outside the sun was shining, she could hear church bells ringing and, her face brightened, she had got hold of some ox tongue to have with the salad.

But there were still things to do. Turning carefully, she put her hands on to the back of the chair and levered herself to an upright position. She waited. Yes – she felt herself again. She would just have to remember in future not to lift anything too heavy. Still, the parlour was done.

With a feeling of satisfaction, she surveyed the room. Pauline, she knew, didn't like the parlour and hated eating meals in there, but Pauline would have to put up with it. No stranger was going to eat in Eliza's kitchen on his first visit.

Pauline, although not actually *saying* anything, made it clear she thought the parlour was full of clumsy old-fashioned furniture and was much too stiff and formal. Well, when she had a few more years on her, she would realize that formality, in small doses, was good for the soul and encouraged self-discipline. As for not liking old-fashioned things, maybe one day her grand-daughter would learn that old things became treasured things because of the memories they held.

Eliza's gaze travelled from Walter's photograph, stopped to admire the highly-polished window and clean net curtains, and then rested upon a large pink seashell perched on the back wall. In Pauline's eyes, the shell was just another piece of Grandma's clutter, but to Eliza it was precious for her brother Wilfred had given it to her long years ago when she was twelve years old.

He had caught her crying at the back of their cottage; hiding behind the outside privy, in fact. Eliza's lips curved in a smile. On a hot summer's day, it had not been the best place in which to hide. She had been desperately unhappy. For some reason she had become the butt of a gang of the village youths who chased her unmercifully, teasing her, pulling her long plait of hair and shouting out that she would never catch a husband because she was buck-teethed and skinny.

Remembering, she sighed. Her hair was silver now and the teeth had gone fifteen years ago, but she was still skinny and still had the seashell, and she could shut her eyes and remember exactly the earnest expression on young Wilfred's face when he had given it to her and told her to listen to the sea.

Then he had squeezed her hand and told her that *he* thought she was beautiful and that one day he'd find a wife who looked exactly like her. Poor lad. Lost in memories, Eliza sniffed and mopped her eyes with her sleeve. Poor lad, he had not lived long enough to court a girl.

Wondering why today, of all days, old memories were stirring, she tried a step but the trembling in her legs warned her it was too soon and she sank back in her chair.

'I'm going to be one of those awful old women who are always harking back to the past,' she told Walter's photograph.

The baby's grin, an echo across the years, comforted her.

She nodded at him. 'Aye, I'm being foolish, aren't I? I'm not that old and I'm fit. I can still cook and clean and do the weekly wash, and I enjoy a game of whist with Mrs Oliver and her sisters, so things aren't so bad. Mind you,' she sighed, 'I wouldn't want to live to be a nuisance. Just so long as I see Pauline settled and happy, then I'd like to go quick, not hang around.'

Despite her brave words the thought of dying, or not dying and becoming senile, depressed her again. 'And I'm starting to talk to myself,' she said aloud. 'That's a bad sign.' She looked away from Walter's photograph and, seeking comfort, surveyed the rest of her treasures.

The two upholstered Victorian chairs with their sturdy plump legs which, so she had been told, had once been covered with cotton slips to conform with ideas of decency, still wore their faded antimacassars, worked in cross stitch. They had been on the backs of the chairs when she bought them at the saleroom, so she had laundered them carefully and replaced them in deference to the unknown needlewoman who had worked them. Continuity was a word unknown to Eliza Verrill, but it was something she believed in.

Most of her treasures had come from the salerooms. She had started going along to auction sales shortly after her marriage, driven there by necessity. There was so much she needed to set up house with Tom and they had so little money.

At first she had bid for everyday utensils, plates, saucepans, a brass jam pan, a kitchen stool, all of which she had borne home in triumph. Then she had made the acquaintance of one of the old men who did the fetching and carrying on sale days. He wasn't the usual saleroom assistant, but a retired teacher of classics who had fallen on hard times.

He must have liked the look of her for they struck up a friendship, and over the months he taught her things to look out for. On the shelf next to her seashell was a memento of him. It was the figurine of a boy playing a lute which he had persuaded her to buy.

Mr Martin, for so he had been called, had been convinced the figurine was a Marieberg. He had shown Eliza the faint mark on the base of the figure, three crowns above a stroke and the letters MB.

She had been unimpressed. The maker's mark was too blurred to be seen properly and, anyway, she didn't like the figurine; the colours were too garish for her taste and privately she thought the little lad looked half-witted and not a bit appealing, but to please her friend she had bid. The piece had gone cheap and, strangely, Mr Martin did not wish to have it himself.

'Too late for me, my dear.' He had sighed. 'But you keep it safe. One day it may be worth a lot of money.'

Eliza doubted it, but she kept the figure because she had liked Mr Martin. What she *did* like, and which she bought on the same day as the figurine, was her best teaset, the one she intended using today. It too had been pointed out to her by the old man.

But her pride and joy, the best buy of her life, was the sideboard. Unfortunately, it was also a source of worry to her, for she lied about it. She had told first her son and later her grand-daughter that the sideboard was a family heirloom. The fact that her parents had never possessed anything of value in their whole life didn't bother Eliza, it was just she loved her sideboard so much, she felt it had been meant to belong to her, and then to the family, and so she had adopted it.

The poor neglected thing had been stuck in a dark corner of a country saleroom on a day when bad weather had cut attendance figures. Badly treated over the years, it had looked a sorry sight. It was filthy, the brass rail fitted along the back discoloured and one of the feet, carved lions' paws, broken and clumsily mended. And yet Eliza had seen that sideboard and coveted it like a miser covets gold.

She had travelled to the sale in her next-door neighbour's milk cart specifically to buy a mangle, but she watched the sale of household goods go by without blinking an eyelid and waited until the afternoon and the furniture sale. Then she bought the sideboard.

Tom had laughed when she went home and told him what she had done. He didn't worry about the lack of a mangle, he never did the washing, and he was a man of sunny disposition who hadn't been married long.

But even someone with a sunny disposition will only

stand so much. When the sideboard was delivered and he had to find five shillings to give to the carrier, his smile flickered. And when, with great effort, they carried it into their two-roomed lodgings and he found it took up so much space and even some of the light from the window, his smile disappeared completely. And finally, when for a whole week they ate stockpot soup and bread and cheese because Eliza had spent all her money, he frowned and they had their first row.

But Eliza explained to him how she was sure the sideboard was worth much more than she paid for it – the reeded legs were very fine and the drawers lined with mahogany. And when she sat on his knee and tickled him behind his ears, where his beautiful corn-coloured hair grew thick and springy, he had smiled again.

Looking now at the rich sheen of the wood, proof of many years' loving care, Eliza's eyes, her mouth, her whole face smiled. Her married life had been painfully short, but it had been packed full of loving. And she still had her sideboard, even though she and her loved ones had suffered a succession of bumps and bruises from squeezing past her treasure – unfortunately, she had never lived in a house large enough for it.

'I'm back, Gran.'

The door slammed and Eliza gasped. Gracious, where had the time gone? Without thinking, she jumped to her feet and then paused, waiting apprehensively. But nothing happened. She felt fine. Her little rest, her trip down memory lane, had done the trick. She wasn't dizzy at all now.

She hurried into the kitchen and looked at Pauline's rosy face and then down at the bunch of freshly picked watercress she held in her hands.

'You found some.'

'Yes, *and* these.' Putting the watercress down on a dish, Pauline took three enormous mushrooms from her pocket.

'Lovely.' Eliza reached for her apron hanging behind the door. 'Let's get to work.'

'That was lovely, Mrs Verrill. It's ages since I've enjoyed a meal so much.'

Grahame was so polite, it was plain to see Gran approved of him. Pauline smiled and looked down at her empty plate with some surprise. She had thought she would be too nervous to eat but when Gran had served up the ox tongue salad, she had realised she was hungry and done the meal full justice.

'I've made a sultana cake for afters.' Eliza shrugged her shoulders. 'It should be all right, but nothing like the cakes I used to make in the days you could get your hands on some butter.'

Grahame laughed. 'Home-made cake? I'll enjoy that, whether or not it has butter in it.'

'Don't you ever have home cooking?'

Gran had risen to her feet and was collecting the salad plates.

'No, I don't really have a settled home any more. Both my parents are dead and I spend most of my time on the road.'

Pauline had also stood up, meaning to help her grandmother clear away the dirty plates, but Eliza gestured to her to sit down again.

'No, stay there, Pauline. Entertain your guest.' She smiled at Grahame before carrying the dishes from the room.

Pauline could almost read her thoughts. Poor lad, all on his own, no family.

Sitting down again, she searched her mind for something to say. It was so silly. She had talked all right to him before, when they had been on their own, why couldn't she now?

She looked across at her father who had cleared his throat before addressing Grahame.

'I'd have thought you'd get better food than we do. Rations don't go far in ordinary households but hotels and such-like, they'll get extra, don't they?'

Well, at least her dad was making an effort, but did he have to sound so stern? Beneath the cover of Gran's best tablecloth, Pauline twisted her hands together. At least Grahame didn't seem worried by her father's curtness. He laughed.

'To say I stay in hotels is a bit of an exaggeration, sir. The places I board in call themselves hotels but mostly they're bed and breakfast. The accommodation's basic and so is the food. And if I try and shop for myself, I don't come off too well. When you're a stranger somewhere the butchers and bakers don't find any titbits from under the counter for you.'

Pauline hid a smile. Grahame was handling things beautifully. He was being modest, her dad would like that. He would also like being called 'sir'.

She glanced shyly across the table at Grahame and thought he looked attractive, even handsome. His features were a little sharp perhaps, but he had a nice mouth and his eyes were an unusual greeny-blue colour with brown flecks in them. She noticed a small strip of peeling sunburn across the bridge of his nose and her heart melted. It was his colouring, of course. He'd have to watch out in hot weather.

'You've got prospects, though?'

She squirmed. Oh, Lord, Dad sounded like one of those old-fashioned fathers in the Victorian novels she had studied at school.

Grahame appeared unperturbed. 'I certainly hope so. The firm's doing well. The difficulty is more in getting hold of the machinery than selling the product.'

Leaning back in his chair, he changed the subject. Perhaps he had noticed Pauline's red face.

'I hear fishing's good at the moment, Mr Verrill?'

'You heard that, did you?' Walter drew lines on the tablecloth with the prongs of a spare fork.

Gran will go mad, thought Pauline.

'And *where* did you hear that?'

'At one of the farms I visited last week, up on the Wolds. The man I was talking to mentioned his brother-in-law was a fisherman and said it looked like being a bumper year for you this year.'

'Aye, that'll be about right.' Walter abandoned the fork and drummed his fingers on the tablecloth instead. 'The farmers around here always think fishermen are rolling in money.' His lips stretched into a thin grin. 'And we tend to think the same about them. They get enough ruddy subsidies from the government.'

'Is that so?'

'Aye.'

There was a short silence and then Walter relented.

'Anyway, it happens your farmer got his facts right this time. The fishing's been grand. It's because of the war, see.' His short laugh held no humour. 'While we've been killing each other, we've done the fish a favour. They've been left to breed in peace. We've been pulling in record catches, and I reckon, when the herring season gets started, it'll get even better.'

Grahame nodded, his face serious. 'That's good news, Mr Verrill. With the food shortages, cheaper fish will be welcome. And it's good to know something worthwhile has come from the last few years.'

'I'll not argue with that.' Walter looked at Grahame with keen eyes.

'Were you . . . ?'

'Yes – North Africa.' Grahame shifted in his seat. 'Pauline tells me you were mine-sweeping?'

'I was.' Walter sighed. 'But this is not the place to talk about it.'

There was a short silence and Pauline, looking from one to the other, thought they had both forgotten she was there.

Then Grahame clasped his hands on the table and spoke.

'I agree.' He studied his entwined fingers. 'Sometimes,' his voice sounded reflective, 'sometimes, I think there's altogether too much talk.'

Walter's stern features relaxed. He stared at Grahame for a moment and then nodded across to Pauline and attempted a joke.

'Your gran's taking her time. Let's hope her cake hasn't dropped in the middle. If it has, she'll stay in that kitchen 'til Christmas.'

Pauline smiled and decided to make another pot of tea. She picked up the teapot, skirted the sideboard carefully and opened the door. As if on cue, her gran sailed in, carrying the sultana cake, placed in the middle of a tray, before her like a prize.

Chapter Five

Grahame's old car bowled along the road at a cracking pace. The mechanic had taken his time repairing the 1936 Morris Minor but he had done a good job. Grahame listened to the purr of the engine, slackened speed and then looked at Pauline who occupied the seat next to him. The rush of air from the open car window was blowing her hair across her pink and glowing face. She looked tousled and pretty.

He smiled. 'Enjoying it?'

She beamed at him. 'Oh, yes. But are you sure it's all right? I thought you said you'd have to rush away after tea?'

'Well,' he glanced out of the window, 'it's such a lovely evening, ideal for a spin, and I can stay another night in Whitby. If I set off early in the morning, I'll get to Stockton-on-Tees in time for my first appointment.'

'I'm glad you changed your mind.' Pauline sat forward in her seat and pointed. 'Look, isn't the view gorgeous?'

He nodded.

They were approaching Ravenscar and could see the sea. For once, the seemingly ever-restless waves were quiet. The scene should have been tranquil but a crowd of kittiwakes were dive-bombing from the surrounding chalk cliffs, searching for food and disturbing the quiet air with their raucous outbursts: *kit-tie-waake, kittiwaake* . . .

Pauline laughed. 'Can we stop here, just for a minute?'

Graham changed gear. 'Yes, of course.'

The sun was close to setting. It floated just above the horizon, its rays painting a pearly pink path across the calm sea.

They left the parked car and walked to the top of the cliffs. Pauline drew closer to Grahame and tucked her hand beneath his elbow.

'This is one of my favourite places,' she confided. 'Of course, without a car I can't come often, but sometimes I bring Gran on the bus.' She pointed to the huddle of cottages clustered together which could be seen in the bay to the right of them. 'She was born in Baytown, you know.'

'Baytown? It's called Robin Hood's Bay, isn't it?' Grahame looked in the direction of her pointing finger.

The setting sun, not content with beautifying the sea, was busily splashing colour on the red pantile roofs of the small fishing village. It looked beautiful and very peaceful.

'Yes. It's just the old folk who call it Baytown.' Pauline laughed, tightening her grip on Grahame's arm. 'Gran has loads of stories about the old days, but sometimes I think she stretches the truth a bit. She says there were still smugglers down there when she was a lass!'

Grahame covered her hand with his own. 'You're fond of your gran, aren't you?'

'I love her,' Pauline replied simply. 'She came and looked after us when Mum died. She pulled us through. I don't know how Dad would have managed without her.' She tilted her head, looked up into his face. 'You and Dad got on quite well today, didn't you? I'm so pleased.' She looked away from him. 'Dad can be a bit difficult sometimes.'

'Parents are like that, don't worry about it.' But Grahame's voice held a strained note.

She looked back at him. 'You *did* get on all right?'

'Oh, yes.'

She gave a small frown, puzzled by the note of irony in his voice, but he said no more. He gazed out over the sea.

He had *thought* his visit had been successful. A bit awkward at first, but by the time the meal had been eaten, pretty good really. But later, when Pauline and her gran had been washing up and he had gone to check on his car, things changed. Pauline's dad had followed him outside.

He had started the conversation genially enough, asking what kind of area Grahame covered and the kind of people he met, and then he had paused and asked, 'Just how old are you?'

Grahame, straightening up from checking the tyre pressure, replied: 'Twenty-six.'

'Twenty-six, eh?' Walter Verrill had cleared his throat, and when he spoke again, his voice had changed.

'Well, to be frank, Grahame, I can't help wondering why a man of twenty-six, a man with experience of life, a chap who meets lots of people on his travels, should want to spend time with a kid like Pauline?'

He waited a moment and then, when a surprised

Grahame did not reply, continued, 'I'd have thought a smart fellow like you could get plenty of girlfriends, so what's so special about my little lass?'

'I – I . . .' To his own annoyance, Grahame heard himself stammering. He took a deep breath and started again.

'Thing just happened that way, Mr Verrill. I didn't especially plan to date Pauline. We met at the Spa and realised how well we danced together. And then Mary mentioned the dancing competition and we decided to give it a go. Then, last night, after we won, Pauline asked me to tea and I accepted. What's wrong with that?'

'Nothing, if that's the whole truth?'

'Of course it's the truth, why shouldn't it be?' Grahame moderated his voice when he realised how loudly he was speaking. Pauline's father was annoying him but he didn't want the conversation to develop into an argument. That would only upset Pauline and her gran. He tried again.

'In some ways, my job makes it hard for me to have a lot of friends, Mr Verrill. I'm never in one place long enough. And to tell the truth, I get a bit lonely sometimes, wonder what to do with myself. I've never been one for spending all night in the pub.'

He glanced at Walter. That should improve the man's mood. Pauline had told him her father was no drinker. But studying the stony expression on Verrill's face, it seemed his small ploy to ingratiate himself had not worked. He sighed.

'I like Pauline. I enjoy her company. She's bright and cheery, and as I said, she's an excellent dancing partner.'

Verrill rubbed his chin. 'Ah, the dancing. Funny

sort of hobby for a man, isn't it?'

A nerve jumped in Grahame's cheek. Oh God, not again!

'Fred Astaire and Jimmy Cagney are wonderful dancers and they're doing all right,' he said evenly. 'No one seems to find them strange.'

A short, mirthless laugh came from the older man. 'Think you're as good as the film stars, do you?'

'Of course I don't. It's just . . .' Grahame had shrugged. 'I suppose you'd rather I was a fisherman or a rugby player, or something?'

'I'm not too happy about your job, Grahame, and that's the truth.' Walter Verrill's expression was less than encouraging. 'Pauline's young and innocent. I don't want a smart-aleck commercial traveller, a man much older than her, sneaking around and filling her head full of nonsense. I don't want her spoiling.'

'That's not fair!' A flush coloured Grahame's face. 'I've played the game straight with Pauline. As for spoiling, she has a mind of her own, you know. I think you underestimate her. And, let's be honest, she's not *that* young! You talk about her as though she was still a child, but she's not. In fact, if you want the truth of it,' he paused, 'it's Pauline who's done all the running up to now.'

He looked into Verrill's stony face and an imp of perversity made him chance his luck. The old sod deserved it, one moment implying he was a homo and the next a seducer of children.

'In fact, if I *was* the "smart-aleck" you seem to think I am, I'll tell you now – I could have had your precious daughter last night, without any trouble at all!'

He shouldn't have said it! He knew immediately, when he saw Verrill's face change.

He took a step backwards. 'I didn't, of course.'

He wasn't quite quick enough. Walter Verrill shot out his hand and grabbed him by the shoulder. Then he thrust his face up against Grahame's until they were almost eyeball to eyeball. Grahame shivered.

The man looked mad. The hostility came off him in waves. And although he was a good four inches shorter than Grahame, he was stronger. His fingers bit like a vice.

'You're saying Pauline's easy?'

'No, no. Of course not.'

By God, he thought, I'm in danger here, real danger. He had seen men look like that before, in the war. But this wasn't the war. For pity's sake, this was a Sunday afternoon in Whitby. What was all the fuss about?

'I'm sorry, Mr Verrill. I should never have made that last remark. I was angry, that's all. Angry that you would think I would hurt Pauline that way. I wouldn't, I respect her too much.'

He was babbling. He forced his words to come more slowly.

'We're friends, dancing partners, nothing else. As you say, Pauline's only a young girl.'

The vice-like grip on his arm relaxed. He swallowed a sigh of relief.

'Pauline would never let you down, I'm sure. As for me, well,' he shrugged, a nervous movement of his shoulders, 'you're right. She *is* too young for me. But nothing's going to come of our friendship.' He wet his lips. 'I probably won't be coming this way again for another two or three months.'

The red glare left Verrill's eyes and he blinked and stepped back. Grahame wondered if he had taken in anything that had been said because, if anything, he looked confused. He said nothing, just stood there swaying, his hands hanging down by his sides. Grahame noticed how the colour had bled from his face, leaving his cheeks grey, turning him into an old man. Then, still without speaking, he suddenly turned and walked back into the house.

Grahame slumped back against his car. Relief possessed him entirely. For a minute, maybe two, he reflected on the danger so narrowly averted. But then the sheer normality of everything relaxed him.

The birds in a tree opposite the house set up a clatter as a tabby cat jumped up on to a wall, settled down and gazed at him impassively. The click of a gate announced that a nearby neighbour was taking her toddler for a stroll. The child did not want to go, he wailed and tugged at his mother's hand and she gave Grahame an apologetic smile as they passed by.

His return smile felt more of a grimace.

It hadn't happened, had it? Walter Verrill was a jealous father and had made it clear he didn't want Grahame to hang around after Pauline, but he hadn't looked at him with murder in his eyes, had he?

He jumped when the door of the house opened again but relaxed when he saw it was Pauline.

She came over to him. 'What's kept you outside so long?'

Grahame swallowed. 'I've been checking the car.'

'But it's just been fixed. Surely nothing has gone wrong with it already?'

He avoided her gaze. 'You can't always trust the garage hands to do a proper job.'

'Well, it *looks* good. It's a lovely car, isn't it?' She

ran her hand over the gleaming exterior.

'It's in pretty good nick, considering its age.' Grahame spoke more naturally. 'But she's getting on. I'm hoping to trade her in next year for a newer model.'

'I'd love a ride in it.'

He swallowed again and this time looked at her properly. 'It's a her, not an "it".'

'Like a ship,' she laughed.

Walter Verrill was wrong. Pauline was not a child. Grahame saw that she had applied lipstick after her meal and the way she was leaning against the car was not at all childlike.

'Yes, like a ship.' He fell silent and caught the beginnings of her pout as he looked away from her again.

'Well,' she moved away from the car, 'I suppose you'll be going soon. Are you coming back in the house to say goodbye to Dad and Gran?'

Pauline's gran was a nice old stick. It would be rude to go without thanking her for her hospitality, but he couldn't face Walter Verrill, not yet.

He rubbed his chin, remembering how he'd burbled on when her father had hold of him. He had thought the army had made a man of him, but he had been afraid of a man twenty years older than himself. He made up his mind.

'Come on, we've time to go for a spin first.' He opened the car door.

'You really mean it?'

'For you, Pauline – anything.'

And he had thrown a defiant glance at the house as they had driven away. But soon it would be time to take her home. He shivered.

'You're not cold, surely?'

'No.' He looked down at her. 'But it's time we were heading back.'

Pauline's chatter deserted her on the way home. She stared out of the window, her face solemn. Grahame wondered why. He didn't think she had heard or seen anything of what had taken place earlier, but her high spirits had certainly deserted her.

'It's my birthday in two weeks' time.'

'Is it?' He attempted to bring a smile to her face. 'Time goes so fast, doesn't it? How old will you be? Twenty-five, twenty-six?'

'Don't you start!' Her voice was harsh.

He gave her a startled look. 'It was only a joke.'

'I know it was, but I don't want humouring. I want you to take me seriously, not make fun of me.'

'I wasn't—'

But she wasn't listening.

'I'll be seventeen. Seventeen, and I'm getting sick and tired of being treated like a child. Good Lord, I know girls of my age who are married and have a baby.'

'And is that a good idea, do you think? Would you like to be in their shoes?'

'No. I mean,' she shook her head, 'I don't know. At least they're regarded as grown-ups. I have to ask permission before I do *anything*. I'm sick of Dad, Gran, and now *you*'re doing it! Talking to me as though I'm twelve years old.' She sighed. 'Sometimes I think Dad would be happier if I still wore short socks, a bow in my hair, and went to play outside with the other kids.'

Grahame stopped the car. They were driving

through moorland and the road before them stretched straight and empty.

He took hold of her hand. 'Don't you think you're over-reacting a bit, Pauline?'

'Maybe.' She slumped in her seat. 'But you don't know what it's like.'

He stared at her. 'What's the actual date?'

'What?'

'Your birthday, what's the date?'

'The fourteenth.' She sat up. 'Why?'

'I'll send you a card.'

The brightness which had started to blossom on her face faded.

'I suppose . . . you could be anywhere on the fourteenth?'

His brow wrinkled. 'Not anywhere.' He thought for a moment. 'Hull area, maybe.'

'I see.'

He looked at her profile, the lips pressed firmly together, the downcast eyes, and sighed.

'I don't suppose I'll be coming to Whitby again for at least six weeks, Pauline.'

She shrugged.

He continued to speak, choosing his words carefully. 'Being a commercial traveller isn't really much cop, you know. Always on the move, never having the time to make proper,' he hesitated, 'friendships.'

She turned her face towards him. Her eyes threatened tears and he cursed inwardly. How had he landed himself in this mess? Her father hated his guts and now Pauline had apparently decided she loved him. God save him from adolescent girls. Next time I pick a dancing partner she'll be well over twenty, he swore to himself.

'Grahame?'

'Yes?' He put aside his threatened depression and forced a smile. She had blinked away the tears, thank God.

'When we won the competition, when I wore the evening dress, you did mean what you said, didn't you?'

'What I said?' His voice was cautious.

'You remember. You said I looked beautiful.'

'Oh, yes, I remember.'

'Did you mean it?'

He stared at her. She sat quietly awaiting his reply. She looked so vulnerable and, yes – childlike. The make-up had gone, melted off, rubbed away, whatever make-up did, and her mouth was pale, the full bottom lip drooping. He remembered how she had looked in the low-cut evening gown and remembered too how soft her mouth had been when he kissed her. His voice deepening, he replied: 'Of course I meant it. You looked fantastic.'

She sighed and looked down at their clasped hands. 'But you don't . . .' Her voice wobbled. 'You don't particularly want to see me again?'

'But I do.' He released her hand in order to touch her cheek gently. 'I just feel it's better we don't get too involved. I'm on the road most of the time and I'm too old for you, Pauline.'

She gave an involuntary shake of her head as he continued.

'I *am*, love. Much better you find yourself a local lad to knock about with for a while. Nothing too serious. A girl like you should have lots of boyfriends before you settle down.'

Her eyes told him she didn't believe him but she didn't argue. She moved away from him and said, 'I suppose we'd better get home.'

'Yes.' He nodded and reached for the ignition key but she suddenly laid her hand on his arm, stopping him.

'Just one last favour, Grahame?'

'Yes?' His voice was more light-hearted. He had sorted it out. He would drop her off at home and then he would be free to clear off. She'd soon forget about him, and so would Walter Verrill.

'I don't care about a birthday card, you needn't go to the trouble, but before we go back, will you kiss me, just once, properly?'

'I . . .'

But it was too late. She had already eased across her seat towards him. She slipped her arms about his shoulders and he felt her hands link behind the back of his neck. She was close to him, too close. He could smell her perfume again. It was light, pleasant, he was only aware of the scent when she was close to him. Her eyes were wide, staring into his, and he could see the down on her upper lip and those soft, parted lips . . .

Without him even realising, his arms had wrapped around her and he had pulled her even closer and just before he kissed her, he realised he could feel the pounding of her heartbeats. They were too fast, a warning to him, but he had stopped being cautious. He forgot she was too young, he forgot Walter Verrill, he only knew the texture of her mouth and the softness of her breasts pressed against his chest.

When Pauline walked into the kitchen only Eliza was there, seated in her chair by the fireplace. For once, she was not busy knitting or sewing. The ginger kitten, foisted upon them by a neighbour four months ago, lay across her lap, purring loudly as her work-hardened hand moved slowly backwards and forwards, polishing its fur. Her eyes were closed. She looked tired.

Pauline looked at her and felt a moment's sadness. Gran was getting old. She hadn't noticed before but it was true. Tears pricked her eyes. Life was cruel because it was short.

But then her moment of sadness was sent packing by a great burst of joy because for her life was just beginning. She wanted to put her arms about herself and give herself a hug because she felt so happy. She was young, and Grahame had found her beautiful and loved her.

She had known all along, ever since he had kissed her after the competition, though it had taken him longer to realise. But in the car he had.

She shivered as she remembered the expression in his eyes when he had unbuttoned her dress and bared her breasts. And his hands had been shaking as he caressed them. He had touched her in other places too, secret places, and it had been beautiful. She hadn't wanted him to stop, it had been so beautiful.

But he had stopped. She flushed, remembering how she had moaned for him to continue but he wouldn't. And now she was glad, for surely that proved that he truly loved her? He had kissed her again and helped her tidy her clothes, but his hands had lingered and he had promised to come and see her soon and to write to her.

'The shop,' she had whispered, 'not at home.' And his face had closed in for a moment, but he had nodded. She had given him the address and he had noted it down in his little leatherbound book. He wouldn't forget. He couldn't, not after this evening. And the next time she saw him she would be seventeen.

She closed her eyes and touched her lips where he had kissed her. She wanted to touch her breasts, feel the nipples tighten as they had when he kissed them, but she couldn't, not here. But after her birthday he would kiss them again and she would make him love her properly.

'You look like the cat that's got the cream.' Eliza's eyes had opened and she was studying her granddaughter, a suspicious look on her face. 'You haven't been doing anything silly, have you?'

Pauline jumped. 'Of course not.' She wished the flush on her face would fade. 'I thought you were asleep.' She glanced round. 'Where's Dad? He's not gone to bed already, surely?'

Eliza's look still held suspicion. 'I hope you're telling the truth, young lady. That Grahame of yours seems a nice enough chap, but you don't know him that well, do you? He's the smooth type, and commercial travellers are always persuasive.'

'That's not fair, Gran. Grahame's a perfect gentleman. That's why I like him.'

'I'm glad to hear it, but I'm thinking of you as well as him. You're a good lass but a mite too eager to dive into life, sometimes.'

'Oh, thank you very much.' Pauline's cheeks were now red hot. 'You mean you don't trust me to behave properly?'

'It's not that, Pauline. It's just . . .' Eliza shook her head. 'It may seem strange to you, but I haven't forgotten what it's like to be young. I remember when I met Thomas.' She looked solemn. 'But just be a bit careful, that's all. I always remember what my mam said to me: "Never rely on love or the weather".'

'Oh, Gran.' Pauline shrugged her shoulders impatiently. 'You and your old sayings! Anyway, I thought your marriage was a happy one? You always told me it was.'

'It was, Pauline, it was. But Thomas and I walked out for two years before we wed. We got to know each other first, and we waited.' She paused. 'If you get my meaning?'

Seeing Pauline's averted face, she said no more. She stood up, deposited the kitten in her chair and moved towards the door. 'I'm for my bed. As for your dad, he's gone down to the boat. The Lord knows why at this time of the night. He mumbled something about meeting Jock Stephens and taking a walk up to the Whitehall Shipyard. It's re-opening, you know.'

Pauline nodded. The news that the shipyard was being re-opened, with the help of the White Fish Subsidy Act, had met with general rejoicing in Whitby. It meant more work for the locals, but even so, nearly ten o'clock on a Sunday evening was a strange time to go and inspect the place and she said so.

'Aye, well. Your dad's in a funny mood tonight. Happen a walk'll settle him down before bedtime.'

Eliza paused to give Pauline a pat on her arm as she passed her. 'It's been a good day. I like your young man. And if I nag you, it's only because I'm fond of you.'

'I know, Gran.' Pauline kissed her soft cheek. 'I'll be up in a minute.'

She was true to her word for she couldn't wait to get into bed and re-live, over and over again, the moment when Grahame had kissed her.

[illegible]

"I meant to buy you a new blouse," [illegible]

[illegible]

Chapter Six

On Pauline's birthday her father gave her a silver bangle and Eliza presented her with a small package containing Avrilla foundation cream, Dusky Rose face powder and Pretty Pink lipstick.

'I meant to buy you a new blouse,' she explained, 'but I couldn't decide which one you'd like so I bought the make-up instead. I had to have a present for you on the day. But take this.' She produced three pound notes from her apron pocket. 'I still want you to get a blouse. I have some clothing coupons, too, if you need them.'

'I don't want the money, Gran. The make-up's enough.' Pauline took off the top of the lipstick and examined the shade. 'Nice colour.'

'You're bonny enough without putting that muck on your face.' Walter, unbidden, had come to look over Pauline's shoulder at the cosmetics.

'Don't be a misery, Walter.' Eliza frowned at him then smiled at Pauline. 'A young woman likes to titivate up a bit, especially on her seventeenth birthday. Oh, and I'm making a cake for you, Pauline. Tea will be ready about half-past five, all right? Will you be going out later?'

'Mary and I thought we'd go to the Coliseum to see

Brief Encounter. It's supposed to be ever so good.'

'So I hear. Well, you'd better be on your way now or you'll be late for work. And, Pauline, take the money, please.'

She kissed her father, admired the bangle again – she was wearing it on her left wrist – kissed her grandmother and accepted the pound notes with a shrug and a smile. 'Thanks. See you tonight.'

As she left the house she heard her father say, 'You spoil her.' But his words didn't disturb her.

For the last two weeks their relationship had been free from strain. Her father had nagged her, but only a little and in the way that fathers did. As spokesman for the Fishermen's Association, he had been kept busy with various tasks around the harbour, and being busy suited him. He had become more relaxed at home and she had never once been conscious of his staring at her in the way that made her feel uncomfortable.

It was funny that he had never mentioned Grahame's visit to their home, but on the whole she was relieved he had not. No questions, no lies, she thought. The thought of Grahame made her footsteps quicken as she hurried to the dry-cleaning shop to see if his card to her had arrived. It had not. She was plunged into black depression for two hours until common sense told her she was being silly. It would come tomorrow.

Work over, she enjoyed the special tea Eliza had prepared then went off to the Coliseum with Mary and another girlfriend. They all cried buckets at the end of the picture but Pauline cried most of all, seeing herself and Grahame as the star-crossed lovers.

Next morning her birthday card was awaiting her at work. She opened the envelope with trembling fingers. The picture wasn't particularly loverlike, a black kitten sitting in a basket of flowers, but it was signed 'with love' and there was a kiss after the signature. She took the card home with her and hid it under the mattress on her bed. Over the next three weeks it was joined by two letters. Grahame wrote no words of love, he wrote as a friend, but he promised to come and see her at the end of July.

A few days after her birthday, when Gran mentioned Grahame and gave an enquiring lift of her expressive eyebrows, Pauline nearly told her about their arrangements, but then she didn't. It seemed more delicious, somehow, to keep everything secret.

For some time after that, she was aware Eliza was keeping an eye on her, but her continuing good humour, the way she was always dashing out with her friends to the beach, on picnics, and on one occasion on a bus trip to Scarborough for the day, finally appeared to allay any suspicions felt by Eliza and life settled down again.

Then one day she left the shop and there was Grahame, waiting outside for her. Her heart flipped like a circus acrobat. He was wearing a white shirt, a hacking jacket, the kind with two vents at the back, and dark brown trousers, and in his hand he held a brown trilby. It was the latest style, Pauline had seen them advertised in a national newspaper, snap-brimmed and turned up at the back. He looked so citified, she wished Mary was here. He smiled at her and came over and took her hand.

She stared up at him. 'You came.'

'Yes. Did you think I wouldn't?'

She looked down and said honestly, 'Oh, no. I knew you would.'

He laughed. 'The car's round the corner, let's go for a ride.'

She bit her lip. 'Gran's expecting me for tea.'

His face creased into lines of annoyance and then smoothed out again.

'Then after tea?'

'Yes, yes.' She squeezed his hand. 'I'll meet you at seven o'clock outside the Empire cinema.'

'But we won't go to the pictures?'

She wrinkled up her nose and laughed. 'No.'

They drove, at Pauline's suggestion, to Pannet Park. They sat on a bench, talked of unimportant things, and all the time they stared at each other, both acutely conscious of their own bodies and the other's nearness.

'So you had a good birthday?'

'Yes.'

She felt she would burst with frustration. They were acting like strangers at a party. Didn't he remember what happened in the car? She stared at him.

He had started to say something but when he caught her intent gaze he stopped, cleared his throat and, bending, picked a long stem of grass from the patch growing near the bench. He bit on the end of it.

'I've arranged to stay over in Whitby for the weekend.'

Pauline noticed how clean his fingernails were and how white and even his teeth.

She asked, 'Where are you staying?'

'A boarding house over on West Cliff.' He shrugged. 'It's not bad.'

'Will you show me?'

At last the paralysis had left her limbs. She leaned over, removed the frayed grass from his mouth and replaced it with her lips.

He held her close, even when the kiss ended. 'If that's what you want?'

She nodded.

The boarding house was tall and narrow and needed painting. The hallway was dark, Pauline was unable to read the room numbers stencilled on the closed doors. She knew which was the W.C. There was a smell of disinfectant issuing from it.

'Which is your room?'

'Upstairs.'

She looked upwards. The stairs seemed to go on forever. She swallowed the flutter in her throat. 'Lead the way, then.'

They sneaked upstairs, avoiding the creaks and whispering, like naughty children.

'Mrs Trenchwell doesn't approve of visitors in boarders' rooms.' Grahame searched in his pocket for his door key.

'Oh dear.' Pauline's legs were already trembling, a mixture of excitement and nerves. Now she exploded into laughter.

'Sorry?'

But she couldn't stop.

Grahame thrust her into the room and hurried in after her. He shut the door, looked at her and joined in her laughter.

And it helped, it really did – for what followed became something sweet and natural and without embarrassment. Even when they were both naked Pauline was unashamed and unafraid, because she was with the man she loved.

The expression in Grahame's eyes when he looked at her made words unnecessary. She held out her arms to him as he came to her.

There was no embarrassment, no pain; only excitement, pleasure and then joy as Grahame taught her inexperienced body how to love. And then came that wonderful moment when suddenly she arched her back and cried out.

'Hush.' Grahame stifled her cry with his kisses. His own body had tensed and they clung together until their climax ebbed, then he asked, 'You're all right?'

'I . . .' Words failed her.

He moved away and tried to read the expression on her face.

She pushed her hair away from her forehead and smiled at him. 'It was wonderful.'

He shook his head. 'It will be better next time.'

She disbelieved him, nothing could be better, but she savoured the thought. Next time.

She sat up. 'What time is it?'

'A quarter to ten.'

'I'll have to get home.'

'I suppose so.' He sighed, and moving off the bed went over to the washbasin in the corner of the room.

She watched him as he washed. He was more muscular than she had imagined. His shoulders were wide and his skin, where it had not been exposed to the sunshine, very white. She watched him and the ripple of heat that stirred in her body alarmed her. What was she, a sex maniac or something?

She looked away from him and around the room. It was pretty awful. The small gas fire was the shilling-in-the-slot kind, and everywhere pipes of various sizes snaked their way up and down the walls. It was obvious the plumbing had been added long after the house had been built. There was a notice over the bed giving instructions about using the communal bath. She shivered. Poor Grahame, spending his spare time in places like this. She wondered whether she dare ask him home again.

But if she did she would face questions from her gran and her father. And if ever Dad found out . . . She pushed the thought away.

'Come on, lazybones!' Grahame moved towards the bed and flicked at her with the towel. 'Your turn to wash, or would you like me to do it for you?' He grinned.

The heat was back in her body. She looked at him from beneath lowered eyelashes, like Vivian Leigh had done in *Gone with the Wind*.

'Yes, that might be nice!'

Disconcerted he drew back, but only for a moment.

During the next two months they met when they could. Grahame drove more miles than he had to in order to visit Whitby regularly and Pauline grew skilled in the art of half-telling the truth. Because it was summer their secret was easy to keep. Her family expected her to be outdoors during her leisure time and Mary was a sympathetic ally.

'Time you had a bit of grown-up fun,' she said.

So, with Mary's help, she was able to spend time with Grahame. They travelled to Middlesbrough to watch the speedway racing at Cleveland Park and went to see the summer shows at Bridlington and Scarborough. They went dancing too, but not in Whitby. There were too many people who knew Pauline there.

And her father continued to be busy, too busy to be suspicious. The bumper fishing continued and now it was time for the herring season to start. Already

Scottish keel boats were arriving in the harbour and it was reported vessels from Poland and Holland were also on their way.

The number of foreign boats sighted alarmed the local fishermen. A meeting was called and Pauline's father was one of the men appointed to a committee set up to safeguard the rights of Yorkshire fishermen.

'A precaution really,' he told Pauline and Eliza. 'There's no need to worry. The way the fish are running, there'll be plenty for everyone.'

When the herring season commenced on the twenty-ninth of August he was proved right. The catches were tremendous. The good news spread and more Scottish boats, ring-netters and drifters, came to join the fleet already assembled. The harbour was a hive of activity. When all the boats were present it was said a man could walk across the tiers of fishing vessels from one side of the harbour to the other without getting his feet wet.

An official from the Herring Industry Board watched over the Scottish and the local boats. Daily quotas for catches were imposed and prices set. The official was obliged to report daily to the Ministry of Food in London and when it was realised there was a glut of herrings, the fishermen were ordered to dump part of their catch back into the sea. This regulation, at a time of stringent food rationing, caused much ill-feeling. Again, Walter's skill at negotiation was called into action.

One evening, when Grahame was in Whitby, Pauline urged him to drive his car down to the harbour to see the mass of boats assembled there. He was reluctant.

'What if your father sees us together?'

She glanced at him. She had no knowledge of the violent argument between them, but realised he was tense so she laughed and patted his arm.

'No, he's away at some meeting or other.' She shrugged. 'We hardly see him nowadays. He's either fishing or attending to business. Getting to be an important man is my dad.'

She waited for him to speak but when he did not, she pointed out a good place for him to park the car.

They walked along together, hands clasped.

Dusk was creeping out from the narrow crooked streets which surrounded the harbour. It shrank within itself as it passed lighted windows and the open door of a noisy public house, but grew and blossomed when it reached the harbour.

There were well over one hundred boats sheltering there. Dusk enfolded them in its dreamy arms. They shifted and creaked with the gentle flow of the water beneath them and masthead lights shone fitfully through the gloom. It was so quiet both Pauline and Grahame jumped when a voice shouted out a few words in a foreign language. A minute later, a reply drifted across over the gentle slap of the sea against the quayside.

'They look like ghost ships, don't they?'

Grahame squeezed Pauline's fingers. 'Yes, I was just thinking of the *Marie Celeste*.'

'They'll be going out to fish in another hour or so and then back about four in the morning.' Pauline snuggled her hand into Grahame's pocket for warmth. 'It will be all bustle and activity then.'

'How do you know?' He was amused. Pauline had said once that she had no interest in fishing but she seemed to enjoy educating him in some of the mysterious ways of the fishing community.

'I've been here sometimes, when they're selling the fish. It's interesting, particularly in the herring season.

' "The silver darlings", that's what the fishermen call the herrings. They bring good money, you see. The fishermen return to harbour, pack the herring into boxes, weigh and tally them, then sell them to the buyers.'

She paused. 'Dad's boat nearly always has the best catches.'

Grahame shivered. 'Can we go now? I'm getting cold.'

She laughed. 'Cold – tonight? You can't be. You'd never make a fisherman, Grahame.'

God forbid, he thought.

Back in the car he asked, 'Where now?'

She sighed. 'Back home, I suppose. I mustn't push my luck.'

He started the engine. 'You haven't said anything at home, have you? About me, I mean?'

'No, I haven't.' She looked anxious. 'Do you mind?'

'No. I think it's much better that you don't, not just yet. Let's see how things go.'

She tried to see the expression on his face. 'You're not going off me, are you?'

'Of course I'm not.'

She wondered whether to tell him how much she loved him but decided not to. The present was so good, she didn't want to spoil it worrying about the future.

'I'll be away for the next three weeks, Pauline. Sorry, but I have to go on a course.'

She was silent so he took his hand from the steering-wheel in order to touch hers. 'I'll write while I'm away and tell you when I'll be through again.'

She relaxed. 'Is everyone doing this course?'

'No, just four of us.'

'Oh.' She tried to inject humour into the situation. 'Does that mean you're one of the best four salesmen in the company, or one of the four worst?'

Her attempted joke misfired. He did not reply.

She filled the silence hurriedly. 'Anyway, I hope you enjoy yourself. Don't worry about me, I'll find plenty of things to do.'

He patted her hand again. 'I know you will.'

She did her best. She sewed herself a new skirt to match the blouse she had bought with Gran's birthday money. She read a book called *Forever Amber* which had received a lot of attention in the newspapers because of the sexy love scenes.

She went with Eliza to a saleroom and watched as she bid for, and bought, a beaten brass coal scuttle. She carried it home for her and became concerned at Eliza's breathlessness before they reached the house. Pauline made tea that day and resolved to do more housework in future, reflecting that being in love made you selfish in some ways.

She met Mary and had long, lovely gossips, not about Grahame but about Mary's many and varied boyfriends. She even went dancing with her friend one night. She circled the Spa ballroom with clumsy partners who trod on her feet, and listened to them talk about themselves. She looked with lofty indifference at their faces. Most of them had spots.

She was so lucky, having Grahame.

One Sunday afternoon, when Mary was busy and Grahame had been away two weeks, Pauline collected

Mary's nephew and niece and took them off to collect cockles.

They were always hanging around the streets nowadays and she felt sorry for them. Their publican parents hadn't much time to bother with them.

Armed with large buckets and spades they went with Pauline to the beach and listened to what she said, eyes wide and serious.

'You follow the trail in the sand, see?' She pointed to the wet sand. 'And then you dig them up quickly and pop them in your buckets. When we get home, I'll boil them and we can eat them up for tea.'

The children set to work with a will and Pauline sat and watched them. Twenty minutes later, a couple strolling along by the water's edge shouted to her and waved. At first she didn't recognise them, then she realised it was Penny Jackson and Brian Jennings. But they looked different.

They came over to her and Pauline saw that Penny was pregnant.

'Don't look so amazed.' Penny laughed at her. 'We're married now. Didn't you see the announcement in the paper?'

'No, I didn't.'

Pauline jumped up and gave Penny a hug. 'I don't have to ask if married life is agreeing with you. You look wonderful.'

'She does, doesn't she?' Brian Jennings put his arm around Penny's shoulders. 'She gets prettier every day.'

Pauline stared at him. It wasn't only Penny that had changed. The last time she had seen Brian he had been a skinny, worried-looking boy. Now he was a man.

His every gesture showed his protectiveness

towards his wife and his pride in her pregnancy. He even looked manly. His shoulders were broader and he stood tall.

'When Dad realised I was pregnant there was a terrible row but after a couple of days, he calmed down. And then he helped us get our little house, and now he says he can't wait to see his first grandson.' Penny grinned. 'I told him it might be a girl.'

'Doesn't matter what the first one is, does it, Penny?' Brian winked at Pauline. 'We both want a big family.'

They talked for a few minutes longer then they went on their way, Brian's arm wrapped lovingly around Penny's swollen body. Pauline stared after them.

Penny and Brian – she and her friends had always laughed, and not in a nice way, when talking about them. Two skinny kids holding hands as they walked around the school playground; two youngsters staring into each other's eyes and sitting on walls to do their courting, no money to spend and nowhere to go. But now look at them – a house of their own and full of joy at the imminent arrival of their first child!

She felt a pang of sorrow and then anger at herself. Surely she wasn't jealous of Penny and Brian when she had Grahame? But did she have Grahame?

She sat down, hunched up her legs and wrapped her arms about them. Angela shouted something to her but she didn't hear.

Grahame was lovely but he never really told her anything about his life. She thought about him all the time but did he think about her when he was away from Whitby?

He had been pleased to discover she hadn't told her family they were seeing each other. She bit her lip.

And when did they ever talk about anything important? Of course, they didn't talk that much.

Her toes curled in her sandals as she remembered their love-making. He was good about that. He always took precautions so she didn't have to worry. But maybe it was *him* that didn't want the worry? Maybe he didn't want anything to tie him to her?

'Auntie Pauline.' A bucket, half-full of cockles, was thrust under her nose. 'I've got more than Malcolm, haven't I?'

'Well . . .'

'No, you haven't.' A second bucket appeared. 'I've got heaps more.'

Pauline sighed and stood up, brushing the sand from her skirt.

'You've both done ever so well,' she said diplomatically. 'Let's go back now and cook them.' She took hold of the buckets in one hand. 'I hope we can find some pins at home. The wiggly tails are the best things to eat, but they're difficult to get out of the shells.'

As they walked along the beach, Angela thrust her sandy paw into Pauline's free hand. 'It's been nice this afternoon.'

The feel of the small fingers curling trustfully within hers made Pauline's eyes smart. She blinked.

'What's the matter, Auntie Pauline?' Angela was looking up at her. Her eyes were round and deeply blue. She looked concerned.

Pauline laughed.

'Nothing, Angela. I've got sand in my eyes, that's all.'

Chapter Seven

The heat bounced off the car as Grahame left the cool greenery of Harwood Dale forest and set off across Fylingdales Moor. He had wound down the car windows as far as he could but still the car was becoming a furnace. The empty road before him shimmered in the heat and whichever way he looked he could see no shade. There was just rolling, uncompromising moorland stretching away in every direction.

He squinted upwards at the sun, burning so brightly in the deep blue of the sky; everything about this place was hostile, telling him he wasn't wanted, he didn't belong.

He loosened his collar. He was tired and the headache which had threatened all morning was now in full swing. Some small devil with a hammer was gleefully bashing away inside his head. He had to stop and rest. He pulled over to the side of the road, there wasn't really any need, he hadn't passed another vehicle for ages, killed the engine and got out, slamming the door behind him.

Immediately a swarm of flies surrounded him. He swore, batted them away and then, in a stubborn mood, stepped off the road and began to force his way through the high, thick bracken. Surely there must be a slight breath of air?

Dry sticks cracked beneath his feet and a lone grazing sheep, the locals called them moorjocks, raised its head and gazed at him, a length of cactus-like greenery drooping from its mouth.

Yes, there was a breeze, so weak it was more of a sigh, but it brought with it a hint of coolness so Grahame walked on, kicking at gnarled roots of gorse and heather with his well-polished, city shoes. He almost slipped a couple of times. He should have been wearing boots, the terrain demanded it.

A spiky, trailing tendril from a gorse bush wrapped itself around his left leg and he winced as he felt a stab of pain. He paused to pull up his trouser leg. Beneath his sock, a long scratch had appeared and beads of blood were welling up.

He gave up then and returned to the car. Before getting in, he opened the door and stood for a few minutes, passing his hand over his reddened, stinging face. He stared across at the distant view. The faraway vista of the moors had a certain charm. He could see the small areas of bright green, which he knew from Pauline meant that bilberries were hiding there, amongst the wilderness of furze and bracken. And amongst the sprawling areas of dried-up brown undergrowth were patches of misty blue and purple heather and larger stretches of brighter purple, which was the plant called ling.

Visitors to the area always pulled up roots of ling by mistake. They bruised their hands yanking the stubborn plant from the stony ground and carted it off to their boarding houses or lodgings, only to be told by the locals that it wasn't the real stuff, it was only 'fool's heather'.

Yes, Grahame's lips tightened, the locals enjoyed

many a laugh at their visitors' foolishness. Yorkshire people were a clannish lot. Take the old chap at Whitfield's farm, this morning. He'd let Grahame talk for an hour about the new reaper he was promoting, then he had removed his cap and scratched his head.

'Thoo's a silver tongue all reet, but dis thoo know hoo ti werk it thesen?'

'Of course I do.' Grahame had flourished his plans and leaflets beneath the old man's nose.

He had waved them away and grinned. Then he had suddenly grabbed hold of Grahame's right hand and turned it palm upwards. He studied it a moment and then let it fall. 'Thoo's nivver done proper work, lad, farm work. Tell yon firm to send someone who knows, then I'll listen.' And he had returned to his battered old tractor and driven away.

Stupid old bastard. Grahame flinched as a fly blundered against his face. Even the bloody flies were bigger here than anywhere else!

Even before going on the course he had known he was getting sick of running after laconic Yorkshire farmers, with their homespun philosophy and sly digs at 'foreigners'. And now he had the opportunity to get out, there was nothing to stop him.

He climbed back into the car, taking half the fly population with him, but instead of starting the engine, he put back his head and closed his eyes.

He'd do well in the South. The course leader had thought so. 'You've a good sales technique, Mr Lossing, and you can think on your feet. You show promise and we've decided to offer you promotion. The firm's doing well enough to consider expansion. How do you fancy moving to the Cotswolds?'

He had been elated and there had been only one

answer. But this thing with Pauline . . . He frowned.

It would have ended sometime or other. In many ways, it would have been better if it had never started. Why did he start it? Grahame opened his eyes and watched a captive fly battering itself against his car window. Was it simply that Pauline and he had fancied each other? He sighed. Perhaps it was as simple as that.

She had so plainly desired him and she was sweet and pretty, how could he not want her? But there had been other reasons.

He had never had a virgin before. The women he had bedded during his time in the army had been slags, with hard eyes and practised hands. Teaching Pauline how to enjoy making love had made him feel masterful, more in control. He winced inwardly when he remembered his first experience with a woman. He had been the virgin then, and she had made a cutting remark when he had come too soon. 'Hardly worth taking your pants off for, was it?'

Well, he liked to think he had made it a more pleasurable experience for Pauline. And he had been careful to protect her from the dangers of pregnancy. No, he hadn't hurt her. But he enjoyed the thought that he had hurt her father, even if the old sod never knew it. All that bosh about protecting his little girl! Grahame smarted as he remembered the humiliation he had endured at Walter Verrill's hands. The man was jealous, wanted her himself. He'd never admit it, of course.

But it was time to move on. Pauline was too young for him and he didn't want to make a commitment to any woman. Sometimes he wondered if he ever would. But it would be bloody awful finishing it. An image of Pauline's face came to him and he sighed. But he'd do it! He wouldn't just creep away. She deserved better than that. And she'd cry and be upset, but she'd get over it. She was a Yorkshire lass, after all. She was tough.

As he turned the ignition key of the car, his lips quirked. What was that saying she had taught him? 'Everyone's queer, except thee and me, and even thee's a bit queer.' No, she'd come to see the sense in their parting, in time.

Mind made up, he put the car into gear and sped off down the road. The sound of the engine faded and silence returned to the moor, silence broken only by tiny sounds: the slither of a grass snake as it glided through the bracken and the buzz of flies.

'Oh, you look ever so well, you've caught the sun. Hasn't it been hot? Did you enjoy the course? I've missed you. Did you miss me?' Without waiting for Grahame's reply, Pauline caught hold of his hands and, beaming, lifted her face for his kiss.

He obliged, and felt his usual confusion. As always, the nearness of her, the smell of her flowery perfume, sent his pulses racing. Everything was so clear when he was away from her, so different when they were together.

'I've got a surprise for you.' She paused, her eyes gleaming, 'Ask me what it is?'

'What is it?' he replied dutifully but felt a touch of irritation. Sometimes, there was a touch of bossiness in her attitude towards him; she liked to manage things. She would probably be a forceful woman by the time she reached middle age. He told himself to remember that.

'We've got the next two days to ourselves, Grahame. Just you and me, isn't that grand? My dad's just left on a fishing trip and won't be back until Monday and Gran's gone off to visit her brother and is staying over a couple of nights.' Pauline walked along with him, her arm through his. 'We can be together all the time. Are you staying at the usual place?'

'Yes.'

'Well, you won't have to tonight. You can come home with me.'

He stopped walking. 'I don't think so.'

She was puzzled. 'Why not?'

He shrugged. 'It just wouldn't seem right. Not in your father's house.'

'Oh, pooh.' She dismissed his objection. 'He'll never know.'

Grahame didn't say any more but, seeing his expression, Pauline sighed. 'Oh, all right, if you feel so strongly about it. I just wanted to be with you in my room.'

'I understand that, but . . .' When should he tell her, when would be the right time? He walked along in silence.

'Mary's got some tickets for us, a dance over at Malton. I thought . . .'

He groaned. 'Have a heart, Pauline. I've been travelling all day.'

'Oh, I'm sorry.' Her face fell. 'Of course we won't go if you're tired. It was just I thought, seeing we haven't seen each other for a while, it would be nice. The crowd's going to Malton by bus but if we went by car, we could have a bite to eat and then meet up with them later.'

She looked at Grahame's unresponsive face. 'We

needn't stay with them. But I like showing you off, you see.' She paused and laughed. 'I've been tempted, Grahame, and I fell. If we don't go dancing, it will be a bit of a waste.'

He looked down at her and then, seeing her expression, couldn't help laughing. 'You've been up to your tricks again?'

She nodded.

After their first few dates, Pauline had told him about her 'borrowing' of the special dress and he had been surprised and amused at her confession. Pauline looked as if butter wouldn't melt in her mouth and yet there were times when she was anything but good. Look at the way she had set out her stall to catch him. He stared down at her and her expression caused him to relent.

'OK. We'll go to the dance.' After all, he thought, it would be their last outing together. And his smile became forced as he listened to her chatter.

Finally, she realised how quiet he was but not the reason. She stood on tiptoe and kissed him. 'Let's go to your place.'

They went to his boarding house and made love. The act, for Grahame, had a poignancy he had never felt before, a feeling of sweetness and shame. If I had any guts, he thought, I would have told her by now. But he couldn't. She was full of laughter and pleasure and he wanted to remember her like that and told himself she would want memories too.

They cuddled together and slept for an hour and then she went home to get ready for the dance.

When he collected her at seven o'clock, he thought she looked beautiful in the figure-flattering white rayon crêpe dress, with her dimpled elbows showing beneath the cape sleeves and her newly washed hair gleaming in the light.

He stared at her. Perhaps he should keep in touch with her? He liked her better than any girl he had ever known. No, he shook his head. It wouldn't do. He wanted a new start.

'You look grim. Don't I look nice?' She swirled round, her skirt flaring.

'You always look nice, Pauline. That dress – it doesn't belong to the same woman as before, does it?'

She laughed. 'No.'

The dance was well attended, the dancers, noisy, exuberant and good-natured. They met up with Mary's friends and Grahame smiled and chattered, but his heart wasn't in it. He noticed the slight pauses in the conversation when he spoke and caught the sideways looks from other young men in the party when he and Pauline danced. It was true, he didn't fit in, he didn't *belong*.

If Pauline noticed anything amiss, she didn't show it. They left the dance before their friends and she was in high spirits as they drove back towards Whitby over the silent moors.

Then she stopped talking and, leaning forward in her seat, peered down the road in front of them. 'See that?'

Grahame looked. 'What?'

'The skyline.'

The night sky was streaked with red, but that was nothing unusual. Grahame said so.

'No, there's something different about it. You'd better stop the car.'

He did so. 'A red sky. It just means it's going to be a fine day tomorrow. What's all the fuss about?'

Without replying she opened the car door and stepped outside. She waited a moment then came round to his side of the car and tapped on the window. 'Get out a minute, please.'

He opened his door. 'What the . . .'

'Don't say anything, just breathe in.'

He lifted his head and sniffed. 'Good God, yes. I can smell burning.'

'It's strong, isn't it?' She looked worried. 'It's a moor fire. There are often little ones around this time of the year, but this smells really bad.'

He looked again at the horizon. Angry red streaks were spreading in the dark grey sky and with each breath that he drew it seemed the acrid smell of smoke grew stronger. He looked at Pauline. 'We'd better get out of here.'

She pulled at her lip. 'Yes, but which way?' She stared at the reddening sky. 'We could try and get home by a different route but I think it would be safer to go back.'

'Come on then.'

They clambered back into the car and Grahame wrenched at the wheel to turn the vehicle. He had almost succeeded when they heard the sound of an approaching motor bike. They looked back.

The bike screeched to a halt next to them. A gangly young man dressed in overalls leapt from the saddle and came hurrying over. He took off his goggles and grinned at them. 'Seen it, have you?'

'Yes.' Pauline answered. 'We thought we'd better backtrack. How bad is it?'

'Getting worse every minute.' The lad grinned again. 'Everything's so bloody dry, see. Old man Felton's got all his farmhands fighting it and t'fire engine's arrived but I don't know how long they can stay. It's not as if there's any water around for them to use and they say there's another bugger started on Spaunton Moor now.' He shrugged. 'I'm off to phone the forestry commission workers, ask them to come. And we need a couple of ploughs.'

'What for?'

The young man assessed Grahame and, realising he was not a local man, answered his question.

'We'll have to mek trenches,' he said. 'There's a lot of bloody peat on these moors, man – it could burn for months.' He sighed. 'And there's a couple of hundred moorjocks in this area, we'll have to move them. Anyway,' he replaced his goggles, 'can't waste time talking. And you'd best get a move on.'

'There's a farm just over that hill. Maybe they have a phone?' Pauline's face was pale.

'Naw, I'll have to go to Saltersgate.'

'Go on then, we'll follow you.' Grahame wound up the car window. The acrid smell of smoke was becoming stronger.

Pauline looked at him in surprise. He grinned at her and raised his eyebrows. 'I think that would be the best thing to do, Pauline. You'll be safe there.'

'And what about you?'

'I'm going back on that chap's pillion, if he'll take me. Looks like they're going to need all the help they can get.'

'You don't know anything about fire-fighting, Grahame.'

'I can learn.'

Many hours passed before the fire was doused. The army of beaters, volunteers like Grahame, farm labourers and forestry workers, worked without a break, methodically flailing away at the creeping, licking flames with the besom-like brooms they had been given.

They coughed away the pall of smoke that attempted to penetrate their lungs, they tied handkerchiefs over their mouths and ignored the blisters which rose on their hands as they worked. Several times they raised a ragged cheer when it seemed they had contained the fire, but each time it broke out again in another patch of moorland.

The smoke and flames panicked the moorjocks. They bucked against the farmworkers as they tried to move them and, eyes rolling wildly, blundered about, hampering the fire-fighters' efforts and ignoring the whistles of the shepherds and the barking of the sheepdogs.

A farm building in the danger area had to be evacuated, and watching the anxious mother and bewildered children being helped into a farm lorry and driven away made Grahame glad he had persuaded Pauline to stay in Saltersgate.

At four in the morning a detachment of soldiers arrived to assist the now exhausted men and the extra manpower showed. As dawn streaked the already blood red sky, the fire chief pronounced the fire out.

Along with other volunteers Grahame clambered into the back of a lorry and was driven away. Dog-tired though they were, the men were in high old spirits.

They quenched their parched throats with the bottles of beer one of the farmers had given them in payment and vied with each other to tell their stories. They took Grahame into their circle, clapped him on the back and told him his borrowed overalls suited him.

He listened to their slow voices, hoarse from the smoke, and looked at their soot-rimmed eyes and white teeth flashing against filthy black faces, and for the first time ever he felt comfortable with them. When, with three other men, he was dropped at Saltersgate, he waved goodbye with a feeling of genuine fellowship. Despite his earlier reservations about Yorkshiremen, he now knew he shared an affinity with them.

He made his way to the pub at which he had left Pauline and tapped on the door. The landlady let him in, clucking at the state of him and telling him to get a hot bath and then go straight to bed.

'Drop those filthy overalls in the basket on the landing,' she said. 'I'll see to them in the morning.'

He climbed the stairs to the small room he had taken for Pauline and entered quietly, expecting her to be asleep, but she was not. She was seated cross-legged on the bed, her eyes wide, her expression anxious.

'Grahame!' She almost fell off the bed in her hurry to get to him. 'You've been so long. I thought something dreadful had happened.'

'No, no. I'm all right.' He held her. 'It took a long time, that's all.'

'Oh, your hands!'

He winced as she touched them. 'They look worse than they really are. I didn't have gloves for the first hour, everything was such a mix-up, but then a forestry chappie kitted me out.' He looked down at himself, his smile tired. 'What do you think?'

'I think you're very brave.' She put up her face to

kiss him, then drew back, her nose wrinkling. 'But, Grahame, you absolutely reek!'

'Yes, I know.'

'I'll go and run you a bath.'

'What, dressed like that?'

She glanced at the low-cut slip, the only garment she was wearing, and shrugged. 'Suppose I'd better not shock anyone.' She grabbed her coat, put it on and disappeared. A moment later, Grahame heard the sound of running water.

He stretched. Every bone in his body ached. A bath would be heaven. And then he would sleep. He couldn't discuss the future with Pauline tonight, he just couldn't. He couldn't even think straight. He went towards the bathroom.

Twenty minutes later, he was flat on his back beneath cool, cotton sheets, welcoming the blessed waves of drowsiness that flowed over him. He heard Pauline give a sigh and then the bedclothes rustled as she snuggled closer to him.

'I was just thinking, Grahame. What a good job Gran and my dad are both away.'

'Um.'

She was trailing her fingers over his belly. It felt good but a warning bell rang in his mind.

'I'm awfully tired, love.'

'I know, I know. I just want to make you relax.' She bent her head and kissed his bare chest. Her hair tickled his chin. 'I'm so proud of you.'

He slid his arm around her bare shoulders. 'Are you?'

'Of course I am. You didn't have to go back and fight the fire. You were wonderful.'

'Oh, no, hardly that.' But he smiled. He thought of

the cheer that went up when the fire was finally defeated. The instinctive handshakes all round, the feeling of comradeship that had flourished. Warmth began to fill him. There had been a few occasions, in the war, when the same spirit of togetherness had occurred, and each time he had felt the same warmth. The pleasure of being part of a group of friends was a rare experience for him. When it happened, he relished it.

And now Pauline, pretty little Pauline, was sliding her hands around his hips, leaning over him with eyes wide and shining in the dawn light stealing through the window. He reached for her.

The noise of a vacuum cleaner downstairs awoke them. Grahame reached for his watch and winced when he picked it up. The blisters on his hands had blown up to the size of walnuts. He'd have difficulty driving the car. He nudged Pauline.

'Wake up. It's nearly half-past ten.'

'So?' She opened sleepy eyes and smiled at him. 'Don't you deserve a lie-in?'

'I suppose so, but the landlady . . .'

Pauline yawned, sat up in bed and stretched. 'She won't expect us to surface yet. You've been up all night, remember?' She grinned. 'And you're a hero!'

Then her face changed when she spotted his hands. 'Oh, Grahame, they look terrible. Do they hurt?'

He looked at them. 'Yes, they do rather.'

She took them carefully in her own. 'You need to get them wrapped up. We'll see about it when we go downstairs.' She pulled a face. 'And I made you make love to me last night.'

'I didn't take much persuading.' He hesitated. 'But,

Pauline, I shouldn't have. I didn't . . .'

'Didn't what?' She wasn't paying much attention to what Grahame was saying. She had bent her head and was dropping feather-light kisses on his poor hands.

He shifted uneasily. Pauline was naked and one rosy, entrancing breast showed above the bedspread. He remembered their love-making and realised he wanted her again.

'I didn't use anything. I'm so sorry. It was just that . . .'

She raised her head and smiled. 'It's all right.'

He shook his head. 'How can it be?'

'It is, Grahame.' She shrugged and her cheeks went pink. 'I've just finished my period, so it's safe. You don't have to worry.' Her embarrassment faded and she gave a little giggle. 'And I'm glad you forgot.' She pulled a face at his expression. 'You're always so careful about taking precautions. What I mean is, you never really let go, do you? It's always lovely, really it is, but I can see from your face there's always a little bit of you standing apart, as it were, telling yourself to be careful.'

He pulled his hand away from her. 'I thought you wanted me to be careful. I was thinking of you.'

'I know that. I've said how wonderful it is. But last night you forgot about being careful and it was even better than usual.' She sighed. 'I can't explain properly.'

She had pushed away the covers and now knelt beside him completely naked. He looked at her with increasing desire mixed with a dash of anger. She was a kid of seventeen and she was telling him how to make love. Apparently he had been too considerate, too much of a gentleman.

He had a sudden flash of memory. It was something that had happened when he was eight or nine years old. He had forgotten, but now he remembered every detail.

School had finished early that day and when he had entered his house by the back door, he had heard something. It had sounded like his mother, moaning. He had followed the sound which led him to outside his parents' closed bedroom door. Then he had been bathed in nervous sweat for, beneath the moaning sound, he had heard his father's voice.

He was terrified of his father but his love for his mother was stronger, and she needed him to protect her. He had clenched his small fist, opened the door, just a crack, and peeped in. Somehow, he would save her. She despised her husband, she had told him so, and now the brute was hurting her.

He had seen his father's back, swaying above his mother, and his terror had been a live bird fluttering in his breast. But he had taken a step forward. And then, beneath the shape of his father, he had seen his mother's face. She had not seen him. Her eyes were closed. She was moaning but her face had worn a silly, idiotic grin.

He had backed away, closed the door softly behind him and retreated to the kitchen. When his mother came in, he had been drinking a glass of milk and studying his school books. She had smiled at him and ruffled his hair and he had smiled back, but he had never trusted her again and he had never fully understood why. Now he did.

He reached for Pauline, clamped his hands on her naked shoulders and drew her towards him, ignoring the pain flaring in his hands. He ground his mouth on hers. She gasped, resisted for a moment, and then her arms went around him. They fell back on the bed.

Her flesh was so soft. His fingers kneaded, pinched her. 'Is this more like it, Pauline?'

She moaned, as his mother had moaned, and clung to him. He took her savagely, watching her face as she rolled her head from side to side and made noises in her throat. He went on and on. He would satisfy her, by God! He would show her he was more than a fancy-talking, soft-handed gentleman.

He had determined not to make a sound himself, but when the moment came, he groaned her name and held her close and his act of petty revenge was transmuted into something more – much more.

And the pub landlady, deciding to make a day of it by hoovering the bar and smoke-room, heard not a thing.

Chapter Eight

'Fancy having to take my second week's holiday in October.' Pauline went to look out of the kitchen window. 'Mrs Denton's just plain mean. If I worked in an ice-cream parlour I could understand, but a dry-cleaner's . . . It's hardly something that relies on the holiday trade, is it?'

'It does seem a bit daft,' Eliza agreed with her grand-daughter, 'but October can be a lovely time of the year.'

'Not today.' Pauline sighed. 'It's starting to rain and I'm meeting Mary at one o'clock. Oh, well – I'll have to wear my mac.'

She reached up to take a raincoat from the back of the kitchen door. Watching her, Eliza frowned. She was sure Pauline was losing weight, and her face was so pale, but it would be useless to say anything. Pauline had been touchy lately and would only snap her head off. Instead she asked a favour.

'If you're off out, will you do a bit of shopping?'

'Yes, of course.' Pauline buttoned up her raincoat and twisted a scarf around her neck. 'But aren't you going round to Mrs Oliver's to play whist? You usually call in at the corner shop on your way home, don't you?' She gave her grandmother a sly look. 'Catch up on the latest gossip.'

Eliza was levering herself, with some difficulty, from her chair. She frowned. 'If it's too much trouble . . .'

'No, Gran. I didn't mean it like that.' Pauline went and slipped her arm around Eliza's waist. 'It's just you haven't been out of the house this week and I thought a change of scene might do you good. What is it, your rheumatism bad again?'

'Well, it's none too good.' Eliza crossed to the table. She picked up her handbag and took some coins from her purse. 'If you pass a chemist, pop in and buy me another packet of Fynnon Salts, will you?'

Pauline shook her head. 'You should go back to the doctor's.'

Eliza handed her the money. 'Doctors aren't magicians, lass. When your joints wear out, there's not much they can do for you. No, Fynnon Salts'll do me fine.' She paused. 'In last night's paper it said Blakelock's were selling army gas-mask haversacks cheap. One would come in useful for your dad's sandwiches.'

'I'll buy one. Anything else?'

'Some kippers would be nice for our tea. We haven't had any for ages. But get them from Fortune's, mind, and bring some spuds back. I'll make a Pan Aggie tomorrow.'

'Oh, good.' Pauline kissed her gran's soft cheek. 'My favourite.'

'Aye, even when you were a little 'un you liked Pan Aggie. Good job too, seeing corned beef was about the only meat we could get during the war.'

'Shall I buy a couple of rashers of bacon, for the top?'

'Being a bit extravagant, aren't you?'

They both laughed. Pan Aggie was a poor man's

meal, but extremely tasty. Potatoes and onions were sliced up and placed in layers in a pot, together with a meagre portion of corned beef or bacon. Stock was added and then the dish was simmered gently over the fire and later popped into the oven to allow the top layer of potatoes to brown and go crackly. Pauline loved it.

Seeing Pauline's quick smile fade away, Eliza rested her hand on her grand-daughter's arm.

'What's bothering you, love? Can't you tell me?'

'Nothing's bothering me.' Pauline turned her face away. 'Everything's fine.'

'Is it? Is it really?'

'Yes.' She glanced at the clock. 'Hey, I'd better run. I'll be late.' She snatched up a shopping bag. 'See you later, Gran.'

Alone in the silent kitchen, Eliza went back to her chair and sat down carefully. A brief ray of watery sun shone through the window suggesting the shower had passed, but her knees, acting as barometers, told her there was more rain to come. She rubbed them gently and looked towards the inner door as it creaked and then slowly opened. Tigger, now a leggy young cat, showed his pointy face. He stared at Eliza.

'Come on then.' She patted her lap. As her movements became increasingly restricted because of rheumatism she had come to value Tigger's companionship.

The cat inched round the door, ran lightly across the kitchen and jumped up on Eliza's knee. He kneaded his paws delicately and then settled down and started purring. She eased him to a more comfortable position on her lap and, when he complained, began to stroke his smooth fur.

'She doesn't fool me, Tigger,' she told him. 'She can

smile all she likes but there's something bothering that lass.'

As her thoughts grew busy her hand stilled and after a few moments the cat laid back his ears and nudged her with his paw, demanding her attention. She looked down at him and frowned. For a split second she felt distaste, almost fear, for Tigger no longer resembled her affectionate little pet.

His long body was sprawled out and relaxed but his claws were half-extended and his gaze, the expression in his flat, green, half-closed eyes, was malicious. His neat pink mouth was parted and his needle-sharp white teeth gave Eliza the shivers.

Shuddering she tipped him off her lap. Sure-footed as always, he landed on his feet. But he arched his back and spat at her before running from the room, tail held high in indignation. She stared after him, wondering what had possessed her to do such a thing.

He was only a little cat. The same cat who played with her wool when she was knitting and kept her company during the long nights when she couldn't sleep, sitting by her feet staring into the flames of the fire with her. She glanced towards the fire now to see if it needed mending. Her body felt cold but the fire was well enough, the coals red and glowing.

'I'm getting to be a potty old woman,' she muttered. She made herself sit upright in her chair, reached for the newspaper which lay on a table nearby. But her feeling of unease wouldn't go away and despite herself her mouth began to tremble because, just as her knees told her rain was on the way, this new feeling told her there was trouble coming.

Pauline decided she might as well go and buy the

kippers before she went into town so, after leaving home, she headed in the direction of Henrietta Street. Fortune's shop was amongst a group of old-fashioned cottages clustered around the bottom of 199 Church Steps in a picturesque area much admired by the summer visitors.

They often climbed all the steps, which led to the parish church, to take photographs but were disappointed when they reached the top. Invariably the view was spoilt by the thick smoke rising from the kippering houses. There were many of them, all supplying the local delicacy, but if you were in the know, you went to one place to buy your kippers and that was Fortune's.

As Pauline entered the tiny shop a bell tinkled, but when no one came to serve her she knew they must be busy in the back so went through and opened the door of the smoking house.

'Hello, anyone there?'

She looked at the tanks where the split herrings were soaking in brine and then up at the rows of fish hanging on hooks from the smoke-blackened rafters, but couldn't see anyone. Then a voice hollered from the back of the shed.

'Get thissen in and shut t'door quick. Thoo's mekkin' smoke whirl everyways.'

'Sorry.' Pauline took a step forward and hurriedly shut the door behind her.

A middle-aged man came forward from the gloom of the shed and studied her. 'Thoo's Walter Verrill's bairn, am Ah reet?'

She nodded.

The man scratched his head. 'By gum,' he marvelled, 'where hast years gan? Thoos wust a skinny little lass the last time I saw thoos, now thoo's a reet grown-up lady.'

'Yes.' Pauline blushed. She had no idea who she was talking to, but he had to belong to the Fortune family. They had been smoking kippers on this site since before the first world war.

'My gran always comes to buy your kippers,' she volunteered, 'but she's not too grand today.'

The man blew out his cheeks in a comical sigh. 'Ah's sorry to hear that.'

He grabbed at a nearby sack, shovelled up a pile of oak chippings and threw them on to a glowing trench of fire, then shook a cloud of sawdust over the top of the chippings. The smoke billowed in the air and Pauline coughed.

'Reet, ow many pairs dost thoo want?'

'Three, please.' She mopped her streaming eyes.

The man took a hook and brought down one of the poles containing the split kippers and extracted three pairs from their hooks. He wrapped them in grease-proof paper and then in a piece of newspaper which he took from a shelf nearby.

'There thoo goes, best kippers in t'county.'

'I believe you.' Pauline took out her purse but he waved it away.

'Nay, have 'em on me this time.' He pressed the newspaper parcel into her hands, ignoring her protests. 'And tell Eliza she mun tek proper care of hersel.'

'I will, thank you.'

Pauline smiled but beat a rapid retreat as she saw the man reach for the sack of chippings again.

Outside, she turned up the collar of her raincoat. The light rain had stopped but the wind was cold. She wrinkled her nose and thought of the lovely summer days when she had been stuck behind the counter at work, and she cursed her employer.

She dropped the newspaper parcel into her shopping bag and walked towards the bridge which linked Whitby's East Cliff to the West Cliff. She was meeting Mary in Flowergate. They had nothing special planned, just a look around the shops and a cup of tea and a natter, but she was looking forward to seeing her friend.

As she stepped off the bridge she saw four men walking towards her but because she wasn't wearing her spectacles didn't recognise her father until he shouted to her. He must have just left the fish pier. She waved her hand in greeting. As he came closer, he asked, 'Now then, Pauline, where are you off to?'

Although the tone of his voice was jovial, now that he was close to her she could see how tired he looked. He had been out fishing for three days and during that time the weather had not been kind. She knew he would be in need of sleep. She smiled at him.

'Dad, I didn't see it was you. How was it? Did you pull in good catches?'

He flung his arm around her shoulder. 'Pretty fair, considering. We landed some skate and good cod and whiting.'

The man to his left snorted. 'Aye, and a lot of muck stirred up by the weather. We caught in a bloody big bream which is good for nowt but cat-food.'

Pauline felt her father's hand tighten on her shoulder. He turned his head. His voice, when he spoke, was cold.

'Watch your language when my daughter's about, Billy Winspear.'

The culprit dropped his eyes to his boots but Pauline saw how the other fishermen looked at each other and raised their eyebrows. She reddened.

They'd be wondering what was so special about Walter Verrill's daughter. All the fishermen swore, she was used to it. She sighed and wished her dad wouldn't make a fuss about unimportant things.

'I'm just off into town, Dad, to do a bit of shopping,' she rushed to fill the uncomfortable silence. 'Anything you want me to get for you?'

'No.' His hand left her shoulder but only to brush back an errant piece of her hair which was blowing about her forehead. 'It's cold today, lass. You should have something on your head.'

'I've got a headscarf, I'll wear that if I need to.' Sensing the hidden amusement of her father's companions, she moved away from him. 'I'll get on then. See you back at home.'

She nodded to the other fishermen as she passed them but avoided looking into their eyes. She knew what they were thinking. She'd overheard snatches of conversation and Mary, when they were both younger, had been a friend who had never pulled her punches.

'The blokes think your dad's soft in the head, you know, the way he treats you and your mam. He seems to think you're made of spun glass. My dad says he wouldn't be so daft if he had a houseful of brats under his feet when he got home. But your mam couldn't have any more, could she?'

Poor Dad. Pauline thrust her hands into her coat pockets as she walked along. The fishermen cursed and cuffed their children but they were proud of their big families, especially when the lads grew up and joined their fathers in the fishing grounds. Dad had no sons, he had lost his wife early in life and he had no friends. Workmates, acquaintances, but no real friends.

Pauline's head came up. But if her dad wasn't well liked, he was respected. For one thing, he owned a quarter-share in *The Enterprise*. That was one reason for the gulf between himself and the local fishermen. They were jealous because they worked for other men and drew a wage, whereas he worked for himself. He had prospered a little too much in their eyes, and he wasn't a Whitby man born and bred.

Just once, Gran had told Pauline about her father's early life and how she and Walter had come to live in Whitby. Pauline remembered it was not long after her mother had died and Gran had moved in to live with them.

Something had happened when the three of them were eating a meal. It was something small, so small she couldn't now remember what it was, but she remembered how her father had pushed back his chair, spoken harshly to his mother and stormed out of the house.

Outraged, Pauline had run across to her gran and hugged her fiercely. Full of pain at the death of her mother, unable to talk to her grief-stricken father, to thirteen-year-old Pauline, her gran had been an angel in disguise.

'I hate him,' she had declared passionately. 'How dare he speak to you like that? You're his mother. If he doesn't say sorry, I'll never speak to him again.'

'You mustn't say that.' Eliza had freed herself from Pauline's grasp and her voice had been stern. 'Your mother was your father's whole life. Half the time, I don't believe he knows what he's saying.'

Then, seeing Pauline's woebegone face, she had shaken her head, made her sit at the table and poured them both some tea while she tried to explain.

'Your dad loves you too, of course, but a man's love for his woman is different, Pauline. When you're older, you'll understand. And particularly in Walter's case . . .' Eliza's voice had faltered. 'Before he met your mother he was a lonely soul. Margaret changed his life.'

She stirred sugar into her tea and looked at Pauline thoughtfully. 'Maybe I should tell you a bit about your dad's life when he was young? It might help you understand.'

'Please, Gran, I'd like that.'

'It's not a happy story but you're old enough to realise life is not always happy.' Her grandmother sighed and began her tale.

'When Thomas, my husband, was killed during the first world war,' she had said, her voice heavy and slow, 'me and Walter lived with my mam. But then my brother Charlie was called up and after he went, we had to make other arrangements.

'There wasn't enough money to live on, see. Me dad and Wilf had been drowned just before the war in a bad storm and there was no way me or my mam could earn a living in Baytown.' She shook her head. 'Eh, those were terrible days, Pauline, there was precious little help for widows and orphans. I tell you, a year after Thomas died, even though I was still grieving, if a halfways decent chap had proposed to me, I would have taken him. I couldn't have loved him, but I'd have tried to be a good wife, and it would have been security for me and Walter.

'But there were no men of marriageable age left. They were all at the front, being gassed and maimed and killed.' She shuddered. 'The only males left at home were old greybeards and little lads.'

She stared at Pauline, her expression bleak.

'There was never a war like that war, Pauline. I say that even though your poor dad is risking his life mine-sweeping and bombs are dropping on poor defenceless . . .' Her voice broke. They sat in silence and then she drank some tea and looked up. 'It's grim stuff I'm telling you here, my girl, but you're almost grown and you've a right to know.'

'So what did you do?' Pauline was sorry to see the sadness on her grandmother's face but she was eager to know what had happened next.

Eliza stared down into her cup. 'What happened next?' she echoed. 'Well, let me see. Your great-grandma went to live with a cousin of hers who was an invalid and was prepared to give her a home in exchange for a bit of cooking and cleaning and looking after. I packed up and moved here to Whitby. I hadn't the money to go any further.

'I managed to rent a room above a public house. It was cold and damp and up lots of stairs and every night you could hear the row from the public bar but it was cheap. And I worked as and when I could, skivvying in the big houses belonging to professional people, ironing in a laundry, whatever was going, and poor little Walter was left with whoever would look after him. He was too young to go to school, see, and I couldn't take him to work. The people who took him weren't your ideal baby-minders; I could only afford to pay a few coppers. A few of the women were kind but many were not. Most of 'em had three or four kids of their own and Walter had it rough. He was considered a foreigner, see?'

Pauline saw. Some things didn't alter.

'I'd leave work all hours, dog-tired, and I'd go and pick him up and he'd stare at me with his big eyes. He wouldn't talk and he'd have a cut lip or a bruise on his cheek, and I'd know he'd been bullied. And God help me, I'd take him back there the next day. There was nothing else I could do, we had to eat.'

Poor Gran. Pauline remembered how she had sighed and put her hand over her eyes.

'Those years damaged us both, but particularly Walter. It was then that he closed in on himself. He was too little to understand, he thought I'd deserted him, and I believe, deep down, he's never really forgiven me.'

'Oh, Gran. Dad's very fond of you.'

'Do you think so, Pauline?' Eliza's voice had been sad. 'He does his duty by me, I'll give you that, but . . .' She pressed her lips firmly together. 'I shouldn't really be talking to you about your dad like this. I just wanted to explain to you why he seems a bit cold sometimes. Things that happen to you when you're young, they affect you.'

'But later on, things got better, didn't they?'

The glimmer of a smile appeared on Eliza's face. 'Oh, yes. After those first few months he learned how to look after himself. When I went for him, he wasn't the only boy with a cut lip! The mothers never seemed bothered, they'd all been brought up in a rough school.

'And I scraped a bit of money together and we moved to better lodgings and Walter started school. Life slowly became easier and then, almost before I knew it, your dad was a strapping lad of fourteen. He left school and took a job with old Sam Parkins. There was a lot of jokes about that. The locals thought he was crazy in the head. No one would work with Sam. He had this leaky old boat, a coble, he was drunk most of the time and when he did go out fishing, he never caught much.

'Cobles are difficult boats to sail, you know. You have to use a lug sail and know when to shift around the bags of sand they carry as ballast. My goodness, I had a fit when Walter told me his plans. But he always went his own way and he knew what he was doing. He fixed up the boat, somehow managed to keep Sam sober before they went out fishing, and after a bit they were bringing in good catches. By the time Walter was seventeen, he'd made enough money to buy the boat from Sam.'

Pauline knew the rest of the story. 'And he went on from there, didn't he? He went deep sea fishing and saved enough to buy shares in a keel boat. And look at him now, he's on committees, speaks for fishermen's rights and everything.'

'Aye, the men respect him now. They know he has his head screwed on right and they admire him for making money.' She shook her head. 'But he's still a lonely man.'

'He doesn't seem bothered, Gran.'

'No, not when he had your mam. But now she's gone he's going to find it terrible hard. That's why you must spend some time with him, Pauline, and try and understand when he's bad-tempered or moody. You're all he's got to remind him of Margaret, and he does love you.'

'I'll try.' Pauline nodded, her face solemn. 'But I

don't know what to talk to him about.'

'Anything, love. Maybe, when a few weeks have passed, you can remember some of the happy times. Eh!' Eliza's face had lifted into a smile. 'Remember how excited your mam was when he had the inside toilet put in, and all the talk that went on?'

'Yes.' Pauline grinned. ' "Too big for their boots, some people," ' she quoted. 'The neighbours were jealous because we didn't have to go outside to the privy any more!'

Eliza smiled. 'Aye, that would be right.'

'You're proud of Dad, aren't you, Gran?'

'I am.' Eliza's nod had been decisive. 'He's a good son. I just wish we could talk, be a bit closer.'

'Hey, Pauline.'

Mary's voice jerked her from the past to the present. She looked up and realised she had walked halfway along Flowergate and her friend was standing across the road from her, waving. She hurried to join her.

Mary gave her an exasperated look. 'You'll have to start wearing your specs outside, Pauline, you're getting worse. Deaf as well as blind!'

'Sorry, I was thinking.'

'Must have been awful important?'

'Not really.' Pauline looked at Mary and wished she had put on some make-up. Her friend always looked so smart. Even on this dull, windy day her hair was in a smart pageboy and in her bright red boxy jacket and a slim black skirt she looked terrific. Pauline sighed.

Mary's nose wrinkled. 'What's that smell?'

'Kippers.' Pauline raised her eyebrows in mock apology. 'Sorry, but I didn't want to trail all the way back to Henrietta Street on my way home.'

Mary held her nose. 'Well, keep that shopping bag on the opposite side of me, please. I'm wearing new perfume and it won't stand the competition.'

Mary was good at cheering people up. She bubbled away, explaining how she had blackmailed one of her brothers into giving her some of his clothing coupons, hence the new skirt, and soon had Pauline laughing when she described a row which had taken place yesterday between one of the milkmen and her boss at the dairy.

They looked round the shops and tried on hats in a local store and then, when their feet began to ache, went into a tea-shop and ordered a pot of tea and toasted teacakes. Then Mary sat back in her chair and looked at Pauline thoughtfully.

'What's up with you, my girl?'

Pauline flushed. 'Nothing. And don't start, I've had enough fussing.'

'Oh, and who else has noticed the change in you?'

'I haven't changed, and it was only Gran.'

'I might have known it. Your gran's no fool.'

'Shut up, Mary. There's nothing wrong with me.'

'Don't give me that. I know you, remember. Look at you! No make-up, a draggy old mac – since when did you come into town dressed like that? And you don't look well, you're getting skinny.' Mary paused 'It's Grahame, isn't it? He hasn't been in touch and you're frightened he's dumped you?'

'He hasn't dumped me.' Pauline hunched her shoulders protectively. 'I haven't heard from him for a while but that's nothing. He's always busy, he may have gone on another course.'

'Then he should have told you. What is it, five

weeks since you last saw him?'

When Pauline didn't answer, Mary's voice softened. 'Want to talk about it?'

'No.'

The waitress brought their order and Mary poured out two cups of tea. She took a bite of teacake, chewed it and said, 'Can I be honest?'

Pauline frowned. 'You will be, whatever I say.'

Mary considered. 'Yes, I will, because I'm your friend.'

She leant forward and touched Pauline's arm. 'Would it be so awful if Grahame *did* fade out of your life?'

Pauline snatched her arm away. 'How can you say that? You know I love him.'

'Perhaps you do, but honestly, Pauline . . . what if he doesn't love you?'

She looked away. 'That's a rotten thing to say.'

'But you have to face facts.' Face serious, Mary persisted in her efforts to get through to her friend. 'He turns up here when he feels like it, has his wicked way with you and buggers off again. You haven't a clue what he's up to when he's away.'

Pauline jumped to her feet, her face white. 'You rotten bitch, Mary! I told you what happened in confidence and now you throw it back in my face. I'll never speak to you again.'

'Hey, wait a minute.' Mary bit her lip. 'Listen to me. I apologise, I didn't mean to upset you. But I know how you feel about Grahame and I don't want you to be taken for a ride. He's never mentioned marriage, has he?'

'He will, in time. I just know he will. He wants to get on in his career first. There's no one else, I know it.'

Talking at feverish speed Pauline snatched up her shopping bag and shrugged into her raincoat. She drew some coins from her pocket and threw them down on the table. 'That's my share of the bill. And until you take back what you've just said, Mary, I don't want to see you again. You just don't understand.' Her voice choked. 'Grahame loves me, I know he does.'

She fled towards the door. Mary watched her go, her face sombre. She built the coins Pauline had left into a tidy pile and then poured herself another cup of tea.

'I hope you're right, love,' she murmured to herself. 'I really do hope you're right.'

Talking at fevered speed, Nadine snatched up her shopping bag and struggled into her raincoat. She drew some coins from her pocket and threw them down on the table. 'That's my share of the bill. And until you take back what you've just said, Mary, I don't want to see you again. You just don't understand. [illegible] Graham loves me. I know he does.'

She fled towards the door. Mary watched her go, her face [illegible] [illegible] [illegible] [illegible]

[illegible]

[illegible]

[illegible] the name of the firm correctly. Yes,

Chapter Nine

Pauline waited for Grahame to contact her. Ten days after her quarrel with Mary she knew she could wait no longer. Even if Mary was right and Grahame had dumped her, she still needed to speak to him, but how? She didn't even know where he was. Then she had an idea.

She made herself act. The next day she left work early and went along to the library. She stood outside the building, nerving herself to go in. A glance at her watch told her it was almost closing time. If she was going ahead with her plan she must not delay. She hurried up the steps, wishing Mary was with her, wishing they were still friends. She pushed open the swing doors.

'Please,' she addressed a thin bespectacled woman who was replacing books on the shelves, 'I need to look up a long-distance telephone number. Someone told me you have copies of all the directories?'

The librarian raised her eyebrows and looked pointedly towards the wall clock, but she directed Pauline to the appropriate section.

She pulled down the relevant book and turned to the pages for Middlesbrough. God, she hoped she'd remembered the name of the firm correctly. Yes, there it was. She gave a sigh of relief and copied down the number of Manner's Farm Equipment Incorporated. She put the precious piece of paper in her coat pocket and scurried past the library assistant just as the closing buzzer went.

'Thank you.'

There was a phone box at the end of the road. She put her piece of paper on the shelf and dialled the number. Would they be cross at her for ringing so near closing time? Perhaps the staff had already left? Maybe she should wait until tomorrow? No, by tomorrow her nerve would have gone. Someone was there.

A woman's voice answered, 'Manner's Farm Equipment, may I help you?'

Pauline pressed button A. 'I hope so.' She cleared her throat. 'You've someone called Grahame Lossing working for you, he's one of your salesmen. I have to get in touch with him, it's quite urgent. I wondered if you could give me a telephone number for him?' Her voice quivered with the intensity of her feelings. Her hand was sweating, the phone felt slippery in her grasp.

'Mr Lossing, you say?' The voice at the other end of the line assumed a cautious note. 'May I ask who's calling?'

Pauline swallowed. 'Miss Pauline Verrill.'

'Do you wish to speak to Mr Lossing about a business matter?'

Pauline hesitated. 'No, it's personal.'

'I see.' There was a pause and then the careful voice spoke again. 'I'm afraid I can't help. You see, we have sales people working all over the country and it's policy to deal only with business matters through the office. If you have Mr Lossing's home address, I suggest you try and contact him there.'

'I don't have his address, that's why I'm ringing you.' Pauline heard the rising hysteria in her voice and checked herself. 'I'm sorry. If you can't give me a telephone number, can you tell me when he's due to visit the Whitby area again?'

Another pause. Pauline shifted the phone to her other hand and waited.

And then: 'Mr Lossing is no longer travelling in the Whitby area, Miss Verrill. He's been given another location down South.'

Pauline gasped.

The woman must have heard, for her next words held a touch of concern. 'Look, if it's *that* important, I'll see he's told of your enquiry. Give me your address and phone number, if you have one, and I'll forward them on. Perhaps he will contact you.'

'Yes, thanks.' Grahame knew her home address, but Pauline gave it anyway, and also the telephone number of the shop. When she replaced the receiver her legs were shaking and she felt dizzy. She closed her eyes.

Grahame had moved away down South, without even telling her – how desperately he must want her out of his life. But why? What had she done? She remembered the last time they had been together and searched for a clue to his behaviour, but could think of none.

She opened her eyes and stared blankly in front of her. He must have become bored with her and when the chance of moving had come up, he had taken it. But how could he have been so loving at their last meeting?

She pushed open the door of the telephone box and

walked down the street in a daze. Mary had been right. Grahame had been using her all these months. He had been lonely, fed up of his own company, and she had been there, throwing herself at him. Her face grew hot remembering how she had made up to him in the car, after he had been to tea with them. Remembering that day, she thought of her father and groaned. Oh God, what was she going to do?

She stopped walking and looked around her. The light was fading and passers-by were hurrying after their day's work but she couldn't bear to go home yet. She realised she was close to where Mary worked and turned her steps towards the United Milk Dairies depot.

'Pauline – God, you look awful!'

Mary was actually standing on the doorstep of the premises, locking up, but after one look at Pauline she twisted the key the other way and, taking her friend by the elbow, propelled her none too gently inside. She opened a door to the right of the corridor.

'In here, quick. You look fit to drop.' She studied Pauline's face and frowned. 'I'll make you a hot drink. You look like you need a brandy but unfortunately a dairy is not the place to find one.' She peeped hopefully at her friend to see if her weak joke had raised a flicker of a smile but Pauline did not oblige. She flopped down on an office stool.

'Anyone else here?'

'No, they all left twenty minutes ago. I had to stay on to finish some lists.'

The girls were in the reception office of the milk company. It was a spartan place. The glazed window was uncurtained, the floor covered with blue and white lino which needed a wash. There were wooden chairs, a couple of square old-fashioned tables piled high with account books and a high counter over which the milk roundsmen submitted their books for checking and paid in the rounds money on Friday evenings.

The wall-mounted ancient gas fire plopped as Mary applied a match.

'There, it'll soon warm up.'

Using the same match, she lit a gas ring standing on a shelf near the fire and shook the battered old kettle to check it contained enough water. Satisfied, she replaced the kettle on the gas-ring and looked back at Pauline. 'Pity I've nothing stronger but tea is better than nothing.'

Loosening the top of her coat, she pulled out a chair and sat down. 'What on earth's happened?'

The concern in her voice broke through Pauline's defences. Tears began to pour down her face.

'I'm sorry about the row,' she sobbed.

'Bloody hell, that's not what's making you look like death, is it? I've already forgotten about it.'

'No, it's not just the row, but I'm sorry, that's all.' Pauline mopped her face with her sleeve but as fast as she wiped away her tears, others followed. 'You were right about Grahame, he didn't love me at all. Oh, Mary!' She paused. 'He's not coming back. I've just rung his firm and they told me he's moved down South and won't say where.'

'The rotten pig!' Mary scowled and reached for her hand. 'Poor old love, you must feel awful. I know how you feel about him but a heel like that isn't worth crying over.' She squeezed Pauline's hand. 'I know you won't believe me, but perhaps it's for the best. Once you get over the shock you'll realise it's not the end of the world. I've been dumped a couple of times by chaps I've been keen on, but I got over it, and so will you, in time.'

Pauline began crying so hard her voice came out in hiccups. 'But it *is* the end of the world, Mary – because I'm pregnant!' She scrubbed at her face. 'I wasn't sure at first, but now I am, and I don't know what to do. Grahame's left me and when my dad finds out, he'll kill me!'

'Oh God, you're not, are you?' Mary screwed up her face in a frown. 'Are you absolutely sure? You always told me Grahame was careful about things like that. How *can* you be pregnant?'

'He wasn't careful the last time we were together, the night of the moors fire.' The tears were fading now, but Pauline was still a pitiful sight. Her face white, dark circles beneath her eyes, she stared at Mary. 'We left the dance early, before you, remember? When we saw the fire was ahead of us Grahame took me back to Saltersgate and booked a room for the night and then he went back and helped the fire-fighters.'

'I see.' Mary's eyes narrowed. 'Oh, yes, I can just imagine.' She jumped up and walked around the room, her steps quick and furious. 'I suppose you greeted him like a conquering hero when he came back, and he was so puffed up with his bravery he threw you on the bed and proved what a fine fellow he was?'

The kettle boiled over on the gas ring. They both jumped.

Mary went and turned off the gas. She took two mugs and placed them by the kettle, then she picked up a tea strainer and waggled it at Pauline. 'Why didn't you stop him, remind him to take precautions?'

'It wasn't like that at all.' Pauline's voice was low. She linked her hands in her lap and stared down at them. 'He came back that night filthy dirty and dog-tired, and after he'd had a bath we went to bed, meaning to sleep.'

'Oh, yeah?' Mary had made the tea, and thrust a mug towards Pauline. 'It sounds like it.'

A tinge of red touched Pauline's cheeks. 'You think you know such a lot about men, Mary – but you don't, you know.'

'I know enough not to get pregnant. Oh, hell . . .' Mary looked startled and her hand went up to her mouth. 'I'm sorry, I really am. Look, I won't say another word. Just tell me what you want me to know.'

Pauline sipped the hot tea. 'I don't know what other men are like.' The ghost of a smile touched her lips. 'I've only known Grahame, but he was always so responsible and careful.' She looked across at Mary. '*Too* careful, if you know what I mean.'

She saw her friend's total incomprehension, and sighed. 'I found it a bit insulting, to tell the truth. He never really "let go". Oh, he enjoyed the love-making and he made me feel good, but it was as if part of him was not involved.' She shrugged. 'I don't know how else to explain it.'

She waited but when Mary simply stared at her, continued: 'When he got back that night he was tired and his hands were hurting, they were all blistered, but he was excited and happy. He told me what had happened, I'd never known him talk so much, and then he had a bath and we went to bed.

'All he wanted to do was sleep.' She hesitated. 'I

couldn't. I'd been waiting up for hours, remember, and I'd got all churned up, wondering if he was safe. So I snuggled up to him and fussed him and after a bit he responded. And do you know, Mary, it was like a different man making love to me.' She paused, remembering. 'He was loving and warm and *involved*, and it was wonderful. I couldn't spoil it by nattering on about . . . you know! And when we woke up the next morning, we did it again.'

Mary wrinkled her brow. 'But didn't you think of the risk?'

'No, I didn't. I was a fool, I know that now. And I thought, What the hell? If anything does happen, we'll get married. We love each other.' Pauline shivered. 'How wrong can you be?'

Mary sighed. 'This place you rang, where he works, what exactly did they say?'

'They wouldn't give me any information but the woman did say she would let him know I've been trying to get in touch with him.'

'So there's a chance you'll hear from him? He might even guess what's happened.'

'I don't think so.' Pauline looked down at the floor. 'I told him it was the safe time of the month.'

Mary gave an exasperated sigh but kept her mouth shut. There was an awkward silence. Then she cleared her throat. 'There could be another solution. It's early days, isn't it? If you're really desperate maybe you could take something?' She winced at the look Pauline sent her. 'You needn't look down your nose. Plenty of women do.'

'I wouldn't.'

'You say that now, but what if Grahame doesn't contact you?'

Pauline shook her head, a stubborn look on her face. 'I won't kill a baby.'

'It's not a baby yet.' Receiving another look, Mary sighed and looked at her watch. 'We'd better go. The cleaner will be coming in soon and she'll wonder what on earth we're doing here.' She took the half-empty mug from Pauline's hand. 'Try not to fret too much, not yet anyway. Perhaps Grahame *will* ring. And whatever happens, I reckon your gran will stand by you.'

'Yes.' Pauline stood up. 'I feel a bit better already, just telling you.'

'If I can help, I will.' Mary switched off the gas-fire and the electric light. 'Trouble is, Whitby's such a narrow-minded place.' She sighed. 'Remember when I talked about leaving, going to Manchester? Pity we both didn't go. Then none of this would have happened.' She opened the outer door of the office. A cold wind swept in and made both girls shiver.

'God, it's been so cold this last week.' Mary shivered then linked arms with Pauline. 'You'll be worrying about your dad and I can understand why, but things might not be as bad as you fear. After all, you're not the first girl in the world to get knocked up. And, let's face it, you've always got round him in the past.'

They went outside and Pauline gripped the top of her coat and held it closer round her throat. 'In the past, yes – but not this time, I'm afraid.'

A few days after Pauline's revelation to Mary, Grahame Lossing whistled as he made his way along Stroud's High Street. Happily aware that the Cotswold area suited him, that he had been introduced to several promising business contacts and that his neighbourhood offered him the opportunities of pursuing a variety of cultural activities, he was at peace with the world. He had even discovered there was a flourishing ballroom dancing society over in St Leonards.

He ran up the stairs to the agency from which his business was conducted and smiled at the receptionist.

'Nice morning, Lesley.'

'Yes, Mr Lossing.'

Her answering smile was a shade too enthusiastic. Lesley was a pretty girl and had made it plain she found him attractive but he wasn't biting. He wanted to stay clear of women for a while. He had plans for his future, the first of which was to save up for a flat of his own instead of staying in digs. Besides which, the memory of Pauline was still strong, uncomfortably strong.

'There's a couple of letters for you and a note from your Head Office.' Lesley handed them over.

'Thanks.' He entered the room he shared with two other salesmen from different companies and kicked the door shut behind him before glancing at the letters. The name printed on the front of the first envelope pleased him. He tore it open. It was from a man he had visited last week who wished him to call again. The second letter was just a circular that he tossed into the waste bin, then he read the memo from Head Office. Oh, Lord – his stomach dipped, he might have known Pauline wouldn't give up that easily.

He threw himself into his chair and stared out of the window. Rationalise as much as he liked, he still felt a heel over the way he had treated her. He should have been man enough to tell her he was leaving, but he hadn't. And he knew, if he was standing in front of her now, he *still* wouldn't be able to explain. How could he say that he loved her, but not enough? If he talked until he was blue in the face, she would never understand. Pauline saw everything so simply, in a way he could not.

He swore, stood up from his chair and paced the room restlessly. Thank God the other two chaps were out. He looked down at the note again.

'The young lady sounded most concerned.'

He could feel the disapproval between the lines. He bet it was a woman who had taken Pauline's call. All women were emotional: they couldn't help it, they were made that way.

His lips set in a thin line. He was away from Yorkshire now. He was free from jealous fathers and pig-headed Wolds farmers and a clinging, if loving, girlfriend. He would not be emotionally blackmailed.

He crushed the note in his hand. Pauline's hurt feelings would heal. In a few months she would be walking out with some other chap. He had been her first boyfriend after all. And what if he had taken her virginity? It was nothing to be ashamed of. Good God, she had practically forced him to. Anyway, it happened to everyone at some time and it wasn't as if he had ever been careless, she couldn't lay that charge at his door.

In the act of throwing the screwed-up paper at the waste bin he paused, remembering their last weekend together, and in remembering he weakened. God, it had been so good. But sex was a small part of life and he had things to do and places to go and wanted to travel light. Thank the Lord the only time he had failed to take precautions was during her safe time.

How easily they could both have been trapped.

He tossed the paper into the bin. He wouldn't ring Pauline, it would be kinder not to. And, as he'd decided on a life without complications, neither would he smile too widely at the pretty receptionist in the outside office.

He didn't ring or write and after a week Pauline knew he never would. Thereafter she went through life like a sleep-walker. She got up, ate her breakfast and worked at the dry-cleaning shop. She went for long solitary walks and listened to Mary when she nagged her to confide in her gran, but it was as if she were behind a pane of glass. She did nothing. When she thought at all, she felt nothing but shame. She had let her family down. Her gran had warned her but she had not listened.

She spent hours imagining how her father would look when he knew, and how the neighbours would react to the news. She shuddered when she imagined the ribald comments of the fishermen, the men who worked with her dad.

'What? You must be joking. Walter Verrill's lass!' Then the laughter. 'By Gawd, that'll put the boss's nose out of joint. Too much of a lady to hear swear words, was she? But good enough to sneak off and open her legs for some lad!'

Oh God, if Dad didn't kill *her* he would kill any man he heard talking about her.

She grew paler, listless. She fended off her gran's questions and thanked God her dad was presently away on long fishing trips. She knew she should visit a doctor but dared not. The family doctor knew her father; he would tell him. She stayed in bed as long as she could during the weekends and told Eliza she had toothache, or a touch of 'flu, or a headache.

Then one Sunday, when the two women were alone in the house, Eliza confronted her. Pauline had trailed downstairs to make a cup of tea. When she turned to go back to her bedroom, her grandmother barred her way.

'Pauline, we have to talk.'

'Not now, Gran.' Pauline edged round her. 'I have a bit of a headache.'

'So have I, but we're still going to talk.'

There was iron in Eliza's voice and an implacable set to her figure. Pauline sat down, a flutter of fear quickening her breathing.

With heavy tread Eliza crossed to the table and sat opposite her. Close up, Pauline saw the tiredness in the old woman's face and suffered another rush of guilt. Gran was already worn out with worry and she didn't yet know the worst.

'It's time for plain speaking, Pauline.'

She was silent.

Eliza waited a moment, then continued: 'I'm not a fool. There's something seriously wrong, something you're too scared to tell me about, but you must. We can't go on like this.' She sighed. 'I've racked my brains to think what it could be. I thought at first that maybe you'd got yourself in the family way.' She shook her head. 'But how can that be? You haven't had a proper boyfriend since you stopped seeing that traveller chap.' A sudden thought struck her. 'Pauline, you haven't been raped, have you?'

'No.' She spoke without looking up.

Eliza sighed with relief. 'Well, that's something. But what is it then, lass? Are you ill?'

Pauline shook her head. Eliza stared at her.

'You must tell me, love. Whatever it is, we'll sort it out. Oh, Pauline, you're ill, aren't you? You've been so pale and tired. Have you seen the doctor? Do you know something you can't bear to tell me?' Eliza put her hand to her mouth. 'I can stand it as long as I know. What is it? T.B.? Cancer?'

'Oh no, Gran, nothing like that.' Pauline was shocked. She rushed to Eliza's side and dropped on her knees beside the old lady's chair. 'I'm not ill at all.' She put her arms around Eliza's waist and hid her face against her breast. 'I'm not ill.' She tightened her hold. 'But I *am* going to have a baby.'

'Ah . . .' Eliza's figure stiffened. She was silent so long Pauline sneaked a look at her face but her expression gave nothing away. Then she rested her hand on Pauline's head and sighed. 'Well, that's bad enough, but it's a lot better than having cancer.'

'Gran!' Pauline exploded into nervous laughter. 'Is that all you're going to say? And why did you think I had cancer?'

'Mrs McBride's lass is seriously ill in hospital. She has it and she looked pale and tired for months before they found out what it was.' Eliza put a hand under Pauline's chin, forcing her to look up. 'And when I've sorted myself out, I dare say I'll have a great deal to say to you, but right now I'm just relieved. If I have to choose between a shamed grand-daughter or a dead one, I'll pick the shamed grand-daughter every time.'

They stared at each other then Eliza shifted in her seat. 'My back's aching. Let's make ourselves more comfortable.'

She stood up and walked, a little shakily, towards her chair by the fireplace. Pauline waited until she sat down and then followed her, crouching on the hearthrug beside her. She took hold of Eliza's hand.

'I wanted to tell you, Gran, I really did, but I was so ashamed . . .'

'So you should be.' The tartness had returned to Eliza's voice. She looked sternly at her granddaughter. 'Who's the father? That Grahame, I suppose?'

Pauline nodded. 'Yes, I've been seeing him all summer. We kept our meetings secret. I know Dad didn't want me to have a boyfriend.'

'And what does Grahame think about your news?'

'He doesn't know.' Pauline began to cry. 'Oh, Gran, everything is such a mess.'

Without comment, Eliza took a handkerchief from her apron pocket and handed it to her. 'You'd better tell me everything.'

Pauline told her story. Her grandmother listened without interruption and when Pauline had finished, said quietly, 'You must try again to get in touch with him.'

'No, I don't want to.' Pauline's voice was stubborn. 'He's made it plain he's not interested in me. I shall manage without him.'

Eliza shook her head. 'You're wrong, Pauline.'

'He left me, Gran.'

'Yes, and you're still hurting, but you must act like a grown-up now, a *real* grown-up. Remember, there's not just you to consider.'

'I know it's going to be awful for you and Dad, but . . .'

Eliza sighed. 'You're still talking like a child. You've rushed into grown-up things and landed yourself in a mess, my girl. Your dad and me can cope, but what about your baby?' She saw Pauline's expression change. 'You haven't thought that far ahead, have you?'

'Well, I . . .'

'Time flies. This time next year you'll be nursing your baby and then, before you know it, that baby will be a growing boy or girl. Do you want your child to be called names by the other kids, shouted after in the street? And a child needs two parents. Don't you remember me telling you what a struggle I had, raising your dad?'

'But things are different now.'

'Not so different.' Eliza touched Pauline's shoulder. 'I'm on your side, love. Grahame has a lot to answer for, but you've admitted you chased after him. He has the right to know he's fathered a child, and knowing might make him face up to his responsibilities. Plenty of men run away from the thought of marriage but end up making good husbands.'

'But if he doesn't love me?'

'Love!' Eliza made an impatient movement. 'There's all sorts of love, Pauline. Life's not just rolling about on a bed, you know.'

'Gran!' She was shocked, but she sat up and stared at Eliza. What if she was right? 'But I can't get in touch with him, I told you.'

'Try once more. Write him a letter and send it to the firm. Send a covering note and ask if they will forward it to him. It's worth a try.'

Pauline pushed her hair back behind her ears. 'All right, if you think so.'

'And while we're waiting, there's practical things to think about. You should see the doctor.' Eliza sighed. 'Ask him for orange juice and those vitamin things.

What with food rationing getting worse and so few fresh vegetables about, your baby will need all the help available.'

Pauline felt a pang of jealousy. Gran seemed more concerned with the unborn baby than she was with her. 'But the doctor will tell Dad.'

'Not yet, he won't. I'll have a word with him.'

'But we'll have to tell him sometime.'

'I know. And *you* must do the telling.' Seeing Pauline's face cloud over, Eliza patted her shoulder. 'I shall be there with you.'

'When shall I tell him?'

'We'll hang on a bit, shall we? Let's see if Grahame gets in touch first.'

'Yes.'

Pauline rested her head against her grandmother's knee and daydreamed. If Grahame came back to Whitby and asked her to marry him, how wonderful that would be.

'Best not to build your hopes too high.'

Eliza knew her so well. Pauline grasped her hand. 'I won't.' She stood up and stared at her grandmother. 'What shall I do if he doesn't get in touch with me?'

Eliza shook her head. 'One thing at a time. Whatever happens, we'll cope.'

'Oh, Gran. What would I do without you?' Impulsively, she kissed Eliza's cheek.

'Get on with you.' Her grandmother gave her a little push. 'That's what families are for, to stick together in the hard times. Now leave me alone to think things out. And stick a bit more coal on the fire, will you? I'll swear it's cold enough for snow.'

What with food rationing getting worse and so few fresh vegetables about, your baby will need all the help available.'

Pauline felt a pang of jealousy. Gran seemed more concerned with the unborn baby than she was with her. 'But my doctor will tell Dad.'

'Not yet, he won't. I'll have a word with him.'

'But we'll have to tell him sometime.'

'I know. And you must let the [illegible].' Seeing Pauline's face cloud over, Gran patted her shoulder. 'I shall be around, anyway.'

'When shall I tell him?'

'We'll wait for a bit, [illegible] Grandad [illegible] get [illegible].'

'Yes.'

Pauline rested her head against her grandmother's. [illegible] If Christopher came back and asked her to marry him, how wonderful the world [illegible].

'Best not to build your hopes too high.'

'[illegible] knew her so well.' Pauline [illegible] her words. She [illegible] up and smiled at her grandmother. 'Who would [illegible] if he doesn't [illegible]?'

Gran shook her head. 'One thing at a time. [illegible] happens, we'll [illegible].'

'Oh, Gran. What would I do without you?' [illegible] the [illegible] know.

[illegible] with you.' [illegible] gave her [illegible] 'There, what [illegible] are for [illegible] of [illegible] times [illegible] to [illegible] and [illegible] it's [illegible] enough for snow.

[illegible]

Chapter Ten

During November the weather worsened. Each day brought new miseries. Fuel ran low, bread stayed on ration and there were rumours that even the humble potato would be in short supply next. Faces grew long and tempers short.

'We were better off in the bloody war' was an opinion often heard as people crouched over meagre fires or blew on their cold hands as they waited in queues outside the butchers' shops. The world shortage of foodstuffs affected everything, particularly supplies of any kind of fat, and 'flu, coughs and colds raged through the population.

One Monday morning Rita Mitchell, despite her hacking cough, turned in for work at Manner's Farm Equipment as usual. She knew the workforce was already depleted, three members of staff being off with 'flu, and she was a conscientious employee. She was even first in the office. She turned on one bar of the electric fire, regulations stipulated the saving of power, and put a double-knit cardigan over her wool jumper. Then she sat down in front of the firm's switchboard.

At nine-thirty Mr Harris sidled up to her carrying a tray which contained the day's post. 'Be an angel,

Rita. Marcia's not turned up.' He grimaced. 'Another casualty, I fear. Will you sort and distribute the post for me?'

'Yes,' said Rita. In truth, she was pleased to be given something else to do. Few people were ringing to enquire about farm equipment in the present weather.

The job was quickly done for the post was predictable, except for one hand-written envelope. It was not the usual buff-coloured business envelope and it was not addressed to any specific person so Rita, feeling rather daring, opened it. Inside was another, smaller envelope and a note. Rita read it, then stared into space for a few moments. She was so lost in thought, she jumped when the switchboard buzzed. She dealt with the telephone enquiry, then returned to the envelope.

The note was signed Pauline Verrill. Rita remembered that particular call, remembered Pauline's voice. Rita Mitchell knew about voices and although the caller enquiring about the whereabouts of Grahame Lossing had carefully phrased her words, Rita had caught the hidden note of panic.

She remembered Grahame Lossing too. A smart young man, intent on making a name for himself. He had been pleasant but aloof whenever he had been in the office. The absent Marcia had developed a crush on him but not Rita. Bit on the cold side, she'd thought.

The rules of the company were strict. By rights she should drop the letter in the bin, but Rita wavered. Pauline Verrill had sounded young and scared. Unable to make up her mind as to what to do, she slipped the envelope into her cardigan pocket.

It snowed again in the afternoon and the office was freezing. Rita's head began to ache and she felt dreadful. Mr Harris, capitalising on her good nature, had passed on more work – fifty brochures to put into envelopes, address and stamp. It was a quarter to five when she finished them. She coughed so hard when she took the envelopes over to Mr Harris' desk he looked at her with belated compunction.

'You don't sound so good, Rita. Why don't you get off home? Someone else can cover the switchboard for the last hour.'

She coughed again. 'Thank you, Mr Harris.'

'That's all right.' He beamed at her. 'However, as you're going early, perhaps you could detour a little? Stick those brochures in the nearest postbox. It's Marcia's night to do the post and . . .'

'Of course, Mr Harris.'

She took off her cardigan, which she kept at the office, and shrugged into her heavy winter coat. The nearest postbox was well out of her way. She'd have to go via Orchard Lane. Thinking uncharitable thoughts, she hung up her cardigan on the peg by her desk and saw the top of the envelope sticking out of the pocket. She removed it and looked at the one line of writing: Mr Grahame Lossing.

On impulse, she crossed to the filing cabinet holding the personnel files and copied the relevant address on to the envelope. She stacked the rubber-banded bundles of brochures into her shopping bag, putting the private letter into the middle of one of the bundles.

'Put that in your pipe and smoke it, Mr Harris,' she muttered.

The slushy roadway and frozen pavements of

Orchard Lane showed it was not a main thoroughfare. Rita walked along cautiously, holding on to garden gates and walls in an effort not to fall. Her boots were at the cobblers' and the shoes she wore had no gripping power whatsoever. She was congratulating herself that she had manoeuvred the most difficult area when she went down.

'Ouch!' She let out a yelp. It was a heavy fall. Her lower left leg and ankle had twisted under her body, she didn't think she could get up unaided.

Fortunately she was near the end of the lane which led out on to a main street and someone had seen her fall. A lady and gentleman came to see if they could help and the man flagged down a passing car.

The bad weather seemed to bring out the best in people. The man with the car put Rita and her shopping bag in the back seat and insisted on taking her home. Twenty-five minutes later she was sitting before the fire at home sipping tea and listening to her mother grumble.

Mrs Mitchell grumbled a lot. She was a forceful lady who believed in expressing her opinions.

'I told you not to go into work today and now look what's happened.' Rita suppressed another bout of coughing. 'My cough had nothing to do with me falling.'

'You must have been mad to try and walk down Orchard Lane in this weather.'

'I've explained, Mother. I was taking the post. Oh!' Rita remembered. 'It's still in my shopping bag.'

'And there it can stay. You don't expect me to turn out in this weather, do you?' Without waiting for a reply, Mrs Mitchell continued, 'Why did *you* have the post? You're the telephone receptionist not the office girl.'

'Yes, but we're short-staffed.' Rita tried to stretch out her leg and groaned. 'Ow.'

'Sit still, for goodness' sake.' Mrs Mitchell had been a district nurse and had attended efficiently to her daughter's injuries. She took the empty cup and saucer from Rita's hand. 'They'll be even shorter staffed tomorrow.'

'Oh, Mother!'

'Don't "mother" me. You need to rest that leg. You'd better stay in bed tomorrow.'

'I suppose you're right.' Rita gingerly moved her foot. 'But what about the post?'

'Oh, stop your fretting. If it's better weather in the morning I'll walk down to the postbox.'

Rita sat back in her chair with a sigh. 'You won't forget?'

'I promise.'

But next day the weather had worsened. It was wet inside and out for a water pipe had burst during the night. The plumber didn't come until the afternoon – rushed off his feet, he said. After his departure, Mrs Mitchell cleaned up and then climbed the stairs to take Rita a bowl of soup.

'Mum, you shouldn't. You've been on your feet all day.' But she drank the soup and snuggled down beneath the warm bedclothes again. Her mother picked up the tray. 'Try and get some sleep. It's quieter now, no more thumping and banging.'

'Yes, but . . .'

'What is it?'

'The post, Mum. You won't forget?

Mrs Mitchell had forgotten. She clumped down the stairs with her heavy tread and went and fetched Rita's shopping bag. As she looked inside she heard the soft rustle of snow outside the windows. She pulled out one of the envelopes and looked at it. It wasn't properly sealed, the flap had been tucked in. The contents couldn't be *that* important. She glanced at the other envelopes. They were the same.

On impulse, she opened the envelope in her hand and took out the single sheet of paper. She read the brochure and snorted. What a waste of time and money. How much had it cost to print all these? She felt angry as she remembered Rita's request for a five-shilling pay rise had been turned down. Mr Harris had said the firm couldn't afford pay rises this year. And yesterday, her daughter had almost broken her ankle carrying rubbish like this!

She looked through the window again and saw it was already dark outside. That made up her mind for her. She transferred the bundles of envelopes into a brown paper carrier bag and went and opened the back door leading to the yard. The dustbin was by the door. She put the carrier bag into the bin and then, as an afterthought, dumped a pile of old newspapers on top. The binmen should be round tomorrow, before Rita got up, but it was as well to be careful. After that she sat down by the fire and had a snooze.

That evening, when Rita asked her if the post had gone, she said yes without the slightest pang of guilt. 'Do to others as they do to you' was her motto. And anyway, it had gone, hadn't it?

After tea, Eliza and Pauline had played cards but Eliza had pleaded tiredness and retired to bed early. Alone at the table, Pauline shuffled the pack and wondered whether she too should go upstairs. But the kitchen was warm and she knew her bedroom would be freezing, and anyway it was too early for sleep. If she went to bed now she would lie beneath her covers, stare into the dark, and listen to the hollow booming of the sea, one of the loneliest sounds in the world. She decided to play patience instead.

She tidied the cards into a neat pack. Her father put down his paper and coughed. Pauline's fingers stilled. The weather had kept the fishing boats in harbour for the last five days but for the first four of those Walter had been busy with his bookwork. She heard his chair creak and wondered if he wanted her to go and sit near him, talk to him. She hoped he didn't.

Although today had gone well enough. Eliza and her father had been there in the kitchen when Pauline returned from work and the three of them had chatted about general things. And after tea, Walter had mended a pair of shoes. He had brought the last out of the cupboard, fitted his shoes upon it, pulled off the old sole and cut new ones. It was the smell of the dubbin he used to soften the leather that had awakened memories. When she was small, she had loved watching her father cobble shoes. She had stood at his knee and chattered to him as she watched him shape and cut the leather, and he had listened to her, nodding his head and smiling.

From the corner of her eye she saw him reach for his pipe which he always kept on a small table next to his chair.

'Your gran's gone up early?'

'Yes.' A worry line creased her brow. 'She seemed very tired. She hasn't been at all well lately.'

And whose fault is that? her conscience screamed at her.

'She'll be all right, it's the rheumatism again.' Walter dismissed his mother's supposed ill-health.

'That reminds me.' He took a pouch of tobacco from his pocket and began packing his pipe. 'Those stockings I put on this morning, very neatly darned they were. Did you mend them?

'Yes.' Pauline began her game. She laid the Queen of Diamonds on the King.

'I thought so.' Walter's voice held a note of pleasure. 'I knew your gran wasn't up to such fine stitching any more, what with her hands and all.'

Why did he always refer to Eliza as *her* gran instead of his mother?

Pauline glanced across at him. He was tamping down the tobacco with his penknife. He looked up and smiled at her.

'I reckon you're growing up gracefully at last, Pauline.'

'Why, because I darned your stockings?'

His brow creased at the veiled hostility in her words but he answered mildly. 'Of course not. But you've been different lately. You've stayed in more, stopped haring all over the place.'

She shrugged. 'It's hardly the weather to go out dancing. Anyway, Mary's got herself a regular boyfriend.'

'And so she hasn't time for you?' Walter shook his head. 'That's a fine, flighty friend you've got.'

Pauline put down the ten of Hearts. Grahame should have received her letter by now. Perhaps she would hear from him tomorrow or the day after? And if he didn't get in touch with her? She pushed the thought away. Gran had agreed they would wait until after Christmas before telling her father. There was still time for Grahame to get in touch.

'Mary's good-hearted, Dad.'

'I'm sure you're right.' Walter lit his pipe and, standing up, walked across the kitchen to stand behind Pauline's chair. 'But she's too empty-headed for you.'

Pauline frowned. 'And I'm clever? Working in a dry-cleaner's doesn't take brains.'

'You're sharp-tongued tonight, lass. That's not like you.' He was annoyed, Pauline knew, and was surprised at her own indifference.

'Mary's shallow, you're not. These past few weeks, I've seen you changing. You're becoming more of a woman, less of a girl.' Her father's voice deepened. 'You're growing up, Pauline, and you're getting more like your mother, God rest her.'

Pauline's hand trembled slightly as she put down the six of Clubs. He'd noticed, had he? He was right, she was changing, and not only because of her pregnancy. Gran had said she must act like a grown-up but now, thinking about it, she realised the process had begun even before their conversation. Maybe it had started during the weekend she had spent with Grahame, or maybe when she learned he had moved away. She couldn't pinpoint the exact moment. She knew only that she had begun to question things she had always taken for granted.

Was it Grahame's desertion that had made her look more critically at her father? She noticed new things about him every day. Like the way he treated his mother. He never thanked Eliza for anything, or asked her how she felt, and yet to Pauline he spoke softly, even when she was being surly. She jumped when she felt his hand on her shoulder.

'Your mother was a wonderful woman, Pauline. I hope you still remember her clearly?' He didn't wait for her to reply, but went on. 'I remember when she told me you were on the way, I was jealous at first. We hadn't been married long and I wanted her to myself. But then you were born and you were so sweet. I was glad you were a girl. I had two lovely ladies to look after then, you see. You have no idea how much it pleases me to see you developing into such a fine young woman.'

He removed his hand from her shoulder but remained just behind her. 'After you left school and Mary encouraged you to go to dances and suchlike, I wasn't too pleased. Dance halls, pubs – what kind of young men do you meet there?' He sighed. 'Young chaps showing off, boozing and seeing how many girls they can pull.' He must have noticed her faint shrug of surprise for he laughed, gently. 'Oh, yes. I know how they talk. I hear them on the boats.

'But they're not for you, Pauline, you deserve better.' He abandoned his stance behind her and came round to her side. 'I'm proud of you. You're not like your mother in looks, but you're beginning to resemble her in other ways. And one day, when the time's right, we'll find you a nice young man, one that's good enough for you. But not yet, eh? You won't leave your old dad just yet?'

He leaned towards her and touched her cheek with his forefinger. A fatherly gesture, Pauline told herself. But then his thumb moved downwards and caressed her chin and then her throat, and his breathing quickened. She jerked her head away and in doing so knocked some of the playing cards on to the floor. She ducked down to pick them up and when she looked at her father again, he had stepped back and was studying the cards on the table.

'You've gone wrong.' He pointed with the stem of his pipe.

'Where?'

'There – you've put the six of Clubs on the seven of Spades.' His voice was conversational, his face calm.

She mustn't start imagining things. 'So I have.' She swept the cards together in a tumbled heap. 'It doesn't matter, I was ready to pack in. I think I'll go up to bed.'

'Off you go, then.' Walter drew on his pipe. 'Sweet dreams, my dear.'

The bedroom was as cold as she'd known it would be. Nevertheless, she lingered long enough, once she was undressed, to study her face in the small mirror. She knew her body hadn't betrayed her yet, her form was still slender, but her face . . . Womanly, her father had said. Yes, she could see what he meant. Her face was rounder, her expression softer, and he had noticed. She shivered and jumped into bed. The stone hot-water bottle her grandmother must have slipped between the sheets earlier in the evening warmed both her heart and her cold feet.

Her darling gran, what would she do without her? To distract her thoughts from her father, and from Grahame, she thought about Eliza. She even chuckled over the way her grandmother had put Doctor Tebbutt in his place.

They had gone to see him last week.

'I'll come with you.' Eliza had looked towards Pauline, waiting for her reaction. She had nodded her head vigorously. She doubted whether she would have dared to go alone.

She didn't know Doctor Tebbutt well. She was a healthy girl, rarely ill. In fact the last time she had seen him must have been when she was eight years old and had scarlet fever. All she could remember about him was his cold hands.

They had sat in the waiting room and listened for his bell.

'Don't let Clarence Tebbutt upset you, Pauline.' Eliza had taken off her gloves and now slapped them together on her lap. 'He's not a bad doctor. The trouble is, these last few years he's become so ruddy sanctimonious. Sometimes he thinks he's God.'

Pauline had given her grandma a startled look, then the bell had summoned them into the surgery.

'So this is the young lady?' Clarence Tebbutt's voice was guarded and his smile tight. Pauline couldn't see his eyes, the light bounced off his glasses. 'Your grandmother has informed me of,' he coughed, 'your sorry situation.'

Pauline blushed crimson.

The doctor shuffled his papers. 'Well, we'd better get on.' He asked questions about her general health, weighed her, looked at her nails and filled in forms. He then asked details about the father. Stumbling over her words, Pauline told him what she knew.

'A normal, healthy young man then, as far as you know?'

'Yes.'

'Well.' His pen paused. 'That's something.'

He handed over chits for Pauline to take to the Health Office for orange juice and cod liver oil. Then he sat back in his chair and studied her. 'You look fit enough. Have you felt sick at all?'

'No.'

Pauline thought he looked disappointed and noticed how he pursed his small mouth when he wrote. She looked across at Eliza for comfort.

Her grandmother hummed the opening line of the hymn 'For all the saints.'

Pauline smothered a laugh and the doctor looked up, took off his spectacles and stared at both of them.

'You're obviously in good spirits, Miss Verrill, and your general health appears to be good. Are you aware that your grandmother has specifically asked me to delay informing your father of your condition?'

'Yes.' Pauline's moment of lightness fled. Her answer was almost inaudible.

'I must say, I'm not happy, not happy at all.'

'But you've agreed, Doctor Tebbutt?' Eliza's voice was serene.

He wriggled like a fish on a hook. 'I've agreed to wait a short period of time. However, I must insist Mr Verrill is told within the month.'

'But I'm your patient, doctor.' Pauline's voice strengthened. 'I thought a doctor was supposed to respect the confidence of a patient?'

'You are also a minor.'

'Oh, don't start quibbling, Clarence.' Eliza stood up. 'These last few years I've brought Pauline up, as well you know. I've already promised you that Walter will be told soon.' She turned towards the door. 'I'd better leave. You'll want to examine my granddaughter, I suppose?'

'Yes.' Doctor Tebbutt waited until the door closed behind Eliza and then gestured towards the couch. 'You'll have to remove your underclothing.'

Pauline's heart sank. She followed the doctor's instructions and, when he began the examination, stared at the ceiling above her. He muttered to himself and told her she must relax, but she couldn't. She clenched her teeth instead.

The last time she had lain on a bed like this she had been with Grahame and there had been laughter and warmth and passion. Now Grahame had left her and a mean little man who heartily disapproved of her was touching her body. She hated Grahame, she hated Doctor Tebbutt and hated his touch. He still had icy cold hands.

On the way home, to take her mind off the examination, she had pestered Eliza. 'How did you persuade the doctor not to tell Dad?'

Her grandmother looked innocent. 'Never you mind.'

'But he wanted to, didn't he?'

'Probably. He makes a great avenging angel, does Clarence Tebbutt.'

Pauline pinched her gran's arm. 'Go on, tell me.'

'Well . . .' Eliza wavered.

'Please, Gran.'

'Let's just say,' Eliza's eyes danced, 'I have a good memory. I remember a time, long ago, when Clarence Tebbutt was younger and not so plump. In those days, he didn't always visit ladies' houses to hold bible readings.'

'Really!'

Eliza pinched Pauline back. 'Now don't you go saying anything. Clarence is a bit pompous now, but he's not such a bad stick. And he has a tartar of a wife.'

Pauline smiled. She was nice and warm now and her feet were glowing. She dived to the bottom of her bed, collected the hot-water bottle and snuggled down, clutching it in her arms. Her next appointment with Doctor Tebbutt was in six weeks' time. She thought that because of Eliza's revelation about him she might find the examination more bearable. She still didn't like him, but at least he seemed more human to her.

Through the wall she heard Eliza cough. If only he could do something to help Gran. The pills she was on now didn't help her much. Each day she looked more grey, more tired.

Following a sudden impulse, Pauline closed her eyes and prayed.

'Please God, give my grandma better health and keep her safe.'

And then, still with her eyes tightly closed, she voiced another request, but this time it was not to God.

'Grahame, wherever you are, whatever you feel about me now, get in touch with me, please.'

Through the wall she heard Tara cough. If only she could do something to help Gran. The pills she was on now didn't help her much. Each day she looked more grey, more tired.

Following a sudden impulse, Pauline closed her eyes and prayed.

'Please God, give my grandma better health and keep us safe.'

And then, still with her eyes tightly closed, she voiced another request. But this time it was not to God.

'Mother, wherever you are, whatever you feel about me now, get in touch with me, please!'

Chapter Eleven

At the beginning of Christmas week, Eliza's brother, Pauline's great-uncle Charlie, came to visit and brought with him his new wife, Winifred. Charlie had been a widower for seventeen years. Eliza knew he had been walking out with a woman who lived in the next street to him, she had been introduced to Winifred when she had visited her brother in September, but his hasty second marriage came as a surprise.

'I can't think what's got into him,' she confided to Pauline. 'He's lived on his own for seventeen years and got used to it. Why rush into marriage now?'

'I suppose he's lonely, Gran.' Pauline studied her grandmother's face. 'Don't you like her?'

Eliza sniffed. 'She seems pleasant enough, but her face doesn't move when she smiles.'

Pauline hid a smile. Was Gran jealous? 'Perhaps he feels the need for company now he's older?' she said. 'He didn't get much chance to meet anyone when he was roaming the world, did he?'

'Aye, you're probably right.' Eliza shook her head. 'I'm being a right misery, aren't I? I expect Winifred will be good for him. I hope they'll be happy together. Poor old Charlie, it's time he had some luck.'

Pauline knew that Eliza's brother had lived with her

for a short time after the first world war, but didn't know he had turned up on Eliza's doorstep all those years ago a mental and physical wreck. Charlie had spent eighteen months in the trenches and then four months as a prisoner of war.

When he left the army he was suffering from gas-damaged lungs and what the medical doctors described as a mild form of shell-shock. Eliza had looked at the pale, shivering creature who was her brother, taken him in her arms and into her home.

But it hadn't worked, it couldn't. Eliza loved Charlie, but she had no money and there was Walter to care for. Her brother was unfit for work and his tiny pension went on drink. Eliza understood. If he drank, he slept without dreaming, didn't wake up screaming and trembling so much his bed shook. But drunk or sober, he was no fit companion for a small boy. So, with tears all round, Charlie left.

Five years later he contacted Eliza again. He had, he told her, pulled his life together again; he had a good job in Newcastle and a sweet little wife called Bella. They were setting up home together and once they got settled, he would bring Bella over to meet his sister.

His next letter was postmarked Brazil. Eliza opened it to read that Bella had died of T.B. and Charlie had sold his home and joined the merchant navy. During the thirties, a letter would arrive every two or three years and they came from every corner of the earth. Then came the war. Charlie stayed in the merchant navy, and worked on the ships which carried food and essential equipment backwards and forwards across the dangerous waters of the Atlantic Ocean. When the war ended he wrote to say he had decided to look for a job ashore. He was too old for the sea life.

It was then Pauline had met him: a thin but wiry little man with a bald head, thick grey eyebrows and the rolling gait of a seaman. She had liked him. He had given her a brief hug, stepped back from her and studied her face seriously.

'She has a look of your Thomas, Eliza.'

Gran had laughed but looked gratified. 'Yes, I think so, too. But I'm surprised you remember.'

'Oh, I remember a lot of things.' Pauline had watched as brother and sister exchanged a long look. Then Charlie had said, 'I want to see more of you in the future, our Eliza. The job in London's well enough, but I can't settle there. I spoke to someone about working in Hull and I've just heard – there's a job if I want it.'

He told them about his new job. He'd be what was called a 'ships' husband', which meant he transferred the large trawlers between the various docks, and also a 'main man', a post which carried responsibilities and a good wage packet at the end of the week. 'I'll be back on board ships again, see. Sometimes a trawler has to go to Goole for dry-dock work, and I'll take it. Then, if a trawler gets knocked about after one of the Arctic runs, I'll be the one to arrange the repairs. Usually a rush job, that. The chaps work all night if needs be to make sure the ship makes the third tide.'

Now, watching his face as he talked to Eliza, Pauline could see his happiness. The old seadog was in his rightful element again. But if Uncle Charlie was top dog at work, Pauline thought that now he was remarried, he wasn't going to be the boss at home. His new wife, Winifred, was small in build, with neatly waved grey hair and soft, pink cheeks but she kept

Charlie on the run. Fortunately, he didn't seem to mind.

It was: 'Get me another cup of tea, Charlie. Fetch me my handbag. Will you just pop down to the corner shop and buy me a bottle of lemonade? It must be the travelling, I feel that dry.'

And Pauline noticed he didn't smoke his pipe indoors any more, simply sucked on the empty bowl.

She sighed as she watched them all, sitting round the fire, laughing, talking – even her dad was chatty. She felt cut off from them, as if she didn't belong. The burden of her worry kept her at a distance from everyone, except Eliza.

But, for her grandmother's sake, she had tried. She chatted to Winifred and praised the wedding photographs, all the time wondering how long they would stay. But Charlie's visit had been good for Gran. Pauline noticed the colour in her cheeks and the way her eyes sparkled. At least *she* had forgotten for a few hours.

Pauline couldn't forget, not for one moment. Grahame had not replied to her letter and in four more days it would be Christmas. In a week, ten days at the latest, her father must be told about the baby. If she hadn't told him by then, Doctor Tebbutt would.

As if sensing her depression, Walter looked across and spoke to her. 'You look lonely over there, love. Come and join us?'

Pauline shook her head, forced a smile. 'Sorry, haven't the time. I'm going out tonight with Mary. Her firm's holding a Christmas dance and she got me a ticket. I told you about it, don't you remember?'

'I'd forgotten.' Walter frowned. 'What time does this dance finish? You won't be gadding about half the night, will you?'

'I won't be late.' Pauline stood up. 'I'd better get ready.'

'What does "not late" mean? I'd like . . .'

'It's Christmas time, Walter.' Eliza frowned at him. 'Pauline's hardly been out of the house these past weeks. Surely at Christmas she's allowed a bit of pleasure?'

Charlie nodded his head, agreeing with his sister. 'Aye, Pauline should get herself out. You're not young for long, you know.'

Walter flushed. 'I want my daughter to enjoy herself but tonight we have company.' He addressed her again. 'I'd have thought you'd put family before friends, Pauline. You can see Mary anytime.'

'I did think twice about going, Dad, but she'd already got the ticket for me.' Pauline clenched her fists. Please don't let him start a row, she thought. To the listeners, her father's objection would sound reasonable enough, but she knew it wasn't the true reason for his displeasure. Since she had stopped going out, stopped meeting her friends, he had become more possessive than ever.

'Well, if you're so keen, you'd better go.' Walter adopted an injured tone of voice. 'But it's a bad business when a man can't speak his mind in his own house.' He looked at the others. 'I just happen to think Pauline should stay at home when we have company. Margaret wouldn't have *dreamed* of going out at such a time.'

Charlie's brow wrinkled. 'We're family, Walter, not company. And Pauline's your daughter, not your wife.'

There was a brief pause. Pauline saw Winifred raise her head and study her father's face and then she looked across at Pauline, touched her rouged lips with her fingers and sent her a knowing little smile. Pauline looked away.

Eliza decided the matter. 'Off you go and get ready, Pauline. You don't want to be late.'

She did as she was told. She put on her best dress, curled her hair and applied lipstick and powder to her face. Then she went to meet Mary.

The hall where the dance was being held was decorated with paper chains and holly, there was a buffet and the atmosphere was festive – but for all the good it did Pauline she might as well have stayed at home.

Mary, sensing her mood, was also quiet. As usual she had a queue of young men wanting to dance with her but she turned several of them down and stayed close by her friend. At the end of the evening she told her most persistent admirer that she was walking home with Pauline.

'You should have gone with him, Mary. I'm perfectly all right on my own.' The night was cold, the breath from Pauline's mouth made a frosty cloud in the air.

Mary linked arms with her. 'I didn't fancy him. Anyway, I feel a bit guilty. It wasn't a good idea, was it? I shouldn't have pestered you to come.'

Pauline smiled. 'Yes, you should.'

'You didn't enjoy it.'

'No, but it was a change of scene and it got me out of the house, I'm grateful for that.'

Mary shivered and turned up the collar of her coat. 'How's the visit going, and how long are they staying?'

'They're leaving tomorrow. Winifred,' Pauline pulled a face, 'wants them to spend their first Christmas alone together.'

'Don't you like her?'

'I don't know her.' Pauline thought for a moment. 'Perhaps we're just a bit shocked, things happening so quickly.'

'But your gran's met her before, when she went to see her brother last September?'

'Yes, but only for a few moments. Gran thought she was just a good neighbour who popped in and cooked Charlie a good meal from time to time.'

'Ah, well.' Mary laughed. 'Men like their creature comforts, don't they?'

'Yes.' Pauline was quiet until they reached the end of the street and then she said, 'Last September seems years ago now. Just think, Mary, if Gran hadn't stayed with Charlie I wouldn't be pregnant.'

Mary sighed. 'You don't know that.'

Pauline nodded. 'I do.'

Her friend stopped walking. 'Have you decided when you're going to tell your dad?'

Pauline shook her head. 'No, but it will have to be soon.'

'That's good.' She hesitated. 'Because tonight, I just thought . . .'

'What?'

'You're starting to show a bit . . . No, listen.' At Pauline's exclamation, Mary hurriedly continued, 'Not much, and maybe it's only because I know about it, but you *are* filling out, Pauline.'

'I can't be, not yet. It's not four months.'

Mary shrugged. 'Maybe I'm imagining things, but I still wouldn't wait too long. Suppose he finds out before you get a chance to explain, before you tell him?'

'But how do I explain?'

They stared at each other and then walked on. Then, just before Mary reached her turning, Pauline caught hold of her hand.

'Thanks for telling me.'

'No, no.' Mary was flustered. 'I didn't want to mention it, I just thought . . .'

'I know, and you're right. But Mary,' Pauline's voice wavered, 'I'm so scared.'

'Oh, love.' Mary hugged her. 'I know you are. That bastard Grahame.'

Pauline rested her head against her taller friend's shoulder. 'Don't say that.'

'Why? You hate him, don't you?'

'I don't know.' Pauline closed her eyes. How could she explain? Sometimes, when she was lying in bed, she imagined he was there, next to her. She could almost *feel* him, hear his slow breathing, feel the weight of his arm across her body. But during the days, when her mind chased round and round the same tired thoughts he faded, became such a pale image it was almost as though he had never existed.

She straightened her weary body. But he had, and in a few months the evidence would be there for all to see. She rested her hand lightly upon her stomach and even managed to smile. 'Grahame's part of the past now and I've this little one to think about.'

'Yes.' Mary regarded her soberly. 'Remember, Pauline, if there's anything I can do . . .'

She nodded, too choked to speak. Mary gave a half-comical, half-sorry shrug of her shoulders and turned away in the direction of her house. 'I'll be in touch.'

'Yes.' Then, remembering, Pauline shouted after her, 'Mary.'

She turned. 'What?'

'Happy Christmas.'

Mary pulled a face, then waved. 'Same to you.'

Eliza was waiting up for her. 'Well, how did it go?'

'All right.' Pauline sat down and eased off her shoes. 'It made a change.' She looked round. 'Everyone else in bed?'

'Yes, Charlie wants to be off early in the morning.'

'Then you should be in bed, too.' Pauline gave her grandmother a stern look. 'I'll get up first in the morning and you can stay in bed until they're ready to leave.' She rubbed her feet. 'They didn't mind too much, did they, me going out, I mean?'

'No, of course they didn't.' Eliza sighed. 'Charlie's too wrapped up in Winifred to worry much about anyone else.' She shrugged.

'She keeps him on the hop, doesn't she?'

'You noticed that, too?' Eliza gave Pauline a close look and said no more about Winifred. 'I think we should both get to bed. You look tired.'

'I am.' But Pauline lingered. 'Mary asked me tonight,' she swallowed, 'when I was going to tell Dad. She said I'd better hurry up because the baby's beginning to show. It isn't, is it?'

'Not so most people would notice, but she's right, of course.'

'I know.' Pauline rubbed her forehead. 'I just wish it was all over and done with, Gran. I'm so scared.' Her voice broke.

'Hush, love.' Eliza came and cradled her head and shoulders. 'There's nothing to be scared of.'

'But there is. You know how Dad feels about me – he's different from other fathers. He seems to think I'm . . .' she shuddered '. . . some sort of saintly version of Mum.'

'No, no. That's just your nerves, Pauline. All this

worry is affecting you and you're exaggerating. As soon as Christmas is over, he must be told. I'm not saying he won't be terribly hurt and disappointed. He'll doubtless rant and rave, but he'll come round, in time.'

Pauline did not reply. Gran was wise, she usually saw things clearly, but with her own son, she was too close.

'Pauline, did you hear me?'

'Yes, but everything's so awful, and there's no way out.'

Still Eliza held her. When she spoke again her voice was quiet. 'I'm going to tell you something. It's something my mam said to me once and I never forgot it. Perhaps it will help. It's one of her old sayings so I don't want you to laugh, mind, like you usually do.'

'I won't.' Pauline shook her head. She had never felt less like laughing.

'It was years and years ago, when I was packing up my few bits and pieces to move here to Whitby with your dad. I remember I couldn't stop crying. My mam was as bad. She was having to leave her home to go and look after someone she hadn't met for years. We'd lost our menfolk and we were going to be separated. Anyway,' Eliza smoothed Pauline's hair, 'when we had packed up, Mam sat me down on one of the boxes, took my hand and said something I'd never heard her say before.'

'What was it?' Pauline leaned against her gran and let her body relax.

'She said "It's a hard life, my dear but remember: When the sky falls down, we will catch larks".'

Pauline frowned and twisted her head around to look at Eliza. 'What did she mean?'

'I didn't know, not then. I remember I was blubbering away and she gave me a handkerchief to dry my eyes, and I told her I didn't understand. She just nodded and said that I would, one day. I was too upset to question her. Then the carrier arrived to take our belongings and I said goodbye to her and I only saw her again once, when she was dying. But I'll never forget that moment or those words.'

'And did you work out what she meant?'

'I think so.' Eliza's voice sounded reflective. 'I mean, I'm not sure the words meant the same to her as they did to me, but it didn't really matter. That old saying has helped me through a few bad times.'

'And now you've told me. But what . . . ?'

'Oh, no.' Eliza gave Pauline a little tap on her cheek. 'It's something you must work out for yourself, young lady, and I am sure you will, one day.'

'I don't know . . .' Pauline's mouth opened in a wide yawn. Listening to Gran's slow voice, feeling her gentle hand stroking her hair, made her suddenly long for sleep.

'Time for bed,' Eliza moved away. 'We've a busy two days in front of us, you know. After all, Christmas is Christmas, whatever worries we have.' She put her arm about Pauline's shoulders and they walked towards the door. 'Keep up your spirits, love. Just think, this time next year all this will be over with. You'll have a baby on your knee and like as not your dad will be out buying a Christmas present for his grandchild.'

On the twenty-eighth of December Pauline left work with a feeling of thankfulness. Never had a day seemed so long.

After the two-day Christmas break the shop had felt icy cold and there had been so few customers the cleaning machines had only operated for two hours. And yet Mrs Denton had found her plenty of work to do and while Pauline worked, her employer moaned.

'Have you seen all this nonsense in the paper about Princess Elizabeth and that Philip Mountbatten? Surely she won't marry him? I mean, he's nice-looking but so are plenty of English boys. Our princess can't marry a foreigner, especially a Greek.'

Then she moved on to more personal matters. 'Our Bill's been put on short time. He works for the Austin Motor Company, you know. He's got a marvellous job but because of lack of coal the factory's only going to work three days a week. Blooming miners.' Mrs Denton had snorted in disgust. 'I can't see nationalisation altering anything, either. This country's going to rack and ruin. You wouldn't think we won the war, would you? Do you know, I couldn't even buy a decent Christmas present for my grandson. I tell you, Germany lost the war and they're doing better than we are.'

'Oh, I don't know.' Pauline recalled recent newspaper pictures of hollow-eyed German children and old people dying among the rubble heaps. 'I think we're still better off than they are.'

'Do you indeed?' Her employer had looked at her, sharp-eyed. 'Well, I must say, the shortages don't seem to have affected you. You've even put on weight. Managed to get some "under the counter" Christmas goodies, did you?'

'No.' Pauline coloured. 'I probably look heavier because I'm wearing two jumpers and a cardigan. It's so cold today.'

'Yes, it is. I'm freezing, too. But the regulations say we have to cut back on heating, so we'll have to put up with it. Maybe a cup of tea will warm us up. You'd better go and make us one.'

Pauline hurried away. For the rest of the day she tried hard to keep her tummy tucked in. And as she went about her work she worried in case something was wrong. Was it normal to start putting on weight so soon? She must ask the doctor.

She left work at five-thirty, hoping Eliza would have a good fire burning. Goodness knows how she'd managed to make the coal ration last, but she did. Pauline just hoped she didn't spend all day in a freezing house in order to do so.

The fire was bright and welcoming but there was a note on the table, which was already laid for tea. Eliza had written that she had gone for a lie-down and would Pauline start the tea? She frowned. That meant her grandma was feeling poorly again. She had to feel ill to go to bed during the day.

She hung up her coat, changed her rubber boots for slippers and put the two filled pans on to the gas stove as Eliza had requested. She was cutting bread when she heard the door slam shut. It would be Dad. Pauline put down the bread knife and, as the kitchen door opened, turned to welcome him, but the words died on her lips.

He looked terrible, and terrifying.

She caught her breath. 'Dad, what is it?'

He looked at her without speaking, and in scared fascination she stared back. She saw his eyes were almost bulging from his head and his face was so pale it held a greenish tinge. She took a step back. *He knew!*

'Dad,' her voice faltered. 'Are you ill?'

Still he stared at her.

She swallowed. She wondered whether to go to him and plead for his forgiveness but she literally couldn't move. Gran had been wrong. This was no normal reaction. Her father wasn't just outraged, disappointed – he looked as though he wanted to kill her. And she could do nothing. She was so petrified with fear, all she could do was stand there and await her fate.

And then, for the first time, she felt her baby move. It was faint, the merest tremble, but Pauline knew and a feeling of calm flowed through her body like cool water. She wetted her dry lips with her tongue, stepped forward and held out her hand.

'Oh, Dad. I'm so sorry, please let me explain. We were going to tell you before Christmas, but we thought . . .'

'We?' His voice was croaky, as though he had not spoken for days. She wondered if he had been drinking, he seemed to have difficulty focusing on her face.

'Yes, Gran and me. We . . .'

'Where is she?'

'She's upstairs. I don't think she's feeling too well. She . . .' Her voice faded.

As if in slow motion her father stepped to one side of the door, took hold of the handle and opened it. 'Get her.'

She hurried past him.

Eliza was only half-awake but when Pauline stuttered out what had happened she rose hurriedly and slipped on her dress and slippers.

'Oh, Lord. I knew we were chancing it, leaving it so long.' She pushed pins into her hair with trembling fingers. 'I bet it was Clarence Tebbutt.'

'It doesn't matter, Gran, it doesn't matter who told him. It's the way he's taken it. He looks . . .'

Eliza cut her short. 'Calm down, Pauline. Of course your dad's in a state. What father wouldn't be? He's shocked.'

'But Gran . . .'

She had already started down the stairs. Pauline, hands and legs beginning to shake again, followed her.

'Now then, Walter, I'm sorry you had to hear the bad news from someone else. I know how shocked you must feel, but we . . .'

As Pauline slipped back into the kitchen she heard Eliza's voice, saw her grandmother's face as she faced her son. She looked pale but determined.

Walter flung up his hand to stop her speaking. 'You *know*, do you, Mother?' The passion in his voice shocked Pauline and also, she saw, her grandmother. Eliza's brow creased in bewilderment.

'Listen to me, Walter. Things seem bad now, but . . .'

His fist clenched as though he wanted to hit her and with his next words there was no mistaking the hatred in his voice. 'You *think* you know, but you know *nothing*, understand? *Nothing*.'

Pauline, seeing Eliza's expression, stepped forward. 'Dad, stop this.'

He ignored her. He glared down at his mother.

'This is *your* fault. Pauline was a fine, sweet girl until you came to live here, but you changed her, you changed everything! Pauline admired, respected and loved me, but you didn't like that, did you? It had to be you she loved. Telling her your old stories, spoiling her. Why did you do it? Was it because there had been precious little love between you and me?'

'Don't, Walter. Please don't say such things.' Eliza's face crumpled. She shook her head so violently her hair escaped from the pins holding it and fell in wispy strands of grey on to her shoulders. 'I loved you as much as Pauline. I tried to make a home for you.'

He never even heard her but ranted on, spittle flying from his lips. 'Was it to spite me? Because I went my own way when I was growing up, because I was strong enough to defy you? I learned how to be strong very early, Mother, remember? But you paid me back, didn't you? You came into my home and deliberately caused trouble between Pauline and me.'

'No, I never meant . . .' Eliza's trembling hand went to her mouth. 'I tried to be a mother to her.'

If possible, Walter's face became even more bleached of colour. 'You spoilt her innocence. You bought her stuff to paint her face with and encouraged her to go about with little tarts. And if I tried to protest, to explain to her how wicked the world could be, you stopped me. Oh, God, why was it you, an old woman, who lived and my wife who died? If Margaret had been alive, this terrible thing would never have happened.' He covered his face with his hands and his shoulders heaved. 'My little girl.'

Pauline shook herself out of her paralysis, forced herself to go to him. 'Dad, please, what you're saying isn't true! It's because you're upset, I know, but you mustn't talk to Gran like that. She loves both of us. The make-up she bought me, letting me go out . . . it's natural, Dad. You have to understand, I'm not your little girl any more, I've grown up. And it's *me* you must blame, not Gran. *I've* caused all this trouble. It's me that's . . .' Her words trailed away when he uncovered his face and stared at her.

'Go on, say it.' He no longer shouted. Now his voice was so soft she could hardly hear him, but it was the look in his eyes that scared her. She wanted to move away from him but couldn't. She stared back at him.

'Say it. You've played the whore, haven't you, Pauline? Who with? Was it that red-haired traveller you picked up, your dancing partner?'

He didn't notice her start, but went on and on . . .

'But no, he left you, didn't he? Your brave young man cleared off after I had a word with him. I suppose it was one of Mary's friends. Perhaps more than one, if what I hear about Mary is true. Did you have fun with any of the lads from the fish pier?' He suddenly grabbed her arm and jerked her closer to him, pushing his face up against hers.

'My, wouldn't that be a joke!'

Pauline began to cry, soundlessly. The slow tears slid down her white face. She stared into her father's eyes like a defenceless rabbit caught in the glare of a car's headlights.

'Let go of her, Walter.'

In slow motion, both turned their heads towards Eliza. She looked ancient. Against the ghastly pallor of her skin her nose and cheekbones showed up starkly, but her voice was firm. 'Let her go – now!'

He did so. Pauline stepped back and sighed with relief. Her head was swimming, she was afraid she might collapse on the floor.

Her father looked at her, his face set into a mask of disgust. 'With pleasure. I have no desire to touch a dirty whore.'

Pauline made a small, piteous sound in her throat and looked at Eliza for comfort but her grandmother's eyes were fixed on her son. Slowly, shakily, she moved to stand in front of him.

'Is that the truth, Walter?' She stared into his face. 'I don't think so.'

He brushed his hand across his eyes. 'For Christ's sake, don't start, old woman.'

Eliza's gaze did not waver. She stared into his face and then nodded her head slowly.

'I've been blind and I've just realised it. You're jealous, aren't you? You wish it had been you. Oh, God.' Her voice broke and her figure suddenly sagged like a discarded puppet's. 'What did I do to you, son, to turn you into such a monster?'

'Gran.' Pauline started towards her but she was too late. Her grandmother collapsed at the feet of her son. Pauline heard an ominous choking sound come from her throat.

She screamed, a strange, weak sound. 'Gran!' She fell on her knees beside Eliza's still figure and fumbled at the opening of her dress. 'Gran, please don't die.'

Eliza moaned and Pauline's panic subsided momentarily. She glared upwards at her father. 'You have to go and ring the doctor, or better still an ambulance. *Quickly*, Dad!'

He stared down at her, his face dazed. '*Go!*' she screamed again. He left the room in a shambling half-run, half-walk.

Pauline sat back on her heels and looked at Eliza. Her closed lids were a pale lavender colour and her face like parchment but as Pauline watched, a spasm of pain contorted her features.

She picked up her hand and kissed it. 'It's going to be all right, Gran. It's going to be all right.' But as she waited for the ambulance to come, she couldn't believe her own words.

Chapter Twelve

Two days later, without regaining consciousness, Eliza died in Whitby hospital. Of the three people who witnessed her passing, only one cried. As the doctor shook his head and drew the sheet over Eliza's still white face, Charlie seemed to shrink in his chair. He cupped his hands over his face and wept.

Pauline didn't look at him. She didn't look at her father, standing across from her, or at the silent, sheeted figure in the bed. And she didn't cry, her sense of desolation was too deep to allow her the comfort of tears.

She stood and let her gaze wander round the white-painted walls of the room. She looked at the trolley at the foot of the bed, set out with machines to help people breathe more easily, pills and potions – they hadn't helped her gran. She looked through the window, at the white snowflakes whirling about outside. The whole world seemed to have turned white. She nodded her head slowly. It was fitting. Hadn't someone told her that in many countries, white was the colour of mourning.

The doctor coughed. 'When you're ready, Mr Verrill, perhaps you would step outside? I'm afraid there are certain formalities to observe, they won't take a moment. Of course, if you'd like to stay a few minutes longer?'

'No. I'll come now.'

She heard her father's voice and his slow, heavy footsteps as he left the room, and wondered if she would ever feel comfortable with him again. The first night at the hospital they had sat in the same room, thanked the nurses who brought them cups of tea and words of comfort, and listened to what the doctors said, but they had neither touched nor spoken. Then Uncle Charlie had arrived and his obvious grief, his many questions, had in a curious way made the waiting easier.

'Pauline?'

She started. Uncle Charlie was mopping his eyes with a large white handkerchief. He put it back in his pocket and looked at her. His face was patchily red and white from crying, but his eyes were shrewd as he asked, 'What's happened here? Why are you and your father acting so strangely?'

She felt weary, too weary to explain. 'I'll tell you, Uncle Charlie, but not right now.' At last she looked towards the bed. 'Gran had a bad heart, the doctor said. She knew, but never told us.'

Charlie saw her shoulders slump and the complete exhaustion on her face. He nodded, then stood up and approached the shrouded figure. 'Why are they always so quick to get them out of sight? It's still Eliza under there, she's not buried yet!' He pulled back the sheet and fell on his knees beside the body of his sister. His lips trembled. 'She was the best friend I ever had.'

'Oh, Uncle Charlie!' His sorrow broke through Pauline's own dumb, tearless misery. She went to kneel opposite him, reaching out to take hold of his hand, and together they grieved for the loss of something precious.

The funeral was held at eleven o'clock. St Mary's had no electricity and so services were always held in the morning. As Pauline walked down the aisle with her father, she was surprised by the number of people who had come to church to pay their last respects to her grandmother.

The parish church was huge, it would have taken an army to fill the place, but the front pews were full of mourners. There were rustling noises and the sound of shifting feet as they stood in response to the strains of the organ. Pauline saw the many beautiful wreaths. The coffin was covered with flowers. She thought what a pity it was that her grandmother couldn't see them.

A rush of tears to her eyes threatened to spill over, but she fought them back. She looked away from the coffin and stared towards the pulpit instead. She even managed a wavering smile when she spotted the ear trumpets. Eliza had told her once that they had been used by the deaf wife of a minister sometime in the last century. She had been full of old tales like that.

The service over, they filed from the church. In the graveyard the bite of the North-East wind was cruel and out at sea the pewter-grey, white-capped waves raced madly across the bay. Pauline stared at them as if mesmerised. She couldn't bear to see Gran placed in the icy grave. She swayed on her feet, then felt Uncle Charlie's hand beneath her arm.

'Bear up, lass. It's nearly done.' He squeezed her elbow. 'Reckon there's a grand view from here, come summer.'

The minister spoke the closing words and the mourners came to offer their respects. At last, a feeling of warmth permeated Pauline's frozen body. Their neighbours were honest folk, their words of comfort sincere. The men twisted their best caps in their hands as they offered awkward condolences and the women's eyes filled with tears as they reminisced.

'A grand woman, your grannie . . . Nivver said nowt bad about onnyan.' And another: 'When Ah went inti labour suddenlike, she was a rock, your gran, a rock.'

Pauline shook hands and smiled and invited them back to the house for a bite to eat. The few words she had exchanged with her father since Eliza's death had been about the funeral tea.

He had thrown some banknotes on to the kitchen table. 'Get what you can find in the shops. Billy Trent's bringing over a lump of pork later today. He killed one of his pigs recently. And I'll get in some sherry and port.'

She had nodded. No matter that he couldn't bear to look at her, there still had to be a wake for Eliza.

In small groups, family and friends trailed back to the house. They took off their coats and spoke in hushed tones but as the plates of food were passed round, the bottles emptied and the glasses filled, the mood lightened. Pauline, offering their next-door neighbour a plate of ham sandwiches, saw a tubby, balding man, dressed in corduroy trousers worn at the knee, tap her dad on the arm.

'Reet sorry about your ma, Walter. She was a good 'un. But thoo still has yon lass. She'll look after thoo.'

Her father nodded and filled his companion's glass, then he glanced at Pauline and his expression made her blench. Eliza's death hadn't softened his attitude. He still hated her. Her hand trembled as she urged the neighbour to take another sandwich.

'Go on, Mrs King. There's plenty to go round.'

'I will then. Eh, it's lovely to taste a bit of decent boiled bacon again.'

The day wore on and eventually the mourners said their goodbyes and drifted away. Last to leave was Uncle Charlie. Winifred hadn't come to the funeral. She had sent a message to say she had a heavy cold and so didn't think it was wise to venture out in such awful weather, particularly as Charlie was already in Whitby and she would have to travel alone from Hull.

If circumstances had been normal, Pauline would have felt outraged at her feeble excuse. Eliza would have travelled to a relative's funeral no matter how ill she had been. But against her other worries, Winifred's non-appearance was as nothing.

Uncle Charlie said goodbye to them separately.

Pauline didn't know what he had said to her father but when he came to her she could see he was troubled. The day after Eliza's death, Pauline had told her uncle she was pregnant. He had given one sharp exclamation of shock and then listened to her stumbling confession intently.

She told the truth about everything until she came to the confrontation with her father. Then, unable and unwilling to put the whole dreadful scene into words, she had implied that Walter had known about the baby before Eliza had collapsed. She also said that although her father was terribly upset, she thought he was gradually coming to terms with the situation.

Now, just before he left for his train, Charlie kissed Pauline on the cheek and grasped her hands. 'I can't pretend I'm not shocked, I would have expected better behaviour from you, but what's done is done. Eliza loved you and now that she's gone I want you to know I will help if I can. If you need help, get in touch with me. Don't forget, will you?'

'I'll remember, Uncle Charlie, and thank you. But I think Dad and me will work things out.'

As she gave her uncle a goodbye wave, Pauline tried to believe her own words. She was Walter's only child, surely he would forgive her? But part of her knew it wasn't that easy, and part of her felt dread at what might happen if he did forgive her. Could she continue living with her father now that Eliza was gone?

But she could see no alternative. Uncle Charlie was kind but she couldn't park herself on him. She had only known him properly for a year, and he was newly married. She couldn't see Winifred welcoming her into their home.

Once her uncle was out of sight, she went back into the house and started collecting up the empty plates and glasses. The idea of holding a wake after someone had died had always seemed a macabre custom to Pauline but now she was glad they had done so. The preparations had kept her busy, kept her thoughts away from the yawning chasm caused by her grandmother's death.

She heard footsteps and turned to see her father standing in the doorway of the kitchen.

He spoke. 'You can leave those.'

'No, I'd rather get things straightened . . .'

'I said, leave them.'

Pauline bit her lips but did as he ordered. She dried her hands on a teatowel and turned to face him. He was a handsome man, particularly when dressed in his best suit, she thought, but his face was like a mask. She swallowed. What now?

'Well, Pauline. We've observed the niceties. We've buried your grandmother and fed and watered the busy-bodies. You can go now.'

'Go? Go where?'

'Wherever you like.' He looked at her as if she was a complete stranger to him.

'But I've nowhere *to* go! I've had no time to make arrangements. Dad, you can't . . .'

'I can do whatever I want, Pauline. Do you want me to feel guilty after what you have done to me? No.' He shook his head. 'You've lied and cheated, you've brought about your grandmother's death, why should I let you stay?'

She pleaded with him. 'If you feel so strongly, Dad, I will leave – but let me stay for another week, until I . . .'

'No, I want you out tonight. I know you and your tricks. You'll try to make me change my mind and I can't risk that.' A tremor of emotion flickered across his face. 'Do you think I could bear to watch you, growing fat with a bastard child?'

She caught her breath. 'I'm still your daughter.'

He shook his head. 'I have no daughter now.'

Hating herself, she searched for something else to say, something that would sway him. If only she could win a few days, give herself time to think. She whispered, 'What will people say?'

'Our neighbours, you mean?' His lips moved in the semblance of a smile. 'Do you think I *care*?' He shrugged. 'This afternoon they lined up to offer their sympathy. I looked at them and remembered. Our neighbours, Pauline, are nothing but hypocrites with short memories.'

She blinked and shook her head, denying that. He did not notice but continued, his voice conversational. 'The older ones, the sanctimonious crowd with their prayers and their platitudes, let their children make my childhood a misery. And then, when I grew a little and worked twice as hard as anyone else to better myself, they laughed. I was the outsider and too big for my boots. "He'll come a cropper", they said, and hated me when I didn't. And now they're as jealous as hell.'

For one brief moment his composure cracked as he added, his voice raw with grief. 'That's why I loved your mother so much. She was different.'

'Dad,' Pauline took a step towards him, 'please don't do this. Surely we can work things out?'

He looked at her with unconcealed hostility. 'No. I hope I never see you again. Make sure you're out of here by the time I come back.'

The front door slammed behind him. There was silence except for the dripping of a tap.

Mary was shaving her legs when she heard the thump of the doorknocker.

'Blast.' She waited hopefully then realised that Jill was upstairs putting the children to bed and Eric, her sister's husband, was listening to the radio. She could hear the signature tune of his favourite programme, *Have a Go*, booming through the kitchen wall.

She'd have to see who it was. She put down the razor, Eric's razor, with a sigh and went to the door.

'Pauline!'

Her friend's face was pale and the corners of her

eyes red. Mary stared at her and at the suitcase in her hand. 'You'd better come in.'

Mary had intended going to the funeral, not just to support her friend but because she had liked Eliza, but Pauline had asked her to stay away.

'It's Dad, you see. He thinks you and I . . .'

'Not to worry.' Mary had guessed Walter Verrill's opinion of her. 'I'm relieved, actually. I hate funerals.'

Now she pulled Pauline in through the door and hurried her into the kitchen. 'What's up?'

'He's thrown me out, Mary, and he won't have me back. I thought, if I could stay here, just for tonight? I know it's an awful cheek, I don't want to upset Jill or Eric, but I can't think of anywhere else I can go.'

'Of course you can stay. Get your coat off. I'll take your case up.' Mary picked up the suitcase and grabbing Pauline's arm, steered her into the passage and through the door leading to the parlour.

'Eric, this is Pauline. You've met her a couple of times, remember? She's my friend, the one who's so good with the kids. Anyway, she's got a bit of trouble on at home right now and I've told her she can stay here and share my room for a few days. That's all right, isn't it? It won't be for long and she'll pay out what she can afford towards her food. Sit down, Pauline. I'll just pop up and tell Jill and then I'll make a pot of tea.'

She disappeared from the room and Pauline heard the thump of her feet on the stairs. She ducked her head and gave Eric an apologetic smile.

He gazed at her blankly, then nodded towards the radio.

'Like Wilfred Pickles, do you?'

'Oh, yes.'

'Good.' He settled in his chair. 'A lass from Barnsley's in with a chance for the top prize.'

Pauline sank into the nearest chair and they sat in silence, both listening as Wilfred Pickles instructed Barney to 'give 'er the money'.

Exactly one week after she moved in with Mary and her sister's family, Pauline was returning from work when a grey-haired, smartly dressed gentleman shouted to her and hurried across the road to speak to her.

'Miss Verrill. It is Miss Pauline Verrill, isn't it?'

'Yes.' She gave the man a cautious look. 'Why do you want to know?'

'My name's John Piper. I'm a solicitor.' He fished in his pocket and produced a card which he handed to her. She read it.

'I attended your grandmother's funeral and intended having a word with you then, but there was such a crowd around you and your father, and the weather was so awful, I'm afraid I headed for home directly after the service.'

'Yes, it was bad weather. But why did you want to speak to us?'

'It's about your grandmother's will; I acted for her.' Seeing the surprise on Pauline's face, Mr Piper hesitated. 'Perhaps you didn't know she had been to see me?'

'No. I didn't know Gran had anything to leave.'

'Well, it's not a large estate, but there are certain bequests.' With his next words, John Piper betrayed traces of embarrassment. 'The thing is, Miss Verrill, I gather you are no longer resident at your father's home?'

‘No.’ Pauline waited for him to continue.

‘I thought so. I wrote, you see. I sent a letter to you and a separate one to your father. Mr Verrill called in to see me two days ago. I told him the contents of the will and he informed me he was no longer in touch with you and couldn’t give me your address. It was quite a poser for me. I was going to put a notice in the local paper, but then I was fortunate enough to see you today. Could you call in to see me before the end of the week, do you think? The address is on the card.’

Pauline nodded her head. ‘But will he – my father – be there, too?’

‘No, just you.’

‘I’ll come, then. Would Wednesday afternoon do? I have half a day off work on Wednesday.’

‘Yes, that will be fine. About three o’clock, shall we say?’

When she kept the appointment Mr Piper told her Eliza had certain monies in a savings bank which came from the sale of her cottage in 1942, and that she, Pauline, was the main beneficiary.

‘It’s not a fortune, of course. There were a few bills and a small sum of money had been left to your father, but I’m happy to tell you the sum of five hundred and twenty-four pounds is yours.’

Pauline gasped. In her precarious situation, the legacy was a marvellous windfall. For the first time in weeks, she smiled.

After listening to Mr Piper’s advice on where to invest the money, and signing the papers he gave to her, she rushed back to tell Mary.

‘I’ll find somewhere else to live at the weekend. I shall be able to find a room I can rent. And I want to treat you and Jill and Eric. You’ve been so kind.’

'Steady on, kid.' Mary shook a warning finger. 'I agree about you finding new digs. Jill's been great about things but there's no denying, it's been a squash. I'm really pleased for you, but you've got to remember you'll be out of a job soon, and with a kid coming along there's going to be expenses. Five hundred pounds sounds a lot, but it will soon spend.'

'I know that, but it's still wonderful news. I never thought about Gran having money, making a will.' Pauline dived into her handbag. 'Mr Piper gave me this envelope when I was leaving the office. He said she gave it to him for safe-keeping when she made the will.' Her face fell. 'It proves she knew she was going to die soon.'

'Maybe not. The medical people probably just told her to take extra care and being the person she was, she decided to sort everything out, just in case.'

'Yes, that sounds like Gran.' Pauline looked down at her letter and Mary, seeing she wanted to be on her own to read it, jumped up from the bed. 'I'll go and tell Jill you've had a little windfall. I won't go into details.' She smiled. 'And although I won't let you splash out too much, you can buy us all a fish and chip supper if you like.'

'You're on.' Pauline grinned, but when she was alone she stared down at the sealed envelope, her face solemn. For Mary's sake she had tried to keep cheerful during the past week but it had been hard. There was the worry about her future and she missed Eliza so much. She sighed and opened the envelope.

There were two pages to the letter, each filled with her gran's large scrawling handwriting.

My Dear Pauline,

I hope you don't read this for a while because

when you do, it will mean I'm not here any more. I hope I shall live to see your baby but if it's not God's will, so be it. This is hard for me, Pauline – I'm no hand at writing, but I'll do my best. It's a stony road in front of you, girl, but I know you'll cope. I pray Walter will be on hand to help you. He's a strange one, but he loves you, I'm sure. Anyway, I hope the money will help. I wish it were more, but it's all I have.

Remember when I told you about my mam, Pauline? Well, love, I don't want to sound silly and sentimental but I do want you to know that you've been my 'lark', Pauline. Will you understand, I wonder?

All my life I've wanted, needed, to give love, but Thomas died early and then Walter never seemed to want me to show affection. He's always been a bit of a mystery to me, which is a terrible thing to say about your own son. But then Margaret gave birth to you and the moment I saw you, I couldn't have loved you more. And you grew up such a lovely lassie. Don't fret about causing me worry, I know you will. That's part of it all, you see. Loving, worrying, joy and tears, and I wouldn't have had it any other way. Take pleasure in life, Pauline, and God Bless You.

Eliza

Pauline cried after she had read the letter, but the tears were healing ones. She smoothed out the pages, read the letter through again and then put it back into the envelope. I'll keep it for ever, she thought.

Two days later, she rented a room from a Mrs Penman

who lived just off Baxtergate, not five minutes from the dry-cleaning shop.

During the following two months, Pauline blessed its closeness to her work for the weather became unbelievably bad. On the twenty-seventh of January the thermometer reading plummeted all over the country and hundreds of towns were snowed in, villages cut off. The thirtieth of January had the worst weather in living memory. Power cuts were long and total and as the days went by everyone in the country began to live a strange half-life. There were cold breakfasts by candlelight and then the struggle to get to work, sliding along footpaths so piled up with snow at each side that it was like walking through tunnels.

Pauline's pregnancy was now obvious but Mrs Denton, although disapproving, agreed to keep her on. Pauline explained that if she worked until she was six months pregnant she would be able to claim a few shillings from the health authority.

Apart from working, her life had come to a full stop. She didn't go out, she didn't see anyone except Mary. About once a week her friend slipped and slithered through the snow to visit her and they enjoyed a good moan together.

'No buses, no trains – God, how long will this weather go on?' Mary rolled her eyes. 'We should have been born into royalty, Pauline. There *they* are, swanning around in the South African sunshine, while we're trying to keep warm.'

Pauline tried to joke about the miserable conditions. 'Remember how I was worried about people staring at me and talking about me? Now the only person I see, apart from you, Mrs Denton and the rare customer who battles through to the shop, is the doctor.'

Doctor Tebbutt was now Pauline's unlikely friend. On her first visit to the surgery after Eliza's death, Pauline had asked him outright if he had been the person to tell her father.

'It seemed the only honourable course. He had the right to know. He . . .' Clarence Tebbutt had been embarrassed. He had blustered for a few moments and then turned bright red and begged for Pauline's forgiveness.

'When I heard Eliza had been rushed into hospital, and on the same day I spoke to your father . . .' his eyes had brimmed with tears, 'I realised I was partly responsible for what happened.'

'Maybe not. Gran had a weak heart,' Pauline reminded him, somewhat brusquely. 'You, of all people, must have known that?'

'Yes – of course I knew. But you can't tell me there wasn't an unholy row which could have triggered the heart attack?'

Pauline studied her hands. 'There was.'

'I thought so.' Doctor Tebbutt paused. 'I've always admired your father. He's a good businessman. He always seemed so calm, but when I told him about you . . .'

Pauline kept her eyes fixed on her hands. 'He went mad.'

'You could say that.' The doctor's voice quivered. 'I was actually afraid.'

'That's why Gran asked you to wait, Doctor. We both knew how shocked he would be although we didn't realise just how badly he would take the news.'

'I can only ask you to forgive me. I gather,' Tebbutt refused to meet her gaze, 'you no longer live at home?'

She sighed. 'No. We don't even speak.'

'Oh, dear! Just at a time when you need help.' He came from behind his desk and sat on the chair next to Pauline. 'If there's anything I can do?'

He looked so distressed, Pauline found it in her heart to be generous. 'Doctor Tebbutt, my father was going to be furious whoever told him so there's no point blaming yourself for my grandmother's collapse.' She hesitated. 'Eliza told me that once you and she were friends?'

'We were indeed and I hope I can be a friend to you, young lady.' A blush crept over the doctor's face and he coughed before, somewhat self-consciously, resuming his professional role.

'Well, we must get on. I think it would be wise to check your blood-pressure.'

He ran checks and professed himself satisfied, except for the weight she was gaining. 'You're sure the dates you gave were right?'

'I'm sure.'

'Well, it must be a big baby you're carrying, Pauline.'

'But nothing's wrong?'

'No. In fact, considering the trauma you have recently experienced, you are remarkably well.' He rubbed his nose. 'You're starting to feel movement?'

'Yes, often.'

'Well then, I don't think you need worry.' He smiled at her. 'Have you thought about when the child is born? Any plans?'

'I'll manage. Gran left me a little money but I'll have to find work later, and make arrangements for someone to look after the baby.'

'It's going to be hard.' He looked at her over his spectacles. 'It's almost a pity the war's over.' When she looked puzzled, he explained, 'Lots of nurseries and crêches were opened to allow women to do war work, but now they've shut down again.'

She shrugged. 'Just my luck.'

He studied her face. 'There are always childless couples eager to adopt a baby.' He saw her frown. 'You really ought to consider the idea, Pauline. You are still so young. In a few years you could marry, have other children?'

'No.' She shook her head. 'I know you mean well, Doctor Tebbutt, but I will never part with my baby, whatever happens.'

Chapter Thirteen

The cold weather continued. During March, in an effort to save fuel, the printing of weekly magazines was banned and, in the daily newspapers, tips were published on how to survive during the power cuts; home page editors explained how easy it was to cook by 'haybox'. By now, over two million men and women had been thrown out of work by the closing of the factories. Pauline thought about Bill, Mrs Denton's son – he was certainly not alone in his misfortune.

The newspapers worked hard to find items of news to raise their readers' spirits, and they found them. They noted that miners had reported in for Sunday work in order to relieve the coal shortage, that workers at the Rolls-Royce works at Crewe were using car engines to generate emergency power, and that a baker in Norwich had used his ovens to cook dinner for one hundred households, for a nominal charge of threepence each. 'You see,' crowed the editorial, 'the British have proved once again that they are at their best in adversity.'

Pauline read about these things but they meant little to her. No longer working, and now over six months pregnant, she had retreated from the world.

Cocooned in her rented room, a bedspread pinned around her shoulders for warmth, she knitted jackets and bootees for the baby.

Grahame's desertion, the loss of Eliza, the split with her father, combined with the atrocious weather – all these things made her content to retreat from reality. She knitted, made lists of names and wondered whether her baby would be born with red hair.

Sometimes, when she looked around at her surroundings, she felt as though she had lived in her rented room forever. It wasn't home, but it wasn't too bad. There was a gas fire which had to be fed with shillings and made a plopping noise which was strangely comforting when she felt lonely, and a table on which she kept her books and the old magazines her landlady passed on to her. There was a shabby armchair in which she sat to do her knitting.

The blue serge curtains at the window were dull, but they were thick and kept the draughts out when she drew them after tea. Her bed was clean but narrow and hard. It didn't matter. She would have slept badly on the finest bed in Yorkshire.

Between one and three in the morning was the worst time. That was when she remembered her grandmother's strangled cry as she slid to the floor and the terrible look in her father's eyes when he told her to leave his house. That was when tears burned her eyes and she knew, without any doubt, that everything was her fault.

But in the early morning, when she awoke from a fitful sleep and heard Mrs Penman switch her radio on, and felt her baby move inside her, she always felt better. She would get up, draw back the curtains and tell herself the weather was definitely improving. And when it did, she would go out.

Just thinking about facing the world again made her shiver, but she knew it had to be done. She must choose a pram for her coming child and thanks to Eliza, she had the money to pay for one. And then, when this ghastly spring finally gave way to summer, she would take her baby for walks, see his or her little limbs grow brown and strong in the sunlight.

She thought about the new pram a lot, what colour it should be, whether she should buy a small pram or a coach-built model, but about other arrangements she would make no decision. 'I've plenty of time,' she said to Doctor Tebbutt when he asked her what arrangements she had made for after the birth of her child. And she told Mary to stop nagging when her friend suggested ideas about work Pauline might do from home, or women who might be willing to look after the baby for her.

It was rarely she thought about her life before Grahame had entered it. When she did, it seemed foreign to her, as though it had been another girl who had 'borrowed' dresses to go dancing in, made eyes at the boys and laughed and giggled with Mary. So much had gone from her life, but not Mary, bless her. No matter how bad the weather, once or twice a week she slogged her way through the snow to visit.

But now things were happening. The ice was cracking, the snow beginning to melt. And after the great freeze-up came the great flood. Rivers from the Bristol Channel to the Wash overflowed and the River Wissey flooded, drowning a vast area of the Fens. Whole areas were devastated and during the Easter holiday it became necessary for giant cranes to be brought over from Holland to fight the rising waters.

'At least Whitby won't flood, it's too damn' hilly.' Mary kicked off her shoes and reached for another cake. She had brought a bag of them along on her visit to Pauline.

She counted the stitches on her knitting needle and then watched as Mary licked the last of the crumbs from her fingers.

'That's the third one you've eaten,' she said. 'Aren't you worried you'll get fat?'

Mary snorted. 'Chance would be a fine thing. That bloke, Stafford Cripps – he's a devil. Cuts in sugar, cuts in flour – what does he think we're going to eat next? Grass?' She shrugged her shoulders. 'Anyway, my new boyfriend likes me plump.'

'Oh.' Pauline's eyebrows arched. 'What's he called?'

For once, Mary was not forthcoming. 'I'll tell you later.' She wandered over to the window, lifted the net curtain and looked out. 'The sun's trying to get out. Why don't we go for a walk?'

'I don't feel like it.'

'Oh, come on, Pauline. That baby of yours needs a bit of fresh air, even if you don't. And you know the doctor told you to try and keep your weight down. A walk will do you good.'

'You sound like a health visitor.' Nevertheless, Pauline heaved herself to her feet. 'Still, I suppose you're right.'

There was a nervous feeling in her stomach as she put on her new swagger coat. She had bought it when she moved to Mrs Penman's but because she went out so rarely, had never yet worn it. At Eliza's funeral she had worn her old coat which was single-breasted with square shoulders and a belt and she had got away with it, no one had realised she was pregnant. But now she was huge. Even the dolman sleeves and swing back of the new coat could not disguise the huge bump she carried in front of her. She donned her serviceable wedge shoes.

'Do I look all right?'

'You look fine.'

Mary was looking particularly attractive. Pauline sighed. Maybe she was celebrating the change in the weather. She watched as her friend retrieved her suede and leather court shoes and slipped them on.

Mary was wearing one of the new fashionable turbans and her coat was flared with a shawl collar. She fastened the buttons and then licked one forefinger and passed it over the arch of her plucked eyebrows. 'Come on.'

Outside, Pauline's apprehension faded when Mrs Chappell, the milkman's wife, crossed the street to speak to her. 'Now then, Pauline. We haven't seen you for a long time. Not long to go now, I see?'

'No.' She nodded and smiled. She thought it might be the welcome sunshine that made Mrs Chappell so friendly.

'By God, Pauline Verrill – what's that you're having, a baby or a horse?' That remark, accompanied by a cheeky grin, was from Sly Roscoe, a lad who had been in Pauline's class at school and who now worked on the fish pier.

Then Mrs Watters, a woman who lived two doors down from her father's house, stopped and patted her arm. 'Reet sorry about all t'trubble, lass. Owt I can do, let me know.' She shook her head. 'Thy dad's a hard 'un, chucking thoo out t'house like that.'

Pauline blushed. 'I can't believe it,' she whispered to Mary. 'I thought they'd all be giving me black looks and whispering about me behind my back.'

'They would, if you were still at home.' Mary pursed her mouth and blew a silent whistle. 'Funny lot, aren't they? You'd still be a bad lass if you were home with your dad, but seeing how he's slung you out, you're the poor victim and he's the villain. Mind, it makes sense, I suppose. You and your gran got on with people, your dad never did, especially folk from this part of the town.'

'No, more's the pity.' Pauline walked the next few steps in silence, remembering her father's bitter denunciation of his neighbours.

Mary glanced at her. 'Feeling all right?'

'Yes.' She rubbed her forehead. 'Bit headachey, though. I've had a few headaches lately. I'm wondering if my specs need changing. Look, Mary, I think I'll call in at the optician's, seeing how we're so close. Is that all right with you?'

'Yes.' Mary pointed across the road. 'I'll go and have a cup of coffee in there. Come over when you've finished.'

The optician too gave Pauline a warm welcome. He gave her an eye test, said her spectacles were OK but that she should mention her headaches to the doctor, and then, when she was about to leave, remarked, 'Antony, my little grandson, is almost three now, Pauline. My daughter still has his nappies and some clothes. They're in good condition. Perhaps you could use them? I know how difficult it is to get hold of anything nowadays. Shall I ask her about them?' He hesitated. 'You wouldn't be offended?'

'No, of course I wouldn't. It's a kind thought, Mr Dennison, thank you.'

She went to meet Mary and over a cup of coffee said, 'I'm glad you persuaded me to come out. People are kinder than you think.'

'Sometimes they are.' Mary's expression was sulky. Pauline looked at her then reached over and tapped her hand with her coffee spoon.

'What have you been up to?'

'Nothing.'

'I don't believe you. Come on, I tell *you* everything.'

'Well, it's nothing earth-shattering.' Mary stirred the dregs of her coffee. 'It's my new boyfriend – some people don't approve.' She sniffed. 'Not that it's any of their business.'

Pauline's eyebrows drew together in a frown. 'What's the matter with him?'

'Nothing. He's lovely, really lovely.' Mary's voice climbed high with indignation, but then sank lower as she said, 'It's just that he's a German.'

'What!' Pauline's mouth dropped open.

'German.' Mary scowled. 'You needn't look like that. He's perfectly normal.'

Pauline tried to hide her shock. 'Of course he is. But tell me, where did you meet him?'

'In a pub.' Mary stared at Pauline and drummed her fingers nervously on the cafe table. 'Stop staring, will you? Where did you think we met, in a prisoner-of-war camp?'

'Sorry.' Embarrassed, Pauline picked up her cup to have a drink and then realised it was empty. She replaced it on the saucer.

'You must have known I'd be surprised. You've got to admit it's unusual.'

Mary sighed. 'Yes, I know it is. Sorry, kid, I didn't mean to bite your head off. But everyone's had a go at me.' She drew her hand across her throat in a cutting gesture. 'I've had it up to here!'

'By "everyone" you mean your folks?'

'Yes.' Mary brooded. 'My four brothers have threatened to beat him up if they see him in the street. Jill seems to think he walks about giving the Nazi salute, and my father has a fit every time he hears his name.'

Pauline sighed. 'What *is* his name?'

'Claus. Claus Brandt. He's a lovely chap, Pauline.'

'Um, I'll take your word for it. He's good-looking, I suppose?'

'Gorgeous. He's tall and dark with lovely brown eyes. When I first saw him, he was leaning up against the bar in the Hare and Hounds. He was wearing one of those chocolate-coloured battledresses, like you see in the war films, and a peaked cap. He looked so gorgeous, my heart did a kind of flip when he looked across at me. And that was it.'

Oh Lord! Pauline looked down into her empty coffee cup. Mary acted so hard-bitten, but she was a romantic at heart. Of course she would be attracted to a handsome foreigner, a man who was living in a hostile land far away from home.

'Well? Say something.'

Mary's voice made her jump. She wondered what she *could* say.

'It's natural your family are upset, Mary. The war's not been over for long and people remember. What about the Blitz, and all the lads who died in the services?'

'But it was the same for them. Claus was wounded and taken prisoner in the war and his mum and dad were killed in an air-raid.'

Pauline frowned and shook her head. 'I still don't understand what a German's doing in Whitby?'

Mary sighed. 'He was in a camp, but he's working

on a farm outside Bridlington now.'

'But won't he be going home, back to Germany?'

'He says not. Poor Claus, he was never a Nazi, he was drafted into the army and hated every minute of it. He was an only child and now his parents are dead, he wants to stay here. Germany's in ruins.' Mary cupped her chin in her hands. 'He likes the British. Of course, some people have been rotten to him but some have treated him well. The farmer he's working for really likes him. He's a good worker.'

'I see.' But she didn't. How could Mary fall for a German?

'Wait until you meet him.' Mary had read her thoughts. 'I'm not just seeing him for devilment, Pauline, please don't think that. He's special, and I think I'm falling in love with him. My dad says he's only making up to me so he can stay in England, but I don't believe that.' She looked at Pauline anxiously. 'You will meet him, won't you, for my sake?'

'Of course I will.' She looked down at herself. 'But I shouldn't think he'll want to meet me, looking like this.'

'That's all right.' Mary raised her hand to attract the attention of the waitress. 'He won't notice what you look like – he has eyes only for me.'

The following Saturday, Pauline did meet Claus and was pleasantly surprised. He proved a gentle giant of a man, with a quiet voice and courteous manners. His English was good and he talked politely to Pauline, but she saw how he watched Mary's every move and realised that he was indeed in love with her. And Mary, although bubbling with happiness, was quieter than usual. Her habit of showing off, as if to an audience, was missing. Watching the couple, Pauline felt envious yet worried. Mary would not have an easy time of it if she decided to marry Claus.

After a couple of hours they left, promising to visit her again, and Mary, hanging back, whispered: 'What do you think?'

'I like him. He's all you said he was.'

'Good.' Her friend hugged her. 'See you next week.'

But they had to wait longer than that before meeting again. Two days after meeting Claus, Pauline's headache was so bad she tapped on Mrs Penman's door and asked her to ring Doctor Tebbutt. He was there within the hour. He took her blood-pressure and frowned.

'I think you'd be better in hospital, Pauline.'

'But the baby's not due yet.'

'No, but I don't want you staying here on your own. Your landlady works, I believe?'

She nodded.

'Now you mustn't get worried, there's nothing seriously wrong, but your blood-pressure's rising and needs monitoring regularly. I suspected this might happen so I took precautions.' He sat down beside her and explained.

'I provisionally booked a bed for you in a mother and baby hospital near York. I think you should go there now. I'll phone from my office and tell them to expect you.'

'But – '

He raised his hand. 'Listen to me. Hopefully, you'll go to full term, but perhaps not. Whitby hospital's small. It can't have you taking up a bed for the next two months. And the place I've mentioned has the latest equipment, should the baby be premature. You must realise that my suggestion is for the best, Pauline? You want your child to have the best medical attention, don't you?'

Her words of protest died on her lips. She looked down at her hands and nodded.

'Good, that's settled. I'll arrange transport for tomorrow morning.' Doctor Tebbutt stood up. 'There's a special annexe attached to the hospital. It's for unmarried mothers. You'll be able to stay there, with any other girls they have in. That means you won't have to go on to the maternity ward until the baby starts.' He paused, pushing up his spectacles. 'There's another bonus. You're allowed to stay on for a month after the birth, if you want to.'

She stood up and walked him to the door. 'You're looking after me very well, Doctor Tebbutt.'

'Well, I promised, didn't I?' He pressed her hand. 'Eliza would likely strike me dead with a thunderbolt from heaven if I let you down.'

She laughed. 'I suppose she would.'

After a sleepless night she was up early to pack. It didn't take long. She checked the cupboards once more then moved restlessly around the room which had been her refuge for the past three months. She knew Doctor Tebbutt was right and was grateful to him but she felt as if she were adrift in the world again.

Mrs Penman had been friendly but had made it perfectly clear that Pauline would not be able to return to her house after the baby was born. 'A single room is not a suitable home for a baby, Pauline.'

She was right. Pauline took a last look around. When she returned to Whitby, if she returned to Whitby, she would have to find a new home. She picked up the note she had written and slipped it in her pocket. She would ask Mrs Penman to give it to Mary when she next called.

The toot of a car horn outside the house made her start. She put on her coat, took a deep breath and picked up her case. It was time to go.

Chapter Fourteen

The hospital was set back from the road and screened by a copse of trees. Close by stood a rambling, two-storeyed house with large bay windows. The mother and baby unit, guessed Pauline. She stared at the windows and jumped when the driver of the cab opened the door for her.

He was a kind little man. He carried her case as he escorted her through the main doors of the hospital.

'You'll be all right here, love.' He nodded to the blue-overalled nursing auxiliary who approached them. 'They'll look after you.'

He turned and gave her a cheery wave from the door. Pauline was sorry to see him go.

'This way, please.'

The auxiliary took her through swing doors and into a waiting room where a nurse asked her to sit down. After ten minutes of nervous anticipation, she was shown into a small office and asked to sit down by a grey-haired woman wearing horn-rimmed spectacles who sat behind a desk.

The interview got off to a bad start. After asking for Pauline's date of birth and other personal details, and noting the replies on a form, the woman asked, 'Have you ever suffered from venereal disease?'

Pauline couldn't believe she'd heard right. She stared. 'What?'

The woman looked over her glasses. 'It's a simple question. Have you ever had venereal disease?'

Pauline shrank back in her chair. 'No.'

'That's something.' The woman wrote on the form. 'Of course, we can't take your word for it. There'll have to be an examination.'

Half an hour later, red-faced and humiliated, Pauline returned to the office and was escorted by the same grim-faced woman across to the adjacent building. In silence they crossed the square-shaped hall and walked up the shallow-stepped staircase which led to the first floor. The woman, she had not told Pauline her name, stopped outside the third door along the corridor and twisted the door-handle. 'Go in.'

Pauline stepped into the room and the woman followed her.

'What's this, a new inmate?'

A black-haired girl, hugely pregnant, was seated by the window. She was smoking a cigarette. She nodded to Pauline. 'Welcome to Stalag 17.'

Pauline's attendant frowned at the girl. 'Put that cigarette out, Noakes. You know smoking's forbidden.'

The girl pulled a face but did as she was told. As she did so, Pauline sneaked a look at her surroundings and was pleasantly surprised. Her welcome, if you could call it that, had made her fear the worst, but the room she was in was bright and cheerful with attractive furnishings.

'Verrill.'

She jumped. The woman's attention was back on

her. She snapped out a list of rules which must be followed and Pauline nodded, aware that the black-haired girl was watching her, a wide grin on her face. When the woman left the room Pauline's shoulders slumped in relief. She was surprised to see her companion take a pack of cigarettes from the pocket of her maternity dress and put one in her mouth.

'Won't she be furious?'

The girl nodded, and producing a match, lit the cigarette. 'Of course she'll be spitting feathers, which is partly the reason for me smoking. But she can't bash me up, can she? I'm pregnant.'

She laughed and coughed and then heaved herself out of her chair and stuck out her hand. 'I'm Muriel, Muriel Noakes.'

Pauline shook hands. 'I'm Pauline Verrill. I've just arrived from Whitby.'

'Whitby, where's Whitby?' Muriel grinned. 'I'm only joking. I've been in this dump four weeks and it seems like forever. Still, with a bit of luck I'll be out soon. This,' she gestured to her huge stomach, 'should appear any minute now and then once the adoption papers are signed, I'm off.'

Pauline looked round the room. 'Is that mine?' She pointed to the bed in the corner and when Muriel nodded, went over and opened her case. 'At least it's a nice room.'

'Oh, yes. Pictures on the wall, flounced bed-spreads.' Muriel grimaced. 'Much better than types like us deserve.'

She began to move restlessly about the place, touching the bedspreads, moving the crocheted mats on the dressing table. Then she glanced at Pauline's face. 'You feeling all right? You don't look too good.'

'It's just a headache – and I'm tired. I didn't know until yesterday afternoon I was coming here. My doctor fixed it up. It's been a bit of a shock.'

'Yeah, I know.' The girl laughed again. 'Bit like getting pregnant, eh?'

Pauline looked down.

'Sorry.' Her companion patted her stomach. 'I'm a bit edgy today. The bump was due to arrive yesterday but nothing's happened yet.'

'Oh.' Pauline thought her room-mate looked young, maybe as young as *she* was. On a sudden impulse, she asked, 'Are you scared?'

'Bloody hell, of course I am, but I can't walk about like this for the rest of my life. I'll be glad when it's all over.'

Muriel started pacing the floor again and Pauline watched her. Greatly daring, she asked, 'You're going for adoption?'

'That's right. What about you?'

'No, I'm keeping mine.'

Muriel stopped pacing. 'Lucky you. The bloke's sticking by you, is he?'

'No.' Colour stained Pauline's cheeks but she did not look away from Muriel. 'But I'm keeping it anyway.'

'Oh.' Muriel plucked at her lips with her fingers. 'One of the saintly ones.'

Pauline lifted her chin. 'I'm doing what I want to do, what's wrong with that?'

Without replying, Muriel walked to the window and looked out. 'Have you noticed how this house has been screened off?' She didn't turn to see Pauline nod, but stared at the view. 'It's not so bad this side, the trees are nice, but wait until you see round the back.

We're near a row of private houses, see, so they've stuck up high boarding all round us. Apparently we're not suitable to be seen by decent families.'

She swung round on Pauline, a scowl on her face. 'I should warn you, it's bloody in here. The staff give you stupid little tasks that don't need doing, and if you go into the sitting-room in the evenings – it's supposed to be *our* sitting-room, by the way – you're only allowed to sit on hard chairs. They pretend to be kind but really they're getting their message over – we're here to be punished for our wicked ways.'

Pauline saw the sheen of tears in Muriel's dark eyes. She said gently, 'Never mind, you'll be leaving soon.'

'Yes, thank God.' Muriel stubbed out her cigarette and flung herself back in her chair. 'Have you worked out what you'll do when you leave?'

'No, not yet.'

Muriel frowned. 'You must. Don't you realise how hard it will be?'

'I know, but I can't seem to concentrate on anything except the baby being born. I'll manage somehow.' Pauline stood up and opened her case. 'Where can I put these?' She held up a dressing-gown and a pair of slippers.

'In there.' She gestured towards the wardrobe.

'Thanks.' Pauline hung up the robe then turned back to her. 'Did you decide on adoption straight away?'

Then was a moment's silence and then Muriel nodded her head. 'Yes, I did. I think it's much the best way. For the baby, I mean.'

When Pauline did not reply she spoke again, and this time a touch of uncertainty showed in her voice. 'Everyone says so. Victor, that's my chap, he said I'd be mad to keep it.' As if conscious of Pauline's silence she changed the subject. 'I've been going with Victor over a year. He's wonderful and he's crazy about me. He'd marry me tomorrow if he could, but he's stuck with a cow of a wife who won't divorce him. Rotten, isn't it?' She shrugged.

'Yes.' Pauline went back to unpacking her case. She took out a nightdress and placed it on the spare bed. 'Yes, it is.'

The door swung open, although Pauline didn't hear anyone knock, and the woman who'd interviewed her stuck her head through.

'Noakes, get a move on, you're due to see the doctor in ten minutes. And Verrill, when you've finished unpacking, go over to the hospital and register with the nurse on duty.'

The door closed and the girls heard the clatter of steel-tipped heels on the corridor outside.

'Stupid old bat.' Muriel struggled to her feet. 'She'd make a good prison warder, she would. Her name's Miss Eames and she's the home's administrator.' She swayed towards the door. 'She hates us. I think she's never had a bloke in her life and she's jealous.'

Muriel did not return to the room and at suppertime Pauline was told she had been admitted to the maternity ward. Lights were doused at ten o'clock by a central switch so Pauline, with nothing else to do, went to bed.

She couldn't sleep. Her thoughts twisted and slithered like fish in a landing net. And she felt just as vulnerable. She wondered how Muriel was doing. Was she in labour? What would it be like to have a baby? How long would she have to stay in this place? Would all the nursing staff be as unfriendly as Miss Eames? What would she do after her baby had been born? Where would she go?

At three am she gave up trying to sleep and went and sat by the window. It was a hunter's moon. The trees looked sinister in the faint light and the utter silence of the countryside unnerved her. She was used to hearing the sea, the wash of the waves and the cry of the seagulls. She drew her dressing-gown closer about her body and felt more alone than she had ever been in her life.

Then, just as tears threatened, there came a low hoot and a ghostlike shape moved in slow flight across the lawn outside her window. She took her spectacles from the pocket of her robe, put them on and peered through the glass. It was a barn owl, the first one she had ever seen in her life. She saw its flattened white head, golden-buff plumage and black eyes, and she smiled. She watched the bird until it disappeared from view and then went back to bed.

'Not quite a lark, Gran,' she murmured, 'but it will do.' Then she fell asleep.

Next day Miss Eames presented her with a list of the light duties she must do each day and she had an appointment with her doctor who told her everything was satisfactory. She discovered that meals were served in the unit and at lunchtime met the only other young woman presently in residence.

Nancy Atkinson was about twenty-five years old and pleasant enough, but she made it plain she wished to be left alone. Pauline was happy to oblige. At seventeen she was awed by the older woman's cool self-possession. She wondered, a little guiltily, how such a person had become an unmarried mother, but Nancy and her past life soon fled Pauline's mind when she found how little spare time she had.

She was visited by a lady from the Health Ministry with yet more forms, then a Catholic priest who, waving away her protests that she was baptised a Methodist, prayed over her for an hour. And, when she returned to the unit, Miss Eames gave her some of the 'little jobs' Muriel had warned her about.

On her second day the doctor told her Muriel had given birth to a little boy and she could visit. Pauline found her way to the correct ward, where the new mother was flat in her bed, her dark hair a beautiful cloud around her tired face. Pauline sat down next to her.

'How are you?'

'Well, it's no picnic.' Muriel smiled at her and pulled herself up to a sitting position. 'I'm OK. A bit sore though. Thanks for coming.'

'Of course I came. You're the only person I know in this place, remember?'

'Even so . . .' Muriel smoothed the already immaculate bedsheet. 'We don't really know each other, do we? No one could call us bosom friends.'

'Oh, I don't know. Right now, we both have enormous bosoms.' Pauline was pleased by Muriel's laugh.

'You're all right, Verrill. Better than these cows.'

'Hush, they'll hear you.' Pauline looked at the three other women in the room; one was reading, the other two were asleep. Reassured, she turned back to Muriel.

'They *are* cows. They don't speak to me.' Muriel shrugged. 'Frightened they might catch something, I suppose.'

'I'm sorry.' Casting about for a more pleasurable

subject, Pauline said, 'I've seen your little boy, he's gorgeous.'

'Is he?'

She shouldn't have mentioned him. Muriel lay down again and closed her eyes.

'Yes.' Pauline bit her lip. She asked, 'Surely you've seen him, Muriel?'

'Yes.' She spoke with her eyes shut. 'When he was born. He was all sticky and bloody.' She shuddered. 'Not a bit appealing.'

'Well, he is now. He's got your dark hair.' Pauline twisted her hands together. 'Don't you think you ought to see him, just once? You might be glad, later.'

'Oh, I see him, Pauline – three or four times a day. I know what he looks like.' Muriel rolled on to her side and looked at Pauline, pain in her eyes. 'I asked if he could be bottle-fed but they refused. "Breast milk's better for the baby," they said. I asked them, what about me – is it better for me?' She choked.

Pauline sat forward in her chair and took hold of her hand. 'You've still time to change your mind.'

Muriel clutched at her fingers. 'I can't, Pauline, I can't. I love Victor. I couldn't bear to lose him.'

'Well, then,' she sighed, 'you must make the most of the time you have with your son.' She dropped a kiss on Muriel's forehead and eased her fingers from her grasp. 'I'm sorry, but I have to go. I've an appointment with Doctor Thorpe, and anyway, they told me I could just stay for a moment.'

'That's all right.' Muriel had turned her face away. 'Thanks for coming.'

Pauline hesitated. 'Like you said, adoption might be best. They'll make sure he goes to a good home, where he will be happy.'

Muriel rewarded her with a watery smile. 'You're a good kid, Pauline. I hope things work out for you.'

Fourteen days later, Pauline watched from her window as Victor, a tall, heavily-built man, swung open the door of his posh blue car for Muriel to enter. Her friend, for Pauline had come to regard Muriel as a friend, looked up and waved a final goodbye. Pauline waved back.

Muriel looked radiant. Her dark hair was upswept in the latest style, her make-up was immaculate and her figure – she was wearing a dark red two-piece costume – was such that it seemed impossible she had recently given birth. She hesitated, staring up at Pauline, then blew an impulsive kiss and stepped into the car. They drove away and Pauline stepped away from the bedroom window feeling a real sense of loss.

'Verrill . . .' The strident voice of Miss Eames sounded in the corridor. Pauline sighed. Moving with some difficulty, she went to the door. Despite eating little, she was gaining weight by the day. She thought of Muriel's slim figure and felt a pang of envy. How lovely it would be to see her feet again.

Chapter Fifteen

Another week limped by. Pauline, deprived of Muriel's company, grew depressed. Another young woman came to stay in the unit but she spent most of the day in floods of tears which did little to raise Pauline's spirits, and there was something about Doctor Thorpe's expression when he examined her that made her worry. He insisted everything was fine but then requested Pauline to find Miss Eames and ask her to see him. The administrator came to Pauline's room later that day.

'You're to be excused all duties from now on, Verrill.' She gave Pauline an odd, swift glance. 'The doctor wants you to rest more. Three hours in the afternoon, he says.' Giving Pauline no chance to ask questions, she turned and stalked out.

So, every day after lunch, Pauline dutifully undressed and went to bed, not to sleep but to worry. However, on the Saturday she received a surprise guest. She was told to go along to the sitting-room at four pm and there she found Doctor Tebbutt waiting for her.

'Pauline, my dear.' He took hold of both her hands, held her at arm's length and studied her face.

'Not a pretty sight.' She pulled down her mouth, her

spirits rising nevertheless at the sight of a friendly face.

'Nonsense. You look fine.' The doctor sat down, grimacing as his ample rump made contact with the hard seat of the chair. 'Are they treating you well?'

'Yes, thank you.' Pauline spoke the truth. Doctor Thorpe was attentive, the food and accommodation good. It was not Doctor Tebbutt's fault some of the staff were lacking in friendliness.

'I'm glad to hear it. Doctor Thorpe says you've been most co-operative.'

They were brought a cup of tea by Nancy Atkinson, chatted for a while and then Doctor Tebbutt came to the reason for his visit. 'Doctor Thorpe thinks your baby will arrive soon, Pauline.' He rubbed his chin. 'I wondered, would you like me to assist at the birth?'

She clasped her hands. 'Oh, yes.'

He laughed. 'I'm glad you're so enthusiastic. Thorpe's the man in charge, of course, but he said he would have no objection to my presence and I thought a friendly face might not come amiss. And I must also admit to a personal interest.'

Pauline put her head to one side. 'Eliza again?'

'Perhaps originally.' The doctor looked uncomfortable. 'But I've developed a high regard for you, young lady, you've coped so well with things.'

'Oh.' She stared at him, lost for words.

'Anyway, now that I know you'd welcome my attendance, I'll ask Thorpe to contact me when the labour starts. Mind you,' the doctor shook his head, 'babies are notorious for their unreliability. You might deliver very quickly, in which case I may not get here in time.'

Pauline had recovered her composure. She laughed.

'I won't complain if that happens.'

'I'm sure you won't.' Smiling, he took his leave of her. 'By the way, your friend Mary sends a message. She hopes to visit you next weekend.'

'Oh, that would be wonderful.' Pauline's smile grew wider. 'Give her my love, won't you?'

'I will.' Doctor Tebbutt consulted his watch. 'I must rush. I'm visiting an old friend who lives the other side of York and I'm late. He'll be wondering what's happened to me.'

Pauline felt better for Doctor Tebbutt's visit and better still when she awoke the following Saturday, the day Mary was due to visit. It was now the month of May and although Pauline had heard the sound of rain during the night, it was a fine morning. By eleven o'clock the sun was out. Too restless to stay indoors, she walked slowly up and down the gravelled path outside the home, waiting for her friend.

From time to time she stopped, raising her face towards the sun. The feeling of warmth in the fresh clean air was wonderful. She was glad her baby would be born in the spring. She listened. The light breeze made the nearby trees sigh and rustle and carried to her the scent of flowers from the hospital garden. She smiled. Despite Miss Eames and her petty restrictions, there were worse places in which to bring a baby into the world.

There was a rattling, clanging noise and a small lorry, the back of it loaded with sacks of produce, came into view. Pauline watched as it pulled up outside the house with a screech of brakes. The window of the cab was wound down and Mary's impudent face peeped out. 'Pauline, it's me. Hang on a minute.'

She rested her hands on her stomach and began to laugh. 'Mary, where on earth did you get that?'

She jumped down from the lorry a second before Claus appeared from the other side of the vehicle to help her down from the high step.

'Don't mock, woman, be thankful for small mercies. How did you think I'd get here, pony and trap?' She dusted down her skirt. 'Why are places like these always in the middle of nowhere? If we'd taken the train to York, it would have cost the earth to get out here by taxi.' She hurried over to Pauline and gave her a smacking kiss on her cheek. 'Great to see you, kid.'

'Great to see you.' Pauline returned the kiss. 'I'm sorry, I wasn't expecting . . .'

'Really? You could have fooled me.' Mary moved her eyebrows rapidly up and down and Pauline laughed again.

'Oh, Mary!'

Her friend grinned. 'Claus sweet-talked his boss into letting us use his lorry. At least those sacks aren't full of manure.'

Pauline mopped her eyes, hugged Mary to her and then turned to Claus. 'Thank you for bringing her.'

'A pleasure.' He shook her hand. 'May I say you are looking delightful?'

'That's one way of putting it.' Pauline smiled to hide her embarrassment.

Mary put her arm around what used to be Pauline's waist. 'He means it, you know. He's got that German thing about motherhood. We're going to have four kids, aren't we, Claus?'

He laughed.

Pauline looked at them both. It was still on, then? She couldn't help wondering about Claus. He was so well-mannered. What had his life been like before the war? She shook her head and smiled.

Mary with her street-wise knowledge and crazy sense of humour and Claus with his old-world courtliness made a strange couple but here they were, still together and looking extremely pleased with themselves.

'We could go indoors.' She glanced back at the house. 'But it's so lovely today . . .'

'Is there anywhere to sit down?' Mary tucked a stray curl back into place and looked round.

'There's a bench just round the corner.' Pauline led the way. 'I'll show you around later.'

Mary eyed the house. 'Looks a bit posh. Are you happy here?'

'It's OK.' Pauline sank on to the bench. 'But it's so far away from anywhere. I feel as though I've been living on a desert island. Tell me, what's been happening at home?'

'You got my letters, didn't you?'

'Yes, and they were lovely.' Pauline shifted position on the bench. 'I'm sorry I didn't write to you much. I've had a few down spells . . . you know.'

Mary's face sobered for a moment, then her vivacity returned as she set out to raise Pauline's spirits. 'Let me see. Everyone in our street thought Mrs Berriman had finally run away with Pete Greaves when she wasn't seen for over a week. Well, we all knew what had been going on, didn't we? Everyone except Mr Berriman, of course. But back she came, large as life. She'd only gone to visit her sister in Nottingham.

'And Titch Coultas holed his coble on rocks near Ravenscar. Actually in the water for two hours he was, before he was rescued. It could have been nasty, but he was tanked up with whisky from the night before so he survived.' She paused, then added thoughtfully, 'Of course, it was probably *because* of the whisky he went on the rocks.'

Pauline laughed. Mary always made her feel better. 'Go on,' she commanded.

'We've got our own genuine "spiv" in Whitby now.' Mary looked at Pauline's incredulous face. 'Honestly. He does black-market deals with the landlord at the Rose and Crown and stands at the corner of Bridge Street selling nylons. I bought a pair but they were no good, laddered the first time I wore them.' She thought a moment. 'I reckon that's about all. Nothing ever happens in Whitby, as well you know.'

'How's things with the family?' Pauline cleared her throat, wondering whether it was a wise question to ask with Claus present.

Mary shrugged. 'You know how they are – it's "out of sight, out of mind" with them. They're fine until I try and discuss important matters with them, then all hell breaks loose.'

'I'm sorry.'

'You needn't be.' Mary slipped her hand through Claus's arm. 'We're sticking together, aren't we, love?'

He nodded. 'I wish Mary to be my wife.'

She beamed at him, then turned to Pauline. 'But what about you?'

Trying to find good things to tell them, she filled in what had been happening to her. Then she hesitated before asking. 'Have you seen my father at all?'

Mary sighed. 'Only once, love – and then he crossed over the road to avoid me. He hasn't been in touch with you, has he?'

Pauline shook her head.

'You didn't really expect him to, did you?'

'No, but I can't help hoping.' Pauline put her hand on the arm of the iron bench and began to get up. 'We'll go in now and – oh!' she gasped and doubled over.

Mary sprang to her feet. 'What is it, Pauline?'

'I'm not sure.' She tried to smile. 'Maybe I've been sitting too long. Oh Lord.' She bent over again.

Mary gasped. 'Hell – it's the baby, isn't it? The baby's starting.' Her hand flew to her mouth and she stared across at her boyfriend.

'There is nothing to worry about.' Slowly, easily, Claus stood up. He touched Pauline's shoulder and when she looked up, smiled at her, then he bent and picked her up, holding her easily in his arms. 'Come on.' He set off at a steady walk towards the house.

'Put me down, Claus. I'm much too heavy for you.' Pauline's voice was small, muffled in the folds of his checked cotton shirt.

He shook his head. 'Save your strength, Pauline. You have an important job to do.'

Another wave of pain grabbed her. She gasped and clutched at him.

'That's right, hang on.' His deep voice rumbled in his chest. He smelt of soap. As the pain ebbed, Pauline closed her eyes and thought, German or not, Mary was a lucky woman.

It had been eleven-thirty when Claus carried Pauline indoors. At three-thirty, Doctor Tebbutt, scrubbed up and masked, bent over her as she lay in the labour ward. 'You're doing fine, Pauline. It won't be much longer.'

'I hope not.' She stiffened and bit back a groan.

'I know it's not easy, you're a small girl and it's a big, strong baby, but things are progressing nicely. When the pain comes again, try and breathe lightly.'

Pauline nodded and closed her eyes. The pain *was* coming back. She felt her forehead beading with sweat. Someone wiped it for her. She didn't open her eyes to find out who, for the pain was now buffeting her body in huge waves. She concentrated on her breathing, determined not to cry out. How long would it take?

Another hour passed. When she had been taken to the hospital she had wondered whether Mary and Claus had left, wondered whether Doctor Tebbutt would make it in time, but now she thought of nothing. She was a frail craft, bobbing rudderless on a powerful sea of sensation.

But at five o'clock there came a change. Her body told her it was time for her to take charge again.

'I want to push,' she gasped.

Doctor Thorpe's face loomed above her. 'That's fine, Pauline. We're nearly there.' Then, a little later, he spoke again. 'Just a few more minutes, my dear.'

She nodded, gritting her teeth, and then the final wave crashed and she threw her head back . . . and heard the cry of a baby.

'It's here, it's here.' She was laughing and crying. She used her hands to try and sit up. 'Is it all right?'

'A lovely girl.' Doctor Tebbutt was back at her side. He was smiling. 'You'll see her in a moment, I promise. But lie still now.' He pushed her back down and placed his hand on her stomach.

'You're sure she's all right?' Pauline moved restlessly under his hand. Her stomach was churning, moving, and, as another wave of pain hit her, she cried out, 'What is it? What's happening?'

'Nothing.' Doctor Tebbutt had moved away, back to the foot of the bed.

Once more she tried to sit up. 'Something's wrong.'

'Pauline, will you keep still?'

He hurried back to her. She relaxed when she saw he was smiling.

'You've fooled us, Pauline.'

Her brow creased in puzzlement.

He smoothed her damp hair back from her forehead. His eyes were twinkling. 'It was the way they were laid, you see. And the first baby was so big.'

She shook her head, dazed. The pain was there but it was weaker, more bearable.

'Here it comes.' It was Doctor Thorpe's voice.

Her body took over again. She gritted her teeth and pushed.

Doctor Tebbutt grabbed her hand. Again she thought, What's happening?

A second later, she knew. There was another cry, weaker than the first one, and then Tebbutt's voice: 'You had another in there, Pauline. You've got twins.'

The lorry swayed and bumped along the country road. The thumping noises coming from the back indicated the loaded sacks were shifting position. The driver took no notice, his foot pressed on the pedal, increasing the speed.

'Must you drive like a madman? You know the state of these roads.'

Claus touched the brake pedal and gazed in some surprise at his beloved. 'We are so late, Mary. Mr Parkin will be angry. He needs the lorry for his work.'

'So that's why you kept on at me to leave, because of your boss? How could I leave Pauline when she was scared and all alone, except for us?'

Claus stared at the road ahead, his lips thinning to a straight line. 'You are being unfair. I was happy to stay, but once the babies had been born, I said we must go.'

'Oh, you men!' Mary drew away from him and hunched in the corner of the cab.

Claus glanced at her. Applying the brake more strongly, he drew the lorry into the side of the lane and stopped.

'What is all this, Mary?'

She refused to look at him. 'Oh, don't stop, Claus. Remember Farmer Parkin.'

'Mary?' He grasped her shoulders, forced her to turn and face him. Then his brow furrowed. 'You are sad? You are crying?'

'I'm not.' Mary sniffed furiously and then her face crumpled. 'I'm sorry, Claus,' she wailed. 'It's nothing to do with you. Let's get back.'

'No, no. I want to know why you are so upset. Is it Pauline? Is there something wrong, something you have not told me?'

'No.' Mary produced a handkerchief and blew her nose. 'Pauline is deliriously happy.'

'Then the babies?' Claus was baffled. 'I saw them for only a moment, they were fine. One is a little small, perhaps, but the nurse said . . .'

'The babies are fine. Everyone's fine.'

'Then why are you sad?'

Mary shrugged. 'You wouldn't understand.'

'Mary,' Claus removed the key from the ignition, 'we are to be man and wife. Maybe I will not understand. I am a man,' he gave a half-smile, 'and also a German, but at least give me the chance.'

'Oh, I love you.' She hurled herself against his chest and he held her close.

'Tell me.'

She sighed. 'I'm sorry for being rotten to you. I know it made things awkward, me deciding to wait until the baby,' she corrected herself, 'babies arrived, but I couldn't leave, Claus. Pauline has nobody else.'

'That is understood.' He nodded his head. 'But now she has her daughters.'

'Yes, daughters – that's why I'm so worried.' Mary caught the look of bewilderment on his face and shook her head. 'I knew you wouldn't understand.'

'I am trying to.' Claus rubbed his forehead. 'Why should Pauline's babies be a problem? She will be a wonderful mother, I'm sure.'

'Yes.' Mary was silent for a moment. 'When they allowed me to see her, just for a minute, I . . .' She sniffed and mopped her eyes again. 'She was radiant with happiness, Claus. She looked tired, of course, I think she had a pretty rough time of it, but that didn't matter. She looked,' a tinge of embarrassment crept into her voice, 'she looked like one of those pictures, you know . . .'

He interrupted her. 'Madonna and Child.'

She stared at him. 'That's right. How did you know what I meant?'

'Some women are meant to be mothers. I saw Pauline with your sister's two youngsters, remember? The day we met her and we all went out for tea. She had a natural affinity with them.'

'Yes, I remember.' Mary was silent so long, Claus had to prompt her.

'So why are you worried?'

'Because she's lost touch with reality, Claus. She's in a dream world. She kept saying, "Two lovely little girls, isn't it wonderful?" '

'So?'

'But it *isn't* wonderful.' Mary pulled away from his embrace and sat up straight. 'To be an unmarried woman with one baby is bad enough, but two . . . What on earth is she going to do?'

'Pauline is a resourceful girl, she'll manage. And didn't you say she had some money? She's not destitute.'

'Not that much money! And how long will it last? She won't be able to work, she has nowhere to live. Her father won't take her back.'

'I see.' Claus touched Mary's cheek. 'You are afraid for her?'

'Yes, I am. Pauline's so unworldly, Claus, and she's so young. She's only seventeen, for God's sake. However will she manage?'

'The father?'

'No one knows where he is.' Mary shook her head. 'There's no help there. As far as I know, there's just one person who might help her and that's her Uncle Charlie.'

'And will he, do you think?'

'I don't know. I've only met him once. He looked a kind man but his wife . . .' Mary sighed.

'Well, we must hope for the best.' Claus replaced the ignition key and restarted the lorry. 'We will do all we can.' He shook his head ruefully. 'But I fear we have our own problems.'

'Yes.' Mary looked at him affectionately. 'You're a good sort, Claus Brandt, and I love you.'

'You'd better.' He leant over and kissed the tip of her nose. 'Now, let's get this lorry back before the boss fires me.'

That night, against strict instructions, Pauline sneaked out of bed and tiptoed into the nursery. A low light burned but no nurse was present. Pauline knew it was the time the night staff had a break. There were only the twins in the nursery and, thank God, they were fit and healthy and needed no special care.

She walked quietly to where the two cots stood side by side and looked at them, gloated over her two perfect, beautiful babies. The first-born, Pauline had already decided to call her Elizabeth in honour of her gran, lay on her back, her tiny hands showing above the cot covers. She had a round face and, deep in sleep, her rosebud mouth worked busily.

'Are you going to be the greedy one?' Pauline touched her face tenderly. She bent over the cot and carefully tucked her daughter's hands beneath the cover.

Then she turned to the other cot. Her second daughter was a smaller baby and dainty as a doll. She lay on her side. Her tiny head was covered with a soft fuzz of brown-gold hair. Pauline's eyes examined her, marvelled at the perfection of the shell-like ear, the faintly marked but plainly visible eyebrow that drew towards the baby's nose as she frowned in her sleep.

'My lovely little girls,' she whispered. There was a sound from the corridor and Pauline straightened up and prepared to leave but no one came in, and she couldn't tear herself away from her babies. She put one hand on each cot.

'Elizabeth Verrill,' she mouthed to the first child.

'How I wish Gran had lived to see you. And Catherine Verrill.' She smiled down at the second baby. 'My favourite name. We're going to be happy together, you'll see. Whatever people say, whatever happens, we will stay together and be happy, I promise you that.'

She started when she heard footsteps outside and someone cough. The nurse was returning. Like a wraith, Pauline moved noiselessly away from the babies and slipped back to her bed. She fell asleep instantly and smiled in her dreams.

PART TWO

Chapter Sixteen

Autumn was Kate's favourite time of year. Because summer was becoming a memory, appreciation of the good things became keener. Things like late roses in the garden, the warmth of the sun and the glorious colours of nature were felt more deeply, because they were transitory.

Her feelings about her husband's job on the oil-rig were similar. Kate was always miserable when Jack left, but in a funny sort of way she enjoyed the build-up to his return, and he would be home tomorrow. She hugged the thought to herself as she admired the clump of trees close by the entrance to the park. They proved her point, she decided. Ten months of the year they were just ordinary trees. Now they were beautiful.

Kate studied the shadings of yellow, brown and orange leaves and thought how they enhanced what was basically an uninspiring place. The place in which she was sitting, the children's play area, was functional rather than attractive.

The woman seated next to Kate said something to her and she smiled and replied, then looked over to where her son sat on the grass. Eleven-month-old Daniel had not moved from the place she had deposited him ten minutes ago. Plump hands resting on his knees, he stared down with intense concentration at the ground in front of him. Kate leaned back and, as much as was possible on an iron bench, relaxed.

'See someone's cleaned up the slide.' The woman next to her lit a cigarette.

Kate nodded. 'Yes, thank goodness. It was a terrible mess.'

The play area was busy. It was just after three-thirty in the afternoon and young mums sat or stood around in groups, watching as their five- and six-year-olds rushed around dispelling the pent-up energy of the classroom. A few slightly older boys kicked a football around on the adjoining grassed areas where large bald patches showed what was thought of the metal notice attached to one of the play tunnels. 'Ball games strictly forbidden'.

Kate watched the footballers. A slim boy with curly hair and freckles on his nose guarded the goalposts, two piles of anoraks and school bags. His grey sweater was thick with mud where he had dived to make a spectacular save and his face was alight with pleasure. A few more years, Kate thought, and Danny will be like that. Oh God, she said an involuntary silent prayer, please let him grow up like that.

The play equipment was elderly. The swings squeaked and the see-saw had to be checked for splinters before infants were given a ride, but Kate knew from experience that it was not just the ravages of time that caused the damage. After six o'clock, gangs of fifteen- and sixteen-year-old boys roamed the park, spraying the ground with broken bottles, tossing the swings over the supports so they were unusable, and inflicting more serious mindless damage.

The incident Kate's companion referred to had taken place last week when the slide had been bedaubed with some kind of grease or motor oil.

'Bloody morons.' The woman took another drag of her cigarette. 'I know what I'd like to do with them.'

Kate nodded, but privately wondered whether a beating would have any effect on the hulking half-men, half-boys who slouched along to the park in the early evenings. She shivered. Once they had been sunny-faced babies like Danny. What made them change into foul-mouthed yobs?

She looked again at her son. Today he was being a model child. He sat on his well-padded bottom, head bent. Even when she shouted and waved at him, he did not look up.

'What is it, Danny, what have you found?' With a deprecating smile at her neighbour, Kate left the bench and knelt down next to the boy.

'It's a beetle, darling. Look.' Carefully she picked a stem of grass and laid it upon Danny's blue-denimed knee. Together they watched as the beetle marched huffily along the blade of grass, scooted along Danny's lower leg and launched itself into a death-defying leap back to freedom. It scurried into the grass and disappeared.

'Oh.' Kate sat back on her heels. 'Never mind, we'll find another one later. Would you like to go on the swings?'

Danny gave her an inscrutable stare, worthy of an oriental potentate, and returned his attention to the patch of grass.

Chastened, she returned to her seat.

'Placid little soul, isn't he? You're lucky.' Kate's

neighbour glanced towards the high slide where one of her children, a boy of about eight years old, appeared to be trying to push his younger sister out of the fenced-in safety area at the top. 'Surprising, really, considering the colour of his hair.'

'Yes, he's usually easy-going, but when he does start he has quite a temper.'

Danny was now rocking backwards and forwards and slapping the ground in front of him with the palm of his outstretched right hand. He was smiling. Presumably he had relocated the beetle.

Kate turned up her face to the sun. Her neighbour did likewise.

'Grand day for the time of year. I don't reckon we'll get many more.'

Kate nodded, her eyes closed. Someone had recently cut the grass, she could smell the sweetness. She listened to the buzz of a bumble bee as it passed over her head and wondered what time Jack would arrive. Then her eyes snapped open as a child screamed. It was not Danny. She watched a mother rush over to the little girl and, when the hurt had been kissed better, she raised her hand in a little wave. The mother was Milly, one of her newfound friends.

Once, when a little boy had cut his hand on a hidden piece of glass, Kate had decided to avoid the local park. For a few weeks she had put Danny in the car and driven over to Roundhay where there was a proper park with a lake, an aviary and masses of flowers, but inevitably she had returned to the playground. The local park was convenient, only fifteen minutes' walk from her home, but more than that, she missed the company.

Kate enjoyed being a full-time mother but she was a

stranger to Leeds and at times she was lonely. Jack was away weeks at a time and her stepdaughter Helen had become, after Danny's birth, not so much *difficult* as a typical teenager. Increasingly over the past six months she had politely withdrawn herself from Kate's attempts at friendly communication. Her school work had fallen off and her only interests appeared to be pop music, fashion, diets and her giggling girlfriends.

When Jack was home, Kate didn't like to burden him with her problems so when he asked if things were running smoothly, she said yes. She was fine, she loved the house and had good neighbours. All this was true, but . . . Kate sighed.

Mr and Mrs Martin were in their seventies and the Blunts, who had recently moved into the house on the other side of her, were young but definitely high-fliers. They had no children and were out at work all day. The only time she ever saw them was at eight-fifteen each morning when she was collecting the milk from her doorstep. Simon and Gill, at least she knew their names, would dash from their house and give her a friendly wave before jumping into their cars, Simon's a white Peugeot and Gill's a brand new Citroen XM.

Kate, noting Simon's sharp three-piece suit and Gill's sleek hairdo, short skirt, long legs and boxy jacket, would wave back, acutely conscious that she was still in her less-than-immaculate dressing gown.

But at the park there were mothers and over a period of time, she had come to know some of them. There was Milly, a timid woman who had two girls and was married to a policeman, and Tracy who was having matrimonial problems, and Joanie who had twin boys. There was Paula with her two girls, Sally and Laura. Sally was five and Laura was three and had something wrong with her. Kate didn't know why Laura couldn't walk or talk properly and didn't like to ask, but she marvelled at the tender way Sally cared for her sister.

Then there was Pam who had a four-year-old son and who brought a huge labrador to the park with her, tethering it to the post securing the swings. Kate had regarded the dog with caution, until she saw it roll over and whimper with pleasure every time a child was brave enough to go near it. Then there was exotic Tamara, who was of mixed blood and beautiful enough to be a model, but who was an unmarried mother existing on social security. All these women became known to Kate and some of them became friends.

Kate listened to them talk about their lives with interest. Most of them were young, but they had experienced so much. Her life had been secure in comparison. She was the oldest woman in the group, but in many ways she felt the youngest.

Once she was admitted to their circle, they gave her advice. They gave her tips on the best way to deal with teething troubles, told her how *they* coped when their children ran a temperature in the middle of the night. They rejoiced with her over small triumphs: Danny's first smile, his first tooth. And sometimes, if she was lucky, Nicky was at the park and the two of them talked of many things.

Nicky had become her first friend in Leeds and Kate found her fascinating. But Nicky wasn't there today and Kate's neighbour on the bench was a stranger, a woman about forty years old with sharp features and a pile of shopping by her feet.

'Kevin, leave your sister alone. If you don't, I'll belt you.'

Her strident voice made Kate jump.

The woman noticed and shrugged her shoulders. 'Sorry, but it's the only way. Kids! If you don't scream at them, they don't take a blind bit of notice.' She sighed. 'You're lucky your little lad's the age he is – lovely they are when they're tiny. But you just wait a couple of years, he'll drive you mad then.'

Kate did not reply. It was not the first time she had been told this and it always annoyed her. She resented the unspoken implication that her child would grow to be unruly. Danny would be taught manners. She looked at him and caught her breath.

Face screwed up in a mask of determination, Danny was getting to his feet. Kate's hand went to her mouth. Two days ago he had stood up for the first time, but then he had been holding on to a chair arm. This time there was nothing to aid him. Hands on the ground, bottom in the air, he straightened his legs and then, grunting, he came upright. For a moment he stood, wavering like a candle flame in a draught, and then he took a step and then another one. He was heading, not to her, but towards the swings. Kate stood up.

'He's done it. Look, he's walking!' She swung round and smiled at the woman. 'It's the first time.'

'That's grand.' The woman nodded. 'How old is he?'

'Only eleven months.'

'Early.' The woman looked impressed. 'Our Kev didn't walk until he was sixteen months, but then he always was a lazy little sod.'

Kate felt a rush of love for her. This woman understood, she was a mother too.

'You'd best go and get him. If he gets to those swings, those lads will knock his block off.'

'Oh, Lord.' Kate set off after her child. From the rear, Danny looked more like a miniature train driver than a baby less than a year old. In his denim overalls he stumped along the grass. Kate looked at his little round head covered in curling auburn hair and the so-vulnerable white nape of his neck above the 'tough-guy' navy blue sweater and was overwhelmed by a rush of love. She reached him, scooped him up in her arms and kissed the back of his neck. 'You clever boy.'

He stiffened and screamed in frustration, flailing his arms around and catching her a blow on her cheek. She took a firmer hold of him and carried him back to the bench.

'See what you mean about the temper.' The woman studied Danny's scarlet face, the fat tears rolling down his cheeks.

'He's just learned how to walk,' Kate answered defensively. 'Naturally he wants to get about.' She put her hands under Danny's arms and held him down in front of her so that he could kick at the gravel with the tips of his shoes.

'Aye, well. You'll never have a moment of peace from now on, you know. Once they walk, you have to watch 'em every minute.'

Kate bit back the desire to remind the woman of her earlier words. Nothing must spoil this moment, Danny had mastered walking. He was her *toddler* now.

The woman looked at her watch. 'Time I was off. The lord and master'll be wanting his tea.' She shielded her eyes with her hand. 'Kevin, Maxime, come here right now. We're going.'

Her children stopped trying to brain each other with

branches broken from a tree and came skidding up to the bench bringing with them a cloud of dust.

'God, look at the state of you.' Exasperation sharpened their mother's voice. 'Your shoes are filthy, Maxime. You'll get them cleaned as soon as we get home. And where's your schoolbag? As for you,' she caught hold of her son's ear, 'what the hell do you get up to at school? I mended that anorak only last week and I see there's another rip in the sleeve.'

Kevin grinned, unperturbed, showing a gap in his front teeth. 'Can we have beefburgers and chips for tea, Mam?'

'I'll give you beefburgers and chips!' But the woman's voice softened and there was a faint smile on her face as she turned to say goodbye to Kate.

And Kate smiled too when she saw the boy take two bags of shopping from his mum's hands and carry them for her as they left the park.

More mothers were collecting their children and preparing to leave. Kate checked her watch. It was half-past four, too late for Nicky to come now. Also the sun was becoming obscured by drifting grey clouds and a breeze ruffled the leaves on the trees. She stood up.

'Come on, Danny. It's time we went home.'

He had stopped crying. He raised his head and looked at her. He had her eyes, large, widely spaced and hazel in colour. She swung him up in her arms. 'In you go.'

He offered no resistance.

Unlike the other toddlers leaving the park, Danny travelled in style in a proper pram. The regular users of the playground were now accustomed to seeing the pram but originally it had caused comments.

No one used full-sized prams nowadays. Mums pushed buggies or carry-cots on wheels. Proper prams were just not seen any more. If you had enough money to run a car, you bought a push-chair to fit in the boot. If you hadn't much money, maybe lived on the nearby housing estate, you still needed something that would fold up small. Council flats were not spacious.

Kate learned how her pram had thrown up barriers between her and the other mothers. Nicky had told her.

'We couldn't make you out, see? The way you talked, dressed, you *had* to have a car, so why the pram? I mean . . .' Her voice had tailed off.

Kate had nodded. She was different, it was silly to pretend otherwise. She spoke without an accent, wore good clothes and low-heeled shoes. She rarely wore make-up and she was older than the other first-time mums. Yes, she was different . . . but not stuck-up.

As Nicky told her: 'If you'd have put on airs and graces, that would have been it! None of us would ever have talked to you.'

'I'm glad you did.' And because she wanted them to know she was glad they had allowed her into their sisterhood, Kate explained.

'Yes, I've a car, and a pushchair too, but I like to walk and I always said I wanted a proper pram whenever I had a baby of my own. I hate to see tiny babies asleep, hanging out of the straps in those flimsy strollers. They always look so uncomfortable.'

She knew Nicky well enough by then, knew she could tell her the truth, even though her friend didn't have a proper pram. Nicky had a twin buggy in which travelled her five-month-old daughter and fifteen-month-old son. And the buggy was pushed slowly, for alongside Nicky walked her three-year-old, Shawn.

Kate thought Nicky was a marvel. She was a reed-thin twenty-one-year-old with cropped blonde hair and heavily mascaraed eyelashes. Kate's adoptive mother would not have approved of Nicky as a friend for her. She would have seen the bleached hair, the large hoop earrings and the three children under four, and tut-tutted.

But Kate saw more than that and Nicky was her best friend. She was not empty-headed, nor irresponsible, and she was a marvellous mother. She cuddled her little ones and occasionally slapped them. She also listened to them, wiped noses, changed nappies, pulled up pants and bottle-fed with an off-hand expertise which left Kate reeling.

Nicky was intelligent and appeared to do five or six things at once. One day, not long after they had started talking to each other, Kate had seen her spoon baby food into the youngest child's mouth, pluck her second child from what looked like certain death from beneath the wheels of a bike ridden by a young hooligan, and continue in her task of advising Tamara how to fill in social security claim forms.

Another day she had explained to Shawn how caterpillars turned into butterflies in between arguing passionately with Kate over whether private medicine was justified.

Back at home, preparing mashed banana for Danny's tea, writing to Jack or hanging out the washing, Kate found herself wondering about Nicky. For a girl who never stopped talking, she said little about her own life. Just once, she confided she had been advised to stay on at school and had studied for three A-levels.

'But there were seven of us at home.' She had shrugged. 'Every time I had the books spread out on the table it was "Shift over, Nicky, I want to lay Dad's tea", or Karen, my sister, wanting to iron a blouse, or Ben wanting to fill in his pools coupon. It was too much hassle. Then I met Richie.' She joggled her youngest baby on her knee.

'Who knows. Maybe one day . . .'

The last time Kate had spoken to Nicky was five days ago when she had confided she was having trouble with her landlord.

'He's determined to get us out this time. Threatening court action now, but just let him try.' Absent-mindedly, she stuck a plaster on Shawn's bumped knee then placed a careless caressing hand on his crewcut. 'If he does, I've told him I'll counter-claim. The back bedroom's running damp and he won't pay a penny towards repairs.' She had frowned. 'Richie's getting depressed about everything, though.'

It was also rare for Nicky to mention her husband. Kate had no idea what he did for a living and didn't even know where the family lived.

Now, as she pushed the pram through the park gates, she wished she had asked more questions. It's my middle-class upbringing, she thought, and sighed. I'm terrified of being too nosey, too pushy.

Nicky had suffered from no such inhibitions. She knew where Kate lived because she had asked her. She had whistled when Kate had said Routledge Gardens.

'We live at the top end, near the church. It's Routledge Terrace, really.' Kate had hurried out the words, anxious that Nicky would not get the wrong impression. Routledge Gardens was an area noted for the impressive houses which clustered around the bottom of a hill. They were of different styles but all shouted money, being sheltered behind high hedges which gave tantalising glimpses of wide lawns, paved driveways and double garages.

Kate's home was not one of these, but before she could explain Nicky had interrupted her.

'Routledge Gardens, eh?' She had laughed, a sound entirely free from envy. 'I thought Danny's clothes hadn't come from Woolworth's!'

Five days was a long time for Nicky to be missing from the park. Kate's brow furrowed as she waited to cross the road at the traffic lights. She hoped nothing bad had happened.

If only she knew more about Nicky. Why hadn't she asked her friend where she lived? Why had she never asked her round for tea? She had thought about it often enough, but innate shyness had made her hesitant. She had never had a friend like Nicky before, and she was so afraid of spoiling that friendship. She had so much, Nicky so little, and Kate was terrified of appearing a Lady Bountiful. Having Nicky round to the house might sour their friendship.

And what about Helen? She had coped with the unexpected arrival of a baby brother but coming home from school with a friend to find Nicky and three more infants running around the house might upset her. And there was Nicky's husband, why did she never talk about him? Did he have a job, was he respectable? Maybe he was a villain who had been in prison; perhaps that was why Nicky mentioned him so rarely? Kate sighed.

Half-way home it began to rain, heavy drops of water which plopped on to the dark blue pram cover and made round dark patches. Kate put a scarf over her hair and then pulled up the hood of the pram to protect Danny. She ducked her head under it and tickled her son's chin. 'There you are, snug as a bug in a rug.'

From the shadowy interior Danny give his best grin. Kate smiled back at him.

'Wait until Daddy hears about you walking,' she said. Then she paused. The strangely familiar rubbery smell of the pram's interior stirred a memory within her. For a brief moment, *she* was in the pram.

She almost felt the bounce of the well-sprung vehicle moving along the road on smooth wheels, but something was different. Without realising, she shut her eyes and breathed in the special smell. Yes, yes – she was in a pram but it had *two* hoods and there was someone sitting opposite her, someone chortling and banging on the pram cover, just as Danny did.

'Baggah.'

Kate opened her eyes. 'What?'

'Baggh, baggah!' Danny smacked the cover with his fists. His eyes gleamed.

'Yes, you're right. Mummy's being silly. She's day-dreaming.' Kate realised she was getting soaked. Turning up the collar of her coat, she walked on. 'We'll soon be home.'

Routledge Gardens came into view. Despite the weather, Kate felt a surge of happiness as she looked up the hill towards the row of houses at the top. She really loved her home, and tomorrow Jack would be here and at leisure for three lovely long weeks. The worries about Nicky slipped away and even the recollection of the letter she had received yesterday failed to disturb her. The appointment wasn't until Tuesday.

She could pick the right time to discuss the matter with Jack.

'Come on, Danny.' Exerting extra effort, for the hill was steep and Danny was getting heavy, Kate pushed the pram up the hill. There was no one else about, so as she walked she sang: ' "The Grand Old Duke of York, He had ten thousand men . . ." '

And Danny, obliging as ever, chuckled and waved fat fingers in the air, as if beating time to the music.

[illegible]

[illegible] door's locked. I can't [illegible] glancing at [illegible]y. At least he was [illegible]ly. In

Chapter Seventeen

The houses at the top of Routledge Gardens were late-Edwardian. They were tall and narrow in appearance, fronted by stone boundary walls and small flower gardens. A few of the houses retained their original leaded light strips of coloured glass at the top of bay windows and in the front door entrances, and Kate and Jack were lucky enough to own one of these.

But today Kate was not in the mood to admire the leaded lights. She wanted to get indoors, and quickly. She looked up at the bedroom window directly above the front door and, for the third time, shouted loudly.

'Helen, are you there?'

She waited. Her scarf had slipped from her head and water trickled from her wet hair down on to her face.

'Helen!'

At last, there was a movement behind the bedroom curtain. The window opened and Helen's face peeped out.

Kate took a deep breath, modulated her voice and asked, 'Will you please come down and let me in?'

'What?'

'The front door's locked. I can't get in.' She waited, glancing at Danny. At least he was warm and dry. In fact, he had gone to sleep. She thought she heard the sound of Helen's feet on the stairs, but it was difficult to be sure. The thumping noise which youngsters regarded as music nowadays issued from her room, drowning out the possibility of hearing anything else. Kate shifted her feet impatiently. To think *her* parents had considered the Beatles far out!

The door opened.

'Thank goodness.' Kate took hold of the pram's handle. 'Give me a lift in with this.'

There was a sulky droop to Helen's mouth, but she took hold of the pram. 'Sorry, I didn't hear you right away, but you did tell me to keep the doors locked when I was in on my own. Anyway, I thought you'd be using the back way, as usual.'

'In case you haven't noticed, it's pouring down.'

They manhandled the pram into the small, square-shaped hall.

'That will do for now.' Kate took off her wet coat. 'I'll move it later. I'm not wading through a sea of mud just to get to the conservatory.'

The Gallantree family lived in the fourth house along Routledge Terrace. Although the properties were not semi-detached they were well-built, spacious, and occupied a highly desirable position. Every window in Kate's home looked out on a pleasant view.

To one side was an ancient grey stone church. The small graveyard and the surrounding land was bright with flowering shrubs and fine sycamore and chestnut trees marked the church boundaries. From her sitting-room and two of the bedrooms, Kate's view was of the velvet lawns and the large houses at the bottom of the hill, and at the back of the house she overlooked her own long narrow garden and those of her neighbours.

The only drawback to their position, and that was only during bad weather, was the lane which divided the terrace of houses from the church's land, and originally Jack had gloated over its existence.

'No more parking problems, Kate. Lots of space for cars. The church people won't let it be built on and look how natural and pretty it is.'

In good weather, the back lane *was* pretty. The road was only partly made up and in spring and summer wild flowers bloomed there; red campions and wild scabious peeped shyly from the uncut grass verges. But in bad weather the back lane became a quagmire. In the winter months, Kate kept a pair of wellingtons permanently by the back door.

They had bought the house just before their marriage and had got it cheap. The old lady who owned the place had taken a fancy to them and had accepted their first offer, one which they had made tentatively, aware the property was worth much more.

'Aye, you can have it for that.' She had laughed at their shocked expressions. 'I could get more, I suppose, but I don't want any hassle. My lad says it's time I moved in with him, and he's right. I can't look after the place like it needs, and that's a fact. Four bedrooms and lots of stairs are all right when you're young, but when you're seventy-five . . .' She had shaken her head.

'If I hung on, I might be offered more money, but how long would it take? No, now I've decided to go, I want to get on with it. And,' she had looked at them slyly, 'I can see you're right taken with the place?'

'Oh, we are.' Jack had looked at Kate and then back at the old lady. 'We certainly are.'

'Right then, it's yours.' She had put her thin,

wrinkled hand on Kate's arm. 'But you mun look after it properly. You're young, you'll want to alter things, but you mun not rip the heart out of it, mind.'

Kate had covered the old woman's hand with her own. 'That's a promise. Anyway, we like it just the way it is.'

And during the three years they had lived in the house, they had altered very little.

The damp-course had been attended to and they had replaced the window in the back room, which they had designated the dining-room. They had repainted the many built-in cupboards throughout the house a soft white for, like many old ladies, Mrs Richards had favoured dark browns and greys. And then, when they had found out that Kate was pregnant, they had left it just as it was. They had plans for the house, but they could wait.

The only room in the house she actively disliked was the kitchen. It was small and narrow, with a tiny window and insufficient working surfaces. Kate prided herself on her cooking, but not in that kitchen.

'Can't you do something with it?' she had pleaded with Jack.

'It needs a total re-think, Kate, and we haven't the money to gut the place. Buying the house has taken all our capital. I'll do what I can for now, but we'd be better waiting a couple of years and then doing a proper job. For instance, if we knocked down the conservatory, we could extend outwards.'

Kate had reluctantly agreed that they should wait and Jack plumbed in a new sink unit and put up another wall cupboard. She said that made things much easier for her. The truth was, she didn't want the conservatory knocked down. It was a good place in which to keep the pram, and anyway she had her own ideas about the kitchen. If the wall between the kitchen and the dining-room was knocked out, she thought, that would give rise to all kinds of possibilities.

Kate had always lived in *small* places. Her adoptive parents had been comparatively well off, but of a cautious disposition, and the family had adopted a modest lifestyle. When Kate was eleven years old, her father had suffered a financial loss and as he was then approaching sixty, had decided it was time to retire from business.

He had moved his little family three streets away from their former home and they had taken possession of a two-bedroomed, modern and easy-to-run bungalow.

After leaving home, Kate had lived in bedsits. Possessing a natural flair for home-making, she had experimented with wallpapers and paint and had succeeded in turning her temporary homes into attractive living quarters, but it wasn't until she married Jack and they bought 8 Routledge Terrace that her creative instincts had fully flowered. She thought her new home was marvellous.

Fortunately, Jack and Helen had been equally enthusiastic about the house. Jack and his daughter had been living in rented accommodation, a flat close to Jack's only sister's home, so that there was someone to look after Helen when her father was away.

Helen liked living in Routledge Terrace for three reasons. It wasn't near to Auntie Pat's, whom she didn't like, but it was a reasonable bus ride from her school, which she did. The third reason was a bonus – her bedroom at Routledge Terrace was large enough to hold more than just a bed and wardrobe.

'Can I make it my own special place?' she had asked, and Jack and Kate, relieved at the way she had taken the news of their impending marriage, had agreed.

Helen, thanks to their trips to the salerooms, duly acquired a small table, a bookcase, a two-seater settee and a standard lamp. When her music centre and tape deck had been set up, she pronounced herself satisfied.

'I've got a bedsit,' she told her schoolmates, and proved it by inviting a different friend round for coffee practically every night.

Jack liked the house because Kate did and because it signified a new start for him. His parents had lived in a council house all their life and when Jack married, he and his first wife, Felicity, had both been very young. Because money was in short supply, they had lived with Felicity's father during the first year of their marriage, then they had moved into rented accommodation. Jack was an electrician and Felicity had continued her teacher-training course. When Helen had been born, Jack had taken a job on the oil-rigs. It meant he was away for two weeks at a time, but he earned better money.

Felicity had completed her studies and when Helen was eighteen months old, had started teaching five-year-olds at the local primary school. She was an excellent teacher and also good at administrative work. Within four years she was deputy head of the infants school and then, at last, they were able to save money. By the time Helen was seven, they had saved six thousand pounds and were asking estate agents to send them details of likely houses. Then, just before

Helen's eighth birthday, Felicity was one of a handful of people in Leeds who contracted meningitis. Two weeks later she was dead.

Because he had a daughter, and because he had to, Jack had continued his life. He worked hard and tried to be both mother and father to Helen and a dutiful son to his parents. When first his mother and then his father died, he was devastated and his life became a bleak treadmill. Only his daughter could make him smile. And then he had met Kate and had begun to live again.

Kate knew Jack's first marriage had been happy and she had no problem with that, but sometimes she felt she had a lot to live up to. Listening to Helen and Jack reminisce, she realised Felicity had been a woman with many talents.

From nineteen until the age of thirty-three, Kate had worked as a librarian, not a record to be compared favourably with Jack's first wife's. But then, still listening to Jack and Helen, Kate realised she had skills Felicity had lacked. Jack's first wife had loved her husband and daughter, but she had been career-oriented; housework and cooking had bored her.

The knowledge had bolstered Kate's self-esteem. She couldn't speak a foreign language or balance books, but she could cook and bake and see the potential of their new home.

Once safely installed in 8 Routledge Terrace, she had scoured salerooms for Edwardian furniture, old prints, anything that suited the house. She chased up the 'For Sale' ads in the evening paper, bought heavy brocade curtains for one bedroom, adapted a set of crystal lustres from an old vase into a central light-fitting for the hall and purchased a shabby chaise-longue which she had re-covered and which now held pride of place in the sitting-room.

Kate loved this room, loved the splayed bay windows, the corniced ceiling and beautiful original fireplace. Behind the living-room was a smaller, square-shaped room with a delicately moulded ceiling, and behind that the dining-room.

'It just goes on and on,' she had gloated to Jack when they had first inspected the property.

'Extra work for you,' he had warned.

'I don't care.' And she didn't, even though the arrival of Daniel had curtailed her more grandiose plans for their home.

During the evenings when Jack was away, Kate liked nothing better than curling up in her large, rose-patterned chair, the one she had purchased from Frinton's salerooms for forty pounds, and studying books and magazines for ideas about materials, patterns and colours for her home.

But there'd be no time for that this evening. She wanted the place spick and span for Jack's arrival tomorrow. Leaving Danny asleep in his pram she walked into the kitchen, looked round and sighed.

The place was a mess. A pile of dirty laundry was dumped by the washer, the floor needed washing and Helen must have entertained friends – there were used cups and plates on the draining board. Not only that, Kate was guiltily aware that the whole house had a neglected air about it.

She was normally houseproud, but since receiving the letter from the Social Services department, had found it hard to concentrate on anything. And Danny had been particularly demanding of her attention since yesterday. She now realised that although she had bought in steak and all the trimmings for the meal tomorrow, she hadn't thought about tonight's meal. She looked in her store cupboard.

It would have to be ham and salad. Luckily there was a tin of ham on the shelf and there was always heaps of salad stuff in the fridge. After eating nothing but hamburgers for several weeks, Helen had recently eschewed junk food. Kate was pleased about her step-daughter's change of diet, but just hoped Helen wouldn't decide to become a vegetarian yet, as many of her friends were. Kate sympathised with the girls' principles, she didn't like to think about slaughter-houses, but neither did she relish the thought of cooking separate meals for Helen as well as for Danny.

She opened the tin of ham, cut bread and butter, washed and prepared the salad stuff and then called Helen down.

They ate their meal.

'Can I go round to Eileen's tonight?' Having refused bread and butter which she said was fattening, Helen put two spoonfuls of sugar into her second cup of tea and without waiting for Kate's answer, went to the biscuit barrel for a chocolate biscuit.

Kate put down her knife and fork. 'I was hoping you'd give me a hand tonight. Maybe hoover upstairs or something? You know I like things nice for your dad coming home but they've got a bit out of hand.'

Helen gave her a stare which asked 'Whose fault's that?' She bit into her second biscuit. 'But Eileen was going to help me with my chemistry homework. It has to be handed in tomorrow.'

'Can't I help?' Kate forced a smile. 'A sort of exchange – you hoover the bedrooms, I'll help with the homework.'

'You can't. What do you know about the influence of lightning on hydrogen or what a trilobite is?'

Helen's tone of voice verged on the insolent but there was nothing Kate could say because she was right. Not for the first time she wished her stepdaughter's talents had been in the Arts. A discussion of a character from *Pride and Prejudice* or *Vanity Fair* she could have coped with. But Helen's mind had a scientific bent which left Kate floundering.

'You'd better go to Eileen's then,' she heard herself saying.

'Great.' Helen crammed the rest of the biscuit into her mouth.

'But wash up first.'

'Oh . . .'

'I mean it, Helen.' Kate's voice was firm, the more so when she heard Danny begin to cry. She stood up. 'It will only take five minutes.'

'Well, why can't you do it then?' mumbled Helen, but Kate did not hear. She was lifting Danny from his pram.

With a sullen expression, Helen collected up the dirty plates.

'What do you think of Mr Morrison?'

Helen and Eileen were sprawled across Eileen's bed eating sweets and glancing through magazines.

'He's all right.' Helen answered Eileen's question cautiously. Mr Morrison had recently joined the staff at school. He was a maths teacher and had taught Helen for the first time that day. Really sarcastic, he had been. She hated sarcasm and privately thought Morrison was the pits. He was tall and thin and his adam's apple shot up and down his scrawny neck when he swallowed, which he did often. She thought he was scared of girls.

'He's got dreamy eyes.' Eileen propped her chin on her hands. 'He reminds me of Mick Jagger – when Mick was younger, of course.'

Helen looked at her incredulously. Was Eileen serious? She saw that she was. 'Yes,' she agreed, 'especially around the mouth.' She flicked over the page of her magazine and unwrapped another toffee. They were Eileen's toffees. Eileen could eat like a pig and never get fat, but Helen shouldn't be eating them, only she needed comfort. There was definitely a spot blooming on her chin and the knowledge depressed her.

'I think I'm beginning to prefer older men.' Eileen put down her magazine. 'Boys of our age are so infantile. Older men know how to treat a woman. Mind you,' she chuckled, 'my dad's still got some of the Stones' records, which is a bit off-putting, when you think about it.'

Helen didn't think all the boys at school were infantile, in fact she would have *died* for a date with Ben Raymond, but she'd never admit it. 'I know what you mean,' she said.

'What do you think of this?' Eileen had picked up her magazine again. She pointed to a model wearing a vivid green suit with a pencil-slim skirt and a jacket with a pinched-in waist.

'Um . . . it's OK.' She'd never, *ever* be able to wear anything like that, her hips were too wide. Was that why Eileen had showed it to her? Helen looked at her friend suspiciously. Eileen was a size ten. 'Bit too old for us.'

'Yeah.' Eileen nodded her head. 'You're right. It

would look good on somebody like your stepmum, though.'

Helen laughed. 'She'd never wear anything like that.' But when she looked at the picture again, she saw what Eileen meant. Kate would look good in the suit. The model actually looked a bit like Kate. Her stepmother didn't wear false eyelashes and scarlet lipstick and she didn't stand with her hip stuck out, like the model did, but she was straight and slim with greenish-brown eyes and a lovely creamy complexion. She wasn't tall enough to be a model, of course, but somehow, she looked tall.

Helen sighed. Kate never had spots, or greasy hair, or walked about with slumped shoulders. Seeking comfort, she took another toffee and then spoke with her mouth full.

'Kate doesn't wear tight clothes. She says she likes clothes that move with her. And since Danny arrived, she doesn't dress up much.'

'Danny.' Eileen flopped flat on the bed and rolled her eyes. 'I don't know how you bear having a baby brother, Helen. It's bad enough for me, having an eight-year-old sister.'

'It's not so bad.' Helen scowled. 'He's a good baby and doesn't cry much.'

'I know, but,' Eileen shuddered, 'it's so *embarrassing*.'

Helen was silent. Of course Eileen was right. It wasn't nice to think of Kate and her dad doing that in bed together. But embarrassing or not, her dad was undeniably happier nowadays. And at least Kate wasn't terribly young, not like Pam Walker's new stepmother who was twenty-two. In fact, because Dad was so happy and bubbling with life, it was almost as if

Kate was older than him. Helen dislodged a piece of her toffee from a back tooth and ruminated. Kate was all right most of the time, although she was a bit prim occasionally.

As for Danny, Helen thought of him when he was in his bath, splashing about with his toys and crowing and giggling, and her insides developed a queer feeling, almost an ache. Abruptly, she changed the subject. 'What are you wearing for the half-term disco?'

Eileen told her, in great detail. When all the toffees had gone, Helen realised it was almost ten o'clock.

'I'll have to go.'

'OK.' Eileen rolled off the bed. 'Shall I walk you?'

'No, there's no need.'

Eileen lived in one of the large houses nestled at the bottom of the hill in Routledge Gardens. Her mother did 'good works' and her father was an accountant. He was a red-faced man who drank a lot of whisky and always draped his arm round Helen's shoulder in a too familiar way when he saw her. He was coming out of the kitchen with an unopened bottle in his hand when the girls came down the stairs.

'Had a good time, girls?' He paused at the bottom of the stairs. 'Beats me what you find to talk about.'

'Yes, thank you.' Helen flattened herself against the wall as she passed him. 'Eileen's been helping me with my chemistry homework.'

'Chemistry, chemistry . . .' He blinked at her owlishly. 'You don't want to bother with stuff like that. What does a pretty lass like you want with chemistry?'

'Helen's going now, Dad.'

She saw the red spots of colour on Eileen's cheeks and felt sorry for her. She grinned nervously, 'Good night, Mr Abbey.'

'Do you want a lift home?'

'Oh, no. I only live five minutes' walk away.'

'Oh, yes. I remember.' He swayed. 'What's the name of your house?'

'It hasn't got a name. I live at 8 Routledge Terrace.'

'Oh, at the top, you mean?'

'That's right.' Helen gave Eileen a little wave, side-stepped Mr Abbey and escaped.

As she walked home, she remembered with a thrill of pleasure that her dad would be home tomorrow. She thought of Mr Abbey and shuddered. Eileen and her sister had heaps of clothes and all the latest pop tapes and records but they had a lousy dad. All that guff about house names, it was pathetic.

The houses at the bottom of the hill didn't have numbers, they were too posh. Instead they had names: Mountjoy, Cornerstones or The Larches. Eileen's house was called Merryvale, but Helen didn't think there'd be much merriment living with Mr Abbey. No wonder Mrs Abbey sat on a lot of committees.

It was really dark now and Helen quickened her steps. She wasn't frightened, but it would have been nice to have company. Not Mr Abbey's though. What would she feel like if Ben Raymond was walking next to her? Her steps slowed for a moment and then quickened. It was no good daydreaming, Ben would never ask her out, especially when she had a spot as big as a tennis ball on her chin. With heavy heart, she trudged the rest of the way home.

'Had a nice time?' Kate's voice floated out of the dining-room.

'Yes, thanks.' Helen paused in the doorway.

'Eileen sorted you out?'

'What?' She remembered the homework. 'Oh, yes.' She dug a floating piece of long-forgotten information out of her memory. 'Did you know, Kate, that flowers appeared about one hundred million years ago?'

'Good gracious, as long ago as that?'

'Yes.' It was easy to impress Kate. She often said herself that she hadn't been very bright at school. Helen felt superior until she noticed the smudges of tiredness beneath her stepmother's eyes. She came further into the room.

'Why are you doing that now?' She gestured to the upright ironing board and the pile of clothes on the chair.

'They needed doing. I don't want to be working tomorrow, when your dad's here, and Danny goes through clothes like there's no tomorrow.'

Helen fingered a tiny sock, bright green in colour with a red engine printed across the foot. 'Mrs Brown at number twenty says she never irons the children's clothes. She says it's a waste of time.'

'What Mrs Brown does is her business, what I do is mine. Anyway,' Kate gave a faint smile, 'Mrs Brown has three boys. I have only the one.'

Helen put the sock back on the pile. 'Would you like another baby?'

Kate stood the iron on its heel. It spat out a puff of steam which sounded loud in the sudden quiet of the room.

'I don't know. At the moment, Danny's enough for me.'

'Oh.' A tide of red had washed over Helen's face. What on earth had made her ask such a naff question? She shuffled her feet. 'I'll hoover upstairs tomorrow, if I wake up in time.'

'Thanks.' Kate had picked up the iron again. 'That

would be nice, but I won't hold you to it.'

They both laughed, knowing how soundly Helen slept.

'Night, then.'

'Night, Helen.'

She went up to her bedroom. She noticed Kate had drawn the curtains and switched on the standard lamp which had a pink shade. She looked round, at the patchwork bedspread on her bed and the poster of Boy George on the wall. Her bedroom was better than Eileen's, for all its frills and flounces.

She undressed and went to the bathroom to wash and check on the spot. It was no larger. Then she got into bed and picked up the photograph of her mother which stood on the table by her bed. She still missed her, of course, but not so much now. She looked at her mother's shining fair hair and full-lipped mouth. Helen was supposed to resemble her but she couldn't see it herself. She thought maybe the spot might go away before the disco, especially if she bought some stuff from the chemist tomorrow.

Chapter Eighteen

'Come on, Danny.'

Kate dipped a toast soldier into the soft yolk of the egg and pretended to eat it. As she did so, she glanced at the clock. Nine forty-five, and still Danny hadn't finished his breakfast.

'Mummy eat it – yum yum!' She rolled her eyes and smacked her lips. Danny watched her thoughtfully and then put out his hand and reached for the toast. She gave it to him. He examined it, put it to his mouth and then, chortling with laughter, threw it at her. The soggy end hit her on the chest before dropping to the floor. Kate looked at the sticky yellow stain on the front of her sweater and shouted at him.

'You naughty, naughty boy. Look what a mess you've made.'

The laughter faded. A look of uncertainty crossed his face and then his eyes shut and his mouth opened wide.

'Oh, no, please don't.'

But he did. Full-blooded howls filled the air.

Kate wanted to howl, too – or go back to bed and start again. What a disastrous morning it had been.

Last night, after Helen had left to visit her friend, she had worked furiously. She had put the dirty washing in the machine, scrubbed the kitchen floor and removed the pram from the hallway, wheeling it round to the conservatory where she had scrubbed the mud from the wheels. Then she had returned to the hall, mopped and cleaned it, then hoovered and polished her way through every room on the ground floor. Finally, when the ironing was finished and Helen had gone to bed, she had taken a long, leisurely bath and washed her hair.

She had fallen into bed tired but content.

Both she and Helen had overslept the next morning. After a panicky half-hour, Helen had dashed off to school without eating breakfast and in a bad temper, and Kate, going into the dining-room to fetch Danny's high chair, had discovered that during the night, there had been a fall of soot.

The fireplace was knee deep in the stuff, and every picture, every ornament, every item of furniture, was covered with a dark, gritty coating. She had grabbed the high chair and backed out of the room, coughing. It must have been the heavy overnight rain, she thought. She remembered the sound had awakened her in the early hours of the morning.

She cursed herself for her lack of foresight. They had never thought to have the chimney swept. There was a wall-mounted gas heater in the dining-room which they had used whenever the weather was cold. They had presumed Mrs Richards had used it too, but from the amount of soot in the fireplace, it seemed the old lady had preferred a coal fire.

Kate had tiptoed upstairs. Danny was still sleeping. She dressed in an old pair of jeans and a baggy black sweater. As an afterthought, she grabbed her shower cap and put that on too. It might help keep her hair clean. Then she hurried downstairs, collected a shovel, dustpan and brush and set to work.

She was carrying the second bucket of soot through the conservatory and out into the garden when she heard Danny. In the mornings, he was not prepared to sit quietly in his cot and play. As soon as he awakened he wanted company and made it plain he was not prepared to wait for it.

Kate dumped the soot, rushed indoors, kicked off her wellingtons and went upstairs. 'Just a minute, pet.'

In the bathroom, looking in the mirror and grimacing at the black streaks of soot on her face, she ran the hot water tap and began to wash her hands. The new bar of soap she had put out last night lost its pristine whiteness and turned a dirty grey, and in the small bedroom Danny's protesting voice rose in volume.

'Just a *minute*.'

Her hands were clean but she'd have to leave her face for he was hiccupping now. If she didn't go to him immediately he would be sick and then all his bedding would have to be washed. She'd have to resemble a chimney sweep for a little longer. She rinsed and dried her hands and hurried into Danny's bedroom.

Her piebald face shocked him into silence and he allowed her to pick him out of his cot without a scene, but once downstairs he had become a little fiend. He was now throwing the remainder of his toast fingers on to the floor and screaming. On her knees, scraping up the mess, Kate didn't hear the sound of a key turning the lock of the front door. It was only when Jack spoke that she jumped and looked round.

'Oh, it's you!' She stared and tears of frustration sprang into her eyes. 'I thought you'd be home about noon.'

Her husband halted in the doorway to the kitchen

and surveyed the scene before him. 'I know you did.' To be audible over his son's yells, he had to raise his voice but his expression remained humorous. 'Shall I go out and come in again?' Without waiting for a reply he strode into the kitchen and hoisted Danny from his chair. 'Pack it in, Danny, there's a good boy.'

Abruptly, the cries ceased. Eyeball to eyeball, father and son studied each other. Then Danny grinned and grabbed at Jack's hair.

'He's got egg all over his fingers,' warned Kate, rising from her knees. She deposited the mashed-up fingers of toast on the draining board and gave her husband an embarrassed smile.

'It doesn't matter.' Jack joggled Danny up and down, talking to her over the baby's head. 'The weather forecast was bad so it was decided the 'copter should set off earlier than planned. Then, as luck would have it, we managed to get an earlier flight to Aberdeen.'

'Oh!' Kate began to rub her hands on her jeans and then, remembering, picked up a dishcloth and used that instead. All she really wanted to do was go to Jack and hug him but she recalled how filthy she was and suddenly she felt a little shy. It was ridiculous, she knew, and yet she couldn't help it. They had been married for three years now, but half that time he was away from her and her life revolved round Danny, Helen and her women friends. Then suddenly Jack was back, filling space with his masculine presence.

Feeling a tiny flutter in her throat, she looked at her husband's tall, lean frame. She noted his hair needed cutting and that there were lines of tiredness around his deep brown eyes, the eyes that were looking at her so intently. She swallowed.

'Are you hungry? Do you want me to cook you something?'

'No, I've eaten, thanks.' Jack continued to stare at her and then he said, 'Kate, what have you got on your head?'

Colour flooded her face. She snatched off the shower cap and her soft shining hair fell about her filthy face. 'It's a shower cap. I forgot. We've had a fall of . . .' Her voice wobbled. 'Oh, Jack, why did you have to arrive *now*, when everything's such a mess?'

'Hey, what's all this?' He moved Danny on to his left arm, came close to Kate and pulled her towards him with his right hand. He held her close. 'You're glad to see me, aren't you?'

'You know I am.' She leaned her forehead on his shoulder. He smelt of pipe tobacco and strong soap. She closed her eyes. 'But I wanted things nice for your return, and instead . . .'

'Everything's fine.' He loosened his grasp on her so that he could tilt up her face with his free hand. 'I'm home, you and Danny are here to welcome me, and presumably Helen is safe and well and at school? What else matters?'

Kate rubbed her nose, not realising she was smudging still further the patches of soot on her face. 'Nothing really, but I worked so hard yesterday and then when I got up this morning, I discovered there'd been a fall of soot in the dining-room, and then Danny turned awkward, and then . . .'

'I came.' There was a grin on Jack's face now. He tickled Danny's tummy and put him back in his high chair. 'Quit worrying.' He shrugged off his jacket and rolled up his shirt sleeves. 'I'll sort out the dining-room. You get this young man washed and dressed. Then . . .' he paused.

'Then what?'

'Then you need a bath!' His grin widened. 'I'll wash your back for you, if you like. In fact,' he touched her cheek, 'I could do with a bath myself, it's been a long journey. What about us sharing the tub?'

Kate blushed and smiled. 'But what about Danny?'

'He can come too.' Jack raised his eyebrows at her expression. 'He'll be all right. He can play with his toys on the bathroom floor, can't he?'

She hesitated. 'I don't know . . .'

'Oh, come on.' Jack slipped his arm around her waist. 'I missed you, Kate, and you look quite fetching with soot all over your face, a bit like a baby panda.'

She laughed, reached up and put her arms around his neck. 'I've missed you, too. All right, after we've got the soot shifted.'

'It's a deal.' He kissed her, a kiss which dispelled her initial feeling of shyness and sent a tingle through her body. 'There's just one thing.'

'What?'

'Don't wear the shower cap!'

Helen came home from school to a scene of snug domesticity. Looking through the open door into the sitting-room, she saw Danny engrossed in building up stacks of large wooden bricks and knocking them down again and her father asleep in front of the television. So she went through to the kitchen, where Kate was busy preparing the vegetables for the evening meal.

Helen, watching her stepmother roll up potato peelings in a sheet of old newspaper, experienced a feeling of sympathetic benevolence. What a totally boring existence middle-aged people led. How awful to have used up the exciting bit of your life and have nothing to look forward to other than growing old.

Kate smiled at her. 'Had a good day?'

'Not bad.' She dropped her school bag on the floor. 'Want a hand?'

Kate's eyes opened wide in amazement but then she shook her head. 'No, thanks all the same, I've just about finished. Go and talk to your dad.'

'I was going to, but he's asleep.' Helen wandered over to the cooker, fished a piece of raw carrot out of a pan and ate it absent-mindedly, wondering whether to tell Kate her stupendous news. Her stepmother was looking good today, she thought, all flushed and smiling.

'Poor Jack.' Kate concentrated on slicing tomatoes. 'I'm not surprised he's having a nap. He's been up all night, remember, and it's a long drive from Aberdeen to Leeds.'

Helen nodded. Her father's life-style was well known to her. Ever since she could remember, he had worked on oil-rigs. When she was small, there had been times when she had resented his absences; when he missed the school play, for example, or the time she had broken her arm. When that had happened, he had requested a flight home, switching shifts with another man so he could arrive quickly, but he hadn't been there for her when it happened. Still, Mum had been with her, of course.

The worst time had been after her mother's death, when he had left her with Auntie Pat and gone back to the rig. She had hated him then and had let him know it, too. He had looked at her, his face all drawn and sad.

'Life goes on, Helen, and we have to go on with it.

I've got to work to keep us both, and you have to try and get along with Pat.'

She *had* tried, but not very hard, because Auntie Pat was bossy and mean and totally devoid of humour. Helen had often wondered how two totally different people, like her dad and his sister, could be born of the same parents. She had talked it over with Eileen who had said maybe her grandma had enjoyed a 'bit on the side'. Remembering her grandmother, Helen had almost choked to death on her lunchtime sandwich.

Still, things evened out. If Auntie Pat had been nice, she'd have been more upset when Dad told her he planned on remarrying. She had met Kate by then, of course, and thought she was all right, though she didn't fancy her as a stepmother. But when she realised it meant she wouldn't have to stay with Auntie Pat when her dad was away, she had given them her blessing.

And Kate was better for knowing. She was fair about things and hadn't asked Helen to call her Mum. Actually, to start with she had been more nervous of about having a stepdaughter than Helen had been about gaining a stepmother, so things had worked out OK. Helen took another piece of carrot and bit into it contentedly. Life was pretty good.

'If you eat any more of those carrots, there won't be enough for dinner.'

'Vegetables taste better when they're raw, and they're good for you.' Helen smiled.

'You're in a good mood.' A few strands of Kate's shining cap of hair had fallen forward. She pushed them back impatiently behind her ear and gave Helen a keen look.

'Yes, I am.' But her smile wavered a little. Kate's hair was *always* shining with health, just like the models in the hair-spray ads. Helen's never did, despite the numerous sprays and conditioners she used. A touch of gloom pervaded her inner happiness as she studied her stepmother. When Kate was off-colour or tired she looked ordinary, and when she was happy, which she obviously was today, she looked extraordinarily pretty.

It wasn't as if she had one enormously beautiful feature, thought Helen, it was just *everything*. Today Kate's eyes sparkled, there was a peachy glow to her clear skin, and of course she never had spots. Helen touched her chin with her fingertips. It was all right, she couldn't feel any lumps. Again, she remembered her good fortune.

'There's going to be a disco at school, at half-term.'

'Oh?' Kate had taken down a stack of dinner plates. The best ones, Helen noticed.

'Yes.'

'Are you going?'

'Well, I wasn't sure . . .' Helen was unable to suppress her smile, 'but I think I will.' She paused. 'Ben Raymond walked home with me. He asked if he could take me.'

Kate put the plates down and, putting her head on one side, gave Helen an old-fashioned look.

'Ben Raymond? He's the boy you like, isn't he?'

'He's not bad.' Helen gave a non-committal shrug. 'Trouble is, I haven't a thing to wear.'

'Helen, your wardrobe's stuffed full of clothes.'

'Yes, but none of them's right.'

'Well, if Ben's taking you,' Kate had turned back to her cooking, 'I suppose something new is in order.'

She gave Helen a nod. 'Better have a word with your dad.'

She returned to the sitting-room. This time she had no compunction about waking her father.

The evening meal was consumed in an atmosphere of family conviviality. Jack told Kate the steak was delicious and the whole meal superior to anything he ate on the oil-rig. She smiled a little shyly, remembering their joint bathing session. Helen tucked into her food, secure in the knowledge she would get a new outfit for the disco, and Danny didn't spit anything on to the floor.

Jack and Helen washed up and then she went upstairs and did her homework. Having been informed of Danny's exceptional walking prowess, Jack took his son for a stroll round the garden and later, when Danny had been bathed and put to bed, the three of them watched an old Bette Davis film on the television.

Kate was a sucker for old films. She shed a few tears during the closing reels but no one made fun of her. Jack put his arm around her shoulder, and Helen . . . Kate thought she must be growing up at last because when Bette said goodbye to her lover with one last brave smile, Helen didn't make one sarcastic comment. Instead, she turned suspiciously red, muttered something about making a cup of tea and suddenly retreated to the kitchen.

Kate and Jack raised eyebrows at each other and then he queried, 'You two getting on all right?'

'Couldn't be better.' Kate snuggled up to him, dismissive of last week's row about mislaid homework and the even noisier row last Saturday when Helen had demanded the right to attend an all-night party at York.

'You've no right to dictate to me,' she had shouted. 'You're not my mother. You can't tell me what to do!' She had flounced out of the house with the parting shot that if she didn't go, she would become a laughing stock at school. 'Everyone's going, everyone.'

When Kate, after a sleepless night, had rung round the other mothers, she had discovered not *everyone* was going to York. In fact, only two girls from the seven families Kate contacted had been given permission.

But she wasn't going to mention that upset, particularly not tonight, when everything and everyone had been in perfect accord.

And, surprisingly, the delightful rapprochement lasted throughout the weekend.

On Saturday Helen went off swimming with her friends and Kate and Jack spent a quiet day at home. After a lazy morning, they gardened a little and then took themselves off for a pub lunch, sitting in the garden behind the pub so that Danny could toddle around and explore. And, on Sunday, the whole family had a day out at Temple Newsam Park.

Helen had been undecided. 'Bit boring, isn't it?'

'I don't think so. There's the house to look round, and the farm, and the grounds are lovely.'

'All right for Danny, he'll like the baby animals, but . . .' Helen had pulled at her lip. 'What can I do?'

'You said you wanted to keep your tan going and it's a lovely day.' Kate was busy packing a picnic. 'We'll sunbathe.'

So Helen, having nothing better to do, went with them.

They walked through Elm and Oak Wood, Danny burbling happily in his pushchair, and admired the deer and the Cascade. They visited the Park Farm and looked at the many and varied animals and fowl kept there. Helen was one of the first to exclaim over the newborn litter of spotted piglets. They toured the cattle sheds and patted the cows and finally found a sheltered, secluded area in which to eat their picnic.

Helen, a piece of cooked chicken in one hand, a can of Coke in the other, flopped down on the short-cut, sweet-smelling turf with a sigh of satisfaction. 'This is nice.'

'I told you it was.' Kate had Danny trapped between her knees and was attempting to put on his bib. 'We're lucky the weather held up.'

'It's always good weather when I'm home.' Jack sat down next to Helen, took his sun-glasses out of his pocket and put them on. 'I order it especially.'

'Oh, you,' she laughed.

He waved his hand. 'It's true. How often do you get a day like this in October?'

It was a glorious day. The nearby flower beds were ablaze with yellow and bronze chrysanthemums and over to the left of them a clump of elm trees were pure gold. The sky above was stainless blue and a mellow sun poured down on them its warming rays.

Although the car park testified there were other visitors to the park, and the farm had been crowded, where they were now was peaceful; apart from an elderly couple walking round the flower gardens, they were alone.

They ate and drank, and gradually conversation ceased. After his minced chicken sandwich and bottle of juice, Danny went to sleep on Kate's jacket. His mother, watching him, thought he looked good enough to eat. His thick, curly eyelashes quivered as he dreamed and his button nose was freckled and sun-flushed. She looked from him to her husband.

Jack, his newspaper folded small, was working on the crossword puzzle. He tapped his pen against his chin and asked, 'Another word meaning satisfaction, beginning with "s"?'

'Sensual,' said Helen.

'Serenity,' said Kate.

Jack counted. 'You're right, Kate. It's an eight-letter word, sensual's only got seven.'

'Sensual's more appropriate,' said Helen.

Kate blushed and hoped they didn't notice. It was silly to suppose Helen didn't think about things like sex and sensuality. At fourteen and fifteen, that's what girls and boys *did* think about, all the time. She hadn't, not that early, but then her mother had been old-fashioned in many ways. Kate had learned about the facts of life from schoolmates. She stole a glance at Jack beneath lowered eyelashes.

Apart from a few fumbled exchanges during her early twenties, Kate's experience of sex had been woefully neglected until she met him. She smiled to herself, remembering. She had been so worried because Jack was a widower and she had so little experience and yet, from the very beginning, their sex life had been totally fulfilling. She had never realised how powerful love could be, how it could transform life. She thought about Helen's word and the one she had chosen. Sensual and serenity – yes, she had been lucky enough to find both in her life with Jack.

Unconsciously, her eyebrows drew together. That was, she had until the last few months. And now, because of her actions, there was the letter, lying in the drawer of the dressing-table like a guilty secret. She must tell Jack about the letter soon. The appointment was for Tuesday.

From previous conversations she knew he would be

upset and probably angry. He was reasonable about everything except this. He had told her he didn't understand.

'If you are as happy as you say you are, why keep chasing the past?'

And she couldn't find the words to explain, but the *need* was there, like a festering wound that would never heal until it was exposed to light and air. Until she did that, true serenity would escape her.

She turned and looked at Danny. How peaceful he looked, and yet it was his birth that had triggered the whole thing off. As she watched him, he stirred and muttered, and Helen, who was getting a little bored, suggested: 'Shall we pack up? I thought you wanted to go round the house before we left?'

'Give him five more minutes.' Kate drew up her knees and hugged them with her arms. It was such a peaceful place, warm, quiet, utterly still; she wanted to stay, hold on to the moment. But then she shivered for the idea suddenly occurred to her that the stillness was because nature was holding her breath. Autumn warmth and colour was all about them, comforting, reassuring, but nature knew the peace was transitory, winter was coming.

Chapter Nineteen

On Monday morning Kate showed Jack her letter. She watched him read it and knew from the tiny white lines that appeared at the corners of his mouth that he was angry. She sat quietly and waited for him to speak.

With studied care he refolded the sheet of paper and returned it to her, then asked, 'How long has it taken you to get to this stage?'

She hesitated. 'I enquired about searching four months ago, but I sent the application form away at the end of August.'

'How did you know what to do?'

'A woman at the public library told me to enquire at the Social Services department. Jack, I . . .'

'And now you've an appointment to see a counsellor?' Jack's lips compressed into a straight line. 'You'll pour out your heart to a perfect stranger, but you couldn't even tell *me* what you were doing?'

'I was going to tell you, at the right time, but the letter came and . . .'

'Ah, yes, the letter.' He leaned forward in his chair. 'Tell me, Kate, if the appointment had been arranged for a time I was away, would you have told me about it?'

'I – I don't know.'

His silence forced her to speak again, to try and explain.

'I knew you wouldn't like it, and as there was a good chance nothing would come from the enquiries, I decided not to worry you. If they did manage to trace any of my relatives, I'd tell you straight away, of course, but I don't suppose they will.'

'Oh, come on.' He ran his fingers through his thick blond hair. 'If they've given you an appointment, it must mean they've found out something.'

'No, it doesn't work like that. I've read leaflets. They ask you to go for counselling at the beginning, to make perfectly sure you know what you're getting into.'

'Do they? Well, if that's the case, go with my blessing.'

Kate reached across the breakfast table and rested her hand on her husband's arm. 'Please, Jack, try and understand. I'm nervous about this afternoon. I could do with a bit of support.'

'Then why do this? Why ferret about in the past? What's wrong with the present?' He moved his arm away. 'You've known since your twenties that you were an adopted child and you never did anything about it. Why now, Kate? You've got me and Danny, aren't we enough for you?'

That was it, she knew. It was hurt that was making him so difficult. She clasped her hands in front of her on the table and spoke slowly and carefully, willing him to believe her. 'I love you and Danny more than life itself, Jack. I love Helen, too, but I *have* to do this. It's just . . . I can't really explain to you why. I know many adopted people have no curiosity about their beginnings. I was like that myself, until Danny was born, but then I changed and there's nothing I can do about it. I've tried, I really have, but it's no good. I need to know where I came from.'

He shook his head, baffled. 'It's now that matters, and the future. Why on earth does it matter where you were born and who your parents were?'

He would never understand. Kate tried desperately to find the right words, but before she could speak again there came a wail from upstairs. Danny was awake. She jumped up.

'I'd better fetch him down.' By the door she paused, looking at his stern face. 'Bear with me over this, Jack, please. It's something I must do. And believe me, whether I find out anything or not, it will never alter how I feel about you.'

Her eyes suspiciously damp, she ran upstairs and said good morning to her son. However, ten minutes later when she carried Danny into the kitchen, her low spirits rose for Jack had brewed a fresh pot of tea and was busy making toast. She smiled at him. 'Thanks.'

He nodded back without smiling and asked abruptly, 'Would you like me to go with you?'

His words surprised her and she paused before answering, phrasing her reply carefully. Her husband may have conceded a truce but she knew she had not won the battle. Jack still couldn't or wouldn't conceive *why* she was making the enquiries.

She fitted Danny into his chair before speaking. Would she ever be able to make him understand? It was unlikely, for how could she explain her motives when she didn't fully understand them herself?

'It's a thought, but it would be more help if you looked after Danny for me. I don't suppose I'll be at the Social Services office for long. We could meet up afterwards.'

'Just as you want.' He poured out two cups of tea,

sat down and hid himself behind the morning newspaper.

She looked at him, wanting to snatch the paper from his grasp and sit on his knee, reassure him he had nothing to fear, but she did nothing. If she went to him now he would think he could dissuade her, and he couldn't. Kate suppressed a sigh.

He was suffering from hurt pride but he had made a gesture of support and she appreciated that. And at least he now knew about her enquiries. It had been awful keeping things from him.

She began to prepare Danny's breakfast. Secrets were funny things – they could be nice, a surprise present or a trip to the theatre – but they could also be unpleasant. She had never felt comfortable keeping secrets from people. She finished pouring orange juice into Danny's feeder mug and fitted on the lid. As she did so, she wondered what would happen at tomorrow's meeting. Had they any information for her? Would secrets be revealed, and if so, would they be happy or unhappy ones?

'Come in, Mrs Gallantree.' The woman ushering Kate into her office had a warm, mellow voice and a welcoming smile.

Part of the service? wondered Kate, with a touch of cynicism. Presumably, counsellors were trained in the art of setting people at their ease. Pity it wasn't working on her yet. The counsellor took her place behind the desk and Kate sat down and tried to place her hands in a position which disguised the fact they were trembling.

'Would you like a cup of coffee or tea, perhaps?' The counsellor, who had introduced herself as Miss

Oliver, lifted her telephone and looked at Kate enquiringly.

'Tea, please.'

'Right.' Tea for two was ordered in crisp, clear tones. Everything about Miss Oliver was clean and crisp. Dressed in white blouse and black skirt, wearing plain court shoes with small heels and with discreet gold hoop earrings showing just below her neat chin-length bob, she looked totally in control.

If she were wearing a long white coat, thought Kate, she would easily be taken for a doctor.

'Won't be long.' The counsellor replaced the phone and sat back in her swivel chair. 'Before we begin, did you bring with you proof of identity, as I requested in the letter?'

'Yes.' Kate fumbled in her handbag and produced her driving licence and a letter from her bank. As Miss Oliver checked the details, Kate looked round the room. Apart from the desk and two upright chairs, the furniture consisted of a filing cabinet, a shelf containing a row of official-looking books and, by the window, a low table and two fawn dralon-covered easy chairs.

That's the area for the counselling work, she thought, and was correct. A young woman entered the room and placed a teatray upon the low table and Miss Oliver, taking a file from her desk, led Kate towards the easy chairs. 'We'll sit here, shall we? Might as well be comfortable.'

If only that were possible. Kate, tense and uncomfortable, perched on the edge of her chair and watched as Miss Oliver poured out the tea, then she asked, 'Have you discovered anything?'

'We've some information.' Miss Oliver's pink-tipped fingernails tapped the cover of the file but she made no attempt to open it. 'I know you're anxious, Mrs Gallantree, but I must ask you a few questions before we proceed.'

'Yes, I know, but . . .'

'Shall I explain?' Miss Oliver did not wait for Kate's permission but began to speak smoothly and authoritatively. Kate realised she must have said the words many times before.

'As you will now know from the leaflets we gave you, since 1975 it has been possible for any adopted person over the age of eighteen to obtain a copy of their original birth certificate. However, the Children Act also stipulated that anyone adopted before the twelfth of November 1975 must attend an interview with a counsellor before receiving the information.'

Miss Oliver paused. 'As a mature woman, Mrs Gallantree, I'm sure you realise the wisdom of this?'

Giving Kate the time to move her head in an acquiescent bob, she continued.

'In your case, adoption took place many years ago, therefore the first thing I must do is to ask you not to set your hopes too high. To be perfectly honest it's a sad fact that even with the information I am about to give you, it is unlikely you will be able to trace your natural parents.'

'I don't see why.' Kate ignored the cup of tea Miss Oliver had placed in front of her. 'If my mother was a young woman when I was born, she'll only be in her fifties now.'

Kate's interruption brought a slightly pained look to her counsellor's face. 'I appreciate that, but consider a moment – the keeping of records in the forties and fifties was not as stringent as it is now and during the last thirty years there have been many changes. Homes and hospitals have been closed, files lost or misplaced. Of course,' she shrugged, 'you may be one of the lucky ones. But that brings me to my next point.' She paused and drank from her tea cup.

'At the time of your adoption, natural parents were assured of future total secrecy. They have lived their lives believing that. Imagine the shock it must be, to be told the child you gave birth to, twenty, thirty years ago, now wishes to meet you. I'm afraid some people can't handle it and, of course, their feelings must be taken into account.' She looked at Kate. 'Suppose you do manage to trace your mother and then find she refuses to see you or to communicate with you in any way? How would you feel?'

Before answering, Kate took her first sip of tea and then, replacing her cup on the saucer, said in a steady voice, 'I would be dreadfully disappointed, but I would accept her decision.'

'You're sure about this?'

'Yes, quite sure.'

The briskness left Miss Oliver's voice. 'I'm not saying it always happens that way, Kate. May I call you Kate?'

'Yes, of course.'

'But I have to point these things out. Every case is different and the outcome can never be predicted.' Miss Oliver finished her tea. 'I have known cases where a meeting with the natural mother has come about and brought joy to the birth parent. But if you go through with this search, you must be prepared for any eventuality. I must also tell you that, statistically speaking, the chance of your tracing your natural father is practically nil.'

She gazed earnestly into Kate's face. 'However, if you do decide to try and concentrate on finding your natural mother and are successful, it's most important to consider using an intermediary before the first meeting. It's for your sake as well as the parent's. Adopted people, sensible middle-aged people, can often have fantasies about their birth parents which are totally different from the reality.'

'I know all that,' Kate twisted her hands together, 'I've read books about it, but I don't think I fantasise and I still want to go ahead.'

Miss Oliver opened a pad and balanced it on her knee. 'Right, then. Could you tell me a little about your life with your adoptive parents?'

Kate shifted in her seat. 'If you want.'

'Are they still alive?'

'No. They were middle-aged when they adopted me. They died several years ago.'

'I'm sorry.' Miss Oliver sighed. 'Still, at least you don't have to worry about hurting their feelings.' She wrote something down. 'Did you ever consider tracing your natural parents earlier in life, before your adoptive parents died?'

'No.' Kate twisted her wedding ring. 'Actually, it was only after my son was born that I began to think seriously about my natural parents. I found myself wondering what they were like and whether Danny, that's my son, resembled them in any way. Then, once the idea was in my head, it just wouldn't go away. I was perpetually asking myself questions and I couldn't stop.' She shrugged. 'I suppose I'm just curious.'

'What could be more natural?' Miss Oliver smiled at Kate. 'We all seek self-identity. With the change in the law, hopefully more people will learn something about their origins. Can you tell me, was your childhood a happy one? Did you love your adoptive mother and father?'

'Of course I did. I . . .' Kate faltered. Had she loved them, *really*? She certainly owed them a debt of gratitude. 'They were kindly and caring.'

'Did they ever discuss the adoption with you?'

'No. I didn't know I had been adopted until I was in my twenties. My father told me after the death of my mother. She never wanted me to know.'

Miss Oliver jotted down another note. 'Nowadays we tend to think hiding the fact a child's adopted is a mistake. Of course, it depends upon the individual. How did you feel when you heard the truth?'

'I don't know; I don't think it bothered me much. I didn't brood about it.'

'Didn't you ask your father about the details?'

'No.' Kate cleared her throat. 'I didn't want to hurt him, and we weren't a very communicative family.'

'What sort of life-style were you brought up in?'

'Fairly middle-class, I suppose. My father had his own business, my mother stayed at home. She kept busy, raised funds for favourite charities, baked for W.I. coffee mornings, things like that.'

'And you had friends?'

'Yes, but mostly at school. Where we lived, it was mainly older couples whose children had grown up and left home.'

'What about aunts, uncles, cousins?'

'No, both my parents were only children.' Conscious she was painting a somewhat bleak picture, Kate added, 'It never bothered me. At home, I liked my own company. I've always loved books so I read a lot, took our neighbour's dogs for walks. And I enjoyed school. I had plenty of friends there but . . .' She frowned, grasping at an elusive cobwebby emotion. 'Sometimes I felt there was something *missing*, a person or—' She broke off, embarrassed. 'I can't explain.'

'It doesn't matter,' Miss Oliver looked down at her notes. 'I won't keep you much longer. You're obviously a sensible person and I'm sure you've thought through many of the possible problems yourself.'

She looked across at Kate and gave her a wide smile, a genuine smile this time, not the official reassuring beam. 'You've been an easy interviewee, Kate. A great many people who come to this office are unable to talk about their lives. They are often rather sad. Their lives have been disappointing and they believe that finding their natural mother will make everything better. It doesn't, of course. Sometimes the reverse is the case.' She sighed.

'Now, I'll give you the information I have, but there's just one more thing. If you feel the need to visit me again, if you want to talk through your thoughts, mull over your failure or success in finding your natural parents, please do. You have my telephone number and if I'm not in the office, you will be given an appointment. If I can help in any way, I will.'

'Thank you.' But Kate was hardly listening to Miss Oliver, kind though she was. Her gaze was fixed on the manila folder which the counsellor was opening.

'My mother's name was Pauline Margaret Verrill and she was only seventeen when I was born.' Kate hung over her husband's shoulder as he studied the form. It was eight o'clock the same evening and she and Jack were in the kitchen. Kate had waited until Danny was tucked up in bed and Helen had gone out before bringing out the precious document.

'She'll only be in her mid-fifties now, Jack. And she wasn't married. The father's surname is different.'

'Grahame Lossing,' Jack read out the name. He looked up at his wife. 'Do you mind?'

'What, being illegitimate?' She laughed. 'No, I expected it.'

He studied her animated face. 'You're really excited about this, aren't you?'

'Of course I am. I've already learned more than I expected.' She took the shortened birth certificate from Jack's hand. 'Poor Pauline. I wonder what kind of life she had just after I was born? I suppose times were tough for unmarried mums in the forties.'

'Depended on what kind of support her family gave her. There's one nice thing.' Jack put his arm around Kate's waist and pulled her to sit on his knee.

'What?'

'Your name on the form, "Catherine" – your adoptive parents retained your original name.'

'Yes, I hadn't realised.' She pored over the form. 'But the most important thing of all is here, look.' She pointed.

'What?'

'Oh, Jack, don't you see? My birth was registered in *York*! I've always assumed I was born in the South. After all, my parents lived there all their lives, and I never heard them mention visiting Yorkshire. But I was born here and perhaps my mother still lives in the county. If she does, she'll be easier to trace. Oh!' She flung her arms around her husband's neck. 'What a good job I married you and came to live in Leeds.'

'I came in useful after all.' His voice was dry but he

dropped a light kiss on her cheek. He was still negative about the whole business, but couldn't spoil her present pleasure. However, he tried a note of caution.

'There isn't a lot to go on, Kate. I . . .'

She interrupted him. 'The counsellor gave me a form so I can send away for a full birth certificate. That will show the place where I was born and details of my mother's address.'

'But it was thirty-five years ago. It's most unlikely . . .'

Her excitement dimmed. She addressed him earnestly. 'I know the odds, Jack, Miss Oliver pointed them out to me, but it's better than nothing. I've taken the first step and found out my mother's name. That's something. And I feel happier now that I'm *doing* something instead of sitting and feeling frustrated. I know you don't approve, but let me have six months. If nothing turns up by then, I'll give up, I promise.'

He cuddled her. 'You're making me feel a real bastard, Kate. I think I'm just beginning to realise how much you need to do this.' His grip tightened. 'OK, we'll give it six months, and when I'm home, I'll help you all I can. Have we got a bargain?'

She kissed him. 'Yes.'

The next morning she posted off her application and cheque to the Registrar General.

Chapter Twenty

Pauline was in the kitchen making herself a milky coffee when the telephone rang. Sighing, she lifted the milk pan from the gas. It wouldn't be anything important, probably someone trying to sell double-glazing. She placed the pan on the draining board and, without hurrying, went through into the hall to pick up the phone.

'Hello.'

'Good evening, am I speaking to Mrs Pauline Bowen?'

'Yes.' Somehow, it didn't sound like a saleswoman, but Pauline couldn't identify the voice. She felt a stir of interest. It was rare for anyone to ring her during the evening. Sometimes, the women at the shop where she worked part-time would phone her during the day, to check on an order or suggest she join them for lunch at the local pub. Without false modesty, Pauline knew she was popular, even though she was much older than them.

'May I just check on a couple of points? I must be sure I'm addressing the right person. Did you spend your early years in Whitby, Mrs Bowen, and was your maiden name Verrill?'

Pauline's knees went weak. How long had it been

since anyone had called her by her maiden name? Her hand clutched the phone tightly. 'Yes, that's me.'

Her caller paused. 'My name's Phyllis Oliver. I work in the Leeds division of the Social Services department. I'm ringing you on a personal matter, Mrs Bowen, and what I am about to tell you may come as rather a shock. Is this a convenient time for us to talk? If it isn't, I could ring later.'

'No, there's no one here, you can speak freely.' Pauline shifted the receiver to her other hand and suddenly wondered if this was something to do with her father. The Social Services dealt with old people, didn't they? She had neither seen nor spoken to her father for years, not since shortly after her twins had been born and, when she thought of him at all, she had assumed he must be dead by now. If he was still alive, he'd be well into his eighties.

She remembered the last time they had been face to face. She had gone home to Whitby after her discharge from the mother and baby home hoping desperately to find a way to make peace with him, but he hadn't given her the chance. He had opened the door and stared at her, his lean figure upright and taut with tension, his eyes hard with anger. He hadn't allowed her to say one word, but had spat out his own venom.

'You've excelled yourself, Pauline – two bastards instead of one. I wish you joy of them, but don't think they're coming into my house.' He had shut the door in her face.

How he had hated her! Perhaps that's what had kept him alive so long? You can feed on hate more easily than you can feed on love. But if he'd now found someone to trace her, perhaps he had decided to make his peace with her at last? She hoped so. In the beginning, she had hated him as much as he hated her, but as she had grown older, she had seen things differently. He had loved as obsessively as he had hated, and he had lost everything he loved. How terrible to look back over a long life and remember only loss, desolation and waste. Perhaps he was ill, lonely, dying, and wanted to see his only child again?

She remembered the two occasions she had tried to make contact with him. The last time was just after her marriage to Lawrence. She had been so happy and wanted to heal old wounds, but he had never replied to her letter. But if he had kept it, if he had saved the address? They had moved to the present flat five years ago but it was only a few streets away. They would have been easy to trace.

Her first letter to her father had been written years and years ago, when little Eliza . . . her mind skittered away from *that* letter like a hare chased by hounds.

'As I say . . .' the woman was continuing. Pauline forced herself to concentrate. '. . . I'm with the Social Services department. I work in the area connected with adoption and fostering.' Miss Oliver had keen hearing, she must have heard Pauline gasp for she paused. 'You all right, Mrs Bowen?'

'Yes, yes. Go on, please.' Pauline needed to sit down but there was nowhere to sit, so she leaned against the wall.

Miss Oliver asked, 'Do you know anything about the changes that have occurred in the laws relating to adoption? Several years ago the newspapers covered . . .'

'I don't read newspapers very often.' Pauline ran the tip of her tongue over her dry lips. 'They always harp on about depressing things.'

Miss Oliver laughed. 'I know what you mean, but sometimes they write about good things, too. I hope you think that what I'm about to say is good news.'

She meant well but Pauline wished to God she'd get on with it. She said nothing.

Miss Oliver continued: 'Under new guidelines brought out in 1975, the law allowed that adult adopted people could enquire about the circumstances of their adoption and be given information about their natural parents. Since then, many people have taken advantage of this right. They have requested, and been given, a copy of their original birth certificate.

'For many applicants, knowing their real name and the names of their natural parents is all they need but,' she paused, 'sometimes the search goes further. People enquire about their birth records for different reasons. Often it's to do with health matters. I've had clients who wished to emigrate and needed to know whether their natural parents suffered from any hereditary health diseases. Then there are others . . .'

Pauline interrupted her. 'This is about my daughter, isn't it? It's about Kate?'

'Yes, Mrs Bowen, it is. Your daughter obtained a copy of her full birth certificate at the end of last year. I helped her to do that. When she saw her birth had been registered at York, she became very excited. You see, she is presently living in Leeds, and the thought that her mother might be living somewhere reasonably close to her crystallised her desire to find you. It has taken her four months, the fact that the adoption was a private one made enquiries more difficult, but at last she traced you to your present address.

'She's very anxious to meet you, but she also appreciates that the news of her interest will come as a shock to you. I have been her counsellor throughout her enquiries. We have discussed the situation at length. When she told me she had found out where you now lived, I suggested I make the first contact with you and she agreed immediately. Your daughter's a sensible young woman, Mrs Bowen. She feels a great need to talk to you but has no wish to cause you any distress or pain. She told me to tell you that if you refuse a meeting, she will understand and will not bother you again.'

'You're saying I don't *have* to meet her, if I don't want to?'

'Yes.'

Pauline's head was spinning and a churning sensation in her stomach warned her she wanted to be sick. 'I don't know, I can't quite take it in.'

'Understandable, in the circumstances.' Miss Oliver's soothing voice floated tinnily through the earpiece of the phone. She waited a moment longer than said, 'Look, there's no immediate hurry. Suppose I ring back tomorrow evening, at about this time? That will give you a chance to think over what I have told you.'

'Yes.' Pauline cleared her throat. 'Yes, if you don't mind.'

'Of course I don't. I'll give you a ring about six forty-five.'

After replacing the phone, Pauline went into the bathroom, sat on the toilet seat and closed her eyes. Gradually, the feeling of sickness ebbed away. She stood up and, leaning her hands on the wash basin, looked through the bathroom mirror. The feelings whirling inside her did not show on her face. She looked the same as always: a blue-eyed, fair-haired, middle-aged woman, wearing spectacles. She took off her glasses and looked again, leaning closer to the mirror to see properly. Her age was beginning to show, the cleft between her eyebrows was getting deeper and, for the first time, she realised her top lip was beginning to thin. But her eyes were still young, staring back at her calmly.

She sighed, splashed her face with cold water, patted it dry and then went into her living-room, unaware she still clasped the towel in her hand. She sat down.

Kate wanted to meet her. Why? What dreams had her daughter woven about her absent mother? Would she be disappointed if they met? Should they meet? Kate was now – without having to calculate, Pauline *knew* – almost thirty-six years old. Miss Oliver had called her a young woman, but she wasn't, she was halfway through her life. Was she married, did she have children? At the thought of grandchildren, Pauline's heart bounded. She should have asked, Miss Oliver would have known. The smoothly competent official she had just spoken to knew much more about Kate than her mother did. But then, she had spoken to Kate recently. Pauline had last seen her daughter thirty-four years ago.

When the Hamptons had carried her away, out of Pauline's life, Kate had been sixteen months old. She had been dressed in her best frock and wrapped in a shawl, because it had been an unseasonably cold day. So very cold. Pauline shivered. And Kate had been coughing, looking over Mr Hampton's shoulder straight at her mother and coughing, not crying.

Pauline, clutching the towel to her body as if for comfort, remembered what an ailing scrap of a baby Kate had been, sweet-tempered but weak-chested and always with a cough or cold. But she had possessed a delicate prettiness which had captured the attention of the Hamptons the first time they had seen her. They had been a cultured, mannerly couple, with quiet voices and good manners. They wouldn't have been drawn to a rowdy, robust child.

Recalling her daughter's pointy little face and beautiful eyes, the way her soft hair had wisped around her delicate ears, an old, familiar pain started up inside Pauline. She huddled in her chair and reminded herself that it was all over. Kate was still her daughter, but now they would pass each other in the street, or sit side by side on a bus, and wouldn't even recognise each other. And maybe, she thought, it would be better for it to remain that way.

The lacerating grief she had felt over the loss of her daughter had long ago faded into a dull acceptance. The pictures she had carried so long in her mind – Kate crooning herself to sleep, the dimple in her cheek when she smiled, the howls that shook her small body when she cried – had slowly faded and become as indistinct to her as an underdeveloped photograph. And the distancing of feeling had been deliberate, an act of survival.

In the days, weeks and months following Kate's adoption, only little Elizabeth, Eliza as she had called her, had kept Pauline sane. For Eliza, who needed her, she had got out of bed each morning and struggled through the day. And as time passed, she had learned to blank out certain thoughts and think only of the future. She had moved to another town, found another job and carved out a new life for herself and her child.

But now, thirty-four years later, one phone call had called forth an army of ghosts and Pauline, immobile in her chair, had to face them. She recognised and acknowledged them and, lost in memories, she did not realise the passing of time until a particularly mean gust of wind buffeted the windows of her living-room and made the window frame rattle. She shivered. February was not a month to sit in a room with no heating.

Moving slowly, she got up from her chair and went to switch on the gas fire, and as she did so, she remembered the day she and Lawrence had bought it. He had been in the early stages of his illness then and had felt the cold. The underfloor electric heating system installed in the flat was too expensive to use on a daily basis, so they had decided to buy a gas fire.

'An attractive one. If we can't have a proper coal fire, let's try and find one that looks as though it's real.'

They had walked round three showrooms before they had found one he approved of.

'You won't scold me if I forget and throw my toffee papers at it, will you?' Lawrence had laughed, and squeezed her arm. 'Now, let's go to a restaurant and celebrate.'

Dear Lawrence, he had managed to make something as simple as choosing a new fire a celebration. What a blessing that man had been. They had spent only ten years together, but it had been a time of great love and contentment. If only he was with her now, to comfort and advise her.

Pauline knelt on the hearthrug and stretched out

her hands to the glowing coals. She supposed she ought to go and prepare herself an evening meal. She wasn't particularly hungry but she had skipped lunch so she ought to eat something. She went into the kitchen and brought out bread and a box of eggs. She couldn't be bothered with proper cooking. She toasted the bread and scrambled three eggs then carried her tray back into the living-room. But after a few mouthfuls of food and a cup of tea, her attention wandered again and, unnoticed, the scrambled egg congealed on the plate.

She wondered how Kate had traced her. The birth registration at York couldn't have been much help.

She had lived all over the place during her last thirty years. She'd now been in Manchester for seventeen years, and before that . . . again, her thoughts wandered to the past.

Like a movie reel played backwards, figures and faces appeared before her. She had switched on the table lamp near her chair before preparing her meal but had not drawn the curtains. As the winter darkness solidified outside, it was as if some portion of it intruded, slipped indoors, for the corners of the room grew indistinct. The photo of Lawrence on her sideboard, her collection of owl plates on the far wall and the figurine of the little boy that had belonged to her grandmother, all drew back into the shadows. Pauline did not notice, she stared into the almost real fire, and remembered.

She had been quietly unhappy when she had met Lawrence and when she finally realised his interest in her, she had been quite rude to him. As she told him, she wanted to be left alone. And although she did not say it in words, she intimated to him that she wished for no involvement or commitment on either side.

He had nodded, and smiled, and he had taken things gently: an occasional five-minute conversation in the corridor at work, sometimes a coffee together at lunch-time, and then the discovery they both shared a passion for old films, especially musicals. They had gone to see *An American in Paris* and then a revival of *My Fair Lady* at the Opera House and, without realising, she had started to look out for him, be disappointed when a day passed without seeing him. His friendship became valuable to her, and imperceptibly her feelings turned into something deeper.

Before her life with Lawrence had been the time she had run a boarding house with Julie Hunter. Where was Julie now? She had met David during that time. Pauline's face relaxed into lines of tenderness.

There had been love and tears with David, but mostly love. No, she would never regret David. But before him . . . that had been the bad time.

Pauline closed her eyes, pressing her fingers so hard against her eyelids that sparks of light shot across her darkness. And behind the sparks, she saw the lithe figure of a young child; a girl in a white leotard with a hint of red in her curling hair and freckles on her nose. The child was smiling a wide, delighted grin as she held aloft a silver cup, her prize for coming first in a junior athletic competition. The first prize Elizabeth ever won, and the last.

'No.' Pauline whispered. Her eyes opened and she concentrated her gaze on the fire, willing her mind to move even further backwards, to earlier ghosts, ghosts less painful.

Mary and her German lover . . . what had his name been? Claus, that was it. Why had Mary stopped writing to her after they had corresponded for six years? And Grahame, Grahame Lossing . . . she remembered his face with little emotion now, yet once she had been convinced he had broken her heart. And dear old Doctor Tebbutt, he had kept in touch with her until his death. She had received a letter from his nephew, also a doctor, a few weeks after his uncle had died. How good he had been to her, even coming to help during the birth of her babies.

She jumped up, upsetting the tray. The toast and scrambled egg landed face down on the hearthrug. She didn't care. She walked agitatedly round the room. It was too much. She didn't want reminding of the past.

When the woman from the Social Services rang tomorrow, she would tell her it was too late, much too late. She had nothing to say to a grown woman of thirty-six. What had happened all those years ago had happened for the best. Kate must understand, her mother wished to be left in peace.

Her decision brought a measure of calmness. She cleared the remains of the meal from the carpet, tidied the room and went up to bed. She took a bath, and as she put on her nightgown, said aloud: 'What is the sense of washing dirty linen in public? Much better for Kate to get on with her life and me to get on with mine.' Nodding her head decisively, she went through to the bedroom.

She sat down on the bed and, in the act of taking off her slippers, remembered someone else.

How often she had laughed at her gran for trotting out old sayings, and yet now she was doing it herself. She must be getting old. Gran had had a saying for everything, 'It's an ill wind', and 'Better the devil you know'. And now, unthinkingly, Pauline was trotting out the same old homilies. A new thought hit her and she sat and clutched her left slipper in her hand.

The past *did* matter. You couldn't pretend what had gone before was unimportant. People grew old and died, but their influence lived on. How many times had Eliza's wisdom helped and sustained her during the bad times? And Kate was Eliza's descendant, it was her *right* to know about her great-grandmother, and about her origins.

Pauline dropped the slipper on the floor and got into bed, once more confused. She also felt a touch of shame. Without thinking, she had just used one of Eliza's favourite sayings but, on this occasion, it had been inappropriate. If there was dirty linen to be washed it was hers, and Kate wasn't public, she was family.

She made up her mind, she would meet her daughter. And then, her inner conflict resolved, she shed a few tears – but not for long. Without realising, Pauline had developed more in common with her grandma than a few old sayings.

As she settled down to sleep, she thought about what she would say when Kate and she met. It would be a strange meeting, hard for both of them, but it was no good worrying. As her eyelids closed in sleep, memories of Eliza were strong and she recalled the letter she had received from the solicitor after her grandmother's death. She still had it, safely tucked up in the back of her writing case.

She drifted into sleep. Catching larks. She wondered . . .

Chapter Twenty-One

'You're sure you don't mind, Nicky? I don't want you to think . . .'

'For goodness' sake, stop flapping.' Nicky looked up from her self-appointed task with a tolerant smile. She was in Kate's dining-room, the table was covered with sheets of old newspaper and Nicky, helped by her eldest son, Shawn, was setting out sheets of drawing paper and jamjars half-full of water. Two large paint boxes awaited use.

'Everything will be fine. You've made the sandwiches for later and there's plenty of juice in the fridge. We'll have a whale of a time, won't we, kids?'

Her question was rhetorical. Danny, struggling away from his mother's grasp as she attempted to dress him in a plastic apron adorned with pink and blue pigs, was not listening. Nicky's baby daughter was fast asleep in her buggy and Jamie, her middle child, was busily absorbed in playing with Danny's red dumper truck.

Only Shawn gave the expected answer. 'Yes, Mummy.' As the eldest of three children under five, he was a sober, sensible little boy.

'If Jack was at home there wouldn't be a problem, but as it is . . .'

‘I’ve told you, Kate, I’m happy to look after Danny at any time. When you’ve already got three kids, one more doesn’t make much difference. Anyway, I’m glad to have a change of scene.’

Her own anxiety forgotten for a moment, Kate looked at her friend sympathetically. ‘Things no better?’

‘Not really. We’ve got six weeks’ grace but then we’re out. The council chap said he’d do his best for us, but I’m not optimistic.’ Nicky shrugged. ‘The housing list’s enormous and there’s not many private landlords prepared to look at a couple with three children.’

‘I’m sorry.’

Kate’s heartfelt sympathy was genuine. When Nicky had finally reappeared at the park playground, Kate had felt a rush of pleasure. She had dashed over to speak to her and, after hugging Shawn, had given her a hug, too. Then, without feeling embarrassed or nosey, she had asked what had kept them away.

Nicky told her. The kids had all had measles and Richie had been ill in bed with his nerves after what had been practically a stand-up fight with their landlord.

‘It’s quiet at the moment but it won’t last.’ Nicky shook her head. ‘We’re going to have to move.’ She’d watched Danny weave his way around the park bench and, apparently dismissing her troubles from her mind, had commented, ‘He’s coming on a treat with his walking, isn’t he?’

An hour and a half later when they left the park together, Kate had asked Nicky back for tea and she had accepted. Three-quarters of an hour later, when Helen arrived home, Kate had waited apprehensively for her reaction. Sometimes, Helen could be quite rude.

On finding three toddlers rolling about the floor in the dining-room and a baby asleep on the sofa, Helen's eyebrows had risen, and her answering nod to Nicky's friendly greeting had been a touch supercilious, but she had made herself a coffee and retreated to her room without comment. When she came downstairs after Nicky's departure, she didn't even mention the visit. Perhaps, Kate had thought, she's too preoccupied with her own life to wonder about my friends.

As autumn turned into winter, the Wednesday tea party developed into a regular weekly feature and Kate looked forward immensely to Nicky's arrival. When Jack was away, she was often lonely. As the weather deteriorated, regular trips to the park had to be abandoned; after a heavy rainfall, the whole area turned into a sea of mud. And Kate saw even less of her neighbours than before.

The elderly couple, the Martins, had gone to stay with their married daughter for a while. Mrs Martin was recovering from 'flu and Mr Martin loved anything to do with ships. Their daughter lived in Southampton. Kate didn't know when they would return.

Her neighbours on the other side, the Blunts, still waved to her when they saw her, but she had a feeling all was not well with them. It was rare for them to leave the house together any more. Gill was away on business trips a lot of the time and Simon's face, when he called hello to Kate, had difficulty in smiling. And on the rare occasions they were home together, they quarrelled. Through the wall, she would hear the sound of raised voices.

So her Wednesday tea parties became events to be looked forward to and she was happy to play the hostess. Sometimes, she wondered if Nicky minded trailing the three little ones over to her house, but Nicky said she did not. And Kate, considering everything, saw the sense of the arrangement. In her house, there was plenty of room for the children to play and when the weather was fine enough, they could go into the back garden. Nicky could hardly invite Kate and Danny to visit her, living as she did in a small flat and presently in dispute with her landlord. But Kate also wondered if another reason for no visitors was Richie, Nicky's husband.

The weeks slipped by and the friendship between Kate and Nicky became closer. Even Helen seemed to enjoy seeing her and the children now. When things were going well with her, that was. If her friendship with Eileen was flourishing and her school marks were good, she would come through to the dining-room and join them for a little while, play with the boys and chat to Nicky. If things were going badly, if Ben did not phone her or she thought she'd gained weight, if *anything* had upset her, she would slam into the house and go straight up to her room. A moment later, the thud of heavy metal music would fill the house.

Kate would apologise. 'I don't know what gets into her sometimes.'

And Nicky would reply, 'Don't you? I do. I was just the same when I was her age.'

They began to talk of things other than their children and to confide certain secrets. One day, Nicky told Kate that three years ago she had had an affair with someone and she wasn't absolutely sure whether Jamie was the child of her lover or her husband.

Kate was both shocked and intrigued. 'But if you were sleeping with this man, how could you leave him, go home and go to bed with Richie? Didn't you feel . . . ?' Her voice faded away.

'Cheap? Not really.' Nicky stared down into her coffee cup. 'You don't understand, do you? I wish I hadn't told you now. You'll think I'm a right cow.'

'No, but . . .'

Nicky interrupted her. 'Your life's been so different from mine, Kate. You were so much older when you married. Richie and me, we were only kids. It was like playing house, we were so full of daft ideas and dreams for the future.

'We'd courted since we were fifteen, neither of us was happy at home. We thought we'd save some money, buy a nice little house cheap and do it up. Then, in three or four years, we'd start a family.' She gave a bitter little laugh. 'Not a lot to ask for, is it? I'd found myself a job and Richie passed his exams and was taken on by a builder. We thought, what could go wrong?'

Kate stared at her. 'You fell pregnant.'

'Almost straight away.' Nicky glanced across the room towards Shawn who was busy building a pile of bricks for Danny to knock down. 'We'd been ever so careful, always taking precautions, then one night we didn't. I can even tell you when it happened. We'd been to a party, we never went out much, and we both got tiddly. And bingo!'

'But you wouldn't be without Shawn, Nicky? He's such a grand little boy.'

'Of course I wouldn't – but once I was pregnant, things went from bad to worse. You'd think we'd done something criminal. We had to give up the flat, the landlady wouldn't have kids at any price. And then, just before Shawn was born, Richie lost his job.' Nicky had looked at Kate defensively. 'His boss told him he was the best worker he'd ever had but the firm was in trouble. Richie and two other blokes got the push. There was only the boss and his son left to run the business. We were upset, of course we were, but I told Richie, we'll get by. Something will turn up. Only, Richie, well – I can't explain, he just gave up.'

Hearing the tremor in Nicky's voice, Kate frowned. 'Don't tell me any more if you don't want to.'

'I do. Now I've blurted out my guilty secret I want you to understand, Kate.'

Nicky had plaited her fingers together and avoided looking at her. 'You know, even at school there was something different about Richie. That's why I fell for him. He laughed a lot and he had things to say. You know what most fifteen- and sixteen-year-old lads are like, but Richie wasn't the same. He was interested in all sorts of things. He painted a mural once, round the gym at school, and the art teacher said he should have gone to art school, but he didn't get the chance. His parents wanted him out at work.

'He didn't mind not going to college too much because we were already planning our life together. Anyway, he was good at lots of other things. He could do anything with his hands, electrical work as well as plumbing and building. But when his job went, he just lost heart, especially when he couldn't get another one. After Shawn's birth I was offered a part-time job, which made things a bit easier on the money front, but we were in a grotty bedsit and that depressed him.

'His parents would visit and have a go at him. He'd married too young. He'd ruined his life. Oh, they were a bundle of laughs, I can tell you. His dad actually told him, in front of me, mind, that he wasn't a proper man, me going out to work and him looking after the baby. There was a fine old row then. We don't see them any more.'

There was a wail. Danny and Jamie had bumped heads. Kate stood up to go to them but Nicky got there first. She picked them both up and absent-mindedly cuddled them. 'I tried, honest to God! I told him it wasn't his fault and things would improve, but he missed one job after another – not enough experience, see – and just went back into himself. And I got fed up, Kate.

'I met Carl at a girlfriend's engagement party and he chatted me up. He didn't know I was married; I'd taken my wedding ring off, slipped it in my pocket. I suppose I went a bit crazy. It was so great to be fancied by someone again. I was only eighteen, remember.

'Anyway, I agreed to meet him. Richie used to sit in our room staring at the television set. He didn't seem to know whether I was there or not. My sister took Shawn a couple of hours a week, to give me a bit of a break. I started to meet Carl when I left work, just for an hour. On our third meeting, I went with him to his flat.'

She looked reminiscent. 'He made love in positions I'd never heard of. I'd be a liar if I said I didn't enjoy it. In fact, it was brilliant, but at the same time it all seemed unreal, it was as if I was outside myself, watching. Back home, I couldn't believe it had happened. I'd cheated on Richie. If he found out, I thought, he'd quite likely top himself, and I swore it wouldn't happen again. But then Shawn would have me up all night and Richie was so full of self-pity and I began to despise him. Not for losing his job, that wasn't his fault, but for being so *beaten*. So I kept on seeing Carl. It was four months before it ended.'

'Did Richie find out?'

'Oh, no, but Carl found out I was married.' Nicky's mouth twisted into a self-mocking grin. 'He asked me to leave Richie and go to him. He even said he'd welcome little Shawn, but I couldn't. The sex was great, but I didn't love him. I still loved Richie.'

She had dropped her eyes before Kate's puzzled gaze, and when her baby cried, she turned to her almost thankfully. The subject was never referred to again, but on her next visit Kate told Nicky all about her own search for her natural mother.

'It's time you were off.' Nicky took Danny from Kate and dumped him on a chair set close to the table. 'There you are, sit next to Jamie.' She placed a cushion beneath his rump and looked at his mother.

'Didn't you say Helen was going through to Manchester with you?'

'Yes. She wasn't too keen but I bribed her. I said I'd give her some money to buy a new outfit. I don't expect her to come with me to meet my mother, I just wanted some company on the train.'

'I can understand that, you must be feeling jumpy.' Nicky dipped a paint brush into a jamjar and then rubbed it vigorously on a block of paint. She handed it to Danny. She watched him as he sploshed a patch of red on to a piece of paper and then waved his hand about wildly, depositing red paint on Jamie's hair. 'That's lovely, Danny.'

She turned back to Kate. 'But considering you've spent the last few months trying to find your mum, you don't look overjoyed at the prospect of meeting her.'

'I can't believe I'm actually going to see her. I keep thinking, what if we've nothing to say to each other? What if we don't *like* each other? What . . .'

'What will you feel like if she doesn't turn up?' Nicky shook her head at the expression on Kate's face. 'Stop worrying. Even if you find you have nothing in common, at least you'll know what she looks like. Now, go and get your coat on. I'll give Helen a shout.' At the door she paused. 'There's one thing, Kate.'

'What's that?'

'Your mother can't possibly be as bad as mine.'

They had agreed the meeting should take place on neutral ground, two o'clock in the cafe on the third floor of a well-known department store. Kate was there by one forty-five. She looked round. A few people were finishing off their lunch-time snacks and a waitress was clearing away dishes.

Kate spoke to her. 'Shall I sit here?' She indicated a table for two in the corner of the room.

'Take your pick.' The waitress loaded dirty plates and cups on to her tray and wiped a table top. 'Do you want to order?'

'May I just have a pot of tea?'

'You can have what you like, it's continuous service.' The waitress gazed into the air above Kate's head. Her face wore the expression of a woman whose feet hurt.

'Er, right. Tea for one, please.'

'Anything to eat?'

She couldn't have eaten if offered one hundred pounds. 'No, thanks.'

The waitress nodded and departed. Kate sat down

and watched as more people drifted out of the cafe. It was approaching the slack time, the period between lunch and afternoon tea. Very few tables were now occupied. Close by Kate, an elderly couple were partaking of tea and muffins and next to them a morose-looking youth was hunched over a cup of coffee. Perhaps, thought Kate, his girlfriend had stood him up. A young mother was cutting up a toasted teacake for her toddler, a little girl seated in a high chair.

The child reminded Kate of Nicky and her brood and she hoped everything was well at home and that Danny was not missing her.

And then she thought of Jack, he was going to ring her tonight to see how things had gone. Since his initial angry reaction to her news about trying to find her mother, he had changed, become both helpful and supportive, but she knew he felt edgy over the proposed meeting. She bit her lip. He wasn't the only one.

A middle-aged woman came into the cafe and looked round enquiringly. Kate tensed, but after a moment the woman's gaze lighted on the child in the high chair and she waved and went over to the little girl and her mother. The waitress brought Kate her tea and she poured herself a cup.

Helen would be rummaging through the bargain rails of Miss Selfridge now. She would probably buy some ridiculous skirt suitable for a thirty-year-old, but it didn't really matter so long as it made her happy. She was still seeing that boy from school, what was his name? Ben something or other? Kate had tried, albeit clumsily, to talk to her as a mother would, but Helen had soon silenced her.

'I'm not a child, Kate. I know all about birth control, but it's not like that between Ben and me. We're just friends.'

She might know about birth control, but did she realise how easy it was to get carried away? And despite her pretence at coolness, she cared about this boy. She fancied herself in love with him. Kate knew that from her moods, one minute starry-eyed, the next minute plunged into the depths of despair. Who'd be a teenager nowadays? When *she* had been fifteen, she had loved her cat! Kate sipped her tea. But then, life didn't get any easier, even when you were grown. Who'd be a thirty-six-year-old woman waiting to meet her mother for the first time?

'Mrs Kate Gallantree?'

'Yes.'

It was a soft, hesitant voice bearing traces of a North Country accent. Kate looked up. A woman with soft, disarranged fair hair, wearing a beige mac, a pink scarf tucked into the neck, stood next to her chair.

'Yes, I'm Kate Gallantree.' The woman must have come into the cafe through the electrical department. Kate saw a small archway which she had not previously noticed. She jumped to her feet. 'I'm sorry, I didn't see . . . Will you sit down?'

'Yes, of course.'

The woman . . . Pauline Bowen . . . *her mother*, took the seat opposite her. They regarded each other. Kate's first impression was that her mother looked ordinary, and she was pleased about that and quite relieved. It wasn't that she had expected an eccentric, or someone peculiar, but you never knew. She looked hard and saw a woman in her early fifties with a good skin, short fair hair and fine features which were slightly blurred by a little too much weight. She asked, 'Would you like some tea?'

'Yes, that would be nice.'

Kate called the waitress over and ordered tea and, as an afterthought, a plate of cakes.

'I hope you haven't been waiting long?' As her mother spoke, she unbuttoned her mac, shrugged it off and hung it on the back of her chair. She smiled at Kate. She seemed quite at ease.

'No, I only arrived a few minutes ago.' Answering, Kate felt a touch of unreality and a nervous desire to laugh. It was so ridiculous, the two of them swopping inanities like perfect strangers. They'd be discussing the weather next. She suddenly realised she blamed her mother for this and felt an unexpected stab of dislike.

She noticed the blouse the woman wore was a little too tight, the third button down was straining against a full bust, and she thought, I'm small like her but my build's different. *I* won't get fat as I get older.

Then her mother took off her spectacles and polished them with a handkerchief and Kate noticed the dark patches of fatigue beneath her eyes, which were a beautiful deep blue colour, and had the grace to feel ashamed.

'I appreciate your agreeing to meet me. I . . .' Kate's voice trailed off. 'I don't know what to call you?'

Her mother replaced her spectacles and gave a tentative smile. 'As you've taken so much trouble to find me, I suppose "Mother" is appropriate, but if you don't want to call me that, call me Pauline.'

'Yes, I will, if you don't mind.'

The waitress came back and deposited another pot of tea and the cakes on their table. They watched her every movement intently and then, after she had retreated, Pauline poured herself a cup of tea.

'How can I object?'

Her face was quite calm but Kate noticed her hand shake a little as she added milk and a spoonful of sugar to her cup. She continued to speak. 'I gave you away when you were a little girl, I have no claim to the name of Mother.'

Kate bit her lip. 'But you must have had a good reason?' She paused. 'There's so many questions, and yet I don't know where to start.' She waited for Pauline to reply but when she did not, went on: 'For example, I'd imagined I was adopted straight after my birth, but when I saw my adoption certificate I realised I was much older.'

'Yes, you were sixteen months old.' Her mother glanced at her. 'Didn't the Hamptons explain?'

'They never told me anything. I didn't find out I was adopted until after the death of my mother. I was in my twenties then.'

Pauline drew in her breath. 'Oh, those silly people, they should have told you.' Her hand covered her mouth. 'I'm sorry, I shouldn't have said that.'

'I don't mind. They *should* have been honest with me.'

'When I first met them, I thought they were such a sensible couple. I was sure you'd be happy with them. They had a comfortable life-style and thought the world of you. I was in a terrible position then and . . .' Pauline's voice faded to a whisper and for the first time, Kate saw emotion change her face.

'I'm sorry. This must be difficult for you.' She reached over and lightly touched her mother's hand. 'But I do need to know.'

'Of course you do.' Pauline's gaze rested on her

daughter's hand, on the gold band on her third finger. 'But first, tell *me* something.'

'If I can.'

'I see you're married.'

'Yes. My husband's called Jack. We have a little boy. He's fifteen months old.'

'What's his name?'

'Daniel . . . Danny.'

Kate's own eyes pricked as she saw Pauline's expression. 'We're very happy,' she added.

Pauline sighed. 'I'm so pleased.' She bent her head for a moment, then looked up and explained.

'I was working in a hotel in Devon when I met the Hamptons. They visited the place regularly, twice a year for a short break. They were nice friendly people.

'They saw you one night when I was taking you out for a walk in the evening, after I had finished work.' Pauline smiled. 'You're a bonny woman now, Kate, but you were an exceptionally beautiful baby and the Hamptons fell in love with you at first sight. We'd spoken a few times at the hotel and they knew about you. I think they realised how difficult it was for me. You worked long hours in the hotel business in those days.

'They asked if they could take you out occasionally, for a walk or on to the beach. I jumped at the chance. I used to worry about you all the time. When I was working, I had to dump you with anyone prepared to keep an eye on you. Anyway, I agreed, and they were cock-a-hoop. They took you out whenever they could. They always used to bring you back with a new toy. I told them they shouldn't spend their money but they insisted, and you liked being with them. You would cry when they handed you back.

'They stayed at the hotel three times while I was there, and each time they couldn't wait to see you. They knew your birth date and said they would send you a card and a present on your second birthday. Of course, there was no question of adoption at that time.' She paused.

'So why did they take me?'

'Something happened and I had to leave the hotel. Oh, don't imagine I did anything wrong.' Pauline frowned at Kate's expression. 'I didn't steal or anything like that, but it was still impossible for me to stay. I had very little money saved.

'I moved into town and rented a room in a lodging house. It was a dreadful place, dark and damp, but it was the best I could manage. You were delicate and, living there, you were always ailing. You were rushed into hospital once with pneumonia. They pulled you round, but you had to come back to the same awful conditions again.

'I was at my wits' end. The season was almost over and I couldn't get another job and the money from the Social Security people just wasn't enough to live on. Then, the Hamptons came looking for me. Well, not me exactly, but you. They came straight to the point, they wanted to adopt you. A private adoption, they said. In the fifties, private adoptions were fairly commonplace.

'At first I refused. I'd kept you for sixteen months, I wasn't going to let you go now. But they made me see I was being unfair. They could offer you a loving, secure home. Still I refused. They went away but they left their address and telephone number, and then you were ill again.

'I remember, I sat up and nursed you through the

night and you felt so light in my arms. You were gasping and coughing. The room was cold and outside the rain was pouring down. The doctor came next day. He looked at you and muttered something about a heart murmur. He arranged for you to be taken into the hospital for tests. I was petrified, but he was smiling when he came to talk to me. He told me you were OK but delicate and needed special care. In winter you had to be kept in a warm room and in summer I had to see you had plenty of fresh air and sunshine. A sheltered, sunny garden, he said. I stared at him. I couldn't give you any of those things.

'It was still raining when I took you home, so I left you with the woman in the next room and I went to the phone box at the corner of the street and rang the Hamptons. They came the next day.'

'And they took me away with them?'

'Yes.'

'They didn't get in touch with you later?'

'No, that was the arrangement. It was fair enough. I might have wanted to claim you back, if my circumstances had improved.'

'But that's terrible! I can't believe you were forced into it like that. It sounds more like something that happened in Victorian times.' Kate shook her head. 'Didn't you have anyone to help, to turn to?'

'No, my father had disowned me. After your birth I spent some time with my great-uncle but that didn't work out. He had just remarried and his wife didn't like me. My mother had died years before.'

'And . . . my father?'

Pauline sighed. 'I'll explain about him. You have a right to know. But will you answer a question for me?'

'If I can.'

'How did you manage to track me down? The birth

certificate wouldn't have given you much information.'

'It wasn't easy. We – my husband and I – followed all kinds of leads, without success. But finally we had a stroke of luck. We found out that your GP was called Tebbutt and lived in Whitby. We went there but discovered the doctor had died some years ago. However, his nephew had taken over his medical practice and had kept some of his uncle's belongings. There was an address book with the name Pauline Verrill and an address in Manchester. That gave us a starting point.'

'Good Lord, old Doctor Tebbutt!' Pauline shook her head. 'He was a kind man. He helped me all he could.' For the first time, she smiled properly. 'Perhaps, because of his book, he did me one last favour?'

'Perhaps.' Kate felt awkward. She was burning to know more, but from the pallor of her mother's face, she realised that relating her story was an ordeal. Also, more people were now thronging the cafe. A group of girls of about sixteen sat down at the next table and began to talk loudly about make-up and boyfriends.

'Not easy, is it?' Her mother was reading her mind.

'No.' Kate decided to be honest. 'But I'd like you to tell me about my father.'

'He was a decent young man. You'll know from the birth certificate he was called Grahame Lossing. He went out of my life before you were born. It's possible he never knew I was pregnant. Oh, and by the way, he was a lovely dancer.' Pauline propped her elbows on the table and rested her chin on her hands. 'But let's get to know each other a little bit first. There's such a lot of catching up to do.'

They talked. Pauline told Kate she was a widow.

'Lawrence was a smashing chap. I miss him.' She looked down at the half-eaten cake on her plate. 'I took my time marrying, though. I was in my early forties before I took the plunge.'

'I was over thirty.' Kate told her mother a little about her early life, stressing the happy moments, and then she spoke about meeting Jack, marrying him and moving to Leeds.

'It's strange, isn't it? The Hamptons adopted me in Devon. I lived in the South until I was over thirty, and then, because of my marriage, I came back to the North.'

'And I was living in Manchester.'

'Yes.'

They stared at each other. Then Kate mentioned that Jack had been a widower when she met him, with a young daughter.

'I brought my stepdaughter with me today, as a matter of fact. She was wanting to buy some new clothes and I, well . . .' She gave a self-conscious smile. 'I wanted company.'

'I know. I could have done with some support myself when I walked in here.' Pauline looked round her. 'Where's the lass now?'

'I said I would meet her at four o'clock.'

'Oh, are you leaving so early?'

'I thought it might be best. I didn't know . . .'

'How we'd get on.' Pauline finished the sentence for her. 'Maybe you're right. We mustn't over-do things.'

There was an awkward silence and then she said, 'I don't know about you, Kate, but I'm glad we've met each other. I've seen you, and I know your life is happy, that's a bonus as far as I am concerned. I won't ask how you feel. I suppose you're as confused as me?'

She looked at Kate who nodded her head helplessly. She wanted to reply to her mother but quite suddenly her throat was tight with tears.

Pauline sighed and, taking out her handkerchief, polished her spectacles again. Then, when they were firmly back on her nose, she spoke briskly.

'We've a bit of time left before you meet your step-daughter. What I'll do is tell you a bit about your dad. After that,' she pulled a little face, 'it's up to you. You've got my address. I hope you get in touch, but if you don't, I'll understand.

'Now, like I said, your father was an excellent dancer. We met at a dance in Whitby when I was sixteen years old. Oh, by the way, he was a good-looking chap, tall and slim with dark red hair . . .'

Chapter Twenty-Two

The loudspeaker system operating on the rig crackled into life and a Scottish voice boomed out instructions.

'Will the following personnel report to the office and pick up their leave cards: Jimmy O'Connor, Del Richards, Ron Blackstone . . .'

Jack Gallantree, trying to have a conversation with his wife, pressed the telephone receiver closer to his ear. 'What was that you just said?'

'I said, she doesn't look at all like me.' Kate was silent for a moment. 'You know, I spent the whole afternoon with her but I *still* can't think of her as my mother. Do you think that's strange, Jack?'

'It would have been more strange if you had fallen into each other's arms.'

'Yes, I suppose you're right.' Kate cleared her throat. 'It was awkward at first, we just talked about silly things, but then we relaxed a little and later she explained about the adoption. She was quite brave about it. She told it straight, gave me the facts. She didn't ask for sympathy but it was obvious she hadn't *wanted* to part with me. I was a sickly baby and she had nowhere decent to live and no job. She was at her wits' end.'

Jack heard her take a deep breath.

'Anyway, I'll tell you all the details when you get home.'

'Did she say anything about your father?'

'A little bit. And guess what?'

'I don't know.' A man passing by nodded to Jack and he nodded back. The man hesitated, and then made a gesture as though he was shooting pool. He raised his eyebrows questioningly.

Jack nodded again and held up his free hand with fingers outstretched, indicating five minutes. The man went on his way.

'She said she'd met Grahame, my father, at a dance when she was sixteen. Apparently he was in his mid-twenties and had served in the army during the war. She said he was tall and slim and he had red hair.'

'Oh.' Jack searched for a suitable comment. 'Did she keep in touch with him? Does she know where he is now?'

'No. I gather they split up before I was born. But just think, Jack, now we know where Danny gets his colouring from.' She gave a little laugh. 'I think it was his hair that started this whole business off.' She waited a moment but when he said nothing, she continued. 'Grahame was a salesman. He travelled around Yorkshire selling farm equipment. Pauline told me the name of the company, Manner's Farm Equipment. Perhaps that will help us to trace him. Anyway,' apparently sensing a lack of response, her voice became uncertain, 'I've been chattering on for ages. I'll tell you the rest of my news later.'

'That would be best.' He shifted his weight on to his right leg. 'There's a fair bit of noise going on in this area, it's difficult to concentrate.' He paused. 'And I'll be home next week. I'll be in Leeds about four o'clock on Wednesday. I'll hire a car in Aberdeen.'

'That's lovely, Jack. I'll have a meal ready for you.'

'Don't go to any trouble.' But he knew she would. She enjoyed cooking for him. Fleetingly, he thought of all the conversations they had shared in kitchens. Indeed, when they had first started going out together, a kitchen seemed about the only place in which Kate completely relaxed; and when they started courting seriously, whenever he had taken her out to a film or to a show, she had always insisted on repaying him by cooking him dinner. It was the least she could do, she had argued, when he had demurred. As a widower he must have had a hard time of it, particularly with a little girl to care for.

Initially, Jack had tried to explain to her that he was quite competent in matters of cooking and house-cleaning. During his first marriage there had been times when Felicity had worked harder and longer than he had, and at such times he had cheerfully accepted his share of household duties. He could hoover, clean and polish, iron shirts satisfactorily, and although not a natural cook, could make adequate casseroles and, at a pinch, rustle up an eye-watering curry. Felicity had once told him he was a better cook than she was, and he had not denied it.

But Kate was different from Felicity. With her, cooking was an act of love, and when he realised that, and saw her at work, he came to enjoy watching her prepare a meal. She would tie a large gingham apron around her trim waist and, as she lit the oven and assembled the various ingredients, her face would become totally absorbed in the details of her task. He learned she loved using herbs, tarragon with chicken dishes, coriander with pork, and chives and fresh rose-mary with lamb.

'Everyone always uses mint with lamb,' she had told

him, on his first visit to her flat to share a meal, 'but that can be really boring.'

He remembered he had looked at her and wondered whether or not to laugh. Surely she was winding him up? But then he realised she was serious and the realisation had made him feel tenderness towards her. He knew she was over thirty years old, but at the same time she was like a little girl playing house – and the meal had been fantastic.

'I never dreamed you could cook like that, Kate. It was wonderful.'

'Honestly?' Her face had lit up.

'Honestly.'

He had kissed her properly then, for the first time. And the way she had responded to him had revealed there were other things he did not know about her.

Remembering, Jack shook his head and smiled to himself. Such a ladylike, earnest young woman Kate was at times, but every now and again another personality would flash out and surprise him.

She had been good with Helen. She'd cooked things for her, too. The first time he had taken his daughter round to meet her, Kate had produced teatime treats of . . . he wrinkled his brow in an effort to remember . . . yes, on Helen's first visit, there had been raspberry and walnut shortbread and chocolate orange soufflé set out on an embroidered teacloth. Jack remembered Helen's startled face as she had surveyed the feast. Before Kate's arrival on the scene, Helen's teatime treats had been a Marks & Spencer's trifle, or cod and chips from the fish shop.

Jack sighed, Helen would eat neither cakes nor fish and chips now, for fear they would make her fat. Still, Danny enjoyed his food. In another year or two, Kate would be in her element, arranging children's parties. The last time he had been home, that rather weird friend of hers had turned up with her three kids and there had been a tray of gingerbread men awaiting them. Kate loved youngsters.

He thought of his wife again, but in the bedroom instead of the kitchen, and he recalled her face as she gently laid their sleeping son into his cot. And then, because he had not held her for almost two weeks, he thought of her figure, flimsily clad in the cream silk nightgown he had given her for her birthday, and his voice deepened.

'It's not just your cooking I'm missing, Mrs Gallantree.' He waited, the phone pressed hard against his cheek. 'Miss me?'

'You know I do.' Her voice was quiet.

'Good.' He smiled. 'Roll on next week.'

'Going to be much longer, Gallantree?'

Jack glanced at the man waiting and straightened up. 'I'm going to have to go now, Kate. Someone else is wanting to use the phone. Shall I ring on Sunday?'

'Yes, of course.'

'After my shift then, about six-thirty?' He paused. 'You've told me about your meeting with your mother, but is everything else OK? What about Helen, is she still desperately in love?'

Kate laughed. 'I think so. I gather the young man's taking her out on Sunday.'

The corners of Jack's mouth turned down. 'Is he? I'd like a look at this chap. Has she said . . .'

'Helen hasn't told me anything about him, Jack.' Kate paused, waiting for him to speak, but when he didn't she continued: 'And don't start worrying that it's anything to do with me being her stepmother.

She's a teenager now, and teenagers are not noted for communicating. But she's OK. I don't think you have anything to worry about.'

'I suppose you're right. It's just it doesn't seem five minutes since she was starting primary school.' He paused. 'You two getting along OK?'

'Yes, pretty well. I went to the school's open evening last week and I gather her schoolwork's continuing to improve, and she went through to Manchester with me when I asked her. But I've told you that, haven't I?'

'Yes.'

'On the train journey home, she actually said she thought my mother was rather nice, but as she only spoke to her for about five minutes I . . .'

The man waiting coughed loudly. Jack interrupted her. 'I'll have to go now, Kate.'

'Just one more minute, please. I need your advice.'

The man next to him leaned against the wall and shut his eyes. Jack smiled apologetically and listened.

'My mother wants us to keep in touch. She mentioned I would be welcome to visit her. She's really keen, Jack, but she says it's my decision and if I don't go, she'll understand. What do you think I should do?'

'I think no one can answer that except you.'

Her silence made him realise he had said the wrong thing – or the right thing, but too abruptly. He tried again. 'You set the ball rolling, Kate. You're happy about the first meeting and you've learned some of the facts about your adoption, but only you can decide whether to take it further. Do you want your mother to become part of your life? It sounds as though she would like that. If you *do* decide to visit her, there'll be no going back later, you realise that?'

'Yes, I do, but . . .'

He cut her short. 'I *have* to go. Sorry. Don't do anything before Sunday, I'll ring you then.' He rang off and stepped away from the telephone.

The man waiting brushed past him. 'Bloody hell, that must have been an important call.'

Jack shrugged. 'Yes, I guess it was.' He put his hands in his pockets and walked away, a thoughtful expression on his face. It wasn't over with yet. He admitted to himself that, deep down, he still regretted Kate's decision to search for her natural parents. Thousands of people grew up with adoptive parents, and they didn't all go dashing about asking questions about where they came from. But she had insisted, and the Lord only knew where it would all end.

The trouble with Kate was that she was so intense. Now she'd actually met her mother, he knew how she would analyse and re-examine every little thing that was said and done. She would lie awake at nights and suffer agonies of indecision before deciding whether or not to proceed with the relationship. And him being away didn't help. She had no one to turn to. If only she could learn to be more relaxed about life, roll with the punches, as he had learned to do. Ah, well. He took his hands from his pockets and rubbed his forehead. He'd be home soon. He'd talk things through with her then. At the moment there was nothing he could do to help. He went off to find his snooker partner.

Over the years, in addition to learning how to ride out life's blows, Jack had also become accustomed to living in two very different worlds. There was his life at home and his life on the rig.

As he walked through the reception area someone

shouted to him. Jack turned his head. Ron Blackstone came puffing up. Ron's name had been one of those called out over the tannoy. Dressed in the regulation bright orange suit, he was heading for the helicopter pad, for his trip to the Shetland Islands and then home.

'We never played that other game of chess, Jack.'

'No, we'll play when you get back.'

'I'll look forward to it. I'd better warn you, though, I've thought up a new move. I'll kill you dead, son.'

'I'd best get practising then.' Jack clapped the older man on his shoulder. 'You'd better get a move on, Ron. They'll be taking off without you.'

'Aye.' But Ron, after nodding farewell, did not rush as he made his way towards the lifts.

Watching him, Jack recalled that Ron had recently been widowed. Poor devil, no wonder he was in no rush to leave. He remembered Ron had two children, but they were grown up now and away from home. Jack thought that Ron would probably become one of the group of oil workers who preferred life on the rig to going home on leave.

It was sad but understandable. During his working life, Ron, like everyone else on the rig, had his food cooked for him. The twenty-four-hour laundry system kept his clothes and kit clean and he was always surrounded by company.

And Ron's main hobby was photography. He spent hours in the darkroom, developing and processing his films. Jack had one of his framed photographs up on the wall in his cabin. It was a dramatic view of the sea, taken during the dawn watch. It showed tumbling restless grey waves, a yellow and grey sky, distant lights from the other rigs around them, and dominating the whole scene, a huge flare of gas against the sky. It was a terrific picture.

Jack went into the sports hall and apologised to his partner for keeping him waiting. They played three games and he won two of them. Then he returned to his cabin, showered, dressed in his working kit and went to the canteen for a meal. He ate grilled haddock, new potatoes and broad beans in parsley sauce and declined a sweet. With the good food on the rig and Kate's cooking at home, it was time he started watching his weight.

He was lucky in that he was naturally lean of build but his last birthday had been his fortieth, and he had no intention of gaining a middle-aged spread. He made a mental note to start working out in the gym more regularly and then checked his watch. He had half an hour to kill before he started work. He went up on deck for a breath of air.

Jack enjoyed company but it was good to be on your own at times and he often spent half an hour up here, just watching the sea. It was something he never tired of for the sea fascinated him. It was like a restless, playful giant, always moving, always twisting and weaving itself into patterns that formed, dissolved then came together again.

Today the giant was quiet, but the power was still there, below the surface.

Staring down into the depths of the ocean, Jack remembered times when, like a capricious child, the sea threw tantrums, storms which caused concern even amongst the well-drilled, well-prepared oil men. Then the waves would rear like wild silver horses, with white foam-capped heads, and the tingle would start inside you, and the phones would begin ringing. The emergency survival crews and the fire-fighting teams would spring into action, and everyone on board would rush to their mustering points, uneasily aware that the impressive structure in which they worked was not invincible after all.

But today's scene was peaceful. The helicopter had disappeared from view and the sky was quiet. Down below him Jack saw the standby boat had arrived and supplies were being brought aboard the rig. He watched the activity for a little while, but the routine was familiar to him, the boats came daily, and so his mind wandered.

He must remember to seek out Ron on his return to the rig. He knew how the old guy must be feeling. Jack had been down the same road himself after Felicity's death. His grief had been deep and it had lasted a long time but now he was happy again and, remembering his first wife, knew she would have approved of his happiness. Felicity had been a fine woman. Thinking about her, and about Kate, Jack reckoned he was a fortunate man for two special ladies had loved him.

Kate was unlike Felicity in every way, but their marriage worked. Thinking back to the party at which they had met, he smiled. He had been one lucky guy to find her. There had been plenty of other women in the room the day he had met Kate, but they had scared the pants off him.

It was true that Felicity had been a strong-willed woman, but that had been different because the two of them had known each other since childhood. Felicity he had been able to tease, and later, after their marriage, when he didn't agree with her they would argue and then he would go off on his own for a bit and she would sulk. Then he would come back and they would kiss and make up and sometimes she would have her way and sometimes he would have his. Boy, oh boy, what rows they had had.

After her death he had never contemplated remarriage. The hurt was too raw and had lasted a long time, and anyway he had been too busy, looking after Helen. He had socialised very little, and his attendance at the party where he had met Kate had come about by accident.

The oil company had sent him down South to attend a week's course in Beckenham. He hadn't wanted to go, but the company insisted their employees kept up to date with the latest procedures. On his third day, a man he had become acquainted with, who lived fairly locally, said that his sister was having a party and would Jack like to accompany him?

He almost refused. He had got out of the habit of socialising, but he had nothing better to do and so he had said yes. Once at the party, he found himself regretting his acceptance. He knew no one except Clive, the man who had invited him, and most of the other guests were in couples, and much younger than he was. He got a drink and tried to join in the conversation, but they were talking about pop groups he had never heard of and alternative comedians he couldn't stand. He had gloomily swallowed his whisky and felt one hundred years old.

There were a few older women. Clive told him they worked in advertising. His sister was a receptionist at a well-known advertising company.

Jack looked at them and decided they were no receptionists; they had the confidence that came with power. They had long red fingernails and their voices were loud and their eyes restless. Jack did not regard himself as a chauvinist but he felt intimidated by these women. They wouldn't be interested in him, they were way out of his league.

He had finished his drink and decided to leave. He edged his way towards the door and bumped into a young woman who, it seemed, was trying to hide behind the leaves of a large potted plant. It had been Kate and he had caused her to spill her drink. He had apologised and then, despite her protests, gone to fetch her another one. Then they had both taken refuge behind the rubber plant, and they had talked. They shared a plate of little sausages and fancy bits and pieces and talked again. When, towards the end of the party, he had asked her out, she had agreed. And that's how it started. Dear Kate, what a bundle of contradictions she had turned out to be, lacking in confidence in many ways and yet competent and tough in others.

Leaning on the rail and looking out to sea, Jack wondered what Kate's adoptive parents had been like. She kept their photograph on her dressing-table, she said her childhood had been happy, but Jack, studying Clive and Olive Hampton's smiling faces, had often wondered.

In the photograph Clive and Olive smiled tight smiles, without showing their teeth, and both of them appeared to be excessively neat. Clive Hampton wore a dark grey suit, immaculate white shirt and maroon tie. Olive was dressed in a matronly knitted twin set, in a lavender colour, and wore pearls.

Jack remembered he had once asked Kate if her old man had ever dressed casually, worn a sports shirt or a sweater? She had said she couldn't remember but added, as an afterthought, that in all his working life, he had never been late for work.

In looks the couple resembled each other. Both were handsome with fine spare features and thin lips. They looked like a couple who had set high standards for themselves and every one else. Had Kate managed to live up to their expectations? Jack wondered. She hadn't gone to university. Had her parents' tight smiles wavered at their adoptive daughter's examination results?

Poor little Kate. He could imagine her at school, a tiny girl seated at her desk, her cap of shining hair falling about her face, stubbornly plodding her way through her lessons. He shook his head.

She had certainly been stubborn in her determination to find out about her *real* parents, and now she had found her mother. Jack hoped she wouldn't be disappointed. She'd go and visit Pauline, of course. She hadn't come this far just to give up now. And from what she had told him, the old girl didn't sound too bad. If the next meeting went well, he'd encourage Kate to ask her mother to visit them. After all, if Pauline was now a widow with no kids of her own, she must be lonely.

Well, he straightened up from the rail, whatever happened, he'd see Kate was OK. And she had him now, and Helen. Although, his brows went up in a rueful expression, perhaps Helen wasn't *always* an asset. And she had Danny.

He stepped away from the rail, leaving the sea to its endless twisting and turning, and went down to level four to clock on.

Time would tell whether the newly-found addition to their family set-up would prove a good thing or not.

And at least it now meant that Danny had one living grandparent. Surely that had to be a bonus.

Chapter Twenty-Three

Jack woke first. He always did, following his first night at home. It was difficult adjusting to normal time-keeping after working twelve-hour shifts. He yawned then rolled over in bed to face his wife.

Kate lay on her back. Her face rosy with sleep, her eyes were closed and her lips gently parted. One of her arms rested across the upper part of her body, but Jack saw the three top buttons of her cotton nightshirt had come undone, and an entrancing glimpse of a small round breast showed.

He looked at her. They had made love the night before, but he found he wanted her again. He sat up in bed, bent over her sleeping form and gently brushed back her hair from her forehead. She sighed and turned her head on the pillow.

'Kate?' Gently, he slid his hand beneath the cloth of her nightshirt and cupped her breast. His thumb brushed against her nipple.

'Ummm.'

He waited.

Her eyelashes flickered, her eyes opened. She smiled. 'Don't stop, that's nice.'

'Good.' He continued to caress her, his fingers moving lightly over her body. He took pleasure in her smooth unblemished skin and rejoiced in her sensitivity, for as he caressed her breasts, her response was immediate. Her breathing quickened and her nipples hardened and lifted beneath his touch.

She gave a little shake of her head and rested her hand against his bare chest. 'Wasn't last night enough for you?'

'God, no.' Now his body was responding. 'It just makes me want you more.'

She smiled again.

He kissed the corner of her mouth and then, with one smooth movement, moved on top of her body and took possession of her. As excitement surged in him, he groaned, 'I'll never have enough of you, Kate, never.'

He couldn't make it last, the taking and the giving was too sweet, and yet, as they lay together afterwards, Jack knew Kate felt as fulfilled and complete as he did. He knew by the utter relaxation of her body, the expression on her face as she turned to look at him.

'Thank you, darling.'

'Oh, Kate. It should be me, thanking you.'

'No, no.' She paused and then laughed, softly. 'Let's pass on the thanks. It was a case of mutual satisfaction, wasn't it?'

He raised her hand, clasped in his, and kissed it. 'I like to think so.'

'We're so lucky.' She rested her head on his shoulder. 'Will we always be so lucky, Jack?'

'Of course.'

'You sound so sure.' Her voice was low. 'And yet so many people make a mess of their life. They start off with such high hopes and then something happens, and everything begins to change.'

'Life can't stand still, Kate. Change brings good things as well as bad.'

She stirred. 'I suppose so.' Then, after a moment's silence, she added, 'Right now, I think I would prefer my life to stay exactly as it is.'

Jack pulled himself up in bed, arranged his pillows and then sat back and looked at her. 'You're worrying about your mother's visit this afternoon?'

'Yes.' She grimaced. 'Silly, isn't it?'

'I think so. What is there to worry about? You said you got on fine when you visited her.'

'But that was different. It was at *her* home, and there were only the two of us there.'

'That could be more difficult than having family milling around.' Jack smiled. 'If Danny puts on his comic act for Pauline, it should defuse any tension in the air.' When Kate did not return his smile, he continued: 'Tell me, when you arrived on her doorstep, was she nervous, like you are now?'

'If she was, she didn't show it.'

He looked at her averted face and kept talking. 'And what about the flat? You've told me something about your conversation, but nothing about her home. What did you think of it?'

She shrugged. 'It was all right – neat, clean, rather anonymous.'

He scratched his chin. 'No clue to her character, eh? What about photographs, books?'

'There was only one photograph on show. A pleasant-looking man with a thin face and spectacles. She said it was her late husband. No books to speak of. Oh, there was a collection of owl plates on one wall, she must admire them.' Kate pulled a little face.

'The bathroom suite was a vile shade of puce.'

Jack laughed. 'Now you're being catty. It's quite possible, you know, that the puce bathroom suite was already installed when she moved in. Ours was!'

Kate had the grace to look ashamed. 'Yes, you're right. I'm not being fair. It's just . . . I'm nervous. I felt the same when I was on my way to visit her. I kept wondering whether she would pour out her heart to me, tell me what she really felt about me tracing her, and I didn't know whether I could handle it.' She shrugged. 'In the event, we just chatted, about most commonplace things imaginable.

'She told me about her childhood in Whitby and about the time she and my father had together. It wasn't very long. To be honest, I don't think she knew him at all, not really. It was just one of those affairs that happen. I think she was young and naive and he took advantage of her and then left her in the lurch.'

She glanced at her husband. 'I suppose I'll still try to find out about the company he worked for then, but if nothing comes of it, I'll let the matter rest.'

Jack nodded sympathetically. 'The counsellor did warn you that natural fathers were difficult to trace. Poor old Kate.'

She tried to smile. 'No honestly, I don't mind. The way I feel at the moment, I wonder why I bothered at all. Nothing is working out as I expected.'

'Oh, don't say that. You have met your mother and it's early days yet. And surely, it's better to take things slowly and steadily. You and Pauline have over thirty years to catch up on.'

'I suppose you're right.' But Kate didn't look at him.

Jack decided to lighten things up a bit. 'Well, the

fact is, Pauline is coming to see us today so we'll try and make the visit a success. And I assure you,' he pulled a comic face, 'you don't have to worry about us.'

'I know all that.'

'So?'

She shrugged. 'I just feel on edge, that's all. I'll be glad when it's all over.'

'But it will never be "all over", will it?' An edge of irritation sharpened his voice. 'Today's supposed to be happy, a celebration, Kate. Your *mother's* coming to see you. Surely that's something you've been working towards for the last seven months?'

'Don't you think I know it?' Kate jumped out of bed and grabbed hold of her dressing-gown. 'And I'm well aware I'm being perfectly stupid. Of course everything will be fine. Anyway, I won't bore you by talking about it any more. I'll go and make breakfast.' She left the room.

After the door closed behind her, Jack sighed. Turning, he punched his pillow a couple of times to release his frustration. He'd been home forty-eight hours and this had been the second sudden outburst. He thought that he, too, would be glad when today was over with.

'This is nice, Kate.' From her place at the table, Pauline smiled first at her daughter and then at her newly met son-in-law. 'I appreciate you welcoming me to your home, Jack.'

'My pleasure, Pauline.' His reply was cordial but careful. Kate's mother was trying hard to please and she seemed pleasant enough, but it was early days.

'It was so awkward, that first meeting at the cafe,

but we coped, didn't we, love?'

Kate nodded, but it was Helen who replied. 'It was more sensible, though, to meet for the first time on neutral ground. I mean, you might have hated each other at first sight.'

'Helen!' Jack choked on his cup of tea but the rebuke that he had intended making died on his lips. His daughter had merely put into words what other people were thinking. He sent her a warning look and she smiled sweetly back at him. He looked away from her, reflecting that his daughter was probably enjoying this tea party. She was no doubt filing away in her memory the best bits of conversation to repeat to her friend, Eileen Abbey. He put the thought from him and helped himself to another of Kate's freshly baked scones.

'Helen's quite right.' Pauline's soft voice interrupted his thoughts. 'Before I met Kate, I did worry over why she had decided to trace me. I went to meet her prepared for angry words. After all, she had every reason to feel resentment towards me.'

'Don't say that, Pauline.' Kate was frowning. 'I don't really remember how I felt on that first day, but I certainly wasn't angry. I was apprehensive, about meeting you and learning the circumstances of my adoption, but I knew it was something I had to do.' She broke off and glanced across at her son, who was in his high-chair next to Helen, busily smearing his face with chocolate cake. 'It was Danny's birth that started the whole thing off.'

'Was it?' Pauline looked thoughtful. 'Yes, I can understand that.' She looked across at Danny with a queer expression on her face, a look Jack couldn't fathom. It was a guarded, closed-in look, compounded of a mixture of longing, resignation, acceptance and . . . guilt? Whatever it was, it unsettled him. He averted his gaze from her face.

Kate was on her feet. She was being the perfect hostess. She brought in a fresh pot of tea and another plate of goodies. 'Try these, Pauline. It's a new recipe I've discovered.'

'Thanks.' Pauline dutifully bit into the cake. 'It's delicious, Kate. You've a wonderful light hand. Eliza would have been proud of you.'

'Eliza?' Kate paused, milk jug in hand. 'Oh, yes, that was the grandmother who raised you after your mother died?'

'Yes. Your great-grandma.'

Pauline's expression was once again serene. Jack, looking back at her, wondered if he had imagined the earlier conflict revealed for one brief moment on her face.

Helen chimed in. 'Did Kate's dad really have hair the same colour as Danny's?'

'Yes. Exactly the same. Gave me a shock, it did, when I first saw your half-brother, Helen.' Pauline looked thoughtful. 'And I seem to remember Grahame mentioning once that his father had been red-headed.'

Helen's questions, reflected Jack, although blunt to the point of rudeness, did not appear to cause Pauline embarrassment and they did bring out more information about Kate's forebears.

The women chattered on and Jack watched his wife's face as her mother spoke about her life in Whitby just after the war and about the time she and Grahame had met and won a dancing competition. It was interesting, but all surface stuff.

Nothing was said about why Grahame departed from the scene before Kate's birth, or why Pauline's father turned his back on his pregnant daughter. That information, he presumed, would emerge more slowly, at a time when Pauline and Kate were better acquainted and there was no inquisitive almost fifteen-year-old present.

'You've a grand house, Mr Gallantree.'

Jack jumped when he realised Pauline was addressing him directly.

'Yes, we like it. And please call me Jack.'

'I will, thank you.'

Pauline was looking at him expectantly. It was time for him to make a contribution to the conversation.

'Kate told me she enjoyed her visit to your flat. Have you lived there long?'

'A fair few years. It suits me well enough. It's handy for the shops and the traffic's not too bad. I envy you your garden, though. Never had a garden myself. I've always lived in bedsits or a flat. I ran a boarding house once, with another woman, but it didn't have a garden.' Pauline's voice trailed off and her eyes assumed a far-away look.

For the first time, Jack felt his own stab of curiosity regarding Kate's mother. This ordinary, middle-aged woman seated at his table was a complete mystery to them all. And it was within her power to tell or withhold information as she wished. She need only tell them what she wanted them to know. He glanced across at Kate and began to appreciate his wife's confusion. For over twenty years she had assumed the Hamptons were her real parents. After she had been told about the adoption her real mother had been a shadow, and yet now she was seated at the tea-table with them, drinking tea and eating cake. After so many years, would the two of them ever be able to establish a close relationship? He felt a moment of depression.

'If we're all finished?'

Kate was collecting dishes, Pauline was stacking plates and Helen was hauling Danny out of his high-chair. As she lifted him, the edge of his slipper caught against the retaining strap and his left leg banged hard against the chair. The impact must have hurt him. Immediately he flung back his head and howled.

Helen flushed. 'Oh, come on, Danny. That didn't hurt . . .'

But Pauline was on her feet and at Helen's side. She took Danny from Helen's grasp and hugged him against her shoulder.

'There, there, little one. It's all right – really, it's all right.'

She rocked him until his cries subsided then cupped her hand defensively around the back of his head and smiled apologetically at his parents. 'You don't mind, do you?'

'No, of course not,' Kate stammered. But she did, and so did Jack.

Pauline's careful conversation and correct manners had been cracked wide open by Danny's cry. She had met her grandson three hours ago, but it was obvious that already she loved him. And her love was powerful, the strength of it showed in the speed with which she reached him, the way she held him and her expression as she looked at him.

Jack stared. Danny was silent now and gazing intently into the face of this stranger who held him. Then, when Pauline's lips turned up in a delighted smile, he smiled back. He slapped one plump hand on either side of her face and, leaning towards her, obligingly rubbed noses with her.

Jack realised he was watching a pact being formed. His son and Pauline were completely oblivious of everyone else in the room. His throat felt tight and dry. He swallowed and instinctively moved to stand next to his wife. He took her hand and squeezed it. She turned and stared up into his face.

He smiled, a little ruefully, and bending towards her whispered, 'We've started something here, love.'

'She's a right card, your mum.' Nicky's voice was approving. 'Not many grannies would dare to go down that slide.'

They were at the park. Nicky was pushing Shawn's swing and Kate pushed Jamie's.

'No, I suppose not.' Kate's push was so vigorous that Jamie screwed his eyes shut as he went soaring high into the air. Kate didn't notice; she was averting her gaze from Pauline who, dressed in pink sweater and purple jogging pants, was shooting down the slide clutching a shrieking Danny on her knee.

Nicky stepped back from Shawn's swing and hoisted Lisa, her baby daughter, higher on her arm. 'Let's go and sit down for a minute. These two will be all right.' She went towards a nearby bench and Kate followed her. They sat down.

'They seem to get on well together.'

Pauline and Danny had deserted the slide and were now playing peek-a-boo through the play tunnels.

Kate sighed. 'Yes, Danny thinks the world of her.'

'Every kid should have a granny like Pauline.' Nicky bent to pick up Lisa's soft shoe which had fallen from her foot and lay under the bench. 'I wish my mam had a bit more life in her. She sees the kids regularly, but she doesn't bother with them much. Mind, she's had so many of her own, I suppose the novelty wore off by the time it came to having grand-children. But it's different for Pauline, isn't it?'

'I should say. I was adopted when I was sixteen months old, she never had any more, and she's only known Danny for three months.'

Kate heard the waspishness in her voice and felt ashamed, particularly when Pauline looked across at her at that very moment and smiled and encouraged Danny to wave to her.

She waved back and then said, 'Sorry, Nicky. I'm a bit grouchy today.'

'No need to apologise.' She bounced Lisa on her knee.

Kate remembered her manners. 'How's the new place?'

For the past six weeks Nicky and her family had led the life of gypsies. Their old landlord had finally claimed back his flat and the local authority had been unable to find them permanent lodgings. A few days ago the council had moved the family again.

Nicky smoothed back Lisa's hair from her forehead. 'It's a nice big room. If we were on holiday there, we'd be thrilled to bits, but living there permanently is a different matter.' She sniffed. 'Ironic, isn't it? When you think of the money they're paying out for us.'

Kate nodded. It was ironic. The council were paying a fortune to keep the family in bed and breakfast accommodation because no council house was available for them. She put her hand on Nicky's arm.

'You'll come back for tea, won't you?'

'Oh, I don't know. Your mum's visiting you and . . .'

'There's no difficulty there. Pauline likes you and the children. Go on, Nicky, say yes. I'd like you to come.'

She gave in gracefully. 'All right then.'

They sat together in a companionable silence, watching their children play. It was a lovely May afternoon. The sky was a deep blue and a light wind fluttered the blossom on the trees. The boys and girls running around the playground wore light tops and shorts. Their arms and legs were becoming tanned. Even Nicky's three children sported freckles and sun-flushed faces. Kate commented on their healthy appearance.

'They should look healthy, I spend most of the day outside with them. You don't think I stay indoors, do you? I'm not holing my kids up in one room when the weather's like this.'

Nicky's voice was over-controlled and tight. Like her children's, her face was tanned, but Kate saw the strain in her eyes and the general weariness of her figure. She felt so sorry for her, but it was difficult to know how to help. She shuddered, remembering the day she had awkwardly offered money – that had been a great mistake. Since then, she had learned to be more careful.

'So, how are you two getting along?'

'Sorry?' Kate collected her thoughts.

'You and Pauline. How's it going?'

'Pretty well.'

'That's good.'

'Yes.'

They lapsed into silence, watching the children.

Things were going well – they *were*! Not exactly how

she had imagined they would be, but well enough. During the last couple of months, a pattern had evolved. Each alternate fortnight, she went through to visit Pauline or Pauline visited her. And they were getting to know each other, even though progress sometimes felt slow.

During the visits, they had tried to fill in the past. Kate had told Pauline something of her childhood and she had told Kate more about her early life. On one occasion, she had suddenly spoken about her father's rejection of her, at first with some passion and then with resignation.

'You can't keep on hating someone, not for years and years.'

Kate had listened to her make excuses for the way her father had treated her. He had still been grieving the death of his wife, Pauline had been his only child, all his hopes had been pinned on her and she had let him down. Things were different in the forties. An illegitimate baby was a dreadful thing, especially in a small place like Whitby. In some ways, his behaviour had been understandable.

'I don't think so.'

At her daughter's words, Pauline had dropped her eyes. It was different then, she had repeated. She told Kate that she had written to her father years later, but he had never replied. 'He must be dead by now. It's so sad.'

By mutual consent, they abandoned that subject and tried another. They talked about themselves, their likes and dislikes, anything they could think of to bridge the gap between them.

One day Kate mentioned she had always liked reading.

'So do I.'

They had smiled at each other and on her next visit Pauline brought with her some of her favourite books. She lent them to Kate who returned the favour. But Kate read literary works and Pauline liked popular novels.

Kate returned her mother's books. 'Sorry, I couldn't get into them. The endings were a bit silly, I thought. In real life, it wouldn't have happened like that.'

And Pauline retorted, 'I don't want to read about real life, I want a bit of escapism.'

And then she complained about Kate's favourite book. 'In three hundred pages, nothing happened. It was boring.'

'You have to read *between* the lines.'

And they stared helplessly at each other.

They never rowed, it was just they kept coming up against walls. Their differences were like weed-killer, sprinkled on the blossoming roots of their relationship. It seemed they could agree on nothing.

They went shopping and that too had been a disaster. The sudden spell of fine weather at the end of April had caught them napping. They had taken Danny and gone to buy summer clothes.

'How about this for Danny?' Pauline held up a romper suit in pale blue, with voluminous knickers and a matching hat.

'It's pretty.' Kate had looked apologetic. 'But a bit childish for him, don't you think?'

'Childish? He's not two yet.'

'I know. But children wear more grown-up clothes nowadays. It's the fashion.'

Pauline had sniffed. 'I've seen them fashionable clothes. Great long trousers on the tiny mites. You ought to let the sun get to their limbs.'

But the suit went back.

By the time Pauline had tried to persuade Kate to buy a short-skirted sundress and some make-up – 'You always look so pale, love' – and Kate had tried to dissuade Pauline from buying the purple jogging pants, the ones she was presently wearing, the atmosphere was spiky, but still polite. They never quarrelled.

They had trailed home. Danny, fed up with shopping, screamed for Kate but went to sleep blissfully in Pauline's arms – another niggling bone of contention.

Sitting next to Nicky, Kate experienced a feeling of resigned sadness. She and Pauline would never be close, and she was beginning to think it must be her fault. Because everyone else liked her mother.

Helen liked her. She told Kate that Pauline made her laugh. The elderly neighbours next-door liked her. She had been round to admire their rock garden and had stayed two hours. The women at the park liked her. Indeed, they communicated with her much more readily than they had with Kate when she had first visited the park. And now Nicky was openly admiring her.

Why couldn't Kate? Why did she, whenever she was with her mother, notice things she *didn't* like about her? They were such small things, too. Kate felt ashamed of herself for letting such things bother her, but they did. Those awful purple pants, for instance.

Nicky admired Pauline for playing with Danny, but when Kate watched Pauline coming down the slide, she just thought how unseemly she looked. In her view, grannies shouldn't wear purple jogging pants, they looked ridiculous. Pauline's hair was dyed, too.

Sometimes, you could see where the roots needed touching up.

And she certainly liked her own way. Kate had seen her mouth set when she had returned that ludicrous romper suit to the rail. Kate had felt quite angry then. Why should Pauline feel she had the right to choose Danny's clothes? If it had been left to her, she would never even have known she had a grandson.

Watching Pauline pick up Danny and swing him round, Kate felt uncomfortable. She was thinking petty thoughts and she knew why. She took a deep breath. She was being petty because she was jealous – but what could she do about it?

At four o'clock they all went back to Kate's house for tea.

'You're quiet.' Nicky wiped the last cup clean and placed it on the draining board, then she folded up the teatowel.

'Am I?' Kate tried to smile. 'Sorry. I've a bit of a headache.'

'Good job Pauline's here then. She's good at entertaining the kids.' Nicky nodded towards the open door.

Pauline had all the children in the sitting-room. She was telling them a story. The two young women listened. There wasn't a sound from the children but a great deal of huffing and puffing from Pauline.

Nicky grinned. 'I think the wolf's trying to demolish the brick house. I always loved that story when I was a kid, especially the end when the wolf fell into the pot of boiling water.'

Kate's lips pressed together. 'I hope Danny feels the same. Otherwise he'll be awake at three in the morning, screaming from a nightmare.'

Nicky's eyebrows twitched. She said mildly, 'I shouldn't think so. In my experience, parents worry too much about their children's delicate sensibilities.'

'Well, of course – you would know.'

The two friends stared at each other and then Kate gasped, 'Sorry, sorry. You're the last person I should vent my bad temper on.'

Nicky jerked a chair forward and made her sit down. 'Explain.'

Kate sat, but shook her head. 'No. It's nothing.'

'Well, if it's nothing, it shouldn't take much sorting out.' Nicky's expression was humorous. 'And why not vent your bad temper on me?'

'Because,' Kate gestured feebly, 'it's nothing to do with you, and you have problems of your own, real problems.'

'So your problems aren't real ones?'

'Not really, I mean . . .'

'Good, then they'll soon sort out.' Nicky pulled out a chair for herself and sat down next to Kate. 'It's Pauline, isn't it?'

Kate gaped. 'Is it so obvious?'

'Not really, but you forget, I'm an expert in family matters.' Nicky's voice held a rueful tone.

Kate's shoulders slumped. 'I know it's mostly my fault, but . . .' And out it all came – her disappointment at the lack of feeling between herself and Pauline, the annoyance her mother's actions caused her, the feeling that Pauline was somehow taking over the family.

'Danny loves her because she plays with him all the time.' Nicky paused. 'She's still a bit of a novelty, remember. He's seen you every day since he was born. Helen probably champions Pauline because she senses you have reservations about her. That's what teenagers are supposed to do, isn't it? Disagree with their parents.' Nicky scratched her chin. 'What does Jack say?'

'I haven't told him how I feel. He's away a lot and I like things nice when he's home.'

Nicky clutched her head in mock dismay. 'You're so close-mouthed, Kate. You'd feel a lot better if you discussed this with Jack. And if you'll pardon me for saying so, you're too intense. Try and relax a bit.' She paused. 'Have you ever let Pauline know how you feel?'

'Of course not. I don't want to hurt her feelings.'

'Why?'

'Because . . . she's my *mother*, and it was I who contacted her. I can't start grumbling because it turns out she's not like I thought she would be.'

'So you're responsible for everything?'

'Yes.'

'Rubbish!' Nicky exploded. 'You're not God, you know. You can't make everything perfect. Just consider, what if you had never been handed over to your adoptive parents? What if Pauline had kept you? Do you imagine she and you would have had a perfect relationship? Do you think all parents and all kids are crazy about each other? If you do then I wonder where you have been all your life.' She stared at Kate. 'Did your mum and dad row much?'

'No. I don't think I ever heard them quarrel.'

'Maybe that's the trouble. A good row can often clear the air.' Nicky broke off. 'That's it.'

Kate moved restively on her chair. 'What is? You think Pauline and me should have a row? A lot of good that would do.'

'Not a proper row, although that wouldn't be the end of the world.' Nicky rested her hand upon Kate's knee. 'But why don't you try being honest with her? Tell her what you *really* think about things.'

'I couldn't. She'd be upset.'

'Maybe not. And consider, maybe there are a few things she'd like to tell you. And if a few home truths develop into a row, so what? Families *do* row, Kate. But they make up again.'

She pulled nervously at her bottom lip. 'I don't know.'

Nicky stood up. 'Well, at least think about what I've said. You know, once you start speaking out, you might find you enjoy it.'

Chapter Twenty-Four

Helen came in from school then and serious conversation ceased. Nicky collected up her brood and departed. Kate gave Helen her tea and then took Danny upstairs for his bath. The fresh air and the sunshine plus the company of other children had tired him and by seven he was tucked up in his cot fast asleep. Kate tidied his toys away, collected up his scattered clothes and put them in the washer. Then she walked through to join Pauline and Helen who were in the sitting-room.

As she entered the room, she heard her stepdaughter explaining to Pauline in lurid detail Nicky's housing problems.

'And now they're stuck in this awful boarding house, all squashed into one room. There's no cooking facilities or anything. Richie, Nicky's husband, is going mad with worry.'

'You've never met Richie, Helen, so how do you know he's going mad with worry?' Kate asked her question in a reasonable way but inside she was shaking with anger. How *dare* Helen discuss Nicky's personal life with Pauline? 'And they're not living in an "awful boarding house", it's a perfectly respectable hotel.'

'Still, it's a ghastly way of living, isn't it? Poor Nicky.' Helen's expression showed not sympathy but avid curiosity, and Kate felt like slapping her.

'Yes, it is a ghastly way to live, but it's Nicky's business and not ours so please drop the subject. Haven't you homework to do?'

Helen's expression changed. Her face registered peevish astonishment. 'You know I have, but I can do it later. I was talking to Pauline.'

'Well, I'm here now, so you're free to go upstairs and get on with your work.'

Helen stared, and then sensing her stepmother's disapproval, she picked up her schoolbag without another word and flounced out of the room. Kate gave a grim smile. Nicky was right. You should let people know how you really feel.

'She didn't mean any real harm, you know.' Pauline sounded anxious. 'Girls that age, they like to dramatise things.'

'I know they do, but she had no right to talk about Nicky's troubles.'

'I'm sorry. I suppose I should have stopped her.'

Kate did not reply and there was an uncomfortable silence until Pauline spoke again.

'Danny's gone to sleep quickly.'

'Yes, the warm weather's tired him out.'

Pauline fidgeted in her chair. 'You know, I feel pretty tired myself.' She avoided looking at Kate. 'I think I might go up, too. I have to catch the early train tomorrow.'

'But,' Kate looked at the clock, 'it's only just after seven.'

'I know, but it's been a busy day for both of us and I dare say you could do with some time on your own.'

I could, thought Kate. Oh, I could. But then she studied Pauline's face and felt a pang of compunction. Her mother did look weary, and somewhat depressed. Kate remembered how she had chased around with Danny and Nicky's children in the park and how she had entertained them after tea. She suddenly realised that her mother was under similar pressure to herself, only more so because Pauline had the whole family to contend with.

'No, don't go to bed yet,' she surprised herself by saying. 'Let's sit and relax for a bit. I fancy a drink. Would you like one?'

'I don't know.' Pauline hesitated. 'I'm not much for drinking, unless it's a special occasion.'

'Well, pretend tonight is special.' Kate stood up. 'I think I'll have a spritzer. What about you?'

'A spritzer? I don't . . .'

'It's white wine and soda.'

'Oh.' Pauline looked dubious. 'I'm not used to wine. Lawrence occasionally bought me a vodka and lime. I like that because you can't really taste the vodka, can you?'

Kate's eyebrows quirked. 'A vodka and lime it is.'

She went and collected the bottles and glasses, put them on a tray and carried it through to the sitting-room. She handed Pauline her drink and they sat back in their chairs and enjoyed the late sunshine streaming through the sitting-room window. And whether it was the fine evening or the alcohol, their desultory chat gradually turned into a natural and unstrained conversation.

'This room has a lovely atmosphere.' Pauline looked around appreciatively. 'And it's so light and airy.'

'Yes, that's one thing we noticed when we first looked round. The high ceiling helps, of course, although it makes decorating difficult. We had to buy rolls and rolls of paper and the deep skirting boards just gobbled up the paint.'

'Was a lot of decorating needed when you first moved in?'

'A fair bit. The old lady who owned the place didn't believe in white paint. Showed up the marks, she said.' Kate laughed.

'And the furnishings.' Pauline shook her head. 'They seem to fit so well.'

'I'm glad you approve. Jack gave me a free hand over those. It's only this last year that this room began to look habitable, because I took ages finding some of the pieces. The house is Edwardian, you see, and I wanted furniture that fitted the period. We couldn't afford genuine antiques so I've cheated quite a bit. The chair you're sitting in is modern, but I liked the shape so I bought it and had it re-covered in material that matched the carpet and curtains.'

Pauline rested her head against the back of the chair in question, and sighed. 'You talking like that, it reminds me so much of Eliza, my gran. She loved old things, too. She had this sideboard, it was her pride and joy. She told me it had been in the family for years and years but because I left home the way I did, I never knew what became of it. Such a pity. It would have looked lovely in this house.'

She took a sip of her drink and looked pensive, then her face brightened again. 'I've got one of her treasures, though. I'll show it to you next time you come through to Manchester. It's a small figurine, a little boy . . .'

Kate interrupted. 'I think I spotted it, the first time I visited you. I wanted to ask you about it then but it seemed cheeky. I didn't get a good look, but if I was right, you must take great care of it, Pauline. I think it's a Marieberg, and if it is, it's worth a lot of money.'

'Well, would you believe it!' Pauline drained her glass. 'Fancy both you and my gran knowing about such things.'

'Yes.' Kate took their glasses, poured out more drinks and handed Pauline her glass back. 'I was talking to Jack yesterday and . . .'

'How did you manage that?'

'What?'

'Talk to Jack?'

'Oh.' Kate laughed. 'Quite easily. There's a telephone link with the rig.'

'Is there?' Pauline's cheeks reddened. 'I never realised. I thought, with him being stuck out there in the North Sea, you'd have to write to each other.'

'We do that too. And the letters are delivered the next day.' Kate looked down into her wine glass and swirled the liquid around. The fresh piece of ice she had added made a soft clinking sound. 'Ridiculous, isn't it? The postal service is much better than the normal one on land.' She gave a faint smile, seeing Pauline's look of embarrassment. 'It's all right, I didn't know anything at all about oil-rigs until I married Jack. Actually, they're like floating hotels, there's everything on them.'

'Except wives?'

'Yes.' Kate sighed. 'Anyway, he told me to ask you if you'd like us to all go through to Whitby one day when he's home again, but only if you want to, of course?'

'Do you know,' Pauline sat upright in her chair, 'I think I'd like that. I have happy memories of Whitby, even though things did go sour at the end, and I've never been back. I suppose I was afraid to, but so many years have gone by and if we all go together, I can show you round.'

'We'll go then.'

'Yes.'

The sun had finally disappeared and Kate stood up and drew the curtains. The distant thump of music from upstairs signified Helen had finished her homework and was relaxing. Kate, her second drink finished, also felt relaxed. Recklessly, she turned back to the tray. 'How about another one?'

'Oh, I don't think so. I'm already feeling the effects of what I've had.'

'Oh, go on. Look,' she held up the vodka bottle, 'this one's almost dead, you might as well finish it off. And it's not as if we have to go out. We can toddle off to bed when we feel like it.'

'All right,' Pauline held out her glass. 'But only if you'll join me.'

The bottle of soda was also empty so Kate filled her own glass to the brim with white wine. She handed Pauline her drink, sat herself down and the two of them smiled at each other.

'This is better than going to bed at seven o'clock, isn't it?'

'It certainly is.' Pauline made a little face as she tackled her third glassful. 'It's a bit strong.'

'Nonsense. Anyway, how do you know? As you say, vodka doesn't taste of anything.' Kate shifted in her seat. She was feeling the effects of the sun, her face and forearms were tingling. She smiled ruefully at

Pauline. 'It's a good job Jack isn't home. I shall have a face like a tomato tomorrow.'

'No.' Pauline studied Kate's profile. 'It's not that bad.' She sat back again. 'You must miss him. He's away a lot, isn't he?'

'Yes, he is and I do miss him, but I'd lived on my own for a long time before we married so I was used to my own company. And looking after Danny and Helen keeps me busy. Of course,' she took a swallow of wine, 'I hate it when he goes back, but I must admit, it's a lot of fun when he comes home again.'

Pauline laughed out loud. 'I'm so pleased to hear you say that. So many marriages nowadays seem to be unhappy, but I can tell you two are well suited.'

'And you were happy with Lawrence?'

Pauline looked down. 'Yes, I was.'

'But what about before then, Pauline? You told me you were in your forties when you married Lawrence. Surely there was someone else after Grahame?' Kate closed her mouth abruptly. 'I'm sorry. I told Helen off for her bad manners and now I am being just as insensitive. Don't tell me if you don't want to.'

'I don't mind you knowing, Kate.' Pauline placed her empty glass on a nearby occasional table. 'Yes, there was someone once. It was all a long time ago.' She stared at her daughter. 'The feelings Lawrence and I had for each other were deep and warm but years before then I experienced the kind of love that makes you feel you're up there on cloud nine.' Her smile widened. 'That's why I'm so pleased about you and Jack. I remember, you see.'

Her expression took on a self-absorbed look and her voice was quiet. Kate strained to hear.

'I was scared off men after Grahame. The way he

left me, the things that happened, well, it took me a long time to heal. And I was also too busy earning a living. My gran had left me a few hundred pounds but it was amazing how fast that evaporated, and then I had nothing. I also had,' she paused, 'certain expenses. I needn't bother you with details. So you see, I had precious little time for romance. Mind you,' she looked up and gave Kate a little grin, 'I did get a few offers.'

Watching her mother's face, Kate believed her. Even now, Pauline was an attractive woman.

She continued her story. 'I was thirty-three, or maybe thirty-four, I can't quite remember. Anyway, I was running a boarding house then, with a woman called Julie Hunter. She was a widow. We'd been in business for two years.

'One day, a young man came to stay. He was training to be an engineer and was attending a nine-month study course at the polytechnic. His name was David, he was twenty-one and he was the most handsome young man I had ever seen.'

'And he was the one . . .'

'Yes.' Pauline adjusted her spectacles and smiled at Kate's look of surprise.

'Are you shocked? I suppose it does seem rather ridiculous, although it didn't at the time. What made matters worse, Julie had a daughter living with her who was seventeen years old. Julie even said to me, Wouldn't they make a lovely couple? And I said yes, only it didn't work out that way.' She paused. 'For some reason, I have no idea why, David set his sights on me.

'I didn't realise at first. I thought he was a pleasant, polite young man, but that was all. When I did realise, I remember I gave him a motherly telling-off. I told him to find a girl at the college, I even suggested he took out Julie's daughter, but he just smiled and looked at me.' She stopped speaking for a moment and Kate gazed at her curiously.

'He would ask me to go out with him, two, three times a week, and I refused. Then one day it was my birthday and I was feeling a bit down, he asked again and I agreed. And that's how it started.'

Kate swallowed some wine. 'And you actually had an affair with him, a boy of twenty-one?'

'I did. It lasted the whole time he stayed with us and I never regretted one day of it.' Pauline's voice was firm.

'But what made you do it? I mean, you were old enough to . . .'

'No, I wasn't, Kate. I wasn't old enough to be his mother, and when I was with David, I felt the same age as him. I was seventeen when you were born, *seventeen*. And for years after . . .' She took a deep breath. 'After the Hamptons took you, I felt old and tired. And then one day there was David, looking at me as though I was the first woman on earth. What was I supposed to do?'

When Kate didn't answer, she shrugged. 'I suppose at first I was just flattered, because he was genuinely involved, Kate, he wasn't trying to make a fool of me. I'd read that young men were often attracted to older women and that's the way David felt about me.'

'And you?'

'As I said, I was flattered. But then it became much more serious. You see, David made me feel young again. We laughed a lot. When I was with him, I believed the world wasn't such a bad place after all. And the sex was wonderful.'

Pauline was feeling in a good humour. She watched

the play of emotions on her daughter's face and smiled. 'Am I shocking you? I don't know why. You enjoy going to bed with Jack, don't you?'

'Of course I do, but he's my husband.'

'You're lucky. I'd never had a husband. Instead I'd had worry and grief. When David made it clear he wanted me, I thought, Why not? Didn't I deserve loving? Didn't I deserve some pleasure?'

'But it didn't last?'

'Bless you, I never thought it would. David did, though. Towards the end of his course, he asked me to marry him.'

Kate just looked at her. Pauline gave a rueful smile and answered her unspoken question.

'I said he'd done me a great honour but for both our sakes, I had to refuse. He was very upset. I had to work hard to make him realise why I had to say no, but in the end he understood.'

'So he went away?'

'Yes.'

'You must have felt unhappy?'

'I did, but I'd prepared myself and we parted on good terms with no recriminations. And I've never regretted our affair. We both derived happiness from it.' She sighed. 'But Julie never forgave me. She really had earmarked David for her daughter. A few months after David left, we ended our partnership.'

'And David?'

'He went on to work in London. He kept in touch for a while and then he stopped writing.'

'Oh, Pauline – I'm sorry.'

'No, it was better that way. I was left with good memories.'

Her voice ceased and there was a moment of

silence. Kate was unable to read her expression.

Earlier in the evening, when she had drawn the curtains, she had not switched on the lamps and now it was dark outside. In the uncertain light, she studied the pale disc of her mother's face and wondered whether she should say any more.

'Maybe I shouldn't have told you.'

'No, I'm glad you did.'

'Are you sure? I suppose to some people the idea of a lover fourteen years younger than yourself would seem disgusting.'

Kate frowned and switched on a lamp.

Pauline's face looked blurred and Kate realised she was close to tears. She also remembered that the last vodka she had poured for her mother had been a large one, and Pauline was not used to drinking. She realised the spirit had loosened her mother's tongue and now she was regretting her confidences.

She went and knelt by the side of Pauline's chair.

'I certainly don't think that. I'm glad you told me about David.' She paused. 'I know you had a rotten time when you were young. Whatever happiness you had later in life, you deserved. Please, you mustn't worry about it.' And on a sudden impulse, she dropped a kiss on Pauline's cheek.

Her mother put her hand to her cheek and stared at her.

Kate smiled. 'Come on, I think it's time we both went to bed.'

'Yes.' A little unsteadily, Pauline stood up. 'I've enjoyed our talk, Kate. You're a good person, I think.'

'I hope so.'

She slipped her hand underneath Pauline's elbow.

Her mother's remark about not being used to drinking was patently true. She swayed as Kate helped her towards the door.

'You sure you're all right, Pauline?'

'Yes.' She gave an unexpected giggle. 'Have to be careful on the stairs, though.'

'Yes.' Kate switched on the landing light.

'I've been thinking, Kate.' Pauline wavered towards the stairs.

'Have you, what about?'

'Those two rooms on the top floor. You don't use them much, do you?'

'No. But you're comfortable up there, aren't you? I know there's not a lot of furniture but . . .' Kate's voice trailed away and her brows drew together. She and Pauline had made progress during the last couple of hours, but she hoped her mother wasn't moving too fast. Suppose she suggested moving in with them! How on earth could she answer?'

However, Pauline's thoughts were not for herself. 'You're fond of Nicky, aren't you?

'Yes.'

'I'm surprised you haven't asked her to stay with you, just until the council finds her something permanent, of course.'

Kate stopped dead on the fourth step of the staircase. Pauline blinked anxiously at her.

'It's just a thought.'

'Yes.' Kate's voice was thoughtful. 'It is.'

She saw Pauline safely into her bedroom, came downstairs to switch off lights and lock up, and then went back upstairs and checked on Danny. He was sleeping peacefully. She went into her bedroom and sat on the bed. Have Nicky to stay here?

But it wouldn't just be Nicky, it would be three small children and Richie, too. Jack wouldn't like it at all.

Not only Jack, a little voice whispered.

No, the idea was really just too ridiculous. She had Danny to consider, and Helen, and Jack would go up the wall at the very idea. And it would mean sharing her cramped little kitchen with Nicky, and the two rooms on the top floor were quite small, too small for a family.

But for each problem posed, she knew there was an answer. Jack was easy-going and liked Nicky, he could be talked round. Danny loved playing with Nicky's children. Helen would roll her eyes and look aggrieved but her interests lay outside the home at the moment. She was more interested in her boyfriend than in anything her parents did. And Nicky? She was proud and might refuse, but as Kate had realised today, she was tired, so tired. She might agree. Surely living in the two top-floor rooms of a friend's house was better than bedsit accommodation in a hotel? And Richie? Kate chewed her nails, a habit she was trying to break. Richie was a completely unknown factor.

She undressed, washed, got into bed, and unsuccessfully tried to forget Pauline had even mentioned the idea.

Jack drove the hired car round into the back lane and parked. He took his bag from the seat and went through the gate into his garden. The paddling pool was out, Danny stopped pouring water over Jamie's head and shouted, 'Dada, Dada.'

'Hey, son.' Jack crouched down and ruffled Danny's wet hair, then he retrieved a yellow plastic duck from a flower border and gave it to Jamie. 'Where's Mummy?'

They both pointed to the kitchen. Jack went indoors.

'Kate?'

Nicky raised her blonde head. She had a dab of flour on her nose and was wielding a pastry cutter. She was busy stamping out rounds of scones.

'Hello, Jack. Kate's upstairs.'

'Thanks.' He made for the door and then hesitated, feeling he should comment on the new arrangements. 'Everything OK, Nicky?'

She gave him a wide smile. 'Yes, it is. And, Jack, I want to say . . .'

He ducked his head. 'No need. I'll just go . . .' He backed out of the kitchen.

Going upstairs he noticed someone had filled in some of the pastel flower prints on the wallpaper with biro and that there were small grubby fingerprints on the polished banister rail. On the first landing he nearly fell over a toy train. Kate was in their bedroom, putting away a stack of freshly ironed clothes.

'Jack.' She came to meet him. 'I didn't expect you yet.'

Why not? It's after three o'clock, he found himself thinking. He pushed the thought away and kissed her. And as he did so, the full realisation of what he had agreed to began to dawn on him.

His house was full of other people. He wondered desperately why he had agreed to their presence. On the rig, Kate's request and the explanations backing up her reasoning had seemed to make sense. Now that he was home, he was not so sure. He hoped to God their lodgers would not be staying too long. He held

Kate away from him and studied her face. How was she bearing up? She smiled up at him. Her brow was unlined and her expression happy.

'I'm so glad you're home. And the weather's great, isn't it? We've planned all kind of things to do these next two weeks.'

'Who's we?' He narrowed his eyes suspiciously.

She laughed. 'Everyone. You know, Jack, things are working out beautifully. I did worry at first, but there was no need. We get on so well. Even Richie's not as bad as I thought. And I see Pauline almost every week now. We've become much closer. At last we're beginning to "jell".

'Nicky and I are taking the children to the swimming baths tomorrow and Pauline's coming, too. Will you? Do you know, Pauline can't swim. She says none of her family ever did. Apparently the fishermen thought it was unlucky to learn, sort of tempting providence. Isn't that ridiculous?'

'Kate . . .' Jack was dazed by her flow of words. 'Kate, I . . .' He bit his lip and stared at her. How could he explain that he felt suddenly a stranger in his own house? How could he tell her he was jealous of all these people crowding in on them?

Perhaps he didn't have to. She looked back at him, her head on one side, then the wrinkle between her brows disappeared and she stood on tiptoe and kissed him.

'Poor Jack, it's all new to you, isn't it?' She kissed him again. 'It's all right, honestly.' She smiled and linked her hands behind his neck. 'I've missed you so much,' she murmured. 'Kiss me properly, please.'

He did so, and in his kiss released his frustration and staked his primary claim on her. He kissed her until she gasped. He pulled her to him possessively and wrapped his arms tightly around her body.

'Umm, that's good.' She opened her eyes and gave him a mischievous look, and then she pulled his shirt free from his trousers and rested her hands on his bare back.

'How do you fancy going to bed with me?'

'Now?' He was astonished.

'Yes.'

'But Nicky and the children?'

'Nicky's broad-minded, and she'll keep an eye on Danny for us. Come on.' Her hands moved up and down his back. 'Helen will be home in half an hour. That should be enough time.' She edged him towards the bed.

He couldn't believe the change in her. He was perplexed but intrigued. Indeed, as he shucked off his clothes, he felt laughter bubbling inside him. This wasn't his normal homecoming. The house wasn't in its usual immaculate condition and he'd bet he wouldn't get a three-course meal tonight, but he wasn't complaining. In fact, as he joined her on the bed and buried his face in her sweetly smelling hair, he felt a distinct change of mood. He thought he might well adjust quite nicely to this new way of living.

Chapter Twenty-Five

Helen pulled a face at the meal Kate was preparing and said she would have poached eggs on toast instead. Ten minutes later she sprinkled salt over her eggs and shuddered at the plateful of sausages, eggs and bacon Kate had placed in front of her father. She put on an innocent look.

'Not your usual fare, is it, Dad?'

Kate flushed, but to Helen's annoyance her father began to eat his food with obvious enjoyment.

'Makes a nice change, Helen. I've always enjoyed a good fry-up.'

He sounded good-humoured, which disappointed her. She had anticipated ructions on his arrival home, when he realised how much had changed now that the house was full of people. 'Fried food causes heart attacks,' she muttered.

'Only if you eat it all the time.' Jack refused to be ruffled. He smiled across the table at her. 'Anyway, what's been happening in your circle lately?'

She stared down at her plate. 'Nothing special. Nothing worth telling you about.' She saw the glance that passed between Kate and her father and she flushed. 'I'm sorry, but I'm not really hungry. I think I'd better get straight on with my homework. I've got heaps to do and I've promised to call for Eileen at half-past seven.'

'But you should eat something.'

'I'll get some fish and chips for supper.'

'You're not worrying about a heart attack, then?'

She did not smile at her father's little joke and so his own smile faded.

'Do you have to see Eileen tonight? I thought we'd spend a bit of time together later, Helen. Just you and me.'

Oh, yes. Time together meant he intended pulling his 'father' act, by asking her lots of questions. She knew, they had been there before. It was almost amusing, except that it was also squirm-making. He'd start off casually, chatting about schoolwork and her friends, but in between the innocent stuff there'd be little comments – like he hoped none of her crowd was into glue sniffing or smoking pot. Then there'd be a lecture on being careful. In other words, 'safe sex'. If only he'd be honest, ask her straight out. Then she could tell him she wasn't a cocaine-using nymphomaniac, and watch his reaction.

She looked at him blankly. 'I can't let her down. I promised. We can talk tomorrow, can't we?'

In her own room, she took out her books and stacked them on the table. She'd told the truth about having lots of homework. She started with her English Literature assignment, reading a chapter from one of her set books. She opened *Return of the Native* and stared down at the closely printed pages. She sighed. How could she concentrate on Thomas Hardy's boring old characters when her heart was broken?

She propped her chin in her hands and when a tear escaped and plopped on to the open page, watched with dreary disinterest as it spread into a small, damp spot. The plain unvarnished truth was that Ben Raymond had dumped her. He hadn't turned up for their date last night and this morning, in assembly, had completely ignored her. And instead of accepting it, she had behaved stupidly and made everything worse. She had gone up to him at breaktime, spoken to him, and he had looked right through her, as though he had never met her in his life!

His friends had giggled as she had walked away. Helen's face grew hot, remembering. She sniffed. Apart from Eileen there was no one she could confide in, nowhere she could go to find comfort. No one had time for her at home any more. Kate was too busy looking after everyone else and there was no peace; the house was full of little kids, it was like living in a kindergarten. She'd even stopped asking her friends round, it was just too embarrassing.

She had waited eagerly for her father's return home. He would hate it, too, she was sure he would. But it appeared he did not. He didn't seem bothered. Of course, it was all right for him, he didn't have to *live* here all the time, and Kate had always been able to talk him round to her way of thinking. Helen closed her eyes. If only she had the same effect on Ben.

Another tear dropped on to the page. Helen blotted her eyes with her sleeve and then tried to concentrate on her reading. Eustacia, the heroine in the book, had also known misery. She too had been crossed in love. *She* had thrown herself into the weir. Helen knew that because Miss Jensen, her English teacher, had read the ending out aloud to the class.

Deserting the book, Helen crossed to the window. She looked down at the front garden. It was a fair old drop. For two pins she'd throw herself out, then they'd all be sorry. She pressed her forehead against the glass and imagined them, Kate, Dad, Nicky, all of them, weeping, and grouped about her limp, broken body. The scene presented was so powerful she shivered and even opened the window a couple of inches, but then she reconsidered. Directly below her was the rockery. Outright death, she could contemplate. Disablement she could not.

She shut the window with a bang, left her room and crept down the stairs. Her parents were still in the kitchen. She could hear Kate's voice. Were they talking about her? She listened.

'No, we don't eat meals together. Before Nicky agreed to come here, we sorted out certain rules. We both agreed there can be too much togetherness. Nicky, Richie and their children have the kitchen and dining-room at certain times. The same goes for the bathroom. It works OK.'

Helen heard her father's voice, but not his reply. She put her ear to the kitchen door.

Kate laughed. 'No, he's not at all as I imagined. He's tall with brown hair and a thin face that has a kind of haunted look. He's terribly shy and doesn't often look straight at you. Oh, and he stammers when he meets someone new, so be prepared.'

She was talking about Richie. That figured. Everyone was more important than she was. She scowled and backed away. Her jacket hung over the banister. She grabbed it and went out, slamming the front door behind her.

'Was that Helen?' Jack looked up and frowned. 'She can't have finished her homework already.'

'I don't suppose she has, but there's no point saying anything.' Kate sighed. 'She's been very difficult these last few days.'

'Is it the extra people in the house?'

'I don't think so. I discussed everything with her before asking Nicky and she was all for the idea. She might have changed her mind, I suppose.' Kate shrugged. 'How am I supposed to know how she feels when she won't tell me?'

'I'll see what I can find out tomorrow.' Jack's voice was troubled.

The back door opened and a tall, thin young man, dressed in jeans and a sweat shirt, ambled in. He stopped short on seeing Kate and Jack.

'Oh, s-s-sorry. I'll . . .' He backed away.

'No, it's all right.' Kate jumped up. 'This is my husband Jack. Come and be introduced.'

Jack presumed the stranger was Richie. He put on what he hoped was a welcoming smile and stuck out his right hand. He wondered whether Richie's clothes were really two sizes too large for him, or whether it was because he was now shrinking into them, like a tortoise into its shell.

'You must be Richie? I'm pleased to meet you.'

'Yes.' His hand briefly touched Jack's. 'I th-th-thought . . .' He stopped and then tried again, speaking more slowly and with deliberation. 'I've g-g-got the plans.'

'Oh, have you?'

Now Kate looked flustered. Jack looked at her questioningly, but she avoided his gaze.

'Thanks. I'll look at them later, when I've more time.' She snatched at the envelope Richie held out to her.

'An archway w-w-would be the b-b-best idea, I th-think.'

'I'm sure it would. Are you going upstairs now? I think Nicky's bathing the children. She could do with a hand.'

Richie nodded and moved towards the door, but then he stopped and turned back to Jack. 'I w-wa-want . . .' He frowned and gestured helplessly with his hands.

Jack, seeing the cords stand out in his neck as he struggled to speak, removed his gaze from Richie's face and looked down at the table.

'I want to thank you.' The words came out in a breathy rush. 'You've been k-kind. We a-a-appreciate it.' He put out his hand again and this time his handshake was firm and a brief smile, like a flash of sunlight, lightened his morose-looking face. Then he was gone.

Jack stared after him.

'He's bad today because he doesn't know you. You'll find him easier to talk to in a couple of days. He's a decent young man, really.'

'I believe you.' Jack transferred his gaze back to Kate. 'What are the plans he was on about?'

'Oh, just something we were discussing.'

'So tell me?'

'Really, it's nothing.'

'Kate!'

She gave in, showed him the brown envelope. 'Richie's worked in the building trade and he's well qualified. He knows all about brick-laying, and plumbing, even electricity. He hasn't a job at the moment, through no fault of his own. The housing market's depressed and, as you can see, he wouldn't impress at a job interview. It's his nerves. The family have had a rough time, housing problems, etc. I told you about it.'

He nodded. 'And the plans?'

Avoiding Jack's gaze, Kate took various papers from the envelope and spread them out on the table so he could see.

'I mentioned that I hoped to have the kitchen altered. He was interested. He's suggested some really good ideas for a conversion job and said he had contacts in the building trade. I thought, well, if he can get the materials we need so much cheaper . . .' She saw Jack's expression change and fell silent.

'We've had this conversation before, Kate. We can't afford a new kitchen yet.'

'But when we talked before about it, we were thinking of employing a proper building firm. And if Richie . . .'

'I wouldn't let that young man change a light bulb! I feel sorry for him, but you have to face facts, Kate, the guy's a nervous wreck.'

'He's only just met you. He's different when he gets to know people, and when he talked to me about his ideas . . .'

'Talking isn't doing. Honestly, Kate,' Jack ran his hands through his hair, 'I sometimes wonder what's happening to you? Since Danny's birth, it's been one madcap scheme after another. You've had me tearing around the country looking for your mother, we've now got a family of five camping out with us, and you're *still* not satisfied. Now you want a crazy chap to work on the kitchen.'

'That's cruel, Jack. Richie's not crazy.'

'He's not far off.' Jack shook his head in

bewilderment. 'What will you think of next?'

Kate's expression hardened. 'You've agreed to everything. I always talked to you first. I didn't just go ahead and do it. Anyway, nothing's decided about the kitchen. I just thought . . .'

'Well, stop thinking.' Jack smacked his hand down on top of the plans. 'We can't afford a new kitchen, and that's that.'

The next day, following a successful swimming session, Kate, Nicky and Pauline were busy in Kate's kitchen. Kate was making sandwiches, Nicky was spooning jelly into small dishes and Pauline was rinsing out bathing suits of various colours and sizes.

'Talk about Little and Large.' With a wide smile, she held up the substantial flowered swimsuit she had been wearing and a minute pair of blue trunks which had adorned Danny's rear end. 'Look at these.' She dropped the swimwear back into the bowl. 'Where are the clothes pegs, Kate?'

'In the cupboard below the sink.' Kate spoke absently. She opened another jar of salmon paste and tackled the next slice of bread.

Nicky and Pauline exchanged glances.

'Is something the matter?'

'No. Why do you ask?'

'Oh, nothing. You've been very quiet today.'

'I'm fine. You might get the children to sit down at the table after you've hung out the swimwear, Pauline, their tea's ready.'

'Right.' She found the pegs and went into the garden and Nicky took the food into the dining-room.

They supervised tea. When the little ones had finished, Kate wiped their hands and mouths and took them through into the sitting-room where they sat down in a row on the carpet to watch children's television. Meanwhile Nicky had made a fresh pot of tea. When Kate returned to the dining-room the three women collapsed into their chairs with a sigh of relief.

'They say swimming's good for you, but I ache all over.' Pauline twisted her neck from side to side. 'Not that I can swim properly yet.'

'You're improving. You were much better than last time. Another couple of sessions, and I reckon you'll manage a width of the pool. Danny's getting much more confident in the water, too. Don't you agree, Kate?'

'What?'

'I said, I don't know who will swim first, Danny or Pauline.' Nicky frowned. 'I wish you'd tell us what's the matter?'

When Kate remained silent, Nicky's face clouded. 'It's us, isn't it? I was afraid this might happen. Jack wishes you hadn't invited us to come and stay with you.'

'No, it's not that.' Kate shook her head. 'And it's nothing to do with you, either.' She smiled briefly at her mother. 'Jack and I had a bad argument yesterday, but it was about silly, stupid things.'

'Rows usually are.' Nicky kicked off her shoes, stretched out her legs and drank her tea. 'Want to talk about it?'

'I'd like to, but I don't think I should. It wouldn't be fair to Jack. You'd just hear my side.'

Nicky interrupted. 'He's gone to see a mate of his, hasn't he?'

'Yes, but I doubt whether he'll tell him about the row. Jack's not one for discussing personal problems with his friends.'

'And the row was personal?' Nicky sat upright in

her chair. 'What an absolutely daft remark. Rows always are personal.'

'It started because of my ideas about altering the kitchen.' Kate told them about the argument, omitting Jack's remarks about Richie.

'But it wasn't just that. He's edgy about lots of things. He says he thinks Helen's unhappy because she's so moody and quiet at the moment.' Kate paused. 'And I gather he's not too happy about me.' She pulled a rueful face.

'He says I'm changing, always wanting things to be different, making decisions without consulting him. Perhaps he's right. But why shouldn't I change? It would be a boring world if we all stayed exactly the same. I'm getting older, I've had Danny, I can't stay exactly the same as when I married him. I don't know what all the fuss is about. I don't feel differently about him.' She blushed. 'I still love him.'

Nicky scratched her chin. 'Oh dear.' She looked across at Pauline. 'I think a weekend away is called for. Do you agree?'

She nodded. 'Decidedly.'

Kate looked from one to the other. 'What do you mean, a weekend? You don't mean me and Jack? It's impossible. We can't just clear off.'

'You could if Helen would agree to spend next weekend with me.' Pauline rubbed her chin thoughtfully. 'I'd be happy to have her and I could meet her off the train. We always get on well together, and a change of scene might be good for her.'

'And I'd look after Danny.'

'Oh, no, Nicky, you do enough already. I wouldn't dream of leaving Danny with you for a whole weekend.'

'It's no problem. In fact,' Nicky spread out her hands and smiled at Kate, 'I'd welcome the opportunity to do *you* a favour. You've been so kind to us.'

'What nonsense. I told you, I love having you here.'

'Just stop right there for a moment, Kate.' Pauline's voice was soothing. 'How long is it since you and Jack were completely on your own?

'That's easy.' Kate sighed. 'It was our honeymoon.'

'There you are.' Her mother nodded benignly. 'It's decided. You're going to have your weekend. There's no use arguing. All you have to do is get Jack to agree, decide where you're going, and pack a bag.' She raised her teacup. 'Agreed?'

The three of them looked at each other. 'Agreed.'

Kate and a slightly bemused Jack departed to the Cotswolds. They booked into a four-star hotel, went for drives, saw the sights, ate good food and drank a little wine. They talked, listened to each other for most of the time and regained their sense of humour. And each night, they made slow, satisfying love in a king-sized bed which had real feather pillows. They returned home relaxed and happy.

Danny, Nicky informed them, hadn't missed them at all. They hoped that was true but were delighted when he gave them a rapturous welcome. He had cut another back tooth during their absence. He showed it to them before opening his present and when the wrappings fell away to reveal a miniature golf set, he beamed and went off to show it to Jamie and Shawn.

Helen and Pauline arrived at the house two hours after Kate and Jack's arrival. They met them on the doorstep and saw, with relief, that Helen looked blooming and had a smile on her face.

'Pauline's bought me a new dress. I'll go and put it on for you to see.' She disappeared upstairs.

'We had a bit of a shopping spree. No, it's all right,' Pauline spoke hurriedly, seeing their expressions, 'I didn't spend too much on her. Most of the stuff came from the market, but we bought the dress in Fenwick's.

'And by the way, I found out why she's been so unhappy.' Pauline lowered her voice. 'That boyfriend of hers, Ben something-or-other, he's dropped her. I didn't know whether or not to mention it, because she told me about it in confidence, but I knew you've been worried. I thought you'd be pleased to know her moods were nothing to do with you, or with Nicky and her family.'

Pauline sighed. 'You know, people laugh about first love and teenage troubles, but they shouldn't. That girl was really upset.' An impish smile appeared on her face. 'But we had a bit of luck. I took her to a tea dance . . .'

Kate choked on the biscuit she was eating. 'You did what?'

'It was in one of the big stores. We happened to be there so we went along to watch. Remember how she's always asking me about my dancing days? Anyway, when we arrived, a formation team was there, giving a display. They were only young, about sixteen years old, but they were good.' Pauline looked dreamy. 'It brought back memories, I can tell you. I used to love Latin American dancing.

'After the exhibition, the group mixed with the rest of the people there and one of the boys came over and asked Helen for a dance. You should have seen her face! She said she couldn't dance properly but he persuaded her to get up. He could have persuaded anyone, I think.' Pauline sighed. 'He was a very handsome boy. His manners were good, too. After the dance he brought her back to the table and thanked her.

'After that, she never mentioned Ben again. I think she's woken up to the fact that there's always more fish in the sea. And do you know, she had me on my feet for two hours when we got back to the flat, showing her how to do the cha-cha-cha. I wouldn't be surprised if she started asking you if she could have modern dance lessons.'

Jack and Kate looked at each other and then he said, 'We don't know how to thank you, Pauline.'

'No thanks needed. I enjoyed myself.' She levered herself from her chair. 'Now where's that grandson of mine? I'll have to go back to Manchester on the early train tomorrow. I'm due into work at half-past twelve. And by the way, Kate . . .'

'Yes?'

'I think I'll have to miss the next swimming session. I've visited you a lot, lately. It's been lovely, but things are piling up at home. If it's all right with you, I'll probably wait four or five weeks until my next visit. Oh, and I'll make it a time when Jack's away on the rig.'

'You don't have to stay away because I'm home, Pauline.' He stared at her. 'Anyway, what about our trip to Whitby?'

'Oh, we'll get there sometime, but not just yet. I really do have things to see to at home, and I also think it's time we had a bit of a breathing space from each other.' Without waiting for their reply, Pauline headed for the door. 'Do you think I have time for a cuddle from Danny before he goes to bed?'

When they were alone, Jack slipped his arm around Kate. 'I think your mother's been doing a bit of thinking.'

'I think so, too.'

'Well, when we *do* go through to Whitby, we'll make sure she has a good time.'

'Yes.' Kate gave him a kiss. 'It's been a lovely weekend, Mr Gallantree.'

Pauline played with Danny until Kate took him off for his bath and then she climbed up to the second floor of the house and tapped on Nicky's door. 'May I come in?'

'Sure.' Nicky was sitting cross-legged on the double bed, sewing. She nodded to the chair opposite her. 'Sit down.'

Pauline did so. She looked around her. 'You've got the place quite cosy now, Nicky.' She nodded approvingly at the picture of a sailing ship which hung on the cream-painted wall, at the full bookcase and the old rocking-chair in the corner of the room.

'That's Kate's doing.' Nicky had finished turning up the hem of a summer dress for her daughter. She bent her head and bit off the thread with strong, white teeth. 'The picture and the bed's ours, the rest of the stuff she conjured up. She's a marvel.'

Pauline smiled. 'That's funny. I've heard her say the same about you.'

'Me?' Nicky's face registered astonishment. 'What have I done except stumble from one disaster to another?'

A fine line creased Pauline's forehead. 'That's nonsense. You've had a spell of bad luck, but you've three fine children and . . .' She hesitated.

'Richie?' Nicky's smile had a bitter twist.

Pauline jumped up and came and admired the little dress. 'This is pretty.' She picked up the garment.

'Yes, it's from a thrift shop. God knows what I'd do without Oxfam.'

Pauline returned the dress. 'It's quiet. Where is everyone?'

'Lisa's already in bed and Richie's out with the boys.' Nicky looked at her watch. 'They should be back any minute.'

Pauline returned to her chair. 'How did the week-end go?'

'With Danny, you mean?'

'Yes.'

'He was fine. What about Helen?'

Pauline told her about the tea dance and Nicky laughed. 'A happy coincidence, eh?' She glanced again at her watch. 'I can't think where Richie's taken the boys.'

Pauline looked at her anxious face. 'How does he really feel, about staying here?'

'He's been happier since we moved. It's not surprising. The last couple of places nearly drove me bonkers, as well as him.' A shame-faced expression dawned on Nicky's face when she realised what she had said. She hurried on. 'He likes Kate, and now he's met Jack he feels more secure. He was terribly disappointed when Kate said he couldn't do the kitchen extension, though. He'd spent hours on the plans, and originally she was so enthusiastic he thought he'd get the job, but now he's accepted that it can't be.'

'That's really what I wanted to talk to you about. I want your reactions to a plan I've dreamed up.' Pauline set forth her ideas. 'What do you think?' she finished.

'From our point of view, it would be marvellous.

But please don't say anything to Richie to raise his hopes, not until you're sure Kate will agree. I know him, he couldn't take another disappointment so soon after the last. But you'll have to be careful not to upset Jack, Pauline.'

'Yes, I know.' She sighed. 'But you think it's worth a try?'

'Of course I do.'

'Then I'll give it one.' She watched as Nicky crossed to the window and looked out. 'Any sign of them?'

'No.'

'Why are you worried? It's not late.'

'He didn't tell me where he was taking them. I always worry when I don't know where they are.' Nicky shrugged her shoulders. 'Just being responsible, I suppose.'

Pauline looked down, studied her hands. 'There's such a thing as being too responsible.'

Nicky turned from the window to look at her. 'What does that remark mean?'

'You know when I said Kate thought you were a marvel?'

'Yes.'

'She's not the only one who admires you.' Pauline still did not look up. She examined her fingernails as she said, 'Kate's my own child and I'm so happy we've got together again and become friends, but there's been an unexpected bonus in that I've also become friends with you.'

Pauline's increasing nervousness showed in her movements. She had now abandoned the scrutiny of her nails and was picking away at an imaginary thread on her skirt. She asked, 'Just how much has Kate told you about my life?'

'She explained why you gave her away to the Hamptons.'

'I thought she might have.' Pauline sighed. 'Well, if you know about that, you'll appreciate that I know what it is to struggle. And because I have first-hand knowledge of hardship, Nicky, I think I understand you, in as much as any one person can understand another.'

Nicky's eyes grew watchful but she made no comment.

'You've had a rotten deal out of life and yet you've come out a winner. Oh, not in any material sense.' Pauline shrugged her shoulders. 'You don't own your own house or run a car, but you've kept your family together, and a loving, close-knit family it is. You've been strong enough to build walls, protect your loved ones. Only,' Pauline hesitated, 'forgive me, but walls also keep people out.' She raised her head and looked into Nicky's face. 'Do you understand what I'm trying to say?'

'Not really.' She had folded her arms. 'But I'm sure you'll tell me.'

Pauline flinched but went on speaking. 'Do you ever feel – forgive me for asking this – do you ever feel that you have *four* children, not three?'

Nicky's eyes widened in shock and she took a step forward. 'That's a lousy thing to say, Pauline.'

'I know.' Her forehead creased. 'I know it is. And I don't want to hurt you, but –'

'So why are you poking your nose in? What the hell do you know about my relationship with Richie? Who do you think you are – Mother Teresa?'

'No, but I see how you are with him.'

'I overpower him, right? I boss him about, is that

what you mean?' Nicky took another step forward. 'Don't you see, I *have* to? You know what he's like. He can't cope with difficulties, he can't make decisions. If I didn't look after him . . .'

'He'd have to cope.'

Nicky shook her head. 'He wouldn't be able to.'

'Are you sure, Nicky? I know he had a nervous breakdown. I know he's still vulnerable, but he's improving all the time. Kate said only last week how much better he is. And I've noticed it, too. Only, when he's with you, he shrinks back inside himself.' Pauline saw the hurt on Nicky's face. 'I'm sorry, love. But it's true.'

'You're saying it's my fault, the way he is?'

'No, of course not. You were there for him when he needed you, but he's getting better now. Only a pattern's been set. The children look on you as the head of the family, and so does he. He knows he hasn't your strength and I think he feels ashamed. He thinks he's let you down.'

'But he hasn't – and I've never felt that.' Nicky gazed unbelievingly at Pauline. 'It's just he's too gentle and sensitive. He can't cope with hassles.' She dashed her hand across her eyes. 'I still love him, you know.'

'I thought you did.' Pauline hurried over to Nicky and took her hand. 'Why do you think I opened my big mouth?' She gave a shaky laugh. 'I knew I was risking your friendship, saying what I did, but I wanted to help, if I could.'

'I believe you.' Nicky pulled away from her and wiped her nose on the back of her hand. 'I wouldn't take what you said from many people, though.' She managed a watery smile. 'And I'm not saying I agree with *everything* you've said. But . . .'

'You'll think about it?'

'Yes.'

They both started at the sound of footsteps on the staircase. A moment later, Jamie and Shawn rushed into the room, closely followed by Richie.

'Dad took us on a rowing boat at the park. We had a smashing time.'

'Goodness, that must have been fun.' Nicky ruffled Shawn's hair. 'But keep the noise down, Lisa's asleep.'

Richie smiled briefly at Pauline then transferred his gaze to Nicky. 'I kn-kn-know we're late back, but they were s-so keen.'

'It's all right. I knew they'd be safe with you.' Nicky smiled at him.

His brow wrinkled. 'I th-th-thought you'd be anxious?'

She went over to him and squeezed his arm. 'Next time I hope you'll take me and Lisa as well.'

He stared at her.

Pauline coughed. 'I'll be off then.' She winked at Nicky. 'Remember what I said about my plan.'

Nicky smiled at her. 'I will, Pauline . . . and thanks.'

Chapter Twenty-Six

The train was approaching Leeds station. Pauline slipped on her jacket and took down her case from the rack. She had arranged to spend four days with Kate and her family and was looking forward to seeing them all again.

It had been two months since her last visit, and it felt more like two years, but Pauline had stuck to her resolution to allow both Kate and herself a breathing space. It had been necessary, she thought, for since their first meeting last February, she and her daughter had been on an emotional roller-coaster of a ride. True, the outcome had been a happy one, but even happy emotions could be exhausting, especially when they were occasionally mixed with moments of apprehension and doubt.

Look how she was feeling at the moment. For over a week she had been eagerly preparing for her visit but now the thought of facing Kate again had made her old guilt resurface. Kate had the right to know the whole truth. She should be told about her twin sister. She must be told.

Pauline stared out of the window but instead of seeing the passing scenery, she saw two little girls, playing together on a hearth rug. The twins had always enjoyed each other's company, even though Elizabeth had been the dominant one of the pair. She had taken Kate's toys away from her when she felt like it and once she had bitten her sister's hand when indulging in one of her temper tantrums, but there had been a definite bond between the two of them. If Kate took a tumble, Elizabeth was often at her side before Pauline. She would help her sister to her feet and give her a reassuring cuddle.

Pauline remembered when, during one of Kate's frequent illnesses, Elizabeth had presented her mother with her favourite toy, a woolly lamb, and indicated Kate should have it. And when Kate was well again she had hung on to that lamb. Kate had neither the strength of her sister, nor Elizabeth's capacity to howl and fight, but she had tenacity. If she really wanted something she would cling on to it like grim death and, at such times, Elizabeth would concede defeat.

Her memories brought a brief smile to Pauline's lips. The problem of telling Kate about Elizabeth haunted her each time they met but her daughter's reappearance had also brought great joy to her. For so long, she had refused to allow herself to think about Elizabeth. She had done so to avoid pain, but now she realised she had also denied herself many happy memories. She bowed her head in shame. The brakes of the train squealed as the station came into view. Pauline stood up, collected her case and made for the nearest exit. When they had spoken on the telephone yesterday, Kate had said someone would meet her. Pauline wondered who that someone would be? Not Jack, he was away. Her daughter then, or Nicky perhaps? No, not Nicky. Pauline remembered that, like herself, Nicky did not drive. Strange, really. Nicky was just the sort of confident young woman to enjoy the freedom of having wheels of her own. Pauline saw hundreds of young wives and mothers every day, bombing along busy roads, dropping off children at school and then rushing off to shop or to work.

How different they were from the young wives of her generation, carrying heavy bags of shopping from the corner shop, not going into pubs on their own, baking and cooking three-course meals every night, making their children's clothes.

Nicky had been sewing for Lisa when she had tackled her about Richie. Remembering their conversation, Pauline felt a jab of apprehension. Had she been right to stick her nose into their affairs? Had her words helped or hindered the young couple? Pauline stood by the door as the train drew to a halt, and as she watched faces in the crowd of people waiting to board, she gave a rueful smile. The worrying was starting already and she wasn't off the train yet. Not only that, she was worrying about Nicky as well as Kate.

She gave a little shake of her head. She couldn't help it. Nicky wasn't family, in the truest sense of the word, but Pauline felt close to her and wanted her to be happy. And one of the reasons for wishing Nicky a bright future was because the young woman reminded her so much of herself years ago.

Nicky had also had to struggle although, thank God, she had never had to part with her children. Pauline knew about having nowhere decent to live and having to count every penny. She sewed for Lisa because she couldn't afford to buy new clothes for her. She couldn't drive because the opportunity, and the money, had never been there for her to learn.

The light on the door came on and Pauline pressed the 'open' button. She held her case in front of her as she stepped down. Some people had no manners. They were pushing past her, standing on her toes in their rush to get a seat.

She stamped smartly on a booted foot with the heel of her court shoe and smiled sweetly into a pain-contorted teenage face. She wasn't so old she was going to allow kids to walk all over her.

She realised once more how keen she was to get back to Kate's house and see everyone. Would Danny like his present? Was Helen in a happier frame of mind? She smiled a reminiscent smile. When the woman from the Social Services department in Leeds had called her, her anxiety and all the other feelings had been wholly centred on meeting Kate. She hadn't realised she was about to become involved with a whole new set of new people, but she was glad, so very glad.

During the past two months she had slotted back into her previous quiet existence. She had worked at the shoe shop. She had gone to the theatre with her next-door neighbour. When one of the assistants at the shop had become engaged, she had accompanied her and her friends to the nearby pub for a bar snack. At home, she had cleaned the flat thoroughly and caught up on her reading. Her old friend Rita had come and stayed for two days and they had talked about taking a holiday together, although nothing was definitely settled.

During that time, she hadn't been lonely, but Kate's weekly telephone call had been eagerly awaited and she hadn't been able to resist writing little cards to Danny. Once she had sent him a parcel containing colouring books and some little cars.

Her face lit up. The young man in her thoughts was tearing along the platform straight towards her.

'Grandma, Grandma.'

Her breath caught in her throat at the strength of her feelings for him and as she smiled and held out her arms she thought, Don't let me lose him.

'He's grown so big!' She said the words to Kate, who was hurrying behind him. She picked him up and kissed his smooth cheek. 'I can't believe how he's grown.'

'I know. He's just had his hair cut, too. I think that makes him look more grown-up.' Kate leaned forward and brushed Pauline's cheek with her lips. 'How are you?'

'I'm fine.' Pauline would have preferred a full-blooded hug, but Kate wasn't that kind of person. 'No, leave the case. I . . .'

But Kate was already walking down the platform. 'We'll have to rush. The car's in a no-waiting area.'

Pauline swung Danny round before setting him on his feet. 'Again,' he demanded.

'Later, when we're home.' She took hold of his hand. It was warm and soft and curled trustingly in hers. She felt her throat close up.

Kate glanced back at them. 'Come on, you two – hurry.'

They hurried.

Kate chattered away vivaciously as they drove home and Pauline relaxed in the seat next to her. She's pleased I've come, she thought, and she sighed happily.

'Nicky's finally had a letter from the council.

There'll be a house or flat ready for them in three or four weeks. Hopefully, it won't be too far away from our place. We've got on amazingly well, you know, and we'll miss them when they go, but it has been cramped. Oh, and the kitchen's coming on a treat. Richie's doing marvels.' She braked to let a woman with a pram cross the road, then glanced at Pauline. 'You know, I still worry about your putting up the money for the alterations.'

'Oh, don't start that again.' She looked through the car mirror at Danny who was in his seat in the back. He was absorbed in running a toy lorry backwards and forwards over the upholstery.

'It was something I wanted to do and I can afford it. I'd never been used to having much money, you know, but after Lawrence died I discovered there was a good pension for me as well as the money in the building society. I'm not extravagant.' She smiled. 'My earlier life-style saw to that, and you and Jack have been so good, welcoming me into your family. I was delighted to find a way of thanking you.'

Kate had turned quite pink. 'But that's what I mean. There's no earthly reason why you should feel obligated to us. After all, you could say I intruded into your life. Just think, if we'd hated each other! That could have been a disaster.'

'But we don't and it isn't.' Pauline hesitated. 'Anyway, there was another reason I wanted to help. I was thinking of Richie.'

'Richie?' Kate frowned and was silent for a moment, then she gave a non-committal smile. 'There's more to you than meets the eye, Pauline.'

'I should hope so.'

When Kate continued to drive without making

further conversation, Pauline asked, 'Well, how is he?'

'As I said, his work on the kitchen is terrific but he's still terribly shy, of course. But he's not sloping off on his own so much. He's spending more time with Nicky and the children. He's still a bit strange, though.' Kate changed gears and took the car smoothly round a large roundabout. 'I do wonder sometimes what on earth Nicky ever saw in him.'

Pauline looked at Kate's purposeful profile and inwardly sighed.

'Anyway, Jack and I have talked things over.' Kate was speaking again so Pauline paid attention. 'He wants you to know he's grateful for your help but he would much prefer to look upon the money as a loan. He's determined to pay you back, but says it may take about eighteen months.'

'I don't want paying back.' Pauline sat upright. 'It was a gift, please don't spoil it.'

Kate shrugged. 'That's what he says.' She glanced at Pauline. 'I think I'll stay out of this business altogether. Jack's stubborn and it seems you are, too. You'll have to sort it out yourselves.'

'Good idea.' Pauline settled back in her seat. 'How is he?'

'Jack? He's fine, we both are. That weekend away did us good. Can't say the same about our neighbours, though.' Kate braked sharply as a car cut in front of her. 'Silly idiot!'

Pauline turned to check on Danny. He was fast asleep. She looked back at Kate. 'Which neighbours?'

'The Blunts, the couple in the house to the left of us. I don't think you've met them. They're rarely at home.' Kate grimaced. 'You know when they are, because you can hear them arguing. Anyway, three weeks ago I saw them putting suitcases into her car, then they both got in and drove off. I assumed they were going on holiday, but now I think it was something more serious because he came back alone and we've not seen her since. I think they've split up.'

'Oh, dear. Have they children?'

'No. I don't think they've been married long. They both have careers and work long hours. I don't mean to be catty, but they don't look the sort of people who are interested in children. They're good-looking, well-groomed and, I imagine, rather sophisticated.' Kate's lips quirked. 'When they rushed off, I did wonder if the sudden influx of kids at our place had driven them away.' She looked at Pauline's puzzled face and laughed. 'Sorry, I was joking – and I shouldn't, should I? If they have broken up, it's not funny.'

'No.'

A few minutes later, Routledge Gardens came into view.

Nicky had the kettle on, which was quite a feat in itself, for a large sheet of polystyrene divided the dining-room and the kitchen, and half the kitchen floor was missing. As far as Pauline could see, the only way to pass between cooker and sink was to edge along the planks of wood laid across the footings.

'Good grief!' She stopped in the doorway to the dining-room.

Kate threw her handbag on to the dining-room table and picked up Danny before he had chance to reach the danger zone. 'Sorry, old boy, but it's the playpen for you. Just stay there a little while until I've shown Grandma the "bombsite".' She dumped him in the playpen.

He frowned, and was about to voice his displeasure when Pauline opened her case and handed Kate a square box. 'Give him this, it should keep him occupied.'

'Oh, Pauline. You shouldn't have.' But she handed the box over to her son. Danny, successfully diverted, held it to his ear and rattled it. Kate took hold of Pauline's elbow. 'Come on, it's quite safe.'

With care, Pauline followed her into what had been the kitchen.

Richie, Kate explained, was building an archway to connect the dining-room and kitchen. 'The arch will support the first floor,' she pointed out, 'and it's an attractive way of opening up the two rooms. Also, there'll be lots more light, which we need, and there'll be a good view of the garden from every angle. Richie put in the new window last week and now the plans have been approved, he can get on with the rest of the work.

'I want a run of cupboards and a working surface along there,' she pointed, 'but we've decided to keep the facing wall plain. Sometimes, fully-fitted kitchens end up looking like hospital operating theatres, don't they? I want to avoid that. I thought I might wallpaper the plain wall with really interesting paper, maybe tiny blue and white old-fashioned flowers on a cream or yellow background, and then get a padded cane settee or a comfy chair for people to sit in. What do you think?' She beamed happily at Pauline.

'Both Richie and Kate are full of ideas.' Nicky walked a tight-rope across one of the planks and handed Pauline a cup of tea. 'I'm just thankful their ideas usually coincide.' She smiled a welcome. 'How are you?'

'Very well. And you?'

Momentarily, Nicky's fingers touched Pauline's hand. '*We're* fine.'

Pauline gave her a long look. 'Is Richie in?'

'He needed to pick up some stuff from a builder over in Bradford. He hired a truck for half a day and he's over there now. He took the boys with him. Lisa's upstairs having her nap.'

'So he's driving again?'

'Yes,' Kate answered for her friend. She leaned over and picked up her mug of tea. 'Keeping busy is obviously good for Richie. He actually seems to enjoy working hard and he does damn' good work, too.'

'I hope you're right.' Nicky propped herself against the kitchen wall, thereby covering her sweater with dust. 'Because after what happened about an hour ago, it looks as though another job may be coming his way.'

'Really, how do you mean?'

'You'd just left to meet Pauline and I went into the garden to collect the washing. Old Mr Martin was pottering about, watering his plants, and he came over to talk to me. He asked about the kitchen alterations. He was quite interested, so I brought him in to see what was happening. I thought I'd better, the poor old soul has had to put up with all the recent banging and clattering. Anyway, he was impressed and asked if he could see it again, when everything's finished. Apparently someone he meets regularly, a friend at the bowling club, is thinking about extending *his* kitchen. Mr Martin said he would mention Richie's name – if he approves of the finished result, of course.'

'That's marvellous, Nicky.' Kate put down her cup with a bang. 'Mr Martin's bound to like the finished kitchen, it's going to look fantastic!'

'I hope you're right. As we're moving into our own place, another job would be a godsend.' Nicky looked at Pauline. 'Did Kate tell you our news?'

'Yes, I'm delighted. Things are working out for you at last.'

'I'm keeping my fingers crossed. We've been let down before, but I've got a good feeling this time.' Nicky grinned affectionately at Kate. 'It's your daughter, she's a good fairy. Things started improving for us when we became friends.'

'Oh, Nicky – that's nonsense.' Kate looked embarrassed. When a yell from Danny told them he had exhausted the play value of Pauline's gift and was demanding his freedom, she went to him with a look of relief.

When they were all out of the kitchen, Nicky and Kate made the area safe. They hauled a large sheet of plywood across the kitchen doorway and made it secure by stacking tins of paint against the base.

'It's to keep the youngsters out,' Kate explained.

'Will it be like that for long?'

'Not too long, please God.'

Nicky laughed out loud at Kate's expression. 'There are advantages. Housework's gone by the board, it would be a waste of time, and we don't have to be fussy about meals. We're relying on the micro-wave a good deal. The kids don't object, so long as they get enough fish fingers for tea and ice pops for sweets.'

'And what does Helen think about it all?'

The two younger women exchanged glances and Pauline's anxiety antennae quivered. 'What's wrong?'

Kate replied. 'Absolutely nothing. Helen is being a paragon of virtue at the moment.'

Pauline looked from one to the other. 'I don't understand?'

'It's true. I was expecting her to complain a lot, moan on about the noise and the mess, but she's been totally co-operative. She's good-tempered, she plays with the children when she gets the time, and she stays home more.' Kate paused. 'And guess what?'

'I've no idea?'

'She's become interested in gardening.'

Pauline looked over the rim of her spectacles. 'Gardening?'

'It's true.'

'But Helen's never shown the remotest interest in the garden.'

'I know. I didn't believe it, either. But she's convincing me. For the past three weeks she's been out nearly every evening, cutting the grass, weeding the flower beds.'

'There must be something you're missing.' Pauline rubbed her nose. 'Perhaps she's interested in a new boy, one that's into plants and things.'

'I don't think so. She's never mentioned anyone.'

'She wouldn't tell you if she was.' Nicky scooped up Danny who had wandered over to the paint tins and was trying to tug them away from the plywood. She bounced him on her knee. 'Anyway, just be glad she's a lot more cheerful than she was two months ago.'

'Yes, you're right. And I dare say we'll find out the truth before long. In the meantime,' Kate took Danny from Nicky, 'the garden's certainly benefiting.'

'What does Jack think about it?'

'Like us, he's amazed, but he didn't want to pry too much. As he said, Helen's happy, so why worry?'

The slam of the front door announced the arrival of

Richie. He came straight through to the dining-room and, seeing Pauline, smiled shyly at her.

'Hello.'

She smiled back. 'Kate's showed me the kitchen. You have been working hard.'

He flushed. 'It w-w-ill soon look better. I've a lad coming in on Saturday to help me with the new floor.'

Pauline noticed he only stammered once.

'So you'll want us out of the way?' Kate looked thoughtful. 'That might be a good day for us to go through to Whitby, Pauline. Remember, we promised ourselves a trip there? What do you think?'

'Why not? If you're sure you won't be needed here.'

'No, Richie will want the place to himself.' Kate looked at him and he nodded his head.

'Maybe we could all go, if we could fit into the car?'

'Not me, I'm afraid. Jamie and Shawn have been invited to a party and I said I'd help out. Anyway,' Nicky looked serious, 'wouldn't it be better for you and Pauline to go on your own? It's not just a day out, is it? It's more a trip down memory lane.'

Pauline stared at her. Perhaps she was right.

'We needn't decide immediately.' Kate made a grab for Danny who had escaped her clutches. He headed straight towards the paint but stopped when Shawn came running into the room.

'Daddy, what about the wood?'

'Yes, I'm coming.'

As he turned to go, Nicky went over to him and linked his arm. 'Want some help?'

He blushed. 'Sure.'

'Me, too. Me, too.' Danny hurried over to Richie and tugged at his trouser leg.

'OK,' he laughed. 'You can all help, you and Jamie

and Sh-Shawn. Come on, then, let's see how strong you are.'

Left in the suddenly quiet room, Kate nodded at Pauline. 'Quite a change, eh?'

'Miraculous.' Pauline laughed. 'Almost as miraculous as Helen becoming a gardener.'

It was getting cold. Helen shivered and looked towards her jacket which she had draped over the garden fence. If it became any colder she'd have to put it on, but she didn't want to.

If she wore the jacket, *he* wouldn't see her in her new top, and she wanted him to, because it suited her and she wanted him to admire her. She had taken a risk in wearing it, but luckily Kate had been talking to Pauline about the proposed trip to Whitby and hadn't noticed. But then, Helen reckoned, just lately she'd been lucky all round.

They had all become so involved in the kitchen extension, it had kept their attention off her. It was pathetic, really. She dug a weed out of the border and threw it into the cardboard box. What did it matter whether or not two rooms were knocked into one? What mattered in life was feelings, whether a person was happy or suffering.

Simon was suffering, but she was helping him through it. He had almost said as much. Helen gave up her pretence of gardening, sat back on her heels and thought about Simon and their very first conversation.

It had been around nine, that halfway time of night when dusk made familiar things seem strange and different. She was in the garden – it must be admitted in a bad temper – because Kate had asked her to go and collect up the children's toys. Although quite late, it was stickily hot and the sky had gone a funny yellowy colour. Kate, Helen remembered, had predicted a thunderstorm.

She had wandered about picking up soft toys, cars and picture books. One of the boys had mixed up some plasticine with mud and water, a disgusting mess, and she had stepped in it and got it all over her new trainers. Disgusted, she had gone to the very bottom of the back garden and behind the white lilac tree, where Dad kept a box for compost, meaning to scrape off the offending substance. And it was then that she had noticed him.

He was leaning over the boundary fence adjoining the two gardens and staring up at the sky. She remembered she had stood still, watching him. His dark profile, outlined against the strangely coloured sky, had seemed strange, almost mystical. It had taken her a minute to realise it was Mr Blunt, their next-door neighbour, and not some mysterious intruder.

And then he had suddenly turned to face her and his face had been all tired and sad and she had suddenly remembered Kate saying she was sure Mrs Blunt had cleared off and that he was now living on his own in the house.

A feeling of sympathy had flooded through her. She coughed hesitantly and then murmured hello. He had nodded to her and smiled and that smile had made her wonder how on earth his wife could have left him.

'Have you come outside to admire the sunset, too? Wonderful, isn't it?'

She had nodded. She wasn't going to tell him the real reason for her coming to the end of the garden. And together they had watched the sky and the huge purple-grey clouds massing above them. A ray from the setting sun had cut a swath through the clouds and Helen thought how dramatic it all was, like a scene from the film *Gone with the Wind* which had been reissued and which she and Eileen had gone to see two weeks ago.

'I can never think of clouds in scientific terms when they are as wonderful as these.' Mr Blunt had put his arms on the wall and leaned towards her. 'They belong in poems, don't you agree?' He quoted: ' "But trailing clouds of glory do we come from God".'

She stared at him. He was definitely behaving strangely, he wasn't a bit like the neighbour she had seen putting out the rubbish on a Friday night, but his voice was thrilling. Helen shivered. It was so deep, it seemed to send out vibrations, a sort of invisible chain which linked the pair of them. She said, 'I know those lines. It's Wordsworth, isn't it?'

'Heavens above, a beautiful young woman who is also literate!'

She blushed. 'We've studied him at school.'

'Congratulations to your teachers. I thought literature was dying.' He had suddenly reached out and caught hold of her forearm. She stiffened in alarm but then relaxed and watched, wide-eyed, as he bent and kissed the back of her hand. And at that very moment the first peal of thunder rolled round the sky and rain began to patter down.

'I fear we must part, fair maiden.' Mr Blunt dropped her hand and turned unsteadily away. 'But I shall look for you again.'

He was drunk. Watching his unsteady gait as he disappeared into the gloom, Helen grinned, but only for a moment. Poor, poor man – he must be terribly lonely. She raised the hand he had kissed to her cheek, ignoring the faint odour of whisky on her skin. He needed a friend, and he had called her a beautiful young woman. When Kate had shouted from the back door, telling her to hurry in, she had walked slowly, despite the rain. She was forming a plan of action.

It hadn't been easy. She had cut the back lawn so often it had been almost bald before they had spoken again. But eventually he had appeared.

She had bobbed her head shyly. 'Hello.'

'Hello, yourself.' He had looked surprised by her greeting. With a sinking heart she realised he had no memory of their earlier conversation. Gamely, she reminded him. 'The glorious clouds, remember – just before the storm?'

'Oh, yes.' He had looked discomfited, like a small boy. Her heart yearned.

'I think I remember. I'm afraid I had too much to drink that night.'

How brave of him to admit it.

'That's all right. I remembered because we discussed Wordsworth.'

'Did we?' He looked astonished. 'It must have been a short conversation. I know nothing about the guy.'

'You quoted him.' At this blank look, Helen changed tactics. 'You have a nice garden, prettier than ours, but with all the kids . . .'

'It's getting out of hand; Gill was the gardener of the family.' He bent his head and studied his shoes and then he looked up again. 'But everything's looking a mess. I thought I'd better tidy up.'

'I'll help, if you like?'

'That's kind of you, but what about your own work?'

'I've finished. I enjoy gardening, but my dad does

most of the work when he's home.' She had looked over the fence. 'I can tell you what bushes need cutting back, things like that.'

He had stared at her helplessly. 'Well, if you're sure?'

And that's how it started. Planning strategy was hard work. She had to try and meet him at the top end of the gardens, so that Kate or Nicky didn't see them. The best times, when a good film was on telly, she was all right. And she had to watch out for him, he didn't appear that often.

In fact the slowness with which their relationship was developing fretted her. He was often silent when they worked together and when he did talk he asked about unimportant things, like what her father did and why so many children had suddenly appeared in their garden.

Several times she had been tempted to give up on him but then something always happened. One day he had come into the garden with a piece of paper scrunched up in his fist – a letter, Helen thought – and his expression had been so bleak she had gone to him and rested her hand on his arm, giving it a little squeeze to express her sympathy. He had smiled then, and covered her hand with his own.

'My little gardener. You're a comfort to me, you know.'

Another time she had told him the hedge should be cut. He had taken off his shirt because he was hot and she had seen the muscles ripple under his smooth skin and had felt anything but a 'little comfort'.

It was almost dark. She shivered. She stood up and went to put on her jacket. It was no good, he wasn't going to come outside tonight. She took the box of weeds up to the compost heap and stood a moment, remembering their first meeting at this very spot.

She'd have to think of something else. Something that would make him call her a beautiful young woman again. She emptied the weeds and trudged slowly back down the path. Kate wanted her to go to Whitby on Saturday but she could make some excuse. Nicky and the children would be away, Richie would be busy working . . . and Simon was home on Saturdays.

[illegible]

[illegible]

She'd have to think of something else. Something that would make [illegible] her a beautiful young woman again. She [illegible] the words and [illegible] slowly back down the [illegible]. Kate wanted her to go to [illegible] Saturday [illegible] Nick, and [illegible] working [illegible] and [illegible] Saturdays.

[illegible]

[illegible]

[illegible] Kate felt ashamed when she saw the pleasure on Nicky's face, particularly when [illegible] was prompted more by [illegible] fact

Chapter Twenty-Seven

The letter arrived on Friday morning and caused quite a stir. A representative of the housing department had written to inform Mr and Mrs Richard Franklin that as the tenants of 28 Darton Road had moved out earlier than originally expected, they were now at liberty to take possession of the property. The keys were at the local housing office.

'We could move in today, if we want.' Nicky fluttered the letter up and down in a sort of victory wave.

'*Do* you want?'

'Why not? Just think, a proper house. We're going to live in a proper house, Jamie.' Nicky grabbed hold of her son who was descending the staircase wearing only his pyjama top and clutching his comforter, a tatty red-checked cot blanket. She jigged the startled youngster up and down the hallway. 'We'll get you and Shawn bunk beds, would you like that?'

'Don't you think you'd better go and check the place out before you start packing? I don't mean to be a killjoy, but perhaps there's repairs needed, or it may want scrubbing out.' Kate felt ashamed when she saw the pleasure die out of Nicky's face, particularly when she knew her remark was prompted more by the fact she wanted her kitchen floor putting in rather than the state of Nicky's new home.

'I suppose I ought to pop round there first.' Nicky stopped jigging, but her smile reappeared. 'I'm sure everything will be OK, though. We've already seen the house once. Don't you remember me telling you about it? The council man let us look round the three properties we were in line for. The people who rented 28 Darton Road were nice and the house was lovely and clean. They told us then how much they had enjoyed living there, but the man's firm was moving him somewhere else to work.'

Of course Nicky wanted to get into a place of her own. Belatedly, Kate tried to make amends. 'If you want, I'll drive you round there after breakfast.'

The keys were collected, the house was visited, inspected and approved of. Kate drove them home again and Nicky went straight upstairs to talk with Richie. Half an hour later, he came downstairs looking for Kate. He found her in the dining-room armed with a dustpan and brush, trying vainly to remove the layers of brickdust which was everywhere.

He looked round. 'It's quiet. Where are the k-k-kids?'

'Pauline's playing with them, in the garden.'

'Good, that gives us more of a chance to s-sort things out.'

Kate rested from her work. She asked, 'Have you decided when to move?'

'Sunday, we think. Nicky's already started to pack. I'm g-going to hire a van, I think that will be big enough, we don't have that much stuff. Nicky's mum has some bits and pieces belonging to us in her f-front bedroom. I'll have to go round and collect them.'

'You're going to be busy.' Kate put down the

handbrush and smiled at him. 'We're really going to miss you and Nicky, you know.'

He blushed. 'Oh, we'll be around, don't you w-w-worry.' He shifted his feet. 'About the kitchen floor . . .'

'It can wait, Richie, until after you've moved.'

'No, I came to tell you I'm going to w-work on it tomorrow, as arranged.'

'But can you spare the time?'

'Yes. I promised I'd d-do it, and I will. Anyway,' he looked away, a hint of a smile on his lips, 'you can't go tightrope-walking along those planks for much longer, you'll end up knock-kneed.'

She laughed out loud, thinking again how much he had changed over the last six weeks. 'Well, if you're sure. I must admit, having a proper floor to walk on would make a difference.'

'I'll try and get an early start. As you're taking your mother to Whitby, and the kids are g-going to a party, I should be able to really get cracking.'

'Yes, and Danny's coming with us.' Kate looked thoughtful. 'But I don't know about Helen. When I asked her about Whitby she didn't seem too keen.'

'She's probably got something arranged with her friends. Anyway, Helen won't be a problem. She's old enough to take care of herself.'

On Saturday morning, Danny turned awkward. Too young to understand what was happening, he nevertheless knew changes were coming and involved his playmates. During Friday afternoon, he had trotted around after Shawn and Jamie, watching silently as they packed toys into cardboard boxes. He whined at bedtime, took a long time to go to sleep, and on

Saturday morning, when Kate tried to take him out to the car, he totally rebelled.

'Don't want to go, don't want to!' he shrieked, clinging to the doorknob as a grim-faced Kate tried to prise his fingers free.

'We're going for a lovely day out, Danny.'

'No, no. Stay here.'

Unable to unclamp his hands without hurting him, Kate straightened up and sighed.

'It's OK, you can leave him with us.' Nicky crouched down before Danny. 'You want to play with Shawn, don't you?'

He nodded and blinked. His long eyelashes were spiky with half-shed tears.

'But, Nicky, you've heaps of things to see to. I can't leave him.'

'No, it's all right. He can go to the party with my lot. Margaret's already expecting fourteen youngsters, one more won't make much difference. And Danny will enjoy himself so long as Shawn and Jamie are close by. Anyway, he knows Margaret and her twins. They've played together at the park. So stop worrying, get yourselves off and make sure you have a good day.'

A few more moments of doubt, more reassurances from Nicky and a hug for Danny, and then they were off. Once the centre of Leeds had been cleared, the roads became bearable. Traffic was heavy but because it was the weekend there were few of the enormous lorries Kate disliked so much. The weather was just right for a day trip out, fine and bright but not too hot.

They travelled via York, turned off at Malton and then headed across the moors. During the first hour they had chatted away happily, but as the journey lengthened periods of silence developed and their quietness was mirrored in the passing scenery, for the moorland roads were quiet and almost empty of cars.

'What a relief it is to have the time and space to look at the countryside.' Kate turned her head and smiled at Pauline.

'Yes, the moors don't alter much over the years.'

Pauline leaned forward and stared intently through the front window of the car. 'We're getting close to Saltersgate, aren't we?'

'Yes. According to the map, we pass through there.'

'Oh.'

Something in her voice made Kate give her a second glance. 'What is it?'

'Nothing special. Just this stretch of road, it brings back memories.'

'Anything you'd like to talk about?'

'No.'

There was a couple of minutes' silence and then, as if to compensate for any unintentional rudeness, Pauline began to reminisce.

'One evening I went to a dance in Malton with your father and on the way back we almost got caught up in a moor fire. We weren't exactly frightened because moor fires often broke out – they still do, during the summer months. In dry weather the bracken becomes tinder-dry, you see, and anything, a spark from an engine or a cigarette butt, can set one off.

'But this particular fire was a bad one. People were evacuated from farms and lots of men were called in to fire-fight and to move the livestock. Anyway, the road to Whitby was closed so Grahame had to turn back. We ended up spending the night in Saltersgate.'

She lapsed into silence. Kate waited a moment and then asked, 'Is that all?'

'Yes. We went home the next morning.'

Kate felt a niggle of annoyance. There was more to tell, she felt sure, but Pauline apparently didn't intend to. They drove through Saltersgate without further comment and headed for Whitby.

As they approached their destination the landscape began imperceptibly to change. Now there were patches of wild flowers by the sides of the road and the scrubby moorland gave way to grass and cultivated fields. The road looped and dropped lower and glimpses of the sea and then of Whitby came into view.

Pauline became more animated. 'Oh, the sea looks so blue today. That's one thing I've always missed, you know, the sound of the sea. And, look!' She pointed. 'That small boat coming into the harbour, that's a coble. My dad had a coble before he went to work on the keel boats. Eventually he bought a share in *The Enterprise*.

'You could make a good living out of the fishing industry in those days. You wouldn't *believe* the catches they netted just after the war. When the boats came in, usually in the early mornings, the fish pier was totally covered with stacked-up boxes, every one filled to the brim with fish. In the herring season you couldn't move for them. The big buyers were always in evidence, of course, waiting for the daily catch, but the local women used to queue up, too.'

She laughed. 'They'd be wearing their aprons and have a plate in their hands. It was five herrings for a penny, if I remember right. They used to cook 'em for breakfast.'

She pointed. 'Look, there's the Abbey and St Mary's.' Her face sobered. 'I'd like to visit the church, Kate, just for a few minutes. My gran's buried in the graveyard of St Mary's.'

'Of course. We'll go anywhere you want.'

Helen concentrated on following the road signs. She drove into Whitby and then pointed the car towards the harbour.

'It's the old town you want to visit first?'

'Yes, please.' Pauline laughed as a seagull bombed the car, screamed abuse, and then soared into the sky again. 'Those damn' birds! They're as bad-tempered and noisy as ever. The residents hate them, you know, but the visitors seem to like them.'

'I suppose it's because the visitors are only here two weeks of the year and the racket the birds make when they wake up reminds them they're on holiday.' Kate was looking about for a place to park the car. She finally squeezed her vehicle between a fish lorry and a stack of crab pots. Then she looked a little anxiously at Pauline.

'Will it be all right to leave it here?'

'Yes. If anyone objects, I'll tell them I'm a native of the town, born and bred. That'll shut 'em up.'

They left the car and, as they walked past a row of stalls selling mussels, cockles and whelks, Kate reflected that Pauline had indeed come back to her native town. For here, in the town of her birth, she seemed different. Her voice was a little louder, she spoke more quickly, and her steps were lighter. And as she walked along, she threw back her head. Kate found herself lengthening her own stride to keep up with her.

'There's Grape Lane over there, I'll show you that later. Captain Cook lived there, you know. Gran told me it was originally called Grope Lane, because it was so dark.'

They walked on. 'And this is Henrietta Street, where we used to buy kippers.' Pauline halted at the bottom of a flight of shallow steps. 'We might as well go up to the Abbey now, Kate? You can get to it via these steps and it's worth seeing. And then, St Mary's church is close by.'

She nodded. 'Lead the way.'

They climbed the one hundred and ninety-nine steps. 'Good lord, you must have been tough to tackle these every day.' At the top of the steps, Kate paused to catch her breath.

Pauline smiled. 'We were.'

First, she showed Kate the Abbey. 'There's not a lot left of it now, but it makes the skyline look good, and the town's proud of the Abbey.'

'So they should be.' Kate strolled around on the short-cut sweet-smelling grass and gazed upwards at the still impressive ruins. 'I've read a bit about this place, you know. The woman who founded it, Hilda, was a cultured, wealthy woman, but also very saintly. She liked getting her own way though. If she hadn't been a nun, I suppose you could have called her one of the very first feminists.' She laughed. 'Quite a formidable lady.'

Pauline put her hand against the sun-warmed ancient grey stones and looked out, over the town. 'I wonder how Nicky's getting on?' she said suddenly.

'I was thinking of her, too.'

Then they both laughed, but their faces were serious when they left the Abbey and went towards the graveyard of the parish church of St Mary's.

'There it is.' Pauline pointed to a small plain gravestone half hidden in grass. 'That's where my gran is.'

'I'll give you a few minutes alone.' Kate squeezed Pauline's arm then retreated to the cemetery boundary wall. The bond between Pauline and her grandmother must have been strong, she thought, as she gazed out at the view. The old lady had been dead for years and years and yet Pauline often talked about her.

Idly, she wondered whether Danny would remember Pauline when he was a middle-aged man. It was very likely, she thought. He had taken to his grandmother straight away, and loved her visits. Kate remembered how his face always lit up when she talked to him on the telephone. She looked back at Pauline's kneeling figure and then she looked out to sea again.

The heat of the sun was increasing. The dry grasses growing by her feet whispered against her bare legs and she could feel the warmth in the old grey stone wall upon which she leaned. She closed her eyes and breathed in the scent of the sea but instead of feeling content, she experienced a mood of depression.

She knew why. Some people found it easy to love, she knew she did not. She loved Jack and Danny, of course, but that was natural, they were her husband and child. But other people – guiltily she wondered if she truly loved Helen. She cared for her, certainly, but loved . . . ? And Nicky and her children, she cared for them, too. Indeed, for Shawn, Jamie and Lisa she cared very much, because they were small and defenceless. Kate thought it was like when you saw a kitten or a puppy in a pet shop, you instinctively wanted to rescue it. But love was more than rescuing someone.

She stole another glance at her mother. Pauline was still kneeling by the grave and now she was holding a handkerchief to her eyes. Kate looked away immediately, ashamed at intruding into someone else's private moment. And looking back towards the sea, she acknowledged that, although she had grown fond of her mother, true intimacy, true *love*, was missing from their relationship.

So if she couldn't love her natural mother, what about her adoptive parents?

She thought about the care they had given her and about her life with them and tried to remember her feelings when she had attended their funerals. Unhappy, upset, yes – but certainly not devastated. She clenched her hands with a feeling of self-disgust. What a cold-blooded creature she was.

'I'm here.' Pauline had come to stand next to her. 'Hope I didn't keep you waiting too long?'

She must have seen the backward glance towards the grave, thought Kate. She unclenched her hands and hid them in her cardigan pockets. 'No, of course not. Take as long as you like.'

'No, I'm ready to go.' Pauline took off her spectacles and polished them on a tissue. 'I had a little chat with her.'

'Did you?' Kate hesitated, frowning. 'Do you really believe she heard you?'

'Well, it's worth trying.' Pauline replaced her spectacles on her nose. 'Anyway, whether she did or not, *I* feel better now. I brought her up-to-date with what has happened to me. I told her about my marriage to Lawrence, and about you and Elizabeth, and I explained how you managed to trace me and that I now have a grandson.' She paused. 'She'll be pleased about Danny. She once told me that "children sweeten labours".'

Kate smiled. 'Your gran had a saying for everything, didn't she?'

'Yes, and I can't tell you how fed up I was hearing them all the time! But you know,' Pauline looked back towards Eliza's grave, 'as I get older, I've begun to realise most of them made a lot of sense.'

'Perhaps you're right.' Kate straightened up. 'We'll go back to the town, shall we?'

They walked back down the steps.

'Who's Elizabeth?'

Pauline stumbled and almost fell. Kate shot out her hand and caught hold of her elbow. 'Careful.'

'Sorry.' Pauline averted her face. 'I tripped.'

'I know. Good job I was here to catch you. There could have been a nasty fall.'

'Yes, I know. Thanks.'

'That's all right.' Kate glanced at her. 'Well, are you going to tell me?'

'She was . . . a friend of the family.'

Pauline was flustered and Kate wondered why. They walked down the rest of the steps until they reached the bottom and then Pauline said, 'Kate?'

'Yes.'

There was a long silence. Looking at her mother's face, Kate wondered if the stumble had shaken her more than she would admit. Pauline had turned quite pale. She asked, 'Are you sure you're all right?'

'Yes.' Pauline moistened her lips. 'I'm hungry, that's all. Let's get something to eat.'

They went and had some Whitby fish and chips. Kate thoroughly enjoyed hers, but noticed that Pauline, despite her talk of being hungry, left some of her food. After leaving the cafe they stood at the corner of Church Street and debated what to do next. Amongst the shoppers passing by was a tall, dark-haired woman. She gave them a casual glance as she walked by and then stopped, turned and looked again. Then she shouted, 'My God, it *is* you. Pauline Verrill, as I live and breathe.'

Pauline's head jerked round. She stared, then gasped out one word: 'Mary!'

Kate watched with interest as the two middle-aged women fell into each other's arms.

'I *thought* it was you but then I thought, no – it couldn't be . . .'

'I never *dreamed* you'd moved back to Whitby. Why didn't you write . . .'

'You look just the same. Well, maybe a bit fatter . . .'

They hugged each other, laughed, and moved apart.

'And who is this?'

Kate, smiling and looking from one face to the other, was disconcerted by the expression that appeared on her mother's face. Pauline hesitated before replying to her friend's question. 'This is my daughter, Kate.'

The dark-haired woman stared. 'Little Catherine?'

'Yes.'

'Oh, how marvellous.' The woman seized Kate's hand and pumped it up and down. 'I was with your mother the day you were born. I saw you and . . .'

'Mary!' Pauline's interruption sounded agonised.

Both the woman and Kate jumped. Kate, who had moved imperceptibly closer to the stranger because of the warmth and enthusiasm of her greeting, looked back at Pauline and saw her shaking her head.

She frowned. 'What's the matter? What is it?'

'Nothing, love, nothing. I just feel a bit strange, that's all. I can't believe I'm here with Mary. We were always best friends, weren't we, Mary? Oh, there's so much to talk about, so many questions.' Pauline raised her hand to her face and Kate saw how it trembled.

She bit her lip. 'Maybe you ought to sit down?'

'No, I'm fine. How's Claus, Mary? You were living with him when we lost touch with each other. Did you ever marry him?'

'Yes.' Mary was looking almost as puzzled as Kate. 'You do look a bit under the weather, Pauline. I only live ten minutes' walk from here, why don't you come home with me? It's daft standing in the street like this. Like you say, we've a lot of catching up to do. Come on, come home. I'll make us a pot of tea.'

'Oh, well . . . I don't know.'

Mary's face showed hurt and astonishment. 'Pauline, you *must*.'

Her shoulders sagged. 'All right.'

The three of them walked down Church Street. Kate and Pauline were quiet, Mary did the chattering.

'We've been back in Whitby fifteen years. If I remember rightly, we were living in Cheshire the last time I heard from you, Pauline? Then you moved and sent me your new address, and then *we* moved, in a rush as it happened. Claus was offered a job in Stockport, but we had to get there quickly. Anyway, with all the rushing about, I lost the paper with your new address written on it. I was upset, I can tell you. I was pregnant at the time and— '

'Oh, so you have a family?' Quite suddenly, Pauline seemed to have recovered from her shakiness. She linked arms with Mary and began walking so fast her friend had to hurry to keep up with her. Kate was left behind. She trailed after the two of them feeling puzzled and annoyed. It wasn't like Pauline to be rude.

But once in Mary's home, everyone relaxed. She

made them welcome, gave them a photograph album to look at while she made the tea and then came to sit with them. She told Kate she was a handsome young woman, although she resembled neither her mother nor her father.

'You knew my father?' Kate sat on the edge of her seat.

'Oh, yes.' Mary glanced across at Pauline. 'I was with your mum when they first met.'

'What did you think of him?' Kate glanced a little apologetically at her mother, but was relieved to see Pauline now looked quite placid.

'He was a smart chap, but I was more interested in his friend.' Mary took a biscuit and bit into it reflectively. 'Do you remember him, Pauline?'

'A little, I can't remember his name.'

'No, neither can I.' Mary smiled at Kate. 'My chap was better-looking, but a bit of a smoothie.' She reflected. 'He was a bit of a heel, really.'

Kate's mouth thinned. 'Well, wasn't my father?'

The two older women looked at each other. 'Well, that's a difficult question, Kate. He'd moved away before . . .' Mary looked uncomfortable.

'Before anyone, including me, knew I was pregnant.' Pauline's voice was low. 'I've told you all I can about your father, Kate. Can't we let it rest?'

She looked down into her teacup and Mary moved on to another topic. 'Have you a photo of your little boy? Pauline tells me she's a grandmother.'

A snapshot was produced and admired. Pauline told Mary how Kate had found her with the help of the Social Services department and how they had become friends.

But after the tea had been drunk, she and Mary

launched into talk of the old days and as name after name was mentioned they embarked on a flood of reminiscences.

'Remember when we went in the sea at Sandsend and that awful brother of Rosie Swales' ran off with all our clothes? We had to come back on the bus in our vest and pants.'

'Remember when you sprained your ankle climbing down the cliffs at Baytown and a fisherman had to carry you down on his back?'

Remember, remember . . .

They laughed and touched hands in affirmation of their long friendship and their faces grew soft and blurry with recollections of long ago. Kate, sitting quietly and watching them, could almost see the girls they had once been.

After an hour of talk, Mary glanced at a clock on the wall of her sitting-room. 'I'd better get the meal started. Claus and the boys will be in soon.'

Jerked back into the present, Pauline sat up. 'How many sons did you say you have?'

'Four.' Mary smiled proudly. 'Brian, Luke, Harry and Steve.'

'And you're back in Whitby. I can't believe it.' Pauline shook her head. 'Remember when you swore you'd never settle in Whitby, and you were certain you didn't want children?'

'Well, I was young and daft then. Anyway, I did see a bit of the country when I took off with Claus. As for the kids,' Mary grinned, 'they just kind of happened along.'

As she cleared away the tea things, she explained, 'My dad went mad every time Claus and me talked of marrying so in the end we didn't, we just cleared off together. My God!' She laughed. 'I bet all the tongues clattered then. But I've never once regretted it, although we had a rough time at first.

'Being a German, Claus couldn't get a decent job for a couple of years but then things started changing. Trade picked up.' She nodded. 'Remember the Festival of Britain, Pauline? Anyway, Claus finally landed a proper job and then we got married.

'After Brian's birth, I sent some photos home and Mum wrote and asked us to visit. We did, mostly for her sake, but it was very uncomfortable. Dad still thought all Germans were Nazis.

'We went back home and I wrote to Mum but I never saw her again. A year after the visit Luke was born, and then a year after that my mum died. She had a heart attack, it was very sudden. Dad got in touch with me, and we came over for the funeral. Then, just before we left, we sorted things out with him. After that we visited him every year.

'He was a stupid old cuss though. He would never visit us. For the next eight years he lived on his own. My sisters kept an eye on him. They cooked his Sunday dinners, things like that. Eventually, a year before he died, he got us all together and said we were to share the proceeds of the house and his savings. He was quite a warm man by then, Pauline.'

Kate, who had been silently listening to Mary's tale, shifted in her chair and frowned enquiringly at Pauline.

'She means he had a fair bit of money saved,' whispered her mother.

Mary didn't notice the interruption, she was too intent on her story.

'Anyway, to cut a long story short, we moved the

family back to Whitby and I persuaded Dad to come and live with us. Claus went to work on one of the keel boats and, later on, Brian followed him.'

'Claus is fishing?'

'Yes. And doing all right, although the cod wars . . .'

Pauline waved her hand. She wasn't interested in the cod wars. 'And your other boys?'

'Luke works for ICI at Middlesbrough. He's a steady lad, married with a little girl. Harry's a bit of a rover, never stays in one place longer than a few months. He doesn't sponge off the state, mind. He can turn his hand to anything. And he's still single, although plenty of lasses have set their cap at him.'

He's her favourite, thought Kate, seeing how fondly she smiled.

'And Steve's the baby, only eighteen. He's the one with the brains. He wants to be a dentist.' Mary laughed. 'Can you credit it?'

'I can credit anything, except that you're the mother of four sons.' Pauline rested her chin on her hands and pondered. 'Where have the years gone, Mary?'

'Don't start getting all philosophical.' She picked up the tray and carried it through to her kitchen. 'We can't turn the clock back, and I'm not sure I want to. I'm happy as I am now. Particularly today.' She smiled at Pauline.

'Yes, so am I.' Pauline stood up and smiled back at her. 'And now we've found each other, we'll definitely stay in touch, but I think we should go now. You've a meal to cook and poor old Kate must be bored to tears with all our talk.'

'No.' She shook her head. 'I've enjoyed listening to you.'

'It's good of you to say that, but I guess your mum's right.' Mary sighed. 'Pity you can't wait to meet Claus though. He would have liked to meet you again, Pauline.'

'Oh, don't worry.' She took a notebook from her handbag and scribbled down a few lines. 'I'll be back. I'm returning to Manchester in a couple of days. If you give me your telephone number I'll ring you from there. We'll sort something out.'

'I will.' Mary took the paper and then gave Pauline a hug and a kiss. 'It's smashing seeing you.'

'I feel the same.' She took a step towards the door, then she turned. 'I'm sorry you lost your mum that way, Mary. She can't have been very old. I remember her. She was a good woman.'

'Yes, she was.' Mary sighed. She was scribbling down her phone number for Pauline. 'Too many kids, perhaps. She never stopped working. Still, other people work hard and live to be ninety. Look at your dad.'

'What?' Pauline stood stock still.

'Your dad. *He's* still around, although he's been in that nursing home for ages.' Mary's voice faded. 'Didn't you know?'

Pauline shook her head slowly. 'I thought he'd died years ago.'

'Oh, no. He's in Redfern House, up on the West Cliff. I'm sorry, Pauline. I never thought.'

'It's all right. You weren't to know.'

'You never sorted things out with him?'

'No.' She bit her lip. 'What's the name of that place again?

'Redfern House. Look, I'll write it down.'

She did so and handed over the sheet of paper.

'Thanks.' Pauline folded it carefully and put it into her bag.

'What will you do?'
'Go and see him, I suppose.'

Chapter Twenty-Eight

Helen Gallantree was quietly sneaking into the partly floored kitchen of her home. She had been out all morning but had returned to the house an hour earlier and gone straight up to her bedroom. There she had changed her clothes, frowning at the noise of banging and clattering downstairs. But the house was quiet now. Richie and the young man helping him had driven off in the hired van. Helen presumed they had gone to fetch materials from the nearby builder's yard, or perhaps they were moving something to their new home. Whatever the reason, she was glad they had left.

Once in the kitchen, she rummaged about until she found what she wanted and then, from the Marks & Spencer's carrier bag she had with her, she brought out the cake. She studied it. Yes, it suited her purposes very well. She put the cake on a plate, opened the biscuit tin she had taken from the cupboard, and took out three blue birthday candles and three candle holders. She arranged them in the middle of the cake. She put the biscuit tin back in the cupboard and carried the now decorated cake back to her bedroom.

In the mirror, she studied her appearance. She was wearing her new straight skirt and a blouse which belonged to Kate. The blouse was just a fraction too tight, Kate was slimmer than she was, but Helen reckoned that didn't matter. It wasn't *terribly* tight, not enough to make her look cheap, but it showed she had a bust. In her usual clothes, teeshirts, jeans and sweaters, she could pass for a boy. She turned sidewards and grimaced. Except for her big bottom, of course.

At school, she preferred wearing sloppy sweaters and cardigans. The boys in her year were so crude, they made rude jokes about any girl who was shapely, but today she wasn't going to school, she was going to call on Simon Blunt.

She brushed a touch of eyeshadow on to her eyelids and outlined her mouth with pink blush lipstick, nothing too obvious, and then, carrying the cake, she went down the stairs and out through the front door. She held the cake in one hand as she juggled the key into the lock and turned it. Then she hid the key behind the loose brick in the wall. She was hoping she wouldn't have to come straight back home and she knew Richie had his own key. She hurried down the path, went through next-door's garden and rang the doorbell. She prayed Simon would answer quickly. He did.

'Hello, Helen.' He seemed surprised and a little disconcerted. She felt a moment of uncertainty, and then she relaxed. Of course, he hadn't seen her dressed up before.

'Can I come in?'

'Er, yes.' He stood to one side to allow her to enter. He was wearing stone-washed jeans and a dark blue polo shirt and he needed a shave. He looked incredibly masculine and handsome, like the men in the catalogues Eileen's mother had in her sitting-room.

Inside the house, she knew at once his wife hadn't returned. She could tell by the state of the hallway. The small table inside the door was an inch deep in dust and the plant standing on it was dying from lack of water. Poor, poor Simon. She suppressed a sigh. He wasn't very good at looking after himself.

She handed him the plate. 'Happy birthday.' She glanced modestly at the hall carpet. 'I made it myself.'

He blinked. 'That's kind of you, but it's not my birthday.'

Her smile wavered. 'Oh, I thought you said . . .'

'It will be soon, on Monday.'

'Oh, I must have got mixed up.' She hesitated. 'I suppose you *could* keep it until then.'

Perhaps he sensed her disappointment, for he smiled. 'Never mind, it was a nice thought. And I think it would be a good idea for us both to have a slice now. We don't want it to go stale, do we?'

'No.' She smiled. 'I really did think your birthday was today, but perhaps it's just as well. You see, my stepmother's having our kitchen altered. You must have heard all the banging? Anyway, by Monday the oven will probably be disconnected.' She put her head on one side. 'Do you like sponge cake?'

'I like any kind of cake.' He lifted the plate higher and examined the sponge. 'It looks terrific. You must be a good cook.'

'Not bad.' She tried to look modest. 'Take it into the kitchen, then.'

'Er, yes.' He hesitated. 'It's in a bit of a state in there.'

'It doesn't matter.' Following him into the kitchen and looking round at the mess, Helen wrinkled her nose. It did cross her mind that Simon could make more of an effort, perhaps wash up a bit more regularly, but then she dismissed her thoughts as petty. When people were experiencing an emotional crisis, they didn't consider mundane things. Hardy's heroine, Eustacia Vye, hadn't washed up before she had chucked herself into the weir.

She asked, 'Do you like the candles?'

'Oh, yes.' He put the cake down on the one part of the kitchen working surface that was relatively clear from clutter. 'Why three?'

'I didn't know how old you were. I guessed around thirty. Anyway, we didn't have enough, so I reckoned one candle for every ten years.'

'Good God – do I look thirty?' He frowned.

She looked at him anxiously. 'Aren't you?'

'I'll be twenty-six on Monday.'

'Oh, sorry.' She blushed but inwardly hugged herself. Twenty-six was much better than thirty. He was only eleven years older than she was.

'It's all right. I suppose to someone of your age, I do seem ancient.' He was recovering. He took down plates from a shelf. 'Anyway, it was a lovely thought of yours, to bake me a cake. Thanks, Helen.'

She nodded, staring up at him. 'Twenty-six is a lovely age to be, and I'm not *that* young.'

He cut the cake, placed a slice on each plate and handed one to her, and as he did so, his gaze flickered rapidly over her figure. He grinned, 'No, I can see you're quite grown-up.'

She felt the heat in her face.

He leaned back against the cupboard. 'We've become quite good friends, haven't we, Helen? Remember our first meeting in the garden on the night of the storm?'

She remembered.

'I thought then you were just a kid. But we talked and as I remember it, you spoke a lot of sense. I remember you knew your Wordsworth. Are you taking English as one of your A-levels?'

A-levels? She opened her mouth to correct him, then shut it again. She had mentioned all the studying she had to do, he had assumed the rest.

'Yes. English, Biology and Maths,' she said demurely.

'Arts *and* Science, that's unusual. You must be brainy, as well as attractive.'

Her heart gave an extra-loud bump. He'd done it again, complimented her.

He had opened a wall cupboard and was studying the contents. 'What about a drink to go with the cake? I've got some sherry, but that's a bit boring, isn't it?' Without waiting for her answer, he brought out two bottles. One contained whisky, the other was a drink she didn't recognise. The bottle was made from dark-coloured glass and was square-shaped. Simon studied the label. 'I think this is still all right. Gill and I bought it last year when we were in Greece, it's some kind of liqueur. It's a bit sweet for me, but you may like it?' He held the bottle towards her, an enquiring look on his face.

'Yes, I'll try a glass. Thanks.'

Two glasses later, they were seated side by side on the settee in his sitting-room. They had eaten three-quarters of the birthday cake and Simon had begun to tell her about his marital break-up. She listened to him intently, even though she felt too hot and a little queasy. The liqueur was very sweet.

'Gill's a wonderful woman but she wants it all, you know.' Simon waved his glass in the air. 'Two holidays a year, masses of clothes, dinner out at least twice a week. That's all very well, but even with two salaries, the mortgage has to be paid and a chap likes to relax at home now and again.'

Helen nodded, her eyes fixed on his face. She suddenly noticed there were tiny flecks of gold in Simon's brown eyes. She shifted in her seat. She was feeling very warm.

'Will she come back, do you think?'

Her words hung in the air. He stared at her and she avoided his gaze by sipping her drink.

'I don't know. Maybe.' He put down his glass of whisky and ran his fingers through his hair. 'We decided on a trial separation. I'm seeing her at the end of the month to talk things through.'

'Oh.' Helen finished the liqueur.

'Do you want another one?'

'No, thanks.' She shook her head vehemently.

'Gill's such fun when she's in a good mood.' Simon had gone back to his main concern. 'But she can be really moody. She's already told me she doesn't want children.'

Helen's eyes opened wide. 'Does she mean it?'

'I think so. Her career's important to her. Of course,' he sighed, 'she might change her mind later. You know, I'd never even thought about having kids, but seeing your lot next-door . . .'

'They're not "our lot"! We've friends staying, three of the kids belong to them – and they're moving out tomorrow.'

'Is that so? I think I'll miss them, although they're a bit noisy in the mornings, aren't they? The little red-head, he's cute.'

Helen smiled. 'He's not going, he belongs to us. He's my half brother.'

'You mean, you don't live with your mother?'

'No, she died years ago. But Kate, my stepmother, she's OK, and Danny's a good kid. Of course sometimes I find him a pain, but usually he's a poppet.'

Helen became aware Simon was staring at her and his face had gone all soft and strange.

'You're a special young woman, Helen. Do you know that? You're caring and warm, and I'm honoured that you took the time to bake me a birthday cake.' He moved closer to her and slipped his arm around her shoulders.

She sat perfectly still, so still she felt her heart pounding. He *did* find her attractive. Maybe he would kiss her. Wait until Eileen heard about this! No, immediately she rejected the idea. This moment was too precious to be shared with anyone.

His breath, somewhere near her ear, smelt of whisky but it was quite a pleasant smell. She was so tense, she jumped when his left arm came across her body, but he only eased her empty glass from her fingers and set it on a table. Then he turned to her again. He *was* going to kiss her, he *was*! Her heart was going like a steam shovel, he must have heard it. If he did, he didn't mention it. He drew her towards him and his left hand gently cupped her chin. As his handsome face came closer, filling her vision, she stared upwards into his wonderful gold-flecked eyes. She relaxed and, greatly daring, put her arms around his neck. His lips came down on hers and they were incredibly soft. Her body seemed to lose all its bones. She gave a little moan.

And then everything changed. Without releasing her mouth, Simon put his hand on her breast and pinched her – and it hurt. Her body tensed and she tried to move away, but he wouldn't let her. He was pressing her down against the back of the settee, and his mouth was no longer sensitive. He was forcing her lips apart with his teeth and tongue.

She felt revulsion and a flicker of something else, something she couldn't understand. She was frightened. She wrenched her mouth away from his.

'Stop it, please. Stop!'

He released her, sat back and stared at her.

She put her hand to her bruised mouth and felt a fool. 'I have to go now, Kate will be back. Thanks for the drink.' She stood up and her legs felt funny. She tried to smile. 'Remember to eat the rest of the cake.'

His brow wrinkled. 'I'm sorry, I didn't mean to offend you.'

'No, no. You didn't. I really do have to go.' She made a bolt for the door.

He followed her. 'I guess I got a bit out of hand? I'm lonely, you see, and you're so sweet, so lovely.' He opened the front door for her. 'Still friends?'

He looked so downcast, she smiled at him. 'Yes, of course.'

She hurried home. As she shut the front door, she heard Richie's voice.

'Helen?'

'Yes?' She approached the kitchen cautiously. Her cheek glowed where Simon's unshaven chin had pressed against hers. She put her hand to her face. Would Richie notice?

He didn't. 'Will you be going out again?'

'No, I don't think so.'

'Good.' Richie stood up from his kneeling position. 'I've about f-finished here and I want to go over to the house and do a few jobs. Nicky's due back any m-minute and I'm not sure whether she has a key. Let her in, will you?

'Yes, of course. Anyway, Kate and Pauline will be back home soon.'

'No, they're going to be late. Kate's just phoned. Apparently, they have to visit s-s-someone before they set off for home. She said to expect them when we see them.'

The property was exactly what a person would imagine a well-run old people's home to be. There was a large rose garden in front of the house with benches in the sheltered areas so that the more active pensioners could sit out in good weather. There were window boxes at the discreet and lightly veiled windows on the first and second floors, and the woodwork and brickwork were immaculate.

A young nurse dressed in a blue and white checked uniform showed Kate into a small waiting-room. 'There are some magazines, and I can get you a cup of coffee if you wish?'

'No, thanks.' Kate sat down and picked up a copy of *The Lady*. She hoped Pauline was having a fruitful interview with the matron of the home, but she also hoped she wouldn't be too long. She wondered whether *she* would be allowed to see Mr Verrill. He was her grandfather, after all.

After ten minutes Pauline put her head round the door. She looked pale but composed. 'I'm going up to see him now, Kate. The matron says he's very frail, and most of the time he doesn't really know where he is.' She sighed. 'Apparently he was mentally and physically in good shape until last year, but then he had a stroke and he's never fully recovered.

Kate stood up. 'Would you like me to come with you?'

Pauline hesitated. 'I'm not sure sure what would be

best.' She thought for a moment. 'I think I'd like to see him on my own first, if you don't mind. Perhaps you could come up in about half an hour? He's in room number twenty-two.'

'Yes, all right.' Kate sat down again. 'Good luck.'

The minutes went by slowly and *The Lady* held little attraction for Kate. She wished she had said yes to the cup of coffee. She left her chair and wandered over to the window. There had been four old ladies sitting outside in the garden when they had arrived at the home, but they had disappeared. They were probably having dinner. Kate glanced at her watch. They were going to be very late home. The day trip had contained more surprises than they had bargained for. She hoped Nicky wasn't too inconvenienced. Her friend was forever obliging, but she had more than enough to see to at the moment. Perhaps Helen would put Danny to bed? She looked at her watch again. She could go upstairs.

The staircase was charming, beautifully proportioned, shallow-stepped and winding. As she walked up to the first floor, Kate thought that if one had to end one's life in an elderly people's home, being in one like Redfern would soften the blow. She turned left and walked along the thickly-carpeted corridor until she found room twenty-two. The door was ajar, she could hear someone speaking. It was Pauline. She hesitated, reluctant to intrude, then moved closer to the doorway and peeped into the room.

The old man – my grandfather, she thought – was propped up on pillows. His eyes were closed and his long, white hair brushed back neatly from his thin wrinkled face. He was dressed in green-striped pyjamas, the jacket too big for his scrawny frame. His hands, knotted with rheumatism, were folded neatly on the counterpane. He looked dead already.

Pauline had pulled a chair close to the bed. Watching, Kate saw her lean forward and place her hand over those of her father.

'Oh, Dad, you can't hear me, can you? You don't even realise I'm here with you. If only I'd known how things were, I would have come sooner.' Kate saw her stroke her father's fingers. 'You must have received my letters, why did you never write back?' Pauline sat back in her chair and stared at her father and with her next words, her voice had strengthened.

'You should have written to me, Dad.' She shook her head. 'You still couldn't forgive me, could you? You were wrong, you know. I made a mistake, I know, but I was young. You were older, and you were my father. You should have forgiven me.'

Kate lowered her eyes. She shouldn't be watching this scene. She was eavesdropping on something very private, and yet she was compelled to watch. She raised her eyes again. She was seeing another side to her mother, she was seeing Pauline as a child with her parent, and she needed to see it if she was to understand.

Pauline was staring at the still figure on the bed. 'I hated you for a long time. I couldn't forget how you turned me away. But then I realised you must have suffered too. All these long, lonely years. Oh, Dad!' Her voice broke. 'Please say something to me? If I can stop hating, surely you can too?'

There were tears on Pauline's face and Kate's own eyes were stinging. She blinked and then looked towards the old man. Remote, locked in his own world, he lay like a graven image, aloof from all human emotion. Kate sniffed and prepared to enter the room, but as her hand touched the door handle she paused because Pauline was talking about her.

'I've my daughter with me, Dad. She's waiting downstairs. Gran once told me that salvation comes when you least expect it. Well,' a tiny smile flickered over Pauline's face, 'she didn't use those exact words. She used one of her old sayings – but that's what she meant. And she was right. Kate and her family have brought me a lot of happiness.'

She saw her mother bend her head. 'Perhaps that was God's reward for my forgiveness of you. I'm not alone any more, you see. I've a little grandson, too. If only you had forgiven me, Dad, you could have known happiness like that. You could have seen the girls growing up. God help me, if only you had forgiven me, everything could have been so different!' Pauline sobbed and covered her face with her hands.

Outside the door, Kate's figure had stiffened. The girls? What was her mother talking about? She waited a moment, then tapped gently on the door and went in.

'Pauline?'

Perhaps the old man had heard some of her words or perhaps the new voice penetrated into his cloudy world for he made a rasping noise in his throat. Pauline looked at Kate and then stood up and bent over him.

'Dad?' Intent on her father, she did not look in Kate's direction. She did not see her walk up to the end of the bed.

'Dad, can you hear me? Oh, please – say something.'

The old man's eyes opened and he made a vain

attempt to pull himself higher on to his pillows. His head turned and he looked into his daughter's face, but his expression remained dazed. Then he looked towards the foot of the bed and an expression of joy spread across his face.

'Margaret!'

He held out a trembling hand to Kate. 'Margaret. Oh, my love, you've come back to me.

After a few brief words with the matron, Pauline and Kate left the nursing home and went back to the harbour to pick up the car. They walked quietly, too lost in their own thoughts to talk.

No one appeared to have challenged their choice of parking space. Kate unlocked the car, climbed in, backed out of the confined space and then opened the door for Pauline. Her mother got into the seat next to hers. They spoke a few sentences, about nothing important, until they were travelling out of Whitby. Then Pauline said, 'He didn't know me. He never said one word, not one word, and yet when you walked in . . .'

'I know.' Kate headed towards the moors. 'But he mixed me up with someone else.'

'He thought you were my mother.' Pauline brushed her hand across her eyes. 'She was only thirty-eight when she died, and now I come to think of it, you do have a look of her.'

Kate was silent. After five minutes, she said, 'Will you visit him again?'

'I suppose so. He's my father, after all.' Pauline sounded flat, dispirited.

Kate glanced at her. 'Why don't you put the seat back and have a rest? You look tired.'

Her suggestion was not entirely out of concern. She, too, was tired, but more than that, she was totally confused. There had been things said today, or implied, that didn't make sense. She sensed there was a secret and it involved her. If only she could sort out all the mixed impressions that were whirling through her mind, she would understand.

She tried to pin down her suspicions, but couldn't. She sighed. It was like having cobwebs in her head. She was missing something, something important.

They travelled in silence. Pauline was asleep before they reached Malton. Kate watched the ribbon of road unwinding before her and tried again. When they were walking to Mary's home, Pauline had rushed her friend away from Kate as if she wanted to tell her something, something *she* must not hear. But Pauline and Mary hadn't met for years and years.

Then there was the mysterious Elizabeth, who was unimportant, but important enough for Pauline to mention over the grave of her beloved gran. And most important of all, those few words she had overheard Pauline say to her father: 'You could have watched the girls growing up.'

All at once, she understood. Oh, God! She looked across at the sleeping form of her mother. Why? Why had she never been told?

There was the sound of screaming brakes. She looked back at the road in front of her and caught her breath. A Range-Rover was heading straight at them. She pulled at the wheel. She had wandered too far over, towards the wrong side of the road. She swerved to the left and slammed on the brakes. She avoided the Range-Rover but went off the road, into the grass verge.

Pauline, thrown forward against her seat belt, put her hand to her head. 'What is it? What's happened?'

'We're all right.'

The other car drove past them. The driver scowled and made a rude gesture. He had every right. Kate took a deep breath, put the car into reverse gear and got them back on to the road. 'My fault, I wasn't concentrating. Are you OK?'

'Yes.'

'That's all right then. Don't worry, go back to sleep if you can.'

Miraculously, she did. Kate, glancing at her, thought wryly that her mother must have great faith in her daughter's driving ability. Of course, she must be emotionally and physically exhausted. Kate was, too. It had been a long day. And when they arrived home, the house would be full of bustle and chatter. There'd be Nicky and Richie, excited about tomorrow's move, and Helen would be asking questions, and Danny . . . hopefully, he would be in bed.

They were almost at York. Kate checked on the petrol situation. Yes, there was enough left to get them home. As soon as they got in, she would go for a long, hot bath and allow herself a period of calm, time in which to think. And then tomorrow, when the house was quiet, she would tackle Pauline. She would insist her mother tell her the truth, about Elizabeth, her sister.

Chapter Twenty-Nine

Kate slept badly and came downstairs on Sunday morning just after eight. Walking into the dining-room she realised someone else had also risen early. The table was set up for breakfast and she could smell bacon frying.

'What's all this?' she said aloud.

'We thought we'd have a slap-up farewell breakfast.' Nicky appeared in the doorway of the kitchen and waved a fork at her. 'Sit down. I'll serve you in a minute.'

'But I never eat a cooked breakfast.'

'You will today.' Richie came into the dining-room carrying a cup of tea. 'We're all having one.'

Kate smiled at him. 'I shouldn't count on Helen, you know she stays in bed on Sunday mornings until after eleven. Anyway, who thought up this idea? You told me you wanted to be off to your new place as soon as possible.'

'We changed our mind.' Richie handed her the tea. 'As Nicky s-said, we can't afford champagne and a house warming, but we can run to a couple of pounds of bacon and a dozen eggs.'

'Helen can have her breakfast in bed. Pauline too if she wants to.' Nicky's voice floated through from the kitchen. 'And the kids can have a plate of bacon sandwiches.'

Kate laughed. 'OK, since it's a special occasion, I'll have the bacon, but no eggs, please.' She grinned at Richie. 'May I have a fried tomato instead?'

'I'll inform the chef.'

As he turned to leave the dining-room, Kate caught hold of his sleeve.

'The kitchen floor's fantastic, Richie. I do appreciate your finding the time to see to it. And Nicky deserves my thanks for looking after Danny.'

She bustled through, carrying a tray heavy with glasses of orange juice and a plate stacked high with toast. 'You needn't thank Richie until he's finished, Kate.' She grinned. 'You still need half a wall and an archway, remember?'

Kate found herself laughing again, which pleased and surprised her. Her thoughts on awakening had been anything but happy. She took a piece of toast and began spreading butter on it, reflecting on how much she was going to miss Nicky's company. She looked up to see her friend smiling down at her.

'I'll be round to visit you pretty soon. How would Wednesday suit?'

Kate nodded. 'Very well. I was just thinking I might need a bit of friendly company next week.'

Nicky's expression became alert. 'Do you know, I had a feeling last night . . .' She paused. 'Anything I can do?'

'No. It's nothing terribly serious.' Kate changed the subject. 'All the packing done?'

'Yep, we're packed and ready to go. Oh!' Nicky raised her head and sniffed the air. 'Hang on, the bacon's burning.

By the time Kate had eaten her breakfast, Pauline had joined them and ten minutes later Helen appeared, still wearing her dressing-gown. The smell of the bacon, the unusual activity on a Sunday morning and the noise of Shawn and Jamie bumping their toy boxes downstairs had awakened her.

She brought Danny downstairs with her. He drank some milk and then wandered about, still wearing his anxious look. But a plateful of bite-sized bacon sandwiches cheered him up and when he discovered the kitchen was within bounds again, he collected his favourite toy cars and went to play in there.

'Talk about getting under people's feet,' Helen grumbled, as she side-stepped him and began to stack the used dishes on the draining board.

'I know, but I'm not risking a scene by moving him,' Kate sighed. 'I keep wondering how he will behave when the boys leave?'

Fortunately for Kate, Danny was no trouble at all when Nicky and her family left the house. Indeed, he refused to go outside to wave goodbye to his friends. His favourite cartoon character had appeared on the television screen and he sat down in front of the set and refused to move. So Kate, Helen and Pauline left him there and went to the gate to witness Nicky and Richie's departure. There was a chorus of voices as they waved goodbye.

'Good luck, see you soon.'

'Look after yourselves.'

'Hope you settle in OK.'

They watched until the van reached the bottom of the hill and then went indoors again. Pauline went to sit with Danny, and Helen said she would go upstairs and do some studying.

'Really?' Kate was surprised. Her stepdaughter rarely worked on Sundays. 'Aren't you seeing Eileen?'

'No.'

Kate wondered if the two girls had fallen out. Then she thought that Helen looked rather pale and wondered if she was sickening for something.

'Do you feel OK, Helen?'

'Of course I do.' She gave an impatient shrug. 'For goodness' sake, it's not so unusual for me to study, is it?'

On a Sunday it is, thought Kate, but she kept her thought to herself because she intended asking a favour.

'Have you a lot of work to do?'

'I *always* have a lot of work. All my teachers seem to think their particular subject should have my undivided attention.' Helen stared at her. 'Why all the interest?'

'I'm always interested.' Kate's voice was casually careful. 'But I was going to ask you to do me a favour.' She took a deep breath. 'Do you think you can spare the time to take Danny to the park this morning, for about an hour?'

'Oh, Kate! Why?'

'I'm sorry. I wouldn't ask, but it *is* important. I need to talk to Pauline about something, and it's impossible trying to have a serious conversation with Danny charging about. And it has to be this morning because she's going back to Manchester after lunch.'

Helen's eyes developed a calculating gleam. 'If I say yes, will you tell me what you're going to discuss?'

'No, I can't. It's something private.'

Helen pouted. But Kate's sombre expression must

have communicated the seriousness of her request for, after a moment's consideration, she nodded.

'OK, if it's that important. I'll go up and get dressed and then we'll be off. I can work this afternoon.'

'Thanks, Helen. I appreciate it.'

Once the television programme had finished, Danny was quite willing to go to the park. He climbed into his pushchair clutching a green plastic lizard and a bag of crisps and allowed Helen to wheel him down the hill. Kate watched them go and then went to find Pauline.

Her mother had gone into the dining-room and was studying the partly built archway. She smiled when she saw Kate in the doorway.

'I wonder when Richie will be able to get back to work on the kitchen.'

'He'll let me know.' Kate realised her voice sounded stilted and rather unfriendly. She walked further into the room. 'Not long, I think.'

'Good. Perhaps next time I visit you, everything will be finished?'

'Yes.' Kate sat down, clasping her hands together on her lap. She was mildly surprised when she realised they were trembling. 'Pauline, we have to talk.'

'Yes, if you like.' She turned her head and listened. 'It's very quiet; what's Danny up to?'

'Helen's taken him to the park.'

'Oh.' Pauline was disappointed. 'They won't be long, will they? I'll be leaving soon after lunch, remember?'

'I asked her to take him out.'

Pauline's brow creased. She studied Kate's face and then came to sit down next to her 'All right, what is it you want to talk about?'

Kate took a deep breath. 'I want you to tell me about my sister.'

She watched as the colour drained from Pauline's face, and waited for her to speak.

'I don't know what . . .'

'Oh, please. Don't lie.' Her own voice sounded harsh to her ears. 'I know you must have had your reasons, I accept that, but please don't lie.' She leaned forward in her chair. 'Listen, *I know* I've a sister. Yesterday you said her name. It's Elizabeth, isn't it?' She stared at Pauline. 'I realised when I heard you talking to your father. You said "the girls".'

Pauline sat as if turned to stone. She had closed her eyes. Kate looked at her sternly. 'You should have told me. I had a right to know.' She sighed. 'I listened to you yesterday. You went on and on at your father about the way he treated you, and yet you've behaved equally as badly to me.'

Her mother opened her eyes and stared at her. A faint tinge of pink had stolen back into her cheeks but her face looked haggard. 'No, it's not the same, Kate. My father was a hard, unforgiving man. I needed him and he closed his door against me. I would never do that to you. As for your sister . . . I wanted so much to tell you about her but somehow it never seemed the right time. Oh God, there's so much to explain. How can I make you understand?'

'I've a sister?' Kate's eyes flashed sparks. 'And you never mentioned her to me. I understand that. She's my *sister*. I want to know where she is now. You must tell me. Can she be contacted? Was she adopted, too?' Her voice softened. 'I'll try and understand, Pauline, really I will. I *can* understand, so long as you tell me the truth. But I must know and only you can tell me. If she was adopted, then perhaps we can find her. I found you, didn't I?' She twisted her hands together.

'You can't find her, Kate. It's not possible.'

'Why?'

'Because she's dead! She died over twenty-five years ago.'

Shock silenced Kate. She gazed blankly into her mother's face.

Pauline looked steadily back at her. The bright blue of her eyes seemed to have faded and her face looked old. She dipped her head and sighed.

'All right, I will tell you. I'll tell you everything.' She gave a weary shrug. 'You *do* have a right to know. Only please believe me, Kate, I always meant to tell you about Elizabeth, when the time was right. And for God's sake,' she choked, 'please don't tell me I'm like my father.'

She waited for Kate to say something but when she realised she had nothing to say, swallowed nervously and began her story.

'Elizabeth was not only your sister, she was your twin. She was born first, ten minutes before you.'

Kate started violently. 'My twin?'

'Yes.'

'That explains . . .'

'What?'

She shook her head helplessly. She remembered the odd fleeting moments of loss she had continually experienced during her early childhood, the feeling that something or someone was missing. And even when she was an adult there were times – she remembered the day she had reached into Danny's pram and felt that there should be someone else . . . there should have been two.

She gazed at Pauline. 'Go on.'

'You were beautiful children, but different. Elizabeth – Eliza, I called her – was much bigger than you were. And she was a noisy baby, either in a temper or full of smiles. You were small, placid, like a little angel. I loved you equally.' Pauline's voice trembled.

'When I left the hospital I went straight to my Uncle Charlie's home. He was my great-uncle really, my gran's brother. He was a lovely man, and I hated imposing on him, but I didn't know what else to do. Poor Uncle Charlie, he was elderly and had just got married for the second time. What he must have thought when I first asked him to take us in I don't know, but he agreed. I had no option, you see. Until the two of you arrived, I had no idea I was carrying twins.'

Pauline's smile was sad. 'When you were born there were no such things as scans and things like that. My doctor was just as surprised at your arrival as I was. Anyway, Uncle Charlie, bless him, put us into his spare room and then he went to see my father. He got no joy there, so he came back and said I was to stay in his home. I thanked him, but I knew it wouldn't work, and it didn't. His new wife was absolutely furious.

'She wasn't a very nice person actually, but I could understand her dismay. Even a saint would have objected. An unmarried mother and two tiny babies moving in with a newly married couple – it was an impossible situation. We struggled along in disharmony for almost three months and then I told Uncle Charlie it was time I stood on my own two feet. Gran had left me some money. I could manage, I said.

'I rented two rooms but there was no way I could work and the money started to disappear at an alarming rate. Then I got the idea of advertising in the local press to see if I could get some kind of resident post. A housekeeper, something like that, but nothing came of it.

'Then Uncle Charlie came to me with a proposition. He had recently been to a wedding. A man he had served with in the merchant navy was the bridegroom. The man had married a widow who owned a small hotel in Devon. Apparently she was finding it hard to get live-in staff.'

Pauline saw Kate look up, and nodded. 'Yes, it was the hotel the Hamptons stayed in. Uncle Charlie told the couple about me, gave me a sort of character reference.' She grimaced. 'It must have been a bit difficult, given the circumstances. Anyway, they finally agreed I should go and work for them, subject to certain conditions.'

An expression flickered over her face that Kate couldn't define. 'Poor Uncle Charlie, he really was trying to do his best for us.' Pauline stopped speaking and tried to smile. It was a pale ghost of a thing.

'Do you want to ask me anything? I promise I'll tell you the truth.'

'No.' Kate cleared her throat and shifted in her chair. She realised the palms of her hands were sore. She had been so absorbed in Pauline's words, she had been clenching her fists tighter and tighter. She spread out her fingers and rubbed them. 'What happened next?'

Her mother shrugged. 'I went to Devon. I had one room in which the three of us lived. I spent my time working hard and creeping upstairs to see if you and Elizabeth were all right. I hated it there. The woman Uncle Charlie's friend had married was a hard bitch. I don't think she even liked children, but she knew a bargain when she saw one, and she knew I couldn't go off and get another job. She was right.

'The only consolation was that she was almost as bad to her new husband. I bet he got a real shock, after the marriage. I think he'd thought he had charmed a rich widow and had landed the life of Riley, but he was mistaken. She ruled him with a rod of iron and he worked almost as hard as I did. He grumbled about her all the time, but he stuck it out. She was older than he was. Perhaps he thought he'd cash in when she died.

'About every two months he'd break out, get blind drunk. One night, after drinking almost a bottle of whisky, he made a grab at me and she caught him. I was out straight away, even though she saw me slap his face.'

She gave a tight-lipped smile. 'She should have known I was too tired to indulge in games with her husband. I had neither the inclination nor the energy. How she punished him I don't know, but I'm sure she did.'

'So that's when my adoptive parents came looking for you?'

'Yes, although it was you they were looking for.' Pauline sighed. 'I think you know the rest.'

'I know about me, but what about Elizabeth? Did you have her adopted, too?'

'No, I didn't.' Pauline looked down at her nails.

There was silence as Kate digested this new information.

'You mean, you gave me away – and kept her?

'I had to, Kate.' Pauline's voice was patient, as if explaining to a child. 'I was out of a job, living in damp, unhealthy accommodation. Elizabeth was never ill, she could stand it, but you couldn't. And the Hamptons pleaded with me, they kept on about the good life you would have with them. I kept remembering what the doctor had said. The worry over whether your heart had been weakened by the conditions you were living in. I did what I thought was best.'

'And you must have thought how much easier it would be, with only one child to care for.' Kate sprang from her chair and paced round the room. 'I can't believe you're sitting there, telling me all this.'

'I never thought anything of the kind. I was heartbroken when you went. But you were wasting away before my eyes and I couldn't look after you properly.' She shook her head. 'I told you all this, Kate, the first time we met.'

'But you didn't mention *Elizabeth*, and that alters everything, don't you see?' Kate's face twisted. 'You gave me away and you kept her. And,' she pressed her hand to her forehead, 'we were twins, we belonged together, and you separated us.'

She paused, paralysed by the enormity of her loss. She'd had a twin sister, they should have grown up together, but she had grown up alone. And now her sister was dead. The waste of it struck her like a physical blow. She felt hatred welling inside her.

She glared at her mother. 'Were we alike?'

'What?'

'Elizabeth and me, were we alike?' She shouted the words.

Pauline flinched. 'Yes, very alike, although Elizabeth had curly hair and a tiny mole on her left cheek.'

Kate touched her own left cheek and felt tears spring to her eyes. 'How did she die?'

'Kate, please.' Pauline closed her eyes. 'Do we have to . . .'

'Yes! I *need* to know, don't you understand? I never had a chance to know Elizabeth when she was alive, so I need to know how she died.'

Very slowly, like an old, old woman, Pauline stood up and moved towards Kate. She put out her hand. 'You must understand, I really had no alternative but to let the Hamptons have you. The doctor had told me . . .'

Kate pulled away from her touch. 'Tell me about Elizabeth.'

Pauline slumped in defeat. She turned away, looking blindly towards the large sheet of plastic which shrouded the partly built archway. She said quietly, 'Three days before her tenth birthday, Elizabeth dashed out of the house to buy an ice lolly. There was one of those ice-cream vans playing away at the bottom of the street.' She shivered. 'I still can't bear the sound of the chimes.'

'And?'

Her mother let out a wavering sigh. 'You read about such things in the newspapers every day. She ran straight out into the road and a car hit her. She died in hospital two hours later. I'd told her before,' Pauline turned to face Kate, 'over and over again I'd told her: "Be careful." We lived on a busy road, you see. But Elizabeth was always impatient, always acted first and thought about things afterwards.'

'Did she?' Kate's face had become as smooth and expressionless as a pane of glass. 'You obviously picked the wrong one, didn't you, Pauline?'

She flinched. 'I don't know what you mean.'

'I think you do. You decided to keep your lively,

vivacious little daughter, only it didn't work out, did it? Hard luck. You should have stuck with the weakling.'

As if hit a physical blow, Pauline's head went back. 'Kate, that's a terrible thing to say. I've explained why I let you go to the Hamptons, surely you believe me?'

The blank expression on Kate's face dissolved into a look of absolute misery. 'I really don't know *what* I believe at the moment. I just know I feel sick, and very tired.' Her shoulders slumped as she turned and walked towards the kitchen. 'I'm going in the garden, I need to pull myself together before Helen brings Danny back. As for you,' she looked back over her shoulder, 'you'll be going for your train soon.'

'But we can't leave it like this. We must sort ourselves out, Kate. We must resolve this thing once and for all.'

'I think the best thing would be for you to just go.' In the kitchen doorway, she paused. 'It's not really your fault, Pauline. It's mine. Jack warned me. When I told him I was going to try and trace my mother he said I might be heading for trouble, but I didn't believe him. I thought,' she hesitated, 'oh, I don't know what I thought. I hoped we'd bring each other happiness. I never dreamed we would cause each other pain.' She looked at Pauline. 'I'm sorry, but I don't want you to come here again. I don't think I could stand it.'

Pauline gasped. 'But, Kate, we're just starting to get close to each other. It's taken time, I know, but during the last few months we've come to understand each other. We can't let all that go. And now you know about Elizabeth, I can tell you things about her. I have photographs. And there's Danny . . .'

Kate's face hardened. 'He's just a little boy, he'll soon forget you.' She saw Pauline flinch and said, 'You see, to be honest, it wasn't really working out even before I knew about my sister. Yes, we've got on all right, but that's as far as it went. I just don't feel . . .' She bit her lip and started again. 'After what we've just been talking about, I think the best thing to do is for us to say goodbye.'

Pushing a sleeping Danny in his pushchair up the back lane, Helen hoped Kate realised she had got good value for money. The trip to the park had gone well and she and her little brother had been out for almost two hours. A girl she knew from school had been there with her little sister and so, as the toddlers played together, Helen and her companion had sunbathed on the grass and talked of teachers, pop music, parents and sex.

A snag had arisen when they had prepared to leave the park. Danny and the little girl had buried Fang, the plastic lizard, in the sandpit and after ten minutes' search, were still unable to find him. Helen had wanted to leave the wretched thing. A boy who lived two doors down from them had given the lizard to Danny. It was a cheap, repulsive toy with foul pink eyes and painted blood dripping from its open mouth, but Danny loved it.

When she had tried to put him into his pushchair, he had screamed and stiffened his body. He wanted his Fang. Helen had finally lost her temper with him. She had slapped his hand and then tapped him smartly behind the back of his knees to make him sit down. He had done so and she had fastened the safety strap on the pushchair with a sigh of relief. But still he cried.

She had crouched down in front of him and tried to make amends.

'Come on, Danny. You have lots of toys at home. And some little boy who hasn't any nice toys will find Fang and love him.'

He had looked at her. He had dirty streaks on his face and his tear-washed eyes were piteous. She had felt ashamed. He was only a baby, after all. She had unbuckled the straps, lifted him out of the pushchair and they had crawled round the sandpit again until they had found his toy. The beaming smile he had given her had made it all worth it.

She reached the back gate of their house. She opened it and wheeled the pushchair up the path. She looked down at Danny. His eyelashes made fans on his flushed cheeks and his right arm firmly clasped his toy to his chest. The ridged tail of the lizard was pressing against his neck. It didn't seem to worry him. Looking round first, to see if anyone was watching them, she bent and softly touched his auburn hair with her hand.

Amy, the girl in the park, had said men were chauvinist pigs and she had no intention of ever marrying. But according to tales circulating at school, Helen knew that her dad had recently run off with another woman so, she reflected, Amy had every reason to be bitter. But she was wrong. There were some decent men about, and some happy marriages. Her dad and Kate were happy most of the time, and they had Danny.

She thought she'd get married, if only to have a couple of babies. Naturally she would never admit to her friends at school that she wanted children, they'd just laugh at her. And anyway nowadays you could have a baby without getting married, lots of people did.

You could even have a baby without sleeping with a man. Her biology teacher had recently explained to the class the method of artificial insemination. That had caused a few sniggers. But she had listened to him very carefully. He had said the recent advances in science were amazing and she supposed he was right but they made life very complicated.

She parked Danny outside the conservatory and went indoors. Everywhere was very quiet. She looked in all the downstairs rooms and wondered where Kate and Pauline were. She went upstairs.

Kate was lying on her bed with the curtains drawn. Helen hesitated by the half-open door.

'I'm back.'

'Oh. Already?'

Helen felt aggrieved. 'It's after one.'

'Is it? I hadn't realised. Where's Danny?'

'He's asleep in his pushchair. I left him outside. Where's Pauline?'

'She decided to go early and called a taxi.'

'Oh!' Helen scuffed the toe of her trainer against the bottom of the door and wondered why Kate hadn't taken her mother to the station in the car, as she usually did. And why had Pauline left without saying goodbye to her and Danny? Something was up, she thought.

'I'm going to make a sandwich. Do you want one?'

'No, thanks. I've a bit of a headache. I'll stay here until Danny wakes up.' Kate raised herself up on one elbow. 'Thanks for looking after him.'

She did look a bit off colour. Helen said generously, 'That's all right. You stay there. I'll look after Danny.'

'But you were going to study?'

'I've decided the weather's too nice to stick in my bedroom all afternoon. I'll get something to eat and then,' she paused, 'I'll do a bit of gardening. Danny can help me.'

'You're sure?'

'Yes.' Helen went back downstairs. Thinking about babies and husbands made her think of Simon. She hadn't seen him lately. She frowned as she slapped pickle on to her cheese sandwich. She had been very childish, running out of his house like that. He had only kissed her. Wasn't that what she had been praying for him to do ever since their first meeting? Eileen said all grown-ups kissed with their mouths open. You'd only got to watch the plays on TV to see that.

She made a little sandwich for Danny, cutting off the crusts. She'd get his paddling pool out for him and he could play in that while she did the gardening. She decided she'd wear her denim shorts and v-necked blouse to garden in. And maybe just a touch of make-up.

Chapter Thirty

It was a Sunday morning in mid-October and Jack, waking in his own bed at home, stretched luxuriously. The bed he slept in on the rig was OK but it was a single and the guy who shared his quarters snored. This bed was king-sized and, more importantly, it contained his wife. He yawned happily and then rolled over to say good morning to her, only to discover she wasn't there. So he lay on his back again and scowled at the ceiling. She still wasn't sleeping too well. She said nothing was troubling her, but he knew it was. She had been tense ever since the fall-out with Pauline.

He'd had four leave periods since the day he had walked into the house to be greeted with the news that Kate had quarrelled with her mother. Telling him about it, looking dark-eyed with fatigue, Kate had become very emotional. The tears had flowed when she spoke about her sister.

'She was my twin, Jack – and I didn't even know she existed.'

Clumsily, he had tried to comfort her but it had been hard to find the right words. Finally, he had said, 'Well, at least you know everything now, Kate. You know the whole truth of the matter, the good things as well as the bad. And as I said right at the beginning, it's the present and the future that's important. You'll always have me and the children.'

She had nodded. 'Yes, you're right.' She had dried her eyes and tried to smile at him and, apart from one occasion, as far as he knew she had not cried again. They had discussed what to tell Helen and had spoken to her that evening. They had told her that something had come to light which made it impossible for Kate to keep on seeing her mother. It was all very sad but it would be better if none of them ever saw Pauline again.

Helen had wanted to know more, of course, but he had shaken his head.

'That's all we can tell you right now. Perhaps later, when things have settled down a bit.'

Helen had protested strongly and a difficult week had followed.

'I don't see why *I* can't keep in touch with her? She hasn't done anything to me. I can go through to Manchester. She doesn't have to come here, to the house.'

Jack had shaken his head. 'It wouldn't work, Helen. Better to make a clean break.'

'But what has she done?'

He had hesitated. 'She misled Kate about several important things. She didn't tell her the truth.'

'That doesn't sound like Pauline.' Helen fiddled with her hair, a sure sign she was upset. 'She was always fair enough with me. Even if she and Kate have quarrelled, I don't see why I should stop seeing her.'

Jack had frowned. 'There's such a thing as loyalty, Helen. You've only known Pauline for a few months and Kate's looked after you for years. I think it's time you got your priorities right.'

Helen had blushed. 'I'm sorry.' She had looked at Kate, who sat silently listening. 'All right, I won't see her again, but can I write to her?'

Jack had hesitated, but Kate nodded.

'Yes, if you want to.' She glanced at her husband. 'We've got to be fair, Jack. It's not Helen's quarrel.' She had looked back at Helen. 'I don't know whether she will write back, though.'

As far as Jack knew, Pauline hadn't been in touch with anyone. Helen pestered to know more details for a few more days but then she left the subject alone. Danny asked about grandma for a little while and then seemed to forget all about her. Of course, he was used to her coming and going. Gradually, the little family resumed their orderly life.

But nothing seemed quite the same for any of them. Pauline was not mentioned but occasionally Helen would come in from school and comment on the quietness of the house. She would sigh and say how she missed Nicky and her children, and Kate would snap back: 'When they lived here, you were always moaning about the noise.' And then Helen would sulk.

Danny demanded more attention than previously, although that could be because he was getting older. He had perfected a peculiar whining noise which he used when he was thwarted in any way. And Kate, back to a strict routine of cleaning and cooking, was irritated by the smallest thing.

Jack sighed and decided it was time to get up. He got out of bed and went to the window, drawing back the curtains to see what kind of day it was. Pretty good, it seemed. The sky was hazy blue and the sun was shining. He stared down into the back garden and noticed how the autumnal tints were beginning to show. The button chrysanthemums were flowering and the copper beech hedge was a picture. He looked at the strip of lawn. Not so many bald patches since Nicky and her crowd had departed. He acknowledged that he, too, missed Nicky, Richie and their children.

Oh, sometimes the noise in the house had got on his nerves, but at other times – he smiled, remembering the sight of the little ones playing together on the lawn and baby Lisa nearby, asleep in her buggy. It was good for children to have playmates, he thought. This silly business with Danny was probably because he was feeling lonely without the constant company of his friends. He had got used to having the boys to play with.

Jack had often felt lonely when he was a boy. His sister Pat had been years older than him and they had never been close. Helen was older than Danny, but at least they got on well together.

Jack wondered whether Kate ever thought about giving Danny a little brother or sister. She never mentioned the subject of another baby and he had been hesitant to ask her how she felt about it. He would have been delighted, but Kate was the one who would have to carry a child and look after it. At thirty-six, maybe she thought one child was enough? A new baby caused a lot of hassle. And, of course, he certainly couldn't broach the subject right now. She was too screwed up about Pauline.

She said she wasn't. She said the whole episode was now far behind her, and indeed she never talked about her mother, but he knew his wife, and he knew the matter was still not resolved. Two leaves ago, he had seen her restless movements, her inability to concentrate on anything for very long, and had asked her, straight out: 'Have you heard anything from Pauline?'

She had flushed, then turned pale. 'No.'

'And *you* haven't reconsidered? You haven't tried to contact her?'

'No. Why should I? It's over and done with.'

He had looked at her expressionless face and felt a slight chill. 'She's still your mother, Kate.'

She had blinked, looked at him in surprise, then turned away. He had caught hold of her elbow. 'Don't you think you're being a little hard?'

'Perhaps.' She had pulled her arm away. 'Don't you think I have the right?'

He had told her then, told her what he really thought about the whole episode.

'No, I don't, as a matter of fact. I feel that, after walking uninvited into someone else's life, you can't just walk out again.' He had softened his voice, seeing the hurt dawn on her face.

'I'm sorry, but I really think we should talk, love. You're not happy the way things are, I'm sure of that. So why not consider trying to sort this mess out? Remember, *you* wanted to find your mother, and you did. You changed her life and you changed our lives, too. But now that you've discovered something about her you don't like, you want to ignore the fact that she exists. You want to go back to before you knew her, but you *can't*. Life isn't like that.'

'You're very wise all of a sudden.' Kate's reply had been bitter. 'You astound me, Jack, you really do. I thought you'd be the one person to understand my feelings, because you loved me.' Her voice cracked and she averted her face.

'Why the hell do you think I'm saying all this?' His voice also sounded rough but his face was gentle as he caught hold of her and held her to him. 'I *do* love you,

Kate, and I can see you're unhappy, although you won't admit it. If only you could make yourself acknowledge that Pauline gave you away because she had to, then you could make your peace with each other and feel better.'

'Never.' She pulled away from him. 'No normal mother would give away one twin and keep the other. It's not natural.'

He shook his head. 'You would have taken the news better if Pauline had allowed both of you and Elizabeth to be adopted, wouldn't you?'

'Of course I would.'

He studied her face. 'You know, Kate, your trouble is you've never had to struggle. You've never known real hardship.'

'And you have, I suppose?'

'Yes, I have. Oh, not at first hand.' He had shaken his head. 'My father always provided for his family. But there was one family in our street where the father was a drunk. His wife had five or six kids. I can't remember the exact number, but I remember them playing in the street. My mum used to send me round to their house with a bag of buns after she had baked or with a spare pint of milk. I'd knock and the woman would open the door.' Jack paused. 'Do you know, the expression on her face haunts me still. She'd force a smile and take whatever was offered, but in her eyes you could see the frustration of *having* to accept charity.'

'You make it sound like a scene out of Dickens. It can't have been that bad. There was social security or whatever name it went under in those days.'

'State handouts buy second-hand clothes and bread and potatoes, Kate. Not an inspiring life-style, is it?

But forget all that. What I'm trying to do is make you see why your mother had you adopted.' He took a deep breath. 'Remember what she told you? You were ill, she was desperately worried. What if you needed specialist care? She couldn't give you a decent home or any of the other things you needed. The Hamptons could afford that, she couldn't and they were crazy to adopt you.'

He had known, looking at her face, that he had failed.

'All right, you've made your point, but we only have her word as to what happened, haven't we?' Kate had shrugged her shoulders. 'And she kept Elizabeth. How did she manage to support her?' She had looked down. 'I'm sorry but I can't forget that, Jack, and I don't think I shall ever be able to forgive her.'

He had looked into her face, felt a flash of dislike mixed with sympathy for her. 'Well, you've got your revenge.'

The word had shaken her. She had frowned, questioningly. 'I don't know what you mean.'

'You still don't see, do you?' He had tried to speak dispassionately, much as she had done. 'You found Pauline and transplanted her into our world. She got to know us, became a part of our family. A family was something she'd never had before, remember? And, as far as I could see, she loved every minute of the time she spent with us. She also came to love certain individuals.'

'Oh, Danny, you mean?'

He snapped at her. 'No, not just Danny. She loved you, Kate.'

When she bent her head, he sighed. 'Didn't you

realise? I did. You could see it in her eyes. And every time she came here, she positively bloomed. But now,' he paused, 'she's out in the cold again.'

'For someone who's away half the time, you seem to have noticed a lot of things. I've never known you be so eloquent, Jack. All this talk of love. I wonder why it's taken this terrible business for you to discuss love with me? Of course, you may have talked to Felicity this way. Maybe she found it easy to show her feelings. I know I'm not like that. I'm not an easy person to get close to, but I had hoped . . .' There was a catch in her voice. Her face crumpled as tears started to flow.

'Oh, Christ. Come here.' He had opened his arms to her and she had come into them. As she sobbed on his shoulder he had kissed her over and over again, smoothing her wet hair from her forehead.

'I love you, Kate. I love you.' He had soothed her as a father soothes a small child. 'I only said what I did *because* I love you. I understand your bitterness, but can't you see? It's eating you up. I just want you to resolve your feelings and put an end to all this.

'Yes, it's true that I have some sympathy for Pauline, but *you* are my main concern. You always will be, you and the children.'

He kissed her until she responded to him and then they had gone upstairs and made love. It had been a frantic, urgent coupling, driven by a mutual need to reaffirm their love for each other, and it had brought them close together again. Since that day he had never mentioned Pauline to her but the problem was still there and both of them knew it. It hung like a dark cloud above their heads, threatening their tranquillity.

Lost in thought, Jack stared at his garden until a movement distracted him. Helen appeared. She carried a pair of shears in her hand and she went towards the beech hedge.

Jack frowned. What the hell was she doing? The hedge was in full glory, the last thing it needed was a shave. And since when had Helen got up to garden on a Sunday morning?

He moved away, grabbed his clothes and went to the bathroom. Washed and dressed, he returned and went straight back to the window. She was still out there, but she had put down the shears. She was poking about in the flower border now with a hoe. It would have been funny if it hadn't been mystifying. He remembered Kate had mentioned his daughter's growing interest in gardening, but she wasn't gardening, she was loitering around.

He watched her with no feeling that he was spying. She was his daughter, his responsibility, and she was up to something. Ah, she had turned her face and he saw her expression of pleasure. Whatever, whoever, she had been waiting for, had appeared. He craned his neck to see who or what it was.

A tall chap was leaning over the hedge. They were talking. The man raised his hands in the air, obviously telling her a story, and she laughed. They seemed very easy together, as though they were old friends. But Helen's companion was no callow schoolboy, he was a handsome man in his late twenties.

Helen was laughing again. Jack noticed how she put her hand to her hair, a feminine, very self-conscious gesture. With a sudden pang, he realised just how grown-up she looked. The jeans, belted tightly at her slim waist, emphasised her shapely hips and breasts. She was wearing a pair of large silver hoop earrings. Jack had not seen them before. She tossed back her head and the earrings caught light from the sunshine. They glinted in the tangle of her shoulder-length fair hair.

Jack stared down at her with a lump in his throat, thinking of his first wife. What would Felicity have thought of her grown-up attractive daughter? And where had the years gone? He remembered a smaller Helen's delight at her first bike. The time she had cut her knee badly on broken glass and had been so brave at the hospital. He remembered her pugnacious little face after Felicity had died when he had been forced to leave her with his sister, Pat.

'I don't like her, I want to go with you.'

He studied the man she was talking to and suddenly realised who he was. Of course, it was Simon Blunt, their next-door neighbour. The chap whose wife had left him. Jack's eyebrows levelled into one straight line. He headed for the door.

Downstairs the scene was quietly domestic. Danny was tucking into a boiled egg and Kate was drinking coffee and looking at the Sunday newspapers. Music and faint voices drifted from the radio. Kate looked up and smiled.

'Oh, there you are. I thought I'd hold breakfast until you came downstairs.'

'Has Helen had her breakfast?'

'Helen?' Kate shook her head. 'I don't think she's up yet.'

'She's up, all right. She's out in the back garden.'

'Really? What's she doing out there?'

'Chatting up our next-door neighbour, as far as I can tell.'

Kate stared, and then laughed. 'Don't be ridiculous.'

'I'm not. Go and see for yourself. She's simpering over the hedge at him like an Edwardian miss.'

'Well then, you don't have to worry. Edwardian ladies were always most circumspect.'

Jack hunched his shoulders. 'It's not a joke, Kate. And it's not her I'm worried about.'

'Now you *are* being ridiculous.' Kate poured him out a cup of coffee. 'Simon's a nice man. He's also in his late twenties; he wouldn't be interested in Helen.'

'If he's so nice, why did his wife leave him? And as for being disinterested, he's been talking to my daughter for the last ten minutes.'

Over her coffee cup, Kate studied him. 'How do you know that?'

'I saw him, from the bedroom window.'

'You mean, you've been spying on them?'

He flushed. 'Of course not. I just happened to see them.'

'For ten minutes?' Kate put down her cup. 'You're jealous!'

'Now *you're* being ridiculous.'

'No, I've read about the insecurities of fathers. Helen's growing into a pretty young woman and deep down you resent it. It's a perfectly natural reaction.'

'I am *not* jealous! I'm perfectly happy for Helen to have a boyfriend, but I don't want her getting involved with a middle-aged married man.'

'He's our next-door neighbour, they'll just be having a friendly chat. Simon Blunt's not the type to be interested in a schoolgirl, Jack. Don't you remember how sophisticated his wife was? Stop worrying.' She stood up. 'Now, what do you want for breakfast?'

At eight-thirty, having eaten breakfast and washed up

her few pots, Pauline went to collect her newspaper from the hallway. 'Oh dear,' she groaned when she picked up the thick wad of paper. The delivery boy had done it again. Instead of the requested paper, he had delivered what she called one of those intellectual things, full of long boring articles about subjects she neither cared for nor understood. She pulled a face as she carried the newspaper into the kitchen, but sat down by the table and attempted to read the lead article, a feature about the current exchange rate.

After a couple of paragraphs, she gave up. It was no good, she couldn't make head or tail of it. Her lack of comprehension upset her. She felt ignorant and ill-informed, she even felt a bit weepy at her failure. Mind you, feeling weepy was nothing new nowadays. Ignoring the newspaper spread out before her, she propped her chin in her hands and her mind wandered. What would Kate and her family be doing today? It was good weather. If Jack was home, perhaps they were all going out for the day.

She frowned. Whatever they were doing, it was no business of hers. Snatching her spectacles from her nose, she polished them fiercely upon her apron, replaced them and turned her attention back to the newspaper. She would search until she found something she did understand. She must keep her mind occupied. No good came of dwelling on sad things that could not be changed.

Ah, there was a travel article on page four. Pauline read about Burma with great attention, even though she had no desire to visit the country. Italy now, she'd love to go to Italy. She finished and turned over a few more pages – the Stock Exchange – she grimaced.

No pictures of the Royal family, no chatty little

article to cheer a body up. And she certainly couldn't tackle the crossword. She'd just read the television page, she decided, and then she'd clean the windows. The window cleaner had done the outsides yesterday so it was a good day to do the insides.

Flipping through the closely printed pages in a vain attempt to find the entertainment section, she spotted a face she thought she recognised. She paused, her hand hovering over the page. It couldn't be! She peered more closely at the photograph. It was him. And then, with a lurch of her heart, she realised what page it was. She closed her eyes for a moment and then looked again. Yes, it was a picture of Grahame Lossing, and in the obituaries section.

She sat and stared down at the grainy newspaper photograph and was surprised at her lack of feeling. The man she had loved, or thought she did, the father of her children, had died, and she felt absolutely nothing. She bent forward and studied his photograph. He looked much the same as she remembered him. Older, of course. His sharp-featured face looked thinner but he had kept his thick hair, although it seemed the redness had faded to grey. He didn't look at all ill, but perhaps the picture was not recent. She read the report accompanying the photograph.

> 'The death is announced of Grahame Lossing, Chairman of Secebush Engineering Group since 1975. A quiet, somewhat solitary man, Grahame Lossing's name will be unknown to the general public but his friends and fellow colleagues at Secebush will miss him greatly. Lossing joined the company as a junior salesman in 1957. His exceptional business acumen was soon recognised

and he rose swiftly through the ranks, becoming Chairman of the Group in 1975.

In the late 70s he was the moving force in fighting off a string of possible predators when the company's shares fell in value due to fierce competition from abroad. He survived to see Secebush retain its former prominence. Grahame Lossing never married, often joking that Secebush was his life and his wife. His one passion, apart from his work, was salmon fishing. His death occurred last weekend, when he was involved in a car accident as he was driving to Scotland to pursue his hobby. He leaves no known relatives.'

So . . . Pauline gave a sharp sigh. Grahame had prospered, but from the newspaper report, it seemed his life had been a lonely one. She had a sudden flash of memory, of Grahame on the night he returned to her after fighting the moor fire. He had been so excited and happy. He had enjoyed being among the fire-fighters, being part of a group, even though there had been possible danger. She wondered if he had felt the same working for Secebush. He certainly had run away from involvement with her.

At last, she felt a burst of emotion, but it was anger that clouded her eyes, not grief. Grahame was dead and there was no one to mourn him. But did he deserve mourners? He had lived a selfish life with no one to please but himself. He had moved up the career ladder, become rich and successful and died at the height of his powers, on his way to something he enjoyed. He had been lucky.

He'd never struggled to keep a roof over his head.

He'd never lost sleep tending a sick child, or faced the prospect of losing that child because he couldn't afford to give her a decent life. Neither had he buried a child, nor felt the pain and the loss. And yet, Kate and Elizabeth had been his children, too.

Pauline clenched her hand into a fist and banged it down on the picture of Grahame Lossing. 'I hate you,' she whispered. 'Damn you to hell.'

Pushing back her chair she stood up and blundered her way out of the kitchen. In the sitting-room the tick of the mantel clock emphasised the silence of the flat. She blinked her eyes clear of tears and looked at the time. It was still early, she had the whole day to fill. The windows, she thought, almost feverishly, there are the windows to clean. She fetched a chamois leather and a duster. She would work. She would not think. But she did.

Kate had abandoned the search for her father. She should be told of Grahame's death. She had a right to know. And . . . Pauline's hand slowed at her work . . . there could be a question over the estate. Grahame's name was on Kate's birth certificate. But Kate never wanted to see her again. Perhaps a letter . . . Pauline rubbed savagely at a spot on the window. She could hardly send her the cutting from the newspaper, without comment.

Head buzzing, she tried to think of other things. She moved to the sitting-room. Being there made her think about Helen, remembering how she had practised dancing the cha-cha-cha. Helen had written a lovely letter, but she hadn't replied because it seemed better not to. There had been a letter from Nicky, too. It had been carefully worded. She had written that she hoped Pauline was well and told her that, if ever she was in Leeds, she was to call and see them. She had even copied down her new address, in case Pauline wasn't sure of it. And at the bottom of the letter there had been a postscript: 'Kate knows I have sent this to you.'

Glancing through the bedroom window, Pauline saw a young woman hurrying by outside. She was pulling along behind her a little boy whose legs were too short to keep up. He kept skipping and running alongside his mother.

Pauline rubbed even harder at the window, telling herself he didn't look a bit like Danny. Grandchildren were not all they were cracked up to be, she told herself. They expected you to spoil them, they whined and tired you out. She rested her head against the cool glass of the window and thought about Danny and then, with a shift of emotion, she recalled the newspaper report on Grahame.

She left her cleaning and walked back into the kitchen. Wearily, she picked up the newspaper.

'You went through life without my pain,' she whispered aloud. 'But then, neither did you share the happiness. Yes,' she nodded at his photo, 'there was that, too.'

She let the paper drop to the floor and went into her bedroom. From a drawer in her dressing-table she took a photograph album. She sat on the bed and with trembling fingers, opened the covers.

There were Elizabeth and Kate together, grinning at her from their old-fashioned twin pram. It was a black and white photograph, faded a little now, but Pauline remembered, their bonnets had been yellow. An old woman, a neighbour, had knitted them. She had been a strict old girl, one of the old school, but with a kind heart. She had always looked into the pram as she passed by, frowning when Elizabeth screamed for attention, but smiling at Kate's serenely sleeping face.

'That bairn's too good for this world,' she had pronounced, touching Kate's cheek with a gentle finger. And Pauline's heart had grown cold, remembering Kate's coughing spells and her gasping for breath. The old lady had got it wrong, though.

Pauline turned over the page. Just one more picture of the twins together, and then Elizabeth, on her own. A sturdily built Elizabeth, beaming at the camera, one knicker leg showing below her short skirt. That photograph had been taken just before she had started school. Pauline remembered how she had blessed the day Eliza had started school. Her little daughter had been such a handful between the ages of three and five, always trying to run away from the various women Pauline had paid to look after her child while she was at work. Elizabeth always wanted to be outside, she had hated being kept indoors.

She had loved outings to the park, loved all living things, too. Oh, the things Pauline had found in her pockets; old matchboxes full of woodlice and snails, the revolting slug she had secreted in her glove one cold day and brought home and hidden in her underclothes drawer. Pauline had been furious when she had found it.

'You bad girl. Look at the mess.' She had thrown up her hands at the sticky, silvery trails all over Elizabeth's vests and pants.

Her daughter had tossed her head. 'The poor thing was cold outside. And I'm not allowed a dog or a cat, so I thought Walter could be my pet.'

Pauline had looked at her. 'You know we can't have a pet while we're living here, it's against the rules.' She had stared at Eliza's frowning face. 'Why did you call it Walter?'

Elizabeth had given her an impish grin. 'He just looks like a Walter.'

And unable to resist that grin, Pauline had unearthed an old, unused goldfish bowl and Walter had taken up residence with them.

When the last page had been turned, she sat quietly savouring the sweet memories she had so long banished from her mind. Whatever happens with Kate, she thought, as she gently laid the album back in the drawer, I feel as though I have got one child back.

And then, because she was Eliza's grand-daughter, she squared her shoulders, went to the telephone and dialled the number of her friend, Rita. She would *not* sit indoors all day and brood about Kate. She waited.

'Rita, are you doing anything special today? No? Well, don't you think it's too nice a day to sit inside and watch the telly? What if I meet you outside the Bellwood Arms at twelve-thirty? We could have a bar-snack and then decide where to go for the afternoon?'

She listened. 'Oh, I don't know. We'll think of something. And, Rita, next week I'll pick up some more brochures from the travel agency. I've always fancied a trip to Venice, what do you think?'

She went into her bedroom and picked herself out a brightly coloured dress, then put heated rollers in her hair. In the bathroom, which had a good, strong light, she peered more closely at her hairline. It was time she had her colour done again. Kate hadn't approved of her having her hair coloured. Pauline knew that, although Kate had never said anything. Pauline hadn't said anything either, but she had kept on having it coloured. It was all right for Kate, she had no grey hairs. She'll learn, thought Pauline. Then her fingers stilled as she replaced a loose hair roller. Perhaps Kate would learn about more than the advantages of colouring her hair as she aged.

Pauline used her little magnifying mirror to help her see to put on her eye make-up. That done, she got dressed, dusted her face with powder, took out her rollers and brushed her hair. She studied her reflection through her mirror. The dress, she decided, would look better if she wore earrings, so she brought out her jewellery box.

She smiled as she opened it, remembering the birthday when Lawrence had given it to her.

'But I've no decent jewellery to put in it,' she had said.

'Well, perhaps I'll get you some. In the meantime, you'll just have to admire the ballerina.'

The little clockwork dancer was still whirling around, even though Lawrence was gone. Pauline watched her for a moment and then searched for her solid gold earrings. Lawrence had kept his promise.

Her hand touched an envelope. She paused. Of course, it was Eliza's letter. She took out the envelope and removed the single sheet of paper, gently smoothing out the yellowing creases. She stared down at it. She didn't need to read the words, she knew them by heart.

Then she gazed thoughtfully in the mirror. It was a strange thing, but even after so many years she still occasionally felt the presence of her grandmother. And today was one of those times.

Without really thinking what she was doing, she

slipped the letter into the back flap of her handbag and then fastened on the gold earrings. She sat back and put on her spectacles. The fuzziness of her faulty vision vanished. She looked and approved of her appearance.

'Not exactly a spring chicken,' she said aloud, 'but not bad, not bad at all.'

And she could almost imagine she heard an approving ghostly chuckle.

Chapter Thirty-One

'Seventeen pounds.' Kate's voice rang out crisply over the subdued murmurs coming from the crowd of people packed into Rannock's salerooms.

'Seventeen fifty.'

'Eighteen.'

'Eighteen fifty.'

Kate's rival was persistent. Jack, who sitting next to his wife, holding Danny on his knee and trying to engage his attention by dismantling and reassembling a Lego car, whispered: 'Remember, we said no more than twenty pounds.'

She nodded and raised her hand. 'Nineteen pounds.'

There was silence. The auctioneer looked enquiringly towards the rival bidder. 'Do I hear another offer? No?' He waited a moment longer and then his hammer went down. 'Sold to the lady in the fourth row.'

Kate smiled jubilantly and squeezed her husband's arm. 'It's a bargain, Jack. I'm sure it's a Copeland and Garrett piece, but better than that, the set will look perfect on the new display shelf in the kitchen.'

'That's great.' He nodded and dumped a wriggling Danny on her knee. 'Here, you have him for a bit.'

Kate laughed. 'You getting fed up, Danny?'

'He's not the only one.' Jack glanced down at the sale catalogue. 'Anything else that interests you?'

'No, we'll leave in a moment.'

Watching the sales assistant carrying away a tray upon which their newly acquired jug and bowl stood, Jack reflected that their purchase was probably the finishing touch to the now finished kitchen extension.

Kate certainly had an eye for colour and line. The jug and bowl would look good on the shelf.

The thought slipped into his mind that it was a pity Pauline couldn't see the new kitchen that her money had paid for. He sighed. They had decided to send Kate's mother a cheque as soon as possible to repay the loan. In another three or four months they would be in a position to do so, but he felt ambivalent about the whole business, although he had been the one who had originally insisted on repaying the money. Pauline had wanted the money to be a gift, but under the circumstances . . . He sighed.

A set of three Allerton's lustre jugs were sold and then a Victorian jardinière, which brought to a close the sale of pottery and porcelain. In the lull that followed, before the 'objets d'art' made their appearance, Jack and Kate vacated their seats and went to the sales office to pay for their purchase.

'The item won't be available until after the end of the sale,' said the desk clerk.

'That's all right, we'll collect it tomorrow.' Jack pocketed his receipt. 'I'll drive over in the morning,' he told Kate. 'Then I'll bring them home and set straight off for Aberdeen.'

'Thanks.' She took a firm hold of Danny's hand as they left the office and went towards their parked car.

'You know, I can't believe you're going back to work already. It doesn't seem a minute since you arrived.'

'Leave time always flies.' He strapped Danny into his carseat and then opened the door for Kate. 'Let's do something tonight, shall we?'

She grinned. 'What did you have in mind?'

He chuckled, rejoicing inside at the sight of her carefree face. At last she was regaining her sense of humour. 'Well, maybe that too – but let's go out for a meal first. What about visiting Angelo's?'

'I'd enjoy that.' Kate nodded. 'OK, you're on. That is, if Helen agrees to baby-sit.'

Jack went around to his side of the car. 'She'll baby-sit.'

Helen waved them off, thinking how nice they both looked. Dad was wearing his new tweed jacket and Kate had put on her cream and ecru two-piece suit, the one that always made her hair look the colour of hazel nuts. She thought they looked happy as they chatted together and walked down the path, and she was glad. The atmosphere at home had been erratic the last few weeks; it had been 'lovey-dovey' one minute and raised voices the next. It was because of the dust-up with Pauline of course.

Helen reckoned that if anyone should be aggrieved, it was her. They'd never really told her what the row had been about and they should have done, she was practically grown-up now and she was family, too. And she *missed* Pauline very much, she really did.

She missed her for all sorts of reasons, but mostly because, with Pauline, she had been able to have proper discussions. Maybe, she thought, it was because Pauline hadn't been close enough to consider everything as directly connected to Helen's future, like Dad and Kate did. And she didn't laugh, either, if Helen talked about something important. Like the time she had thought about joining Greenpeace. Helen scowled, remembering. Eileen had cracked up at the very idea, but Pauline had been really interested.

And then there was the problem that still bothered her, whether or not to aim for university. It was all right Kate and Dad saying she should, but did she *want* to go to university? Would it be best for her? As she had said to Pauline, nowadays there was no guarantee of a good job, even with a degree. And the thought of all that studying, for years and years, was just too awful.

'It seems to me,' she had told Pauline, 'that what should be the happiest time of our life is totally spoilt by worrying over O-levels and A-levels. I bet it was a lot more fun when you were young. You didn't have to worry about such things.'

She had been gratified when Pauline had actually agreed with her. She had said examinations hadn't been important in her day because by the time you were fifteen you were expected to leave school and get a job. But then she had pointed out, in a very matter-of-fact way, that the jobs available for fifteen-year-olds were poorly paid and usually uninteresting. She spoke about her own experience, and said that working in a dry-cleaning shop nine hours a day had been pretty boring.

And then she had pointed out that if Helen *did* manage to get a place at university, there could be a number of choices when she finished.

'You wouldn't automatically have to decide on a

career straight away, Helen. I read something about how lots of graduates go and work overseas for a year. You're interested in the environment, maybe you could do something like that? And if you studied Science subjects – who knows – you might end up joining some scheme to help people in underdeveloped countries.'

Helen hadn't thought of that.

And then Pauline had advised her to stop worrying so much about the future.

'Concentrate on your O-levels, get them over with, and then let your hair down for a bit.' She had laughed. 'You know what they say. "Why worry about something today, when you can worry about it tomorrow?" Or if you want something more unusual, my grandma said something similar: "Fair and softly goes far in a day." And she knew what she was talking about, young lady.'

Yes, Helen sighed, she still missed Pauline.

She went upstairs and listened outside Danny's bedroom. There wasn't a sound, he was fast asleep. It was boring being in the house on her own. She wouldn't have minded if he was awake. Then she could have sat on his bed and read him stories from the big blue book of fairy stories.

Everywhere was so quiet. Too quiet. Kate had said she could invite Eileen round, but she hadn't bothered. Eileen had got very silly lately.

Last week she had gone out on a date with a boy from the Sixth Form College and ever since she had gone on and on about the violent necking session they had indulged in. It had sounded totally repulsive. Helen had said as much and Eileen had simpered and told her she was 'too naive for words'. She thought about Simon and the kiss he had given her the day she had taken the birthday cake round to him. That had been a bit scary, but not repulsive. She sighed. She'd been stupid that day. Stupid and childish.

Downstairs again, she looked at the TV page in the newspaper. There was nothing she wanted to see, but she switched on the set anyway, and then she went to get a bag of crisps out of the kitchen. There was only cheese and onion flavour left. She took a packet and returned to the sitting-room and perched on the chaise-longue.

A new programme had started, something about a threatened tribe living in the Amazon jungle. Helen watched the screen as thin natives with bones through their ears loped about hunting game, and sweet-faced young women giggled at the camera and nursed their babies.

If I'd been born there, she mused, I'd be like that. I wouldn't be fretting about global disaster or whether I should try to get into university. I'd be suckling a baby and waiting for my man to return home, with a dead rabbit or something. She wondered, did they have rabbits in the Amazon?

She thought again about Simon Blunt. Would he make a good hunter? He'd certainly look good in a loin-cloth. She had been in the garden on Tuesday evening when he had returned from a run. He had been wearing shorts and she had seen his legs. They had been lovely, not a bit hairy, but strong and golden-looking. She didn't like hairy men. He had stopped to speak to her and they had chatted, but not for very long because she wasn't sure where her father was.

She and her father had engaged in a very curious

conversation on Monday. She still wasn't sure what they'd been talking about. He had mentioned Ben Raymond, who had so completely disappeared from her thoughts that she had thought: Who? And then, out of the blue, he had said what a pity it was that Gill Blunt had left her husband. She had agreed it was a shame. Agreed also that Simon Blunt seemed a decent young man. Then her dad had gone waffling on about how most young couples fell out, but they usually made up again.

He said he was sure the Blunts would sort out their problems and she had nodded, and even yawned a little, to show him how nonchalant she was about the whole subject. He had shut up then, and given her a fiver to buy herself something. She had accepted the money gratefully, but his mentioning Simon had made her wary.

Still, he was out for the evening and Simon wasn't. Helen knew that because his car was parked outside. Maybe he too was slumped in front of the TV watching Amazon women pounding corn? An amazing idea popped into her mind. She frowned and chewed her lip. It was a bit way out, but why not? She turned off the television set and went to the telephone. She dialled.

'Simon? Hey, it's me, Helen. Look, I'm sorry to bother you, but do you by any chance have a copy of Wordsworth's collected poems?' She waited, crossing her fingers. He'd studied Wordsworth at school, he had told her so, but that didn't mean he had kept his books. 'Sorry? Oh, yes, of course I'll hang on.'

He returned to the phone, spoke to her.

'You have! Oh, that's great. You see, I should have written an essay on some of his poems, but I've mislaid my book. Could you possibly bring it round for me? I'd come for it, but my parents have gone out and I'm baby-sitting and I don't like to leave Danny in case he wakes up. You will? Thanks.' She put down the phone and smiled. Then, remembering the onion-flavoured crisps, she rushed upstairs to brush her teeth.

By a quarter to eleven, Kate and Jack were on their way home. They had enjoyed their evening out. The carafe of wine chosen by Jack had complemented their choice of food and the service had been excellent. Jack had suggested they end the meal with coffee and a brandy but Kate demurred, saying she didn't want to leave Helen on her own for too long. Walking up the path towards the house, they were surprised to see no lights showing.

'Perhaps she's gone to bed?' Jack put his key in the lock quietly.

'No, I doubt that.' Kate was peering through the window. The curtains were drawn but she could see a dim blue light from the television set. 'She's probably watching a late-night horror movie. They're always more scary in the dark.'

'On her own?' Jack gave a mock shudder. 'Then she's braver than me. I remember I nearly passed out the first time I saw *Pyscho*.'

'Ah, but that was a classic, Jack. Tonight's offering is probably a sixties vampire film with female vampires sporting beehive hairdos and forty-inch busts.'

They were laughing as they pushed open the door and walked into the sitting-room. Then the laughter faded and there was an appalled silence.

The television was showing some old movie but the sound was turned down and Helen certainly wasn't watching it. She was on the chaise-longue with her arms around Simon Blunt and he was kissing her with great thoroughness.

Jack's eyes flashed sparks and he ground out, 'What the hell . . . ?'

The couple sprang apart. Simon Blunt looked at them with an embarrassed expression on his face. Helen, her eyes blinking rapidly in the sudden light, looked petrified. Hand to her throat, she gasped, 'Dad, I didn't expect you back so soon.'

Jack opened his mouth to make a caustic comment, but words literally failed him. Silently, he took in the scene before him.

There was a bottle of whisky on the table. *His* whisky. There were also two glasses, one empty, the other one half-full. Helen's shoes were on the carpet where she had kicked them off and she . . . Jack found it hard to look at his daughter.

Helen looked like a tramp! Her hair was mussed up and her face was flushed with alcohol. Her mouth was blurred-looking, as if from too much kissing, and – with a pain that was almost physical – Jack saw her blouse was unbuttoned and gaped open. He could see the swell of her breasts and her bra, a white cotton schoolgirl's bra, heartbreakingly plain and simple. At least the bastard hadn't got that off. The blood drummed in his temples.

He clenched his hands and took a step towards them.

'Jack.' Kate's voice held a warning note.

He looked at her.

'Give them chance to explain.'

'I don't need a bloody explanation. I can *see* what they've been up to.'

Simon Blunt sat forward, partly shielding Helen from her father's gaze. 'I apologise, Mr Gallantree. I'm sorry you walked in on us like that.' He coughed. 'It's rather embarrassing, isn't it? But I think we should keep things in proportion.' He shrugged. 'You see, I brought a book round that Helen needed to borrow for her work. We talked a little and she offered me a drink.'

'You call what you were doing *talking*?'

'No, of course not.' Blunt looked irritated. 'Helen's a very attractive girl and I guess we're attracted to each other. I suppose you object to me because I'm a married man? But Helen knows about Gill. We're separated and anyway, let's face it, when certain signals are being given out, a man would have to be a fool not to take advantage of them.'

'Why, you . . .'

'Oh, Dad!' Helen had finished buttoning up her blouse. Now she interrupted her father. Indeed, she glowered at him. 'Please don't make a scene.'

Simon Blunt put his arm around her shoulders. 'Yes, you are over-reacting a bit. Don't tell me you've never . . .'

Jack's control went. Pulling his arm free from Kate's restraining grasp, he strode towards Blunt, grabbed his shirt collar and twisted it.

'You filthy bastard! No, for your information I never did. I never gave a fifteen-year-old girl whisky to drink, and then tried to seduce her in her own home, not even when I was a single man!'

The genuine shock which appeared on Blunt's face disconcerted him and caused him to ease his grasp on his neighbour's throat. When Kate begged him to release the man, he did so.

Blunt fell back on to the sofa. He put up his hand to ease his collar. His face had gone bright red, whether from lack of breath or discomfiture it was hard to tell.

'Helen's only fifteen? I didn't know, I swear it.' He glanced at her sidewards. 'I thought she was at least seventeen.'

'You thought wrong then, didn't you?' Jack thrust his hands into his trouser pockets to stop himself hitting Blunt. They were still clenched into fists. 'I've a good mind to call the police.'

'Wait a minute, Jack.' Kate looked at her stepdaughter. 'What have you to say about all this, Helen?'

'I never thought to say how old I was.' Her voice was jumpy with fear and suppressed tears. 'Age is immaterial anyway. It's how you *feel* that's important.' She drew breath, and from somewhere courage to defy her parents. 'We were fine until you came back. Now you've spoilt it. You've made everything seem dirty, and it wasn't.' She buried her head in her hands and burst into tears.

'I'd better take her upstairs.' Kate frowned at Jack. 'It's no good going on at the poor kid.' She went up to Helen and put her arms about the girl's heaving shoulders. 'Come on, love.' Helen allowed herself to be led to the door. She was too busy crying to look at anyone. Kate totally ignored Simon Blunt, but she gave Jack a hard look as she left the room.

When they'd gone, Blunt spoke again. 'Honestly, I thought she was seventeen. I never would have touched her if I had known she was only a schoolgirl.'

Jack's shoulders slumped. The anger had burned out of him but he felt flat and depressed. 'I accept that may be true, but you're still way out of line. Even if she were seventeen, you're still too old for her, and you're a married man, for God's sake. What the hell were you doing in *my* house, trying it on with *my* daughter?'

Blunt hung his head. 'I guess I've had too much to drink. I'd been at the whisky at home before she telephoned. I brought her the book she wanted and she asked me to come in.' He paused. 'She made it pretty plain she liked me, Mr Gallantree. I was flattered, and I've been very lonely. I suppose you know that my wife and I . . .'

'I know a little bit.' Jack spoke hastily. He felt dead beat and he didn't want to hear about Blunt's emotional problems. He had more than enough of his own. He went over and opened the door. 'The best thing you can do is go home and sleep it off.'

The younger man walked towards the door. As he came within touching distance, Jack caught hold of his shirt sleeve. 'I'm prepared to forget about tonight, Blunt. But,' he fixed his neighbour with a gimlet stare, 'if I ever see you being over-friendly with Helen again, I *will* involve the police. Understand?'

'Yes. Yes, I do.' Blunt nodded his head emphatically.

'And another thing.'

He waited, his face showing apprehension.

Jack gave him a thin-lipped smile. 'You owe me a bottle of whisky.'

After locking up, Jack went upstairs. Kate was coming out of Helen's bedroom. She closed the door quietly behind her and then whispered to him, 'Has he gone?'

'Yes.' He looked at the closed door. 'Should I go and talk to her?'

'No, she's worn out. Talk tomorrow, if you feel you must.' She went through into their own bedroom and he followed her. He sat down on the bed and stared down at his hands. 'That creep! I could have killed him, you know, when we first walked in.'

'So I noticed.'

'Just think, if we'd have stayed on in Angelo's, if we'd had coffee and a brandy, he might have—'

'Seduced her?'

Kate's voice was light, almost ironic. He stared at her. 'You're not upset, are you?'

'I was. It was as much of a shock to me as it was to you. But I'm not any more. These things happen, particularly nowadays. Anyway, there's no point in me fretting. You're worrying enough for both of us.'

'Haven't I reason to?' He was getting angry again. He frowned. 'I can't understand your attitude, Kate. You saw the two of them.'

'Yes, and they weren't exactly stretched naked on the rug, were they?' She came to sit next to him. 'Put your fatherly concern to one side for a moment and try and look at things a bit more rationally. Helen's growing up, Jack. She's at the stage when she's in love with love.'

She sighed. 'Simon's a good-looking chap, and he lives next door so he's accessible. Helen's been out with a schoolboy. Now she's seeing if she can land a bigger fish. She's an adolescent, Jack. She's practising being an adult, that's all.'

'And adolescent girls never get pregnant, I suppose?'

He felt her stiffen and move away from him. 'Yes, of course they do, but I trust Helen to be sensible. Don't you?'

'Not after what I've seen tonight.'

She just looked at him. She was making him feel guilty, as though everything that had happened was his fault. He burst out, 'It's not Helen I'm thinking of, it's bloody Simon Blunt.' Recalling the scene that had greeted them when they entered the sitting-room, his blood began to run hot again. 'I *knew* that guy was up to no good. I told you, remember? But you wouldn't listen.'

He stood up, yanked his shirt over his head and threw it on to the floor. 'It's not often you do listen to me, Kate. And you know why? Because you always think you know best.

'You knew best about going ahead with the search for your natural mother, didn't you? And then, when things turned out not to your liking, you knew best about how to deal with it. You decided to cut Pauline out of our life.'

Behind the shield of his anger, he saw her hurt expression, but he couldn't stop. The words came pouring out of him. 'You didn't think that Danny might miss his grandmother, did you? Or that Helen had become great friends with her? Because you think you even know what's best for my daughter, don't you? *My* daughter, Kate, not yours.'

Now he stopped, appalled at his own words. He had gone too far and knew it. 'Kate, I'm sorry. I didn't mean . . .'

Blank-faced, she stood up and collected her nightgown from the bottom of the bed. 'I'll use the bathroom first.' By the door, she paused and glanced back at him. 'Don't wait for me to come back in here. I'll sleep in Danny's room tonight.' She went out.

He sat on the bed again and gazed blankly into

space. Who'd have thought that such a pleasant evening would end so disastrously? And tomorrow he was going back to the rig. He swore and smacked his clenched fist into the palm of his left hand.

Why the hell did I have to open my big mouth? he asked himself.

Chapter Thirty-Two

Pauline was halfway through her breakfast when the newsflash interrupted the early morning music programme on the radio. It was November now, and a wild blustery day. She had turned the heating up the night before because the weather had turned so cold. She listened to the newsflash and watched the bare branches of the tree outside her flat tossing in the wind. She frowned at the gravity of the announcer's voice, and turned up the volume of the radio so that she could hear him properly.

> 'Reports are coming in that a helicopter, engaged in a routine task of ferrying oil-workers to the Shetland Islands, has crashed into the North Sea. A rescue search had been launched but coastguards in the area state weather conditions are severe and it is feared there will be casualties. It is believed the helicopter was carrying a crew of two and sixteen passengers. A telephone number is being set up to allow relatives to ring in for further details. We hope to broadcast the emergency number within the next few minutes. We will bring you further information as and when available. We now return you to normal service.'

The soothing strains of a Nat King Cole classic came over the air. Pauline stared down at her breakfast and watched as a blob of marmalade slid off her knife and spread across the plate. There was no reason to believe Jack was on that helicopter. Hundreds of men worked on oil-rigs. But she remembered Kate telling her that Jack regularly flew by helicopter to the Shetlands because it was the first lap of his trip when he was coming home.

Realising her breathing was becoming too rapid, she consciously slowed it down.

Nat King Cole's velvet voice died away, and she strained her ears for the promised telephone number. Not that she intended phoning. She knew that once the number was given, there would be hundreds of anxious wives and mothers reaching for their telephones. How could she steal their time and space?

Another record was playing. No telephone number yet. She stood up and walked round the kitchen. Had she *imagined* the newsflash? No, of course she hadn't. She clenched her hands. If only there was someone she could talk to. The telephone shrilled and she jumped, then ran to answer it. It was Rita, asking whether she had booked their holiday yet. She wanted to know if . . .

Pauline cut her short. 'Sorry, Rita, I'll have to ring you back. I'm expecting a very important call and I have to keep the line clear. I'll ring you later and explain.' She replaced the receiver and heard the announcer's voice again. She rushed back into the kitchen and caught his last three words: '. . . seven, two, four.' She could have wept with frustration. She waited until the hands of the clock crawled round to eight-thirty and then she rang Kate's number. The line was engaged.

At nine o'clock, Helen rang her.

'Pauline, have you heard the news?' She sounded upset.

Pauline bit her lip. 'Yes, love. And I wondered if . . .'

'A man rang us. He spoke to Kate. Dad was on that helicopter, Pauline. The one that crashed.'

She clutched the phone tightly.

'I've been trying to get hold of Nicky, but she's not in.' There was a pause and Pauline could tell Helen was fighting to keep her tears at bay.

'And Kate . . .'

Pauline interrupted her. 'Is she there? Will she talk to me?'

'I don't think so. She's acting really strange, Pauline, as if nothing has happened. She's brought Danny downstairs and she's playing games with him.' Helen's voice went up a notch. 'And when I mention Dad, she just stares at me and I don't know what to do.' She started crying.

Pauline felt her own heart fluttering. She tried to keep her voice calm.

'I'll come straight away, Helen. I'll catch the first available train. But you'll have to manage for the next couple of hours. Stay close by the phone and write down any messages you get from the oil people. Keep trying to get hold of Nicky. And about Kate.' She paused. 'I think you should ring your doctor. If she should want to go out, try and persuade her not to. I don't think she will, but just in case . . . Is there a neighbour she's particularly friendly with?'

She heard Helen blow her nose. When she spoke again, her voice was calmer. 'No. I asked her if she wanted anyone, but she shook her head.'

'Well, at least that means she's taking in what

you're saying.' Pauline's fears subsided fractionally. 'Perhaps it's just her way of dealing with the news, Helen. Everyone acts differently under stress. And *you* must keep calm, too. Can you do that?'

'I'll try.'

'Good girl. Do you know what the man said to Kate?'

'Yes, she dropped the phone and I picked it up and explained who I was and he said that Dad was on the missing helicopter. He and the other men were starting their leave. He said a massive search was going on. He said we mustn't lose heart because they've pinpointed the exact area.' Her voice wobbled. 'They've spotted the wreckage.'

Pauline bit her lip. 'I'm on my way. Hang on, love.'

She put the phone down and then picked it up again and rang for a taxi. She collected her coat and handbag. She checked her purse. Yes, she had enough money. While she was waiting for the cab, she remembered Rita, so rang her and tersely explained the situation.

'So you see . . .' She heard the taxi-driver peep his horn. 'Oh, the cab's here, I'll have to go.' She slammed down the phone and made for the door.

Kate looked . . . dislocated. She was tidily dressed, wearing blue jeans and a deep pink sweater, and she was sitting on the floor, still playing with Danny. Pauline saw her hair was neat and well-brushed but her face was a bluey-white colour, like skimmed milk.

Mother and child looked up at Pauline's entrance. Danny grinned, Kate look blank.

'Grandma!' Danny stood up and ran towards Pauline.

She bent and put her arms around him. 'Hello, darling.'

'Come back here, Danny, you haven't finished colouring this picture.' Kate's expression, as her gaze swept over Pauline, held no animosity but equally no welcome. She held out her hand to Danny.

'You see?' Helen's eyes were enormous and panic lurked in them.

Pauline released Danny. 'Go and finish your picture, Danny. Grandma wants a cup of tea, then she'll play with you.' She backed out of the sitting-room and went into the newly furbished kitchen with Helen.

'Would you make me a drink, love? The train was packed and the heating was on full blast. I'm parched.' She didn't really need the tea, but Helen, she thought, needed to keep busy.

The girl took down the tea-caddy with hands that trembled, but her movements became more sure as she put the kettle on the gas and set out cups and saucers.

'Shall I make one for Kate? I took her a drink about an hour ago, but she didn't touch it.'

'I'll take one through later. Tell me, Helen, what time did the man ring you? I caught the newsflash about eight o'clock, I think. I know I was finishing my breakfast. Of course, I thought immediately of your father.' Pauline kept up a smooth flow of conversation, without pausing for replies. 'I hadn't a clue what to do, whether to come straight here or whether I should wait and see if anyone rang. I was so glad when you did get in touch.'

'I'm glad, too.' Helen handed her the cup of tea and then sat down and stared at her.

'Aren't you having one?'

'No.' She fidgeted with her hair for a moment and then blurted out, 'Do you think he's dead? Do you think my dad's dead?'

The pathos in her voice caused Pauline's fingers to tremble and she tightened her grasp on the cup and saucer. I must *not* spill it, she told herself, not when Helen's been brave enough to make it for me. She looked across at her honorary grandchild and ached to comfort her, but Helen's self-control was too fragile and she did not want to shatter it. So she said, 'I don't know, Helen. But I do know that if anyone could survive a crash into the sea, your dad could. He's an excellent swimmer, isn't he? And he keeps himself fit.' She sighed. 'If only we had more information.'

Helen, wordless, nodded.

'And remember, he'll be wearing special clothing to keep the heat in, and don't they wear bright colours so that they're easily spotted? I remember, when we were talking once, your father said safety regulations were very strict. And rescue teams are marvellous nowadays. They have all kinds of sophisticated equipment.'

Helen bent her head. 'But if the helicopter ditched quickly, and it sounds as though it did, they'd have been trapped inside. Being strong wouldn't help them. They'd all have drowned.' She began to cry, slow, silent tears, and then to apologise. 'I'm sorry, I shouldn't. Crying doesn't help anyone.' She scrubbed savagely at her wet face.

'But you should cry. Of course you should.' Now was the time for comfort. Pauline put down her tea and hurried to Helen's side. 'And crying *does* help.' She paused, thinking of Kate's unnatural calm and wishing she would let her grief out.

She picked up Helen's hands and held them tightly

in her own. 'I feel like crying, too, and I've known your father less than a year.' She forced a smile to her face. 'But don't cry too long, will you? For all we know, your father may already have been found. He could be walking in through that door in a few hours, and you don't want to be looking like a wreck when that happens, do you?'

She was rewarded with a watery smile and a shake of Helen's head.

Pauline hugged her. 'And I tell you one thing. When he does walk in, I shall tell him he has a terrific daughter.'

'Will you?' The smile widened. 'Why?'

'Because of the way you've coped. He'll be really proud of you, Helen.'

She shook her head. 'I'm not so sure. I upset him on his last leave, just before he went back to work. We had an awful row, and then I think he and Kate rowed about me, because when he left the next morning they were glaring at each other and there was a horrible atmosphere. And if he never comes back . . .' Her eyes brimmed over again.

'Good Lord, Helen, you mustn't worry about a family argument. Some families row all the time. It's the families who never row you have to worry about.'

Helen sniffed and sat up straight in her chair. 'You won't tell Dad I cried?'

'Not if you don't want me to.' Pauline hesitated. The poor girl still looked exhausted but the strain had eased from her face. 'Feel better now?'

She nodded.

'Good, because I'm asking you to be brave for a little longer. Can you hold the fort while I go and sit with Kate for a little while?'

'Yes, of course I will.' Helen produced a handkerchief

and blew her nose vigorously. Then putting her head to one side, she asked, 'What happened between you and Kate, Pauline? You seemed to be getting on so well, and then Dad told me you wouldn't be coming here any more.'

'Kate found out I didn't tell her the whole truth about what happened when she was a baby. She thinks I was deceitful and let her down.' Pauline's face set in sad lines. 'She was hurt and angry and I understand why she should feel that way, but there were reasons I acted as I did.' She broke off and sighed. 'It's complicated, Helen, and I'd rather not talk about it now. What about this emergency number?' She stood up. 'Shall we ring to see if there's any more news?'

'No. The man who rang this morning said he would contact us again, immediately they had any more information.'

Pauline rubbed her chin. 'Well, perhaps you should try to reach Nicky again. She is Kate's best friend and I know she would come immediately if she knew what had happened. I didn't know she was on the phone, by the way?'

'She isn't, but her next-door neighbour is, and she's been really good about me ringing up. I'll try again in a minute. But what about Danny, Pauline? He's been stuck in the sitting-room with Kate all morning. He's been so good, maybe he senses something's wrong, but he must be getting restless by now. He'll start playing up soon.'

'Yes, you're right.' Pauline ran her fingers through her hair. 'That's one of the reasons I wanted Nicky to come round. I thought she could talk to Kate and then take Danny back to her place for a few hours.'

'Well, I'll ring the neighbour again, although I did

leave a message before.' Helen got to her feet. 'And I can look after Danny.'

'Are you sure, love?'

'Yes, it will do me good, give me something to think about.' Helen managed a genuine smile. 'He's only had a few biscuits since his breakfast so he'll be hungry. I'll cook him some sausages; he likes those.'

Pauline nodded approvingly. 'And try and eat something yourself. I'll make some fresh tea and take it in to Kate and we'll see what happens.'

She went to put on the kettle on, reflecting that her daughter was going to be much harder to comfort than Helen had been.

When she walked into the sitting-room she saw Kate was trying to get Danny to play with his bricks, but he wasn't interested. He was rolling about the floor and whining, 'I want to go out, I want to go out.' His face brightened when Pauline entered the room. He sat up and asked. 'Walk, Grandma?'

'In a bit, Danny, when I've talked to Mummy.' Pauline sat down. Her daughter was kneeling on the carpet.

Without looking at Danny or Pauline, Kate placed a triangular-shaped wooden brick on top of a piled-up tower, and then sat back on her heels. 'Look, Danny, we've made a castle.'

Disenchanted with the game, he stood up and ran to Pauline instead of his mother. He demanded to sit on her knee.

With hidden misgivings, she lifted him up. 'How are you managing, Kate?'

'Fine.' She stared at the bricks. 'Come and see, Danny. It's like the tower in your fairy-tale book. A king could live there, or a magician.'

Danny was more interested in Pauline's spectacles. He grasped the side pieces in his chubby hands and joggled them, laughing as they bobbed up and down on her nose.

'Careful. Grandma can't see without her glasses.' Pauline rescued her spectacles and then smoothed back the hair from his forehead and smiled at him. 'I know a story about a lady who was locked up in a tower. A handsome prince came and rescued her, and they married and lived happily ever after.' She glanced at Kate. 'The lady had long, beautiful, nut-brown hair.'

The little boy looked at her doubtfully and touched his head. 'Long hair,' he echoed.

She smiled again. 'Yes, much longer than yours, but don't worry about it. You're not really old enough for that story, I was really telling it to your mummy.'

'Me?' Kate frowned. 'Why are you telling me a fairy story?'

There was a knock on the door and Helen popped her head round. 'Still no Nicky. I've reminded the neighbour to ask her to ring us as soon as she comes home.' She looked uncertainly towards Kate and then grinned at her little brother. 'Hey, Danny, want to play ball in the garden?'

He scrambled off Pauline's knee. 'Yes, play ball.'

Kate's head went up. 'But . . .'

'Let him go, Kate. Helen's only taking him in the garden for a few minutes, and then she's getting him something to eat. And you need a rest from him.'

Seemingly for the first time, Kate focused on who she was. She frowned. 'Why are you here? I didn't ask you to come.'

Pauline flinched, but nodded to Helen to take

Danny from the room. Then she said quietly, 'Helen did. She rang me because she was upset and frightened, Kate, and she was worried about you.'

She shrugged her shoulders. 'I'm all right.'

Pauline folded her lips. 'But Helen wasn't. Try to think about her for a moment, Kate. Jack's her father as well as your husband. The child needed comforting.'

She had spoken sharply, hoping to provoke a reaction from Kate, and she got one.

'Don't you dare to lecture me!' The words were shouted.

'My God, you don't change, do you, Pauline? In the house for five minutes and already you're taking control.' Kate glared at her mother. 'How pleased you must have been to get Helen's call. It gave you the perfect opportunity to come back here and start interfering in our lives again.'

Pauline's eyes widened but she answered her daughter quietly. 'I haven't come to interfere, Kate. I thought you might need help. And as soon as this business is settled, I'll leave. Or I'll leave when Nicky comes, if you want me to.'

'This business?' Kate's voice was shaking. 'You mean, when we know whether Jack is alive or dead?'

Pauline bowed her head. 'Yes.'

'Well, I don't think you will leave.' The pupils of Kate's eyes were dilated. She shook her head violently. 'If Jack's dead, you'll stay on, playing your favourite role of "wise woman". You'll dispense tea and sympathy,' she gestured to the tea Pauline had brought in, 'and everyone will think you're wonderful. And you'll tell us to be brave, and spout words of wisdom you learned at your grandma's knee. But can't you understand?' Her face contorted. 'If Jack's dead, I don't *want* comforting, and I refuse to be brave.' Her kneeling figure slumped as she wrapped her arms around her body. 'If Jack's dead, that's the end of me too. He's the only person I've ever been happy with, the only person I have truly loved.'

Pauline stared down at her and then said, in a quiet voice, 'I hope to God he *isn't* dead, Kate, but if he is, you'll find it's not always possible to give up. You'll have Helen and Danny to think about, remember?'

'I don't *care* about Helen and Danny. They're young, they'll get over it.' Kate raised her head. Her eyes were burning in her pale face. 'There, I've said it. And to you, of all people.'

She made a sound that was a twisted parody of a laugh. 'We're a fine example of mother and daughter, aren't we, Pauline? After all our talk of family ties, too. You gave me away and your other child died, and I'm following in the family footsteps because I'm not interested in Helen's pain or Danny's needs. I've no room for them. I just want to mourn my husband in peace.' She covered her face with her hands, her shoulders heaved, and, at last, she cried.

Pauline sat quietly, waiting for the storm of tears to cease, and as she waited, she thought about her daughter's words. When Kate's sobs began to die away, she asked, 'Do I really interfere so much?'

'Yes, you do.' Kate's voice sounded terribly tired. Pauline saw that although her eyes were red and swollen, her gaze was lucid. Her next words confirmed that. There was a hint of conciliation in her voice as she continued, 'I suppose you can't help it. You were alone for most of your life and you had to fight to survive, but that doesn't mean you know what's best for everyone. But you think you do.'

'But surely I don't . . .' Flags of colour flared in Pauline's cheeks.

'You do! You can't help it. You give out messages every time you open your mouth. We all have to be "brave and courageous". We have to "keep smiling". Don't you realise, not everyone *can*?'

Kate's head dropped. 'Jack and I fell out because of you. He said I was too hard, that I shouldn't have sent you away. He just didn't understand.'

'I don't either, but I'm trying to. Please, Kate, keep on talking.'

Her words were painful, but Pauline knew they had to be said. And while Kate was revealing her true feelings to her, she was momentarily diverted from worrying about Jack's fate.

She looked at Kate's tear-stained face and tense body and added, with a touch of asperity, 'And for God's sake, get up off that carpet. It's a wonder you haven't got cramp.'

Kate did as she was told. She sat on the chaise-longue opposite her mother and twisted her hands together. 'I know it sounds ridiculous, but in a way you frighten me. You change people's lives. I think it's because you involve yourself *too* much with other folks' problems.'

Pauline was bewildered. 'What do you mean?'

'Well,' Kate frowned, 'you've been a big influence on Helen, and you insisted on lending us the money for the kitchen. You meant well, but Jack was upset about that. He felt beholden to you.'

'But I explained why. And, anyway, I thought if Richie did the work . . .' Pauline stopped abruptly.

'You see. You were interfering there, in Nicky and Richie's marriage.'

Pauline frowned. 'Yes, I did.' She lifted her chin

defiantly. 'It worked, didn't it?'

'That's not the point. Their marriage was none of your business.'

'But, Kate, we all influence each other, that's what life is all about. We can't avoid involvement with people. We make friends and enemies, and from some people we take and to others we give. There's no alternative as far as I can see. We can't live our lives totally alone. We can't shut ourselves up in a box.'

'I know that, of course I do. But I hate it when I see you taking over. And all this "family" business.' Kate lifted her shoulders. 'Look, I'm your daughter, but I'm nothing like you. You're always manipulating people. I hate being with people I can have an effect on.'

Pauline frowned. She had to think about that one.

Seeing her mother's bewilderment, Kate tried, clumsily, to explain her own feelings. 'It's too much responsibility for me, Pauline. I always think, what if I influence them wrongly?' She glanced across and sighed. 'About the only time I've deliberately tried to influence a situation is when I traced you.'

Pauline winced. 'And that's been so bad?'

'No, no. I didn't mean that. But things never turn out as you expect them to. I'm not laying blame, but I think we've both been disappointed in each other, and I have to take the responsibility for that. I should have left well alone.' She looked sadly at her mother. 'You still don't see, do you?'

'I'm beginning to.' Pauline sat back in her chair and gave Kate a long look. 'For what it's worth, I've never felt disappointed in you.'

The uncomfortable silence held until Kate stood up. 'There may be more news.'

'There's nothing we can do, except wait and talk. Helen explained to me about the man who contacted you. They'll ring again when they have anything to tell you.'

Kate looked towards the door. 'Yes, but there's Danny. I should see to him.'

Pauline smiled. 'You said Danny wouldn't matter if Jack died.'

'I know, but he'll be wanting some lunch and . . .' Kate's figure froze. 'That's a rotten thing to say.'

'I didn't mean Jack was dead.' Pauline leaned forward and talked rapidly and earnestly. 'I just wanted you to realise what you've said. Danny *does* matter to you, doesn't he? He's in your thoughts all the time. And I'll tell you something, Kate. If that phone does ring and someone tells you that you're a widow, part of you will still think about Danny. And because of him, you'll never give up – you won't be able to.'

She shook her head. 'You see, Danny, and Helen too, they *need* you. And I'll tell you now, that's one involvement you will never be able to avoid. There'll be times when you hate as well as love them, but you'll stay involved.'

She sighed at the look on her daughter's face. 'You think you're unnatural, don't you, for feeling so little for Danny right now?' She took off her spectacles and rubbed her eyes. 'You should have seen *me* after the Hamptons took you. Poor little Elizabeth. She must have thought her mother had turned into a monster. One minute I was hugging and kissing her, the next minute I was screaming at her. I went a bit crazy, you see. I'd lost you. I knew I would never see you again. And Elizabeth had lost her sister. Twins should be brought up together, everyone knows that.'

Pauline was gazing into space. It was as if she had forgotten Kate's presence. 'Some days I would smack her for nothing. I put her to bed early because I couldn't bear to see her and not you, and then I would get her up again because I couldn't bear to be alone.' She shook her head. 'So many years ago, but I still feel guilty. A two-fold guilt, because I parted with you and I was cruel to Elizabeth. But then,' she sighed and replaced her spectacles, 'I tell myself I was so young, and there was no one to advise me.'

She looked back at Kate and smiled. 'And I came to my senses. One day I looked at Elizabeth's little face and saw her wary expression and I realised what I was doing to her. From then on, I was a proper mother again. Inside I didn't feel normal, but I acted as if I was because there was no one else to look after my daughter, and she needed me. And, bless her, she forgave me. Within a couple of days she was wrapping her arms around my neck again. Children are like that, you know, they put no conditions on love.' She stopped for a moment, overcome by her memories, then she blinked and said: 'Involvement is something that goes with being a mother, Kate, but I'm sorry if my involvement has been a burden to you.'

Kate was staring at her mother, a curious look on her face. 'You really *did* want to keep me, didn't you?'

Pauline made a helpless gesture with her hands.

'And then you lost Elizabeth?'

'Yes.' There was the usual little dig of pain, fainter now but still hurtful. Pauline ignored it. Instead she concentrated on the look on Kate's face. Her daughter was looking thoughtful.

She asked, 'Can you bear to talk about Elizabeth, just for a few minutes?'

'Of course I can.'

'You say we were alike?'

'In looks. But in nature, she was the dominant one. I had to watch her. She would take your toys from you and pull your hair when you tried to get them back.'

'We had a twin pram, didn't we?'

'Yes. I bought it second-hand,' Pauline blinked. 'Surely you don't remember it?'

'Not really, just a feeling I had one day when I was pushing Danny in his pram. A feeling that someone or something was missing.'

'Oh, my Lord.' To her own astonishment, Pauline found her eyes were filling with tears. 'Fancy you feeling like that. I knew it was wicked, separating the two of you. I remember thinking, after Elizabeth's death, I deserved God's punishment.'

'That's ridiculous, Pauline. You did what you thought was best. And as you say, you were young, only three years older than Helen is now.'

Her daughter was defending her. Pauline's mouth went dry. She swallowed. 'Do you have any more memories of your sister?'

'Not really. When I was young, just now and again, when I was in my room, I used to feel that something was missing, but I didn't know what. There was a sort of "incompleteness".' Kate shrugged. 'I can't explain it properly.'

Pauline's eyes misted over again and she dropped her head on her hand. 'I'm so sorry, Kate.'

'No, it's all right.' She jumped up and came to kneel by her mother's side. 'I understand now. I should have realised before but I'm no good at understanding people.' With sudden bitterness she added, 'The Hamptons did a good job on me. They believed emotions should always be kept well under control. Materially they looked after me very well, and they never shouted at me, but they never hugged me either. A chaste kiss on the cheek was good enough for them. When I plodded along in the middle stream at school – I wasn't very bright, I'm afraid – they looked depressed but never told me off or helped me with my homework. It was as if they just accepted everything that happened.' She looked up at Pauline. 'They were the most neutral couple I have ever known.

'And then I met you and you were so different. It confused me. I wanted us to get closer, but I was scared.' She shook her head. 'Perhaps I'm more like my adoptive parents than I realised.'

Pauline had been listening to her with a sad expression on her face. Now she smiled widely and patted her hand. 'No, you're not like the Hamptons, Kate. You're very like your father.'

'What!'

'I've only just realised.' Pauline nodded. 'He was a nice young man, so you needn't look scared. I'd forgotten, but while you were talking I remembered certain things about him.' Seeing how hard Kate was listening to her, she explained.

'I was a bit of a rebel, I just couldn't grow up fast enough. I'd started work and I thought that meant I was an adult. My mother had died, and my father,' she paused, 'he wanted me to stay his little girl, so he was very strict with me.'

'I met Grahame and encouraged him like mad. I was flattered by his interest in me because he was a lot older than I was and I thought he was terribly sophisticated. Actually, he was a quiet young man and self-contained.' She touched Kate's cheek. 'Like you. Anyway, because I was totally smitten by him, I threw myself at him. He tried to keep things on a casual basis, but I practically forced him into bed with me. And once we'd made love, well . . .' She lowered her eyes. 'He became as keen as I was. We saw each other for a whole summer and it was wonderful.'

She sighed. 'But I was dreaming of weddings and Grahame wasn't, and looking back, I can see he tried to warn me. He was too cautious to rush into marriage with a girl of seventeen. He used to take care of me, though. He made sure about things. He made sure I didn't get pregnant.'

She smiled ruefully at Kate's look of surprise. 'Yes, he did. There was just one time when he didn't, and that's when you and Elizabeth were conceived.'

She glanced at Kate. 'I know this is hardly the right moment, but you did get my letter enclosing the cutting?

Kate nodded. 'Yes.' She looked down at her hands. 'I didn't reply. I'm sorry. It's just that I didn't want to think about anything to do with . . .' Her voice trailed away.

'Your natural parents?' Pauline tried to keep the hurt out of her voice. 'I did wonder whether to keep the knowledge of his death to myself, but I couldn't. You had a right to know.'

'Yes. I realised that.' Kate glanced at Pauline's face. 'Were you very upset?'

'Not really, it was so long ago.' Pauline stirred in her chair. 'He was rich, you know. You could get in touch with the company, perhaps . . .?'

They both froze when they heard the telephone ringing.

Chapter Thirty-Three

The voice of the oil company representative was low and controlled. His message was terse and to the point. Six bodies had been recovered and identified. The families of the men had been informed. Jack Gallantree was still on the missing list. The search was continuing although seas were high and visibility poor. Waiting families should rest assured that everything possible was being done. The man speaking to Kate paused.

'You mustn't give up hope, Mrs Gallantree. It may seem rather a brutal thing to say, but chances of survival may well depend on some small thing, which seat your husband was in when the helicopter went down, for example. And another point in our favour is that although the bad weather is hampering our search, the air and sea temperatures are relatively warm which means anyone who did get out in time could survive in the water for some time yet. Anyway, I'll ring you again, probably in a couple of hours. You'll appreciate I have other people to talk to.'

Kate put down the phone and quietly relayed his message. Her earlier detached strangeness had disappeared and now her face was composed, but every line of her body betrayed utter fatigue. She held out a hand towards Helen and her mother and the three women drew together and wept a few silent tears. Then Danny fell over the back door step and cut his arm. His roar of alarm and the sight of blood got them moving again. Kate picked him up and kissed him better and Pauline and Helen hunted for the first-aid box.

With a prominent plaster covering what turned out to be a rather small cut, Danny again demanded to go out.

His mother shook her head. 'No, love. It's beginning to rain.'

Not only was a light rain now falling but the wind was becoming stronger. Their thoughts far away, the women jumped when a window suddenly slammed upstairs.

'I'll see to it.' Pauline thought she would give Kate and Helen a few moments alone together. She went upstairs into Helen's room and shut the window in there. She looked out at the wildly waving shrubs in the garden and shuddered, thinking of Jack. Was he alive or dead? And if he was still alive, was he struggling to stay afloat in huge seas, afraid and alone? She closed her eyes and said a little prayer, then went back downstairs.

Danny was still grizzling but she was pleased to see Kate was sitting next to Helen and had her arm around her stepdaughter. When Pauline entered the room she stood up.

'I think I'll make us some coffee, Pauline. Would you like a cup?'

'No.' She wandered restlessly round the room. 'I think I'll take Danny out.'

'But it's so miserable outside.'

'I won't take him far, and I'll wrap him up well. A breath of air will do him good.'

'All right, but don't be long, will you?'

She put on her raincoat and wrapped a scarf around her head. She dressed Danny in cord trousers and his zip-up jacket with a hood. She didn't take the pushchair. She had no intention of going far and her grandson would stay warmer if he walked. As they went down the hill the wind buffeted his face and blew back Danny's hood. He laughed, and to her surprise, she laughed too. The wind was cold but clean, and somehow, full of life.

She grasped Danny's hand tightly as he skipped along at the side of her. They battled their way down the hill and a gleam of optimism lightened her misgivings. No news was good news.

As they came to Routledge Gardens a bus pulled up and a woman alighted. It was Nicky. Pauline shouted and waved and Nicky came running over.

'Pauline, I didn't expect to see you.' Nicky's eyes were wide and anxious. 'What's the news? Have they found Jack yet? I didn't know anything about all this until my neighbour came round and told me to ring Kate. I tried her number straight away but the line was engaged, so I thought the best thing to do was come straight round.'

'A man from the oil company rang not long ago, it was probably him on the line. They haven't found Jack yet.' In a low voice, so as not to alarm Danny, Pauline recounted the events of the last few hours.

Listening, Nicky put her hand to her mouth. 'Oh, my God! That's horrible.'

'Yes, I know. But at least we still have hope.'

'Yes, you're right. Those poor men and their

families.' Nicky bit her lip. 'And how is Kate? How's she taking it?'

'She's terribly shocked, of course, but bearing up. Helen's being very brave. They're comforting each other.' Pauline cleared her throat and spoke up more clearly. 'Danny and I thought we'd like a walk.'

Danny was trying to unzip his jacket. He wanted to show Nicky his plaster. Pauline stopped him. 'She'll see it when we get home, pet.'

'I'll hurry on, then.' Nicky shook her head. 'I'm sorry I wasn't around earlier. I took the kids round to see my mother. My sister was there and we ended up rowing, as usual. What with the row, and five kids running around and my mother complaining, I had no idea what was happening outside. If I'd been at home I would have heard the news on the radio.'

'Where are the children now?'

'The neighbour said she would take them. They'll be all right. Richie will be home in half an hour.'

Pauline touched her arm. 'It was good of you to come so quickly.'

'Nonsense.' Nicky turned in the direction of Kate's home but then paused. 'Thank God you were in and were able to come over.' She gave Pauline a brief smile. 'Kate rang you, I presume?'

'No, Helen did.' Seeing her smile fade, Pauline hurried on, 'But Kate and I have talked, really talked, I mean, and I think things will work out between us.'

'I'm so pleased.' Nicky bent her tall figure and dropped a swift kiss on Pauline's cheek, then she tweaked Danny's nose before setting off up the hill. Pauline watched her eating up the distance with her long, swift strides.

'Park, Grandma?' asked Danny, hopefully.

'No, it's too wet and cold.' Pauline looked down at

his disappointed face. 'What about the sweetie shop?'

At five-thirty the phone rang again. Silently they watched Kate's face as she took the call. When her lips trembled into a smile, they knew the news was good. They waited in an agony of suspense for her to put the telephone down and tell them the news. She listened intently, nodded a couple of times and then grabbed a pen and wrote something down on the pad near the telephone. Finally she said goodbye and turned to face them.

'He's alive. They've found them, Jack and four other men.'

'Oh, thank God. How? Where? Is he hurt?'

She put up her hand. It was trembling. 'I'll tell you what he told me. The helicopter was on the very last sweep because the light was so bad.' She swallowed. 'They had really given up all hope, but then the pilot thought he saw something. He went down even closer. He was brave. The man speaking to me said it was a tricky manoeuvre, the seas were running high. It was the orange suits the pilot spotted. There were five figures clinging to a life-raft. They managed to pick them up and,' she looked down, 'they also retrieved another body which was floating nearby.

'Jack and the other men have been taken to the hospital in Lerwick. They're suffering from hypothermia, shock and minor injuries but they're going to be OK.' She picked up the pad. 'It's the Gilbert Bain hospital and I've got the number. We can ring there for more details.' She smiled across at her stepdaughter and then emotion overwhelmed her and she burst into tears. 'I can't believe it!' she cried. 'He's coming home, he's safe.'

She swayed and Nicky caught hold of her. The tears

were rolling down her face, too. Pauline put her arms round Helen and then they were all crying. Nicky recovered first. She patted Kate's shoulder and asked, 'Where's the telephone number?' She waited until they had composed themselves and then dialled the number. She listened and then handed the phone to Kate.

'Hello, is that the Gilbert Bain hospital? I'm Mrs Gallantree. My husband . . .' She listened. 'Yes, thanks. And he's all right? Yes, thank you so much.' She put down the phone and faced them. 'He's asleep now. He needs rest, and they think he'll need some counselling before he returns home, but he won't have to stay there long. He should be home within forty-eight hours.' She smiled at them, and then closed her eyes and put her hand to her head.

'He's not the only one that needs rest. I think you, and Helen, too, should go up to bed.' Pauline took charge.

'Oh, I couldn't. What if there're more calls?'

'And I wouldn't be able to sleep.' Helen's face set mulishly.

'If there are more calls, I'll fetch you immediately, Kate. And even if you don't sleep, Helen, you'll rest.'

'But . . .' Kate wavered.

'Pauline's right, Kate.' Nicky picked up Danny, who was demanding attention. 'You must be exhausted. Take the opportunity to rest while you can. You'll be busy when Jack gets home.' Like a sheepdog circling two errant lambs, she gently moved Kate and Helen towards the door and persuaded them to go upstairs.

When she came back into the room she saw Pauline had produced Danny's giant box of Lego. 'Good idea, that should keep him busy.' She dumped Danny on the carpet. 'Build Auntie Nicky and Grandma a lovely big house,' she requested.

He puckered his lips but then picked up a handful of the red and white bricks.

Nicky dropped into a chair. 'You must be exhausted too, Pauline. I've been here no time at all, and I feel tired out.'

Pauline smiled. 'It's the emotional strain.' She paused. 'And you have been visiting your mum.'

'That's true. Oh!' Nicky jumped up again. 'I'd better ring my neighbour. She can tell Richie the good news.'

She did so and then made a pot of tea and ferreted about in one of the kitchen cupboards.

Pauline enquired what she was looking for.

'This.' She came back into the dining-room, waving a whisky bottle in her hand. 'I think we deserve a dram, don't you?'

'Oh, I don't know, I can't handle spirits. The last time I drank in this house Kate gave me some vodka and I can't remember going to bed.'

Nicky laughed. 'Good for her. But I promise not to get you drunk. Just a little tot of whisky in our tea, to pep us up.'

'Go on then.'

They drank their tea and watched as Danny, sprawled on the floor, built himself a strangely proportioned boat.

'Now the alterations are completed, Nicky, I want to say they look marvellous. I would have mentioned it sooner, but of course I've had other things on my mind.'

'Yes, Richie does a good job. As well as practical

knowledge, he always comes up with great ideas about a room's possibilities. And Kate's good on colour and design, as you know. I'd forgotten you hadn't seen the finished result. It's been a long time since your last visit, hasn't it?'

'Yes.' Pauline nodded. 'The last time I was here there was plastic sheeting everywhere.'

Nicky poured more tea into her cup, and then a splash of whisky. She looked enquiringly at Pauline, who shook her head.

'Working on Kate's new kitchen changed Richie's luck, you know. He's landed another job on the strength of it, and the new customer says he's delighted with the work up to now. With a bit of luck, he'll put the word out among his friends. And who knows?' Nicky sipped at her tea. 'And, really, we have you to thank for everything.'

Pauline blushed. 'That's not strictly true. If Richie's work hadn't been so good . . .'

'Yes, we know all that, but you started the whole thing off. You put up the money for this alteration. And from little things Kate has let slip, I believe it was your suggestion that we move in here. You got us out of that ghastly bed and breakfast accommodation.'

'It wasn't just me. Kate and I thought up the plan between us.'

Nicky looked unconvinced, but moved on to something else.

'I'm so pleased you two have sorted yourselves out. You know, you're not a bit alike, more like chalk and cheese than mother and daughter, but you're good together.'

'You think so?' Pauline didn't know whether to be pleased or annoyed.

'Yes.' Nicky laughed. 'And don't try and look disapproving, you'll never match Kate in that field.'

Pauline really did bristle. 'As Kate's supposed friend . . .' she began.

Nicky cut her short. 'There's no "supposed" about it. I *am* Kate's friend. I think a lot of her. She's loyal and kind and straight as a die. I'd trust her with my life and, more important, the lives of my children. But, like the rest of us, she's not perfect.

'She's touchy, a bit snobby at times, and I think that's because she's riddled with self-doubt.'

Pauline looked grim. 'And your analysis of me?'

Nicky raised her eyebrows and gave a wry grin. 'Honestly?'

She nodded.

'You're good-hearted. You act first and think later. You look for the best in everyone, and you're generous to a fault.'

The colour sprang into Pauline's face. 'My goodness, haven't I any faults?'

'Well . . .' Nicky paused. 'You're inclined to be bossy, you take over rather, and you believe everyone should think as you do.'

'I see.'

Nicky looked contrite. 'Was I too hard on you? If you want to know *my* faults, I'll tell you. I have hundreds, and I know every one of them.' She recited: 'I'm a loud-mouth. I'm bossy. I act without thinking. I don't respect my parents. I'm domineering and I offend people.' She paused. 'You look stern. Have I offended you?'

'No. I was thinking of something Kate said earlier today.'

'And?'

'She said I caused trouble by interfering too much in things that don't concern me.'

There was a short silence. Nicky looked out of the window. 'It's late. Richie will be here with the van soon, to take me home.' She looked back at Pauline. 'If it makes you feel better, I'm glad you interfered in my life.'

Pauline's face was expressionless. 'Are you sure?'

'Oh, yes. You made me face up to myself, you see. I'd got into a rut. Having no settled home, an out-of-work husband and three kids in five years, you either turn into a drudge or a bossy cow.' A wry smile flitted across her face. 'I definitely fitted into the second category. I didn't mean to be that way, but during Richie's breakdown *someone* had to take charge. Unfortunately, it became a habit I couldn't break. I never really gave him the chance to be a man again. Anyway, your little talk shocked me into realising what was happening, and I'm trying to change. I'm still a bit pushy, but Richie has a say in a lot of things and now he's working again, his confidence grows every day. We are both much happier, and a lot of credit for that goes to you.'

'It's kind of you to say so.'

'It's not kind. It's the truth. You know,' Nicky looked pensive and a tinge of embarrassment crept into her voice, 'I wish my mum was more like you.'

Pauline's brow creased. 'Even though I'm bossy?'

'Oh, yes. My mum's not bossy, she's like a limp rag. She sits around and moans all the time. She says she lives for her children, but I'm not so sure. Whenever she visits one of us, she always ends up complaining. She tells me when my sister Karen has borrowed money from her and never paid her back, and when one of my brothers has been talking about me and Richie, and whatever she talks about, it's never anything good. It's as if she wants us all to argue. It's not a nice thought.' Nicky looked down and then up again. 'Like I say, you and Kate have fallen out, but you haven't known each other long, have you? I think you'll build up a really good relationship, given time, and you're a smashing granny for Danny.'

They looked across at him. He was curled up among the scattered Lego, fast asleep. They both laughed. Then they heard a quiet knock on the back door.

'That will be Richie, I'll have to go.' Nicky yawned and stretched. 'Tell Kate I'll be over tomorrow. If she'd like me to take Danny for a while, I will.' She slipped on her coat. 'Are you staying?'

'I'll stay until lunchtime, see that everything is still all right, but I'll have to go home tomorrow. I left in a terrific rush. The milk will still be on the doorstep and my neighbours will wonder what's happened to me. And I'm due in at work the following day.'

'Well, thank God that you were home when Helen phoned.' By the door, Nicky stopped. 'Where is Jack's sister, by the way? I know they're not too close, but I thought she would have come round?'

'She's away. She and her husband are abroad on a winter holiday. We did wonder about contacting them but Kate wasn't sure where they were staying and until there was any definite news, there didn't seem much point in alarming them.'

'I see. Oh, well. I reckon you were better for Kate and Helen than Pat would have been.' Nicky pulled a face. 'I've only met her once, but she seemed a sour sort of individual.'

'I've never met her.'

'You will, I'm sure. In due course.' Nicky opened the back door. 'You'll be coming again, Pauline?'

'Oh, yes.'

Chapter Thirty-Four

The following afternoon, Kate came through the kitchen to find Pauline phoning for a taxi.

She frowned. 'Why on earth have you called the taxi firm? I'll drive you to the railway station.'

'No, I want you to take it easy today. Nicky's taken Danny, and Helen's busy with her own affairs. I think you should rest. Jack will be home tomorrow, remember.'

A smile lit up Kate's face like sunshine. 'How can I forget?'

Pauline consulted her watch. 'I've time for a cup of coffee before I go. I'll make it.'

They went into the kitchen.

'Nicky told me Richie's working on another kitchen extension?'

'Yes. A neighbour came and saw what he had done here and hired him straight away.'

'I'm not surprised.' Pauline made the coffee and carried a tray through the archway and into the dining-room. She set the tray on the dining table and then looked round appreciatively. 'I love the silvery-green colour in here, it makes the room look as though it's part of the garden. That wall looks a bit bare, though.' She gestured to the wall facing the window.

'Yes, I know. I haven't been able to find anything that "belongs", if you know what I mean. I was thinking about a french dresser but I'm not sure.' Kate shook her head. 'I'd rather wait for a while and then buy something I really like. I chose the colour for the walls and Richie made that corner cupboard.'

'It's lovely.' Pauline handed her a coffee then sat back in her chair to enjoy her own.

Kate hesitated. 'You know, you're very welcome to stay a bit longer. Jack would be pleased to see you.'

'He can see me in a couple of weeks. After the ordeal he's been through, he needs peace and quiet.' Pauline sent Kate a shy glance. 'He doesn't want an interfering old woman in the house on his return home.'

'Oh, no, you're not . . .' Kate's anxious look faded and she dissolved into laughter when she saw Pauline smile.

'Will you ever forgive me?'

'Of course. I already have. But, for my own sake, I might not forget.'

They drank their coffee and chatted and then Pauline glanced at her watch. 'I think I should get my things together.'

'So soon?'

'Yes. I hate to rush.'

Both women stood up.

'When you come again,' said Kate, 'why don't we go through to Whitby? You can call and see your friend Mary, and I'll drive up to the nursing home and you can visit your father.'

Pauline's forehead creased in a frown. 'I never told you, did I? My father died a month ago.'

'Oh, Pauline. I'm so sorry.'

'Don't be. I'm not.' She sighed. 'That sounds terribly hard, but you have to understand, my real goodbye to my father was many years ago.' She smiled softly at her daughter. 'I regretted our separation for a long time but even regret dies in the end. Now I feel nothing.' She paused. 'Remember how we talked about people living in a box? That's what my father did, and much good it did him.'

Kate nodded. 'Did he know you, at the end?'

'No. The matron phoned me and told me he was dying. I went through and sat by his bedside, but he died without recovering consciousness.'

Pauline sighed again, looked down and smoothed her skirt.

Kate moved closer to her mother and touched her shoulder. When Pauline looked up, she said, '*Please*, let me cancel the taxi?'

'For goodness' sake, why?'

'Because *I* want to drive *my* mother to the station.'

They arrived ten minutes before Pauline's train was due to leave. As Kate switched off the engine of the car, Pauline opened her handbag and scrabbled about inside, looking for her ticket. 'I know it's in here somewhere,' she said. She opened the zip at the back of the bag. 'Ah, here it is.'

As she took out her rail ticket, a tattered old envelope fell out also. She stared down at it. 'Well, fancy that! I'd forgotten I had that in my handbag.'

'What is it?' Kate was interested. From the look on her mother's face, she could tell the envelope was important.

'It's a letter my grandma wrote to me, when she knew she was dying.' Pauline picked up the envelope, handling it carefully, and then she thrust it towards Kate. 'Here, take it. Read it. But, please, take great care. I would hate to lose it.'

'Are you sure?' Kate took the envelope from her with some reluctance. 'Of course I'll take care, but if it's private?'

'I think Eliza would have liked you to read it.' Pauline smiled. 'I think you know how much I cared for her? That letter might explain why. When we have more time, I'll tell you all about her. That is,' she raised her eyebrows, 'if you can stand to hear a few "old sayings"?'

Kate blushed. 'OK, I deserved that.' She put Eliza's letter in her jacket pocket. 'Thank you.' She locked the car windows. 'I suppose we ought to go now and find out which platform your train leaves from.'

Pauline looked at her watch. 'We have five minutes.' She studied her daughter's face. 'In the letter, you'll see she called me her "lark". Perhaps I should explain a little, is that all right?'

Seeing Kate's nod, she continued: 'You see, Kate, when I first realised I was pregnant, I was terribly afraid. I was young and I knew how furious my father was going to be when he heard the news. Eliza knew how frightened I was, so she told me about a time when she had been young and equally afraid of the future.

'Her husband was killed in the first world war, and she was left with a young child and no money. She was very close to her mother, but because of family circumstances they had to split up, go their separate ways. Eliza had no idea of what the future held for her.

'Her mother comforted her by quoting an old, old,

proverb. You see,' Pauline smiled ruefully, 'this thing about old sayings must run in the family.'

'Which proverb was it?'

'Oh, you won't know it.' Pauline shook her head. 'I'd never heard it until Eliza told me, and that was back in the nineteen-forties. Anyway, as I remember, Eliza's mother told her to have courage because, after someone had struggled through the blackest of times, there was always something to rejoice in.'

'Sounds encouraging, but do you believe it's true?'

Pauline hesitated. 'I didn't at first, but now, yes, I believe it's true.'

'What was the proverb?'

' "When the sky falls down, we will catch larks." '

'What a strange saying.' Kate frowned.

'Yes.' Pauline shrugged. 'When Eliza said those words to me, I didn't have a clue what they meant. But it's strange, I never forgot them. And every time I was terribly down, I remembered those words and felt better.' She put her head on one side. 'I nearly quoted the proverb to you when we were waiting to hear about Jack, but I didn't dare.'

Kate laughed. 'I'm glad you didn't. I probably would have flown at you.'

'Yes, well. Times are different now, I suppose. Anyway, I thought if I explained the story behind the proverb, it might help you to understand the letter.' She looked again at her watch. 'Oh, dear, I've talked too long. We'll have to rush.'

She got on the train just in time. Kate waved her goodbye and then went back to the car. Once inside, she took out Eliza's letter and read it, then she leaned her head back against the car's headrest and closed her eyes.

'Joy and tears.' She smiled faintly. Yesterday she had felt as though she was the only woman in the world to experience those emotions. How foolish of her. Pauline had been there before her. And before Pauline there had been Eliza, and before her, her mother. A whole chain of women who had cared for their men and their children, enduring the hard times and rejoicing in the happy days.

And all those women had woven their life pattern into the fabric of her history. Kate's smile widened. All her earlier worries, her doubts and fears, vanished. She had been right to search for her natural mother. For if she had not, she would not have met Pauline and would never have known about her forebears. And perhaps she would never fully have known herself.

She shook her head, remembering Pauline's words. 'Times are different now.' Her mother was wrong. As she refolded the letter, placed it in the envelope and slipped it into her pocket, she murmured, 'They're not so different, Pauline.' She turned the car key in the ignition and drove home.

Jack was outside the house, paying off a taxi. She screeched the car to a halt, opened the door and fell out, snagging her tights as she did so.

'Jack! Jack, I'm here!' She waved and ran towards him. 'Oh, darling, I thought it would be tomorrow!' She hugged and kissed him and then fumbled to find her key. She opened the door with clumsy fingers and ushered him inside. 'Let me look at you.'

With stoic good humour, he stood and allowed her to fuss around his tall, upright figure. He allowed her to remove his coat, lead him into the sitting-room and push him gently down on to the chaise-longue. She sat down next to him, not bothering to remove her jacket.

'You look so tired, Jack. And, oh!' She started, noticing that his left hand was heavily bandaged. 'What happened?'

'Calm down, Kate, please.' He held out his undamaged hand.

She took it and covered it with kisses. 'It's so wonderful to see you. The woman I spoke to at the hospital, she said you wouldn't be home until tomorrow.'

'I know. They told us that, too. But all we wanted to do was get home, so they finally agreed to let us loose. They made two of the men, Clive Tyler and Tommy Bolter, stay overnight. I suppose because they are older men and physically and mentally they're still not over the shock. They keep going on and on about . . .' Jack's voice faded and this face suddenly became grey and pinched-looking. He gripped her hand tightly.

'Why did it happen, Kate? I've done that flight up to fifty times and nothing like this has happened before. The chap sitting behind me, Angus McNeil, only joined us last month. He was on his first trip home.' Jack closed his eyes. 'He was only twenty-four years old. Why did he die and not me?'

Kate felt his body begin to shake. 'Oh, Jack.' She pulled her hand free in order to put her arms about her husband. 'There's no answer to a question like that, and there's no point torturing yourself. There'll be an enquiry into the crash, won't there?'

Jack nodded his head.

'Well, maybe they'll find out what really happened. But whether they do or not, you just have to accept some things happen for no accountable reason. Right now, try and concentrate on the fact that you're home and safe. And Helen, Danny and me – we're so relieved and happy.'

Jack took a few deep breaths and nodded.'You're right. I'm sorry, Kate. I didn't want this homecoming to be sad.'

'Oh, darling.' She buried her face in his neck. 'How could it be otherwise? As I say, I'm overjoyed to have you back, but beneath the delight, I can't help thinking about the other families.' She was silent for a minute and then asked, 'What happened to your hand?'

'I cut it.' Jack had put his arm about her and as he talked, she felt his fingers digging into her waist.

'The flight was going fine, everything was normal, and then suddenly the helicopter banked and went down, straight into the sea. God knows why. Everything happened so quickly, there was no time to think. One minute we were reading our papers, laughing and joking about what we were going to do when we got home, and the next minute, the water was pouring in and we were sinking.'

He shook his head. 'Me and the other guys who survived were just plain lucky. We were in the best place to get out quickly. While I was pulling myself out of the wreck, my hand caught on some jagged metal. It's nothing.' Jack glanced at his hand impatiently. 'But we couldn't do anything for the other men, Kate. There was no time.' He sighed and put his head in his hands.

She stood up. 'Can I get you anything? A whisky?'

'No, thanks.' He tried to smile. 'They made me take some pills. I guess I'd better leave spirits alone for a while. I'd like to go to bed for a few hours, if that's all right?'

'Of course, darling.'

She put her hand under his elbow and helped him up.

Once on his feet again, he wrapped his arms around her and buried his face in her hair. 'I thought I'd never see you again, Kate. And I thought, when we were bobbing about in the water, clinging to the raft, that the last words I had spoken to you had been said in anger.'

'Don't think about it. It doesn't matter, it doesn't. I was angry too, but words are nothing. We both know that we love each other.'

'Yes.' He drew away and looked into her face. 'Yes, you're right.' He held her close again and asked, 'It's quiet. Where are the children?'

'Nicky's looking after Danny, and Helen will be in soon. She was wonderful, Jack, so brave.'

'She's a good kid.'

Kate thought she heard the smile in his voice and, encouraged, she went on: 'And Pauline came through to be with us. She was a great help. It's all sorted out, Jack. We're friends again.'

'Good.' He nodded, but she saw the grey shadow of fatigue on his face.

'Come on.' She eased herself away from his grasp. 'Bed for you. We can talk later.'

As she helped him up the staircase, he leaned heavily upon her slight frame and in their bedroom was content to let her help him undress. Within a minute of his head touching the pillow, he slept.

She sat by the bed and watched him. His head moved restlessly as he slept and once he jumped violently and his eyes opened. She stroked his forehead and quietened him. Once he mumbled the name

'Angus' and flung his arm over his eyes.

Kate's own eyes stung with unshed tears. Joy and tears, she thought. Joy and tears.

Chapter Thirty-Five

Once again, Pauline was travelling to Leeds, but this time she was going to celebrate a birthday. Tomorrow Kate would be thirty-seven years old, and she was having a party.

Six months had elapsed since the helicopter crash and it was now mid-May. Pauline's train was not crowded. She had even managed to find a vacant window seat. She sat back and watched the passing scenery and thought, as she had thought so many years ago, that May was positively the best month of all in which to have a birthday.

The train was passing through a wooded area, and she looked upwards, studying the tall trees which lined the side of the railway tracks. In winter, she remembered, they had looked so ugly. The hard light had shown up their scarred trunks and bare, wildly waving branches. Now spring had transformed them. Soft green moss spread like a salve across rough trunks, and their branches had been covered by a dressing of delicate green foliage. And further back, deeper in the woods, Pauline could see drifts of shadowy blue and knew the bluebells were out.

The sight of them brought back vivid memories of her youth. She, Mary and her other school-friends had always gone bluebelling. They had picked great armfuls of the flowers and then carried them home, mixed with sprays of tender green beech leaves. And on other days, if the May weather had been kind, they had packed a picnic and walked for miles across the moors.

She rested her arm along the window-ledge of the train and remembered the giggles and the chatter as they had slogged over the furze and bracken, looking for a suitable place to sit and eat.

She closed her eyes, remembering the feel of the hot sun upon her bare legs, and the annoying, ever-present buzzing of the flies. There had been patches of blue up on the moors. Not bluebells but the tiny flowers they had called 'birdseyes', and clumps of delicate harebells which grew in the hollows, sheltered from the sun and the wind by granite rocks. And from the wide, wide skies would come the call of the curlew.

'Tickets, please.' The voice of the conductor made her jump. She smiled her apology, and fumbled in her pocket for the train ticket. He clipped it and moved down the carriage, and she looked out of the window again.

One May, she and Elizabeth had travelled this same route. For once, she had managed to save a little money and she had taken her daughter to Scarborough for a long weekend. Eight-year-old Elizabeth had been bubbling with excitement. Pauline smiled, remembering how heavy their cases had seemed when they changed trains at York.

'What on earth have you got in this case?' she had panted as they struggled up the steps of the footbridge at York station.

'Nothing much,' Elizabeth had replied. She had

been carrying her mother's case, which was considerably lighter.

Unpacking at their boarding house, Pauline had discovered a layer of long-playing records spread neatly between Elizabeth's clothes.

'What on earth . . . ?' she had gasped.

Elizabeth had hunched her shoulders. 'I couldn't leave them at home, Mum. You know what the Donaldson kids are like for pinching things. And the lock on my window's dodgy. They might have broken in and stolen them while we were away.'

Pauline had bitten back her reproof. The family living to the right of them were noted for thieving and the records were Eliza's most treasured possessions. An old gentleman who had lived on the ground floor of the building had given them to her daughter two months earlier. He had recently emigrated to Australia to live with his daughter and her family.

Elizabeth had been a great friend of Mr Lloyd. She had visited him every week and they had drunk tea together and listened to music.

Pauline didn't point out to Elizabeth that the tearaway Donaldson boys would not appreciate her records. Ravel's 'Bolero' or the '1812 Overture' were definitely not their kind of music. It was Elizabeth's, though.

She would bounce in, after a visit to Mr Lloyd's, with her eyes glowing. 'It's so exciting. There's this bit where the bells start pealing and all the cannons go off.'

It had poured down with rain on their first day in Scarborough. But they had played shove-halfpenny in the amusement arcades and shrieked their heads off on the ghost train, passing the day pleasantly enough.

The next day the sun had shone and Elizabeth had enjoyed her best birthday ever. She had ridden on the donkeys, they had taken a trip on a steamer and when they returned to their lodgings, the landlady had produced a birthday cake.

'She's such a bright little thing,' she had said, when Pauline had told her she shouldn't have gone to such bother. 'Really enjoys life, doesn't she?'

Pauline sighed and looked again at the scenery.

The wood had been left behind. They were travelling through farmland now, neat and well cared for. They passed cultivated fields and then a meadow where lambs skipped and jumped, watched by their placid amiable-faced mothers. They passed a hedgerow over which May blossom rioted with total abandon. But now there were increasing signs of habitation. First a farmhouse, tucked under the fold of a hill, and then a pond at which a sole angler fished. The train passed a row of cottages, a church and a pub.

Five minutes later factory buildings came into sight and a car park full of cars. Then more houses, begrimed with soot, with clothes flapping from washing lines in the gardens. Pauline glanced at her watch. They would be in Leeds in ten minutes.

Jack was waiting for her. He kissed her cheek and picked up her case. 'Hello, Pauline. How are you?'

She smiled at him. 'Well, as you know. If you remember, it's only three weeks since I last visited you.'

'Ah, yes. But a lot can happen in three weeks.' He set off towards the barrier. 'For one thing, Helen's got herself a new boyfriend.'

She quickened her pace to keep up with his long

strides. 'Is that so? What's he like?'

Jack shrugged. 'Hard to tell. We've only had a glimpse of him. He's tall, with flowing blond locks, and he plays a guitar. I think he's a student at the College. However, we'll know more tomorrow. She says he's coming to the party.'

'I look forward to meeting him.' They reached the car and Pauline settled herself comfortably in the passenger seat. Jack fastened his seat belt and gave her a smile before setting off. It was a warm smile but Pauline saw the shadow at the back of his eyes and felt a moment's sadness. The ugly scar on the back of Jack's left hand was not the only legacy of the helicopter crash.

He must have noticed her serious expression. His eyebrows went up. 'Why so glum? It's not the prospect of the party, is it? I thought you would be looking forward to it.'

'I am. I love parties, although I must admit I was surprised when Kate told me she was having one. I mean, thirty-seven isn't a particularly important birthday, not like a fortieth.'

'Please don't talk to her about being forty.' Jack laughed. 'She's gloomy enough about this one.'

Pauline sighed. 'Thirty-seven's young. I wish I was thirty-seven again.'

Jack took a right turning and then glanced at her. 'Sure about that?'

'Yes – no.' She smiled and shook her head. 'You're right. I don't want to go back in time. I'm quite happy as I am.'

'When the present's good, let's appreciate it, eh?

'By the way . . .' Now the busier roads were behind them, Jack could afford to relax a little and talk.

'Remember our conversation, when you last visited, and we talked about whether to pursue the matter of Grahame's estate?'

Pauline nodded.

'Well, we agreed it made sense. Kate set the thing in motion and we had a letter from a firm of solicitors a few days ago. It's early days of course, but it sounds as though she may inherit something.' Jack glanced sidewards at Pauline's face. 'You may be contacted to verify certain facts. Will you mind that?'

'No,' she smiled at him. 'I expected it.'

Jack cleared his throat. 'That's all right then.' He was silent for a moment and then said, 'The thing is, as I think you know, we don't want much. Kate never knew her father and he never knew her. But Grahame Lossing was a wealthy man. The solicitors' letter said that the bulk of his money was willed to various charities. Well, we don't want to change that.'

Pauline interrupted him. 'I know you and Kate are not greedy people, Jack. You don't have to explain. I encouraged Kate to contact the people dealing with Grahame's affairs. You provide very well for my daughter, I know that, and I know you always will, but a nest-egg for young Danny wouldn't come amiss, would it?'

He grinned at her. 'It certainly wouldn't.' With some relief, he reverted back to their original conversation.

'I think it was a mixture of things that made Kate decide to have a party.' He glanced towards Pauline. 'That business with the crash altered her, you know.' He grimaced. 'It altered all of us, but Kate most of all, I think. And one of the things that's happened is that she's become more out-going.'

'I've noticed.' Pauline nodded. 'When she told me she was joining the local amateur dramatic society, I was astounded.'

'So was I.' Jack checked the car at a pedestrian crossing. 'It was a teacher at Danny's playgroup who suggested the idea to her. She was involved in one of the plays the company was putting on and got Kate interested in it, too. She went along to a few rehearsals, but I never thought she would actually join.'

'She enjoys it, doesn't she? Last week, when she phoned me, she was telling me all about the coffee morning she'd arranged to raise funds for the company.'

'Yes, it went well. Kate's a good organiser. She's made some new friends there, too. I'm pleased about that. It makes me feel better when I'm leaving her to go back to the rig.' He paused. 'It's still difficult for her.'

'For you, too, I should think.' Pauline rested her hand on Jack's sleeve.

'Of course.' He nodded, staring ahead. 'But accidents can happen anywhere, and life has to go on.' He smiled briefly. 'You'll be meeting some of Kate's new friends at the party.'

'And Nicky, I hope?'

'Oh, yes. We couldn't have a party without Nicky and her family.'

They drove for a few minutes in silence and then Pauline said, 'I had been wondering, now that Danny's started playschool, whether Kate had ever considered going back to work? So many young women do nowadays.'

She waited for a reply and when none was

forthcoming, she sighed and put her fingers to her lips. 'Oh dear, I'm doing it again.'

'Doing what?'

'Being nosey.'

He laughed. 'That's all right. You're part of the family now, Pauline. And families *are* nosey.'

She sat quietly next to him and enjoyed the warm glow his words had invoked. She quite forgot that Jack had not replied to her question.

They were almost home when he slowed the car and said to her, 'By the way, your present arrived yesterday.'

She looked him anxiously. 'Did she like it?'

'Like it! She was absolutely speechless. She *loved* it, Pauline, really loved it.'

'Honestly?'

'Honestly.'

She relaxed. 'I hoped she might.'

They reached Routledge Terrace and Pauline had time to leave the car, go though the gate and admire the lilac tree blooming by the path before the door flew open and Kate hurried out.

She hurried to greet her. 'Oh, Mum, it's the most *marvellous* birthday present. I wondered, when the furniture van turned up yesterday, and then I saw it! Thank you.' She threw her arms around Pauline and hugged her.

Pauline blinked hard. Those damn tears again. They sprang to her eyes whenever Kate called her 'Mum'. And the funny thing was, she knew Kate hadn't even realised when she started using the word.

The first time had been a couple of weeks after the helicopter crash, when Pauline had come through on the train to see Jack. The three of them had been sitting talking when Kate had suddenly jumped up and said, 'I'll make a pot of tea; would you like a cup, Mum?'

There had been a pause, and then Jack, bless his heart, had averted his gaze from her face and said smoothly, 'Of course she would. Let's have some chocolate biscuits, too.'

But Kate was still chattering. 'Come and see it.'

Pauline allowed herself to be rushed through the house and into the dining-room.

Eliza's sideboard stood resplendent by the far wall, opposite the window. Sunlight was slanting through but Kate had partly drawn one curtain to protect the piece of furniture. Nevertheless, the sideboard gleamed. The wood shone with a gentle sheen, the brass rail fitted along the top-piece glittered and the lion-shaped feet looked magnificent, planted proudly on the bluey-green textured carpet. Pauline stood and stared. She had never seen Eliza's pride and joy look so magnificent.

'I went straight out and visited my friend at the saleroom. I persuaded him to come and see it. He said it was a lovely piece of craftsmanship and told me what to buy to use on it. It's a special oil and paste mixture the restorers use.' Kate clasped her hands together. 'That's all right, isn't it?'

'Of course it's all right. It's your sideboard now.'

Pauline's gaze travelled over the carved drawers and cupboards and down the reeded legs of the sideboard. 'Oh, I wish Eliza could have seen it looking like this, and in this room, too.' She smiled at her daughter. 'She always said it should be in a large room. I'd forgotten all about it, you know, but after my father's death, the matron at the home gave me some of his papers. When I checked through them, I found a receipted bill from a furniture storage firm. It acknowledged payment for the storing of "an item of furniture". I couldn't think what it could be so I rang them, and they told me it was a sideboard.'

She rested her hand on the warm, glowing wood. 'My father had put it into store when he went into the nursing home. Nothing else. He must have sold the rest of his furniture. But he kept the sideboard, and every year thereafter he paid for it to be stored.'

She looked questioningly at Kate. 'Do you think he kept it in memory of Eliza? He never showed her much affection when she was alive.'

'Perhaps. But perhaps,' Kate answered her mother slowly, 'in his heart, he hoped that one day you would turn up and claim it.' She came to stand next to Pauline. 'And you did.' She put her hand on her mother's arm. 'Are you sure you want me to have it?'

'Of course I am. Anyway, it seems to belong in here. And I have no room in my flat for a piece of furniture that big.' Pauline reached out and touched the brass rail with her finger. 'You know, I can almost see Eliza polishing that.' She smiled at Kate. 'I know you'll look after it.'

'Oh, I will.' Kate clasped her mother's hand. 'And, when the time comes, I shall pass it on to Danny. Just think, Pauline, this sideboard belonged to his great-great-grandma.'

'Where's Grandma?' As if on cue, the door burst open and Danny pelted in, closely followed by Helen. A babble of conversation broke out. Danny wanted to sing his newly learned nursery rhyme for her. Helen wanted her to come upstairs to see her newly decorated room. Pauline looked at Kate helplessly.

'Do what you want to do, Mum, only don't let them monopolise you for too long. I'm going to shut myself in the kitchen now and make some more goodies for the party.'

'Don't you want some help?'

Kate smiled. 'Of course, but later. Then I'll find you all a job.'

Helen was now talking about a new tape she had bought and Danny had launched himself into his rendition of 'Itsy-bitsy-spider'. Pauline ruffled his hair and joyously allowed herself to be monopolised.

Next morning, about eleven, Nicky and her sons arrived. 'Hello, Pauline. Lovely to see you.' Nicky embraced her. She turned to her children. 'Go and find Danny, you two – and try and keep *clean*!' She grinned at Pauline. 'I've come a bit early to help. How are you getting on?'

'OK. I could do with some earplugs, though.' Pauline laughed as Danny and his friends whooped their way through the kitchen and out into the garden. Blasts of music were heard from upstairs.

'Yes, I suppose it is noisy.' Nicky stole a cheese straw from a nearby plate and nibbled at it. 'You get so you don't notice after a while.' She grinned. 'Whenever my house is quiet, I'm frightened I've gone deaf.'

When Kate put in an appearance, Nicky produced a card and a gaily wrapped present. 'Happy birthday.' She handed over the parcel. 'You needn't open it yet. Keep it for the party. Now, give me a job.'

'Thank you, Nicky.' Kate was flustered, her face was pink and flushed. 'At this moment I don't know why I wanted a party.'

'It's going to be great.' Nicky surveyed the work surfaces of the kitchen which were covered with cling-filmed platters of food. 'Your guests certainly won't starve to death.'

Jack put his head round the door. 'We're definitely eating in the garden, are we?'

They all looked through the window at the cloudless blue sky.

'Yes.'

'Right. Richie's here with Lisa. She's gone to sleep, so we've put her in Danny's cot. Richie has offered to help me set up the tables.'

During the next two hours, the house and garden turned into a hive of activity. Jack and Richie set up the tables and chairs. Nicky mixed salads and then transferred some of Danny's large toys to the bottom of the garden near his slide. She told the children firmly that they must play there. Then she came back indoors and started on the endless task of washing up.

Helen appeared and, under Kate's watchful eye, mixed up a bowl of punch. Then she put white linen tablecloths on the tables and decorated them with green trailing ivy and small pots of flowers, and Pauline and Kate checked on the food and drink.

When Pauline saw her daughter taking china and glasses from Eliza's sideboard, she was delighted. Impulsively, she said, 'I'm so glad you're *using* the sideboard, not just having it as a sort of ornament.'

Kate's eyebrows shot up. 'Why should you say that? Of course I'm using it.'

'Well,' Pauline felt embarrassed, 'I know you're keen on design. And I had noticed . . .' Her voice trailed away.

'Go on, tell me what you noticed.'

'I just wondered whether you'd put anything in it? You see, I noticed the top was completely bare, except for that lace cloth, and I remembered that Eliza had all sorts of things on top of the sideboard when she had it. There was a framed photograph and her favourite little ornaments.' Pauline stopped talking and her cheeks flushed.

Kate sighed. 'I'm going to put something on top of the sideboard, Pauline, when I find the right thing. And of course I'm using it to hold my crockery. I'm surprised you'd think I wouldn't.'

Pauline blushed.

The doorbell rang. 'I'll get it.' She rushed away to answer it and came back a moment later carrying a beautiful bouquet of flowers. 'They're for you.'

'Oh.' Kate held out her hands. She took the flowers and breathed in their scent then opened the card. 'They're from Jack.'

'They're gorgeous.'

'Aren't they?' Kate grinned at her mother, the earlier spat forgotten. 'I must go and thank him.'

An hour later, the guests began to arrive. Pauline, dressed in her new blue dress, found herself in demand.

'Pauline, this is a friend of mine, Adam Collins. Adam knows quite a bit about the fishing industry, and he lived in Whitby for a few years during the seventies. Adam, this is my mother-in-law, Pauline Bowen.'

Jack's friend was a grey-haired man with a kind face and the long-sighted gaze of a former seaman. He said he was retired now and lived in the village of Pudsey. Pauline found him easy to talk to. He even knew about the Whitby ceremony of Planting the Penny Hedge, which always took place on Ascension Eve.

'My father took me one year,' she reminisced. 'You were supposed to cut wood with a knife "of penny price" and help build the fence in the upper harbour, at the brim of the water. My dad didn't allow me to use the knife, in case I cut myself, but I remember the hedge.'

'And someone blew a horn.'

'Yes, that's right.' Pauline smiled. 'I wonder why?'

'I have no idea.' Adam returned her smile. 'Perhaps we ought to go through to Whitby one day and find out what it was all about? They still continue the custom, I believe.'

She blushed a little, and turned with some relief to find out why Danny was tugging at her skirt.

'Yes, Danny?'

'Grandma, I want to wee-wee.'

She was escorting her grandson back from a trip to the toilet when Helen caught her arm. 'Pauline, this is Michael. I've told him about you and he said he would like to meet you.' Her anxious expression told Pauline that the encounter was important. She smiled at him.

'Hello, I hope you're having a good time?'

He hung his head and mumbled something. Helen looked anguished. Then Pauline spotted the 'Save the Whales' badges they both sported. 'I see you and Helen have a lot in common. I read an article in a newspaper last week, about the conservation of the rain forests. I think . . .'

Ten minutes later it was Kate's turn. 'Mum, I'd like you to meet Ruth and Tony Stannard. Tony produces plays. He . . .'

Pauline gave Helen an apologetic glance and turned

to smile at Ruth, a tall woman with bold features and dark hair, and her stocky, attractive husband.

'We're so pleased to meet you. Kate has mentioned you often.'

'Has she?' Pauline sent her daughter a look of alarm.

Kate shrugged and laughed.

'. . . I'm sure Kate has the makings of a good actress. A bit shy, of course, but she's tackling her first stage role in October.'

Pauline nodded and listened, talked and nodded, and moved on. After an hour she helped Kate and Nicky serve the food, which was voted delicious. After clearing away some of the empty glasses, she slipped into the kitchen and sat down for a rest.

Nicky was in there. 'Bit hectic, isn't it?'

Pauline nodded and waved a serviette in front of her face to help her cool down.

'It's going well though, and Kate's thoroughly enjoying herself. Look and see.' Nicky pointed through the window.

Pauline stood up and watched as Jack and Kate mingled with their guests. They were both laughing and talking and she noticed how Jack kept his arm firmly around his wife's waist.

She smiled. 'They look as though they haven't a care in the world.'

'Good. After that scare with the crash, they deserve a good spell. There's Helen.' Nicky laughed. 'What an earnest couple they make.'

'Life is earnest at their age.' Pauline permitted herself a grin. Then, sobering, she enquired: 'Do you know what happened about the next-door neighbour? Blunt, I think he was called.'

Kate had told her in confidence about the baby-sitting episode.

'Oh, that's sorted out. Apparently, he's not such a bad chap. His wife's come back and now they seem to be a model couple.' Nicky rubbed her nose. 'Helen's totally lost interest in him. In fact, they might have been invited to the party, but they're away visiting in-laws at the moment.'

Pauline reflected. 'It's funny, isn't it? Something, or someone, can seem so important one minute, and then the next . . .' she blew on the open palm of her hand '. . . it's gone.'

'Yeah, it makes you wonder why we worry so much.' Nicky yawned and stood up. 'I'd better go and rescue Richie. He's got a pile of kids climbing on his back and they're threatening to smother him.' She smiled and sauntered outside.

Pauline had a drink of water and then followed her.

She collected some food and sat down in the shade of the beech hedge. She hadn't had time to eat earlier. A few minutes later, Adam Collins came across to her. 'Mind if I join you? Perhaps I can fetch you a drink?'

She didn't mind at all. He brought two glasses of wine.

By eight-thirty, the last of the guests had left and Danny was asleep in bed. Helen had gone for a walk with Michael and Jack was snoozing in the sitting-room.

Pauline helped Kate put away the last of the plates and glasses.

'It was a lovely party, Kate. You must be very pleased.'

'I am. Everything went smoothly and I've had a

lovely birthday.' She closed the doors of the sideboard and sat down in a nearby chair. She sighed and kicked off her shoes.

'You must be tired.'

'Not really. I feel very well.'

She looked it. Pauline thought she had never seen Kate looking so healthy. Her hair shone and her eyes sparkled. She appeared to have gained a little weight. It suited her. The few extra pounds had rounded her cheeks and made her look far younger than she had fifteen months earlier, when they first met.

'Did you enjoy the party, Mum?'

'Of course I did. It was lovely to meet your friends and see Nicky and Helen and everyone enjoying themselves.'

Kate looked down. 'Forgive me for asking, but did you think about Elizabeth at all?'

Pauline nodded. 'Of course. It was her birthday, too.'

'I see.' Kate looked down at her hands. 'I thought about her, too. This morning I looked at the photo you gave me and wished that she could have been here to share today.' She raised her head and smiled at Pauline. 'You don't have to go straight back home tomorrow, do you?'

'No, I could stay on for a few days, if you'd like me to.'

'I'd like that. We all would.' Kate was twisting her wedding ring round and round on her finger.

Pauline, watching her, thought she wanted to say something. When Kate remained silent, she spoke instead.

'Actually, it would suit me to stay over because that nice man Jack introduced me to . . .' She paused.

'Adam Collins, do you know him?'

'Yes, I've met him a couple of times. When Jack's home, they play bowls together.'

'He's asked me out tomorrow night. I've agreed to let him take me to dinner.'

'Mother!' Kate's head went up.

'What's so surprising? We like each other and neither of us is exactly in our dotage.'

Kate stared at her and then burst out laughing. 'You never cease to surprise me.'

'Good.' Pauline nodded her head. 'I hope I never do.'

'Well, then. Let's see if I can surprise you.' Kate went to the corner cupboard and produced a cardboard box. She carried it over to the table. 'Come and see.'

'What is it, another birthday present?' Pauline went over to her.

'No. Something I found at the sales, about a month ago.' Kate took off the lid and removed two bundles, wrapped in tissue paper.

'What do you think of these?' Carefully, she unwrapped the paper and stood two porcelain figures, about twelve inches high, upon the table.

Pauline stared. 'They're beautiful.'

'Yes, I thought so, too. They're Derby bone china, made about 1860, I think. They're fairly valuable, but I didn't buy them because of that.' Kate paused. 'Do you know what they are?'

Pauline studied the porcelain figures. They were birds, and one was slightly larger than the other. The larger bird was coloured brown, streaked darker and paler beneath. It had a noticeable crest, thin beak, and white feathers showed in the tail. The second figure was also in shades of brown but was a little smaller. This bird had no crest and was a rounder, plumper shape. Both birds perched on a delicately coloured, flowery support.

Pauline touched the larger bird with a gentle finger. 'They look so real,' she marvelled.

'Yes, the earlier soft-paste porcelain they used then for work like this was ideal. But they moved to the harder paste because it was more hard-wearing.' Kate studied her mother's face. 'Do you know what kind of birds they are?'

'No.'

'They're skylarks, Mum. A parent figure and a fledgling.' Kate smiled at her mother's startled face. 'I remember Eliza's old saying, about catching larks, and I knew I had to buy them. I want you to have one of them. And the other,' she picked up the figure of the smaller bird and carried it across to the sideboard, 'will stand here.' She put the piece of porcelain on top of the lace cover and stood back to admire it.

'But, Kate, the two pieces belong together. You can't split them.'

'I can.' Kate gave her skylark a last approving pat and then came back to Pauline. She picked up the second figure and handed it to her.

'You must take it, Mum. This one's the parent bird.'

'Oh, Kate.' Pauline's voice broke and she fought back tears.

'There's nothing to cry about.' Kate was smiling.

'It's a lovely thought.' Pauline shook her head. 'But I still think they should stay together.'

'One day they will be, but not yet. Please take it, Mum.' Seeing Pauline was still undecided, Kate hurried on. 'Remember when you gave me Eliza's letter to read?'

'Yes, of course.'

'After I'd read it, I kept thinking about her, and about you and me. And when I thought about the "lark" quotation and all her other old sayings.' Kate shrugged her shoulders. 'It may sound funny, but I thought they seemed like a chain, binding us together. Does that make sense?'

When Pauline nodded, she said, 'Maybe it was because I didn't find you until last year, but I feel now that if I can do anything to strengthen that chain, then I should.'

Pauline shook her head. 'Things, old sayings, they don't bind people together. Only love does that, Kate.'

'I know. But I like the idea of me looking at my skylark every day, and you looking at yours. Call it a stupid whim if you like.' Kate took a deep breath. 'And you should humour me, particularly now.'

'Why should I?' Pauline had been staring down at the birds. Now she looked up into her daughter's face and caught her breath. 'Do you mean what I think you mean?'

Kate nodded, her face glowing. 'Yes, I'm nearly four months pregnant.'

'Oh, that's wonderful news.' A huge smile lit up Pauline's face. 'At least,' she hesitated, 'if you're pleased?'

'I'm delighted, and so is Jack. Danny may have reservations, of course.' Kate laughed. 'We haven't told him yet, or Helen.' She paused. 'I wanted to tell you first.'

'Well, I'm thrilled to bits. And, yes,' Pauline nodded, 'I will take the lark and cherish it.' She sighed. 'What a lovely way to end the day.'

'Yes.' Kate was staring at her. 'Just one last thing, Mum?'

'Yes.'

'If I have a girl, would you mind if we called her Elizabeth?'

Pauline was speechless. Her eyes opened wide and tears filled them.

'Oh, Mum, I'm sorry.' Kate was dismayed. 'I didn't mean to upset you.'

'Upset me!' Pauline's tears escaped and rained down her face. 'Upset me? It's the best present you could ever give me, Kate.'

'You're sure?'

'Yes.' She put her hand out to her daughter and Kate took it. Now both women were weeping.

'Oh, Lord.' Kate sniffed distractedly and mopped her face. 'I hope Jack doesn't come walking in here. What would he think? I keep telling him how happy I am, and I *am* happy, and yet here we are, blubbing away as though the sky had just fallen in.'

Pauline gulped and moved away to stare at her daughter.

Kate, brushing away more tears, looked up and her forehead creased into a frown. 'What is it? What's the matter?'

'Do you realise what you've just said?'

'I said . . .' Kate thought for a moment and then her puzzled frown turned into a look of surprise.

'I said something about the sky falling in.' She looked at Pauline's quizzical expression and started to laugh.

'Oh, my God, I'm starting to sound *exactly* like Eliza!'

'That's right.' Pauline nodded, holding on to her

quizzical look. But when Kate, now rocking with laughter, held out her hands to her, she took hold of them and she too began to laugh.

They laughed until their stomachs hurt. They couldn't stop. And, when they were weak from laughing, once more they clung to each other, and once more they cried. But this time the tears were of mirth and happiness.